Fantasy Lover

Sherrilyn Kenyon

piatkus

PIATKUS

First published in the US in 2002 by St. Martin's Press, New York
First published in Great Britain in 2005 by Piatkus Books Ltd
This paperback edition published in 2011 by Piatkus
Reprinted 2012

A CIP catalogue record for this book
is available from the British Library.

ISBN 978-0-7499-5506-9

Typeset in Great Britain by Action
Printed and bound by CPI Group (UK) Ltd, Croydon, CR0 4YY

Papers used by Piatkus are from well-managed forests
and other responsible sources.

MIX
Paper from
responsible sources
FSC
www.fsc.org   FSC® C104740

Piatkus
An imprint of
Little, Brown Book Group
100 Victoria Embankment
London EC4Y 0DY

An Hachette UK Company
www.hachette.co.uk

www.piatkus.co.uk

Acknowledgements

As always, this is for my wonderful family who supports me unreservedly.

For Nancy Yost, who believed in an idea that was completely different, and for all the faith you had, and encouragement you gave.

Jennifer Enderlin and Kim Cardascia for sharing my vision, and allowing me to explore the outer reaches of my imagination.

For my friends who are always there to share my laughter and my pain: Rickey Mallory, Celeste Bradley, Cheryl Lewellyn, Valerie Walton, Diana Hillock, Rebecca Baum, and Kim Jones (thanks for the psychologist insights). And for Lisa Rich, who was the original Moon Mistress.

And most of all, to you, the reader, for wanting to take a stroll with me on the Wild Side, where with a little faith, imagination, and love, all things are possible.

Hugs to all!

An Ancient Greek Legend

Possessed of supreme strength and of unrivaled courage, he was blessed by the gods, feared by mortals, and desired by all women who saw him. He was a man who knew no law, respected no quarter.

His skill in battle and his superior intellect rivaled the very names of Achilles, Odysseus, and Heracles, and 'twas written that not even the mighty Ares himself could ever defeat him in arms.

As if the gift of the mighty War God wasn't enough, 'twas also said that on his birth, the goddess Aphrodite kissed his cheek, and secured his place forever in mortal memory.

Blessed by Aphrodite's divine touch, he grew into such a man that no woman could deny him her body. For when it came to the Art of Love, he knew no equal – his stamina far beyond that of any mere mortal man. His desires hot and wild, he could never be tamed.

Or denied.

Golden in skin and hair, and flashing the eyes of a warrior, 'twas said his presence alone was oft enough to satisfy women, and once touched by his hand they would become blinded by pleasure.

None could stand against his charm.

And so out of jealousy came a curse to endure. One that can never be broken.

Like poor Tantalus, 'tis his plight to forever seek his satisfaction, and never fulfill it. To yearn for his summoner's touch and to bring about her complete and utter pleasure and satiation.

From full moon to full moon, he will lie with her, make love to her, until he is again forced from this world.

But beware, for once his touch is felt, it is branded into his lover's memory. No other man shall ever satisfy her again. Because no mere mortal male can compare to a man of such beauty. Such heat. Such intrepid sensuality.

Behold the cursed.

Julian of Macedon.

Hold him to your breast and call for him three times on the wings of midnight under the weight of a full moon's light. He will come to you then, and until the next full moon cycle, his body will be yours to command.

His only goal will be to please you, to serve you.

To savor you.

In his arms, you will learn true paradise.

Chapter One

'Honey, you need to get laid.'

Grace Alexander flinched at Selena's overly loud voice in the small New Orleans café where they sat, finishing up their lunch of red beans and rice. Unfortunately for her, Selena's voice possessed a lovely octave that could carry plainly through a hurricane.

And it was followed by a sudden hush in the crowded room.

Glancing at the nearby tables, Grace noted the men had stopped talking, and turned to stare at them with a lot more interest than she cared for.

Ah jeez! Will Selena ever learn to keep her voice down?

Worse, what will she do next, strip naked, and dance on the tabletops?

Again.

For the millionth time since they had first met, Grace wished Selena *could* get embarrassed. But her flamboyant, often extravagant pal didn't know the meaning of the word.

Grace covered her face with her hands and did her best to

ignore the curious onlookers. An urge to slink beneath the table, followed by an even greater urge to kick her companion, consumed her.

'Why don't you speak a little louder, Lanie?' she whispered. 'I don't think the guys in Canada were able to hear you.'

'Oh, I don't know,' the gorgeous brown-haired waiter said as he stopped by their table. 'They're probably headed south even as we speak.'

Heat stole up Grace's cheeks as the obviously college-aged waiter gave her a devilish grin. 'Is there anything else I can get you ladies?' he asked, then looked pointedly at Grace. 'Or more precisely, is there anything *I* can do for *you*, ma'am?'

How about a bag for my head, or a stick to beat Lanie with?

'I think we have it,' Grace said, her cheeks scalding. She was *definitely* going to kill Selena for this. 'We just need our bill.'

'All right, then,' he said, pulling their ticket off and scribbling across the top of the paper. He set it down in front of Grace. 'Just give me a call if I can be of any further service.'

It was only after he left that Grace saw his name and phone number on the top of the bill.

Selena took one look at it and laughed out loud.

'Just you wait,' Grace said, suppressing a smile as she totaled her portion of the food on her Palm Pilot. 'I *will* get you back for this.'

Selena ignored the threat as she fished in her beaded bag for her money. 'Yeah, yeah, so you say. If I were you, I'd hang on to that number. He is a cute little thing.'

'*Young* thing,' Grace corrected. 'And I think I'll pass. The last thing I need is to be locked up for contributing to the delinquency of a minor.'

Selena slid her gaze over to where the waiter leaned with one hip against the bar. 'Yeah, but Mr. Brad Pitt look-alike over there might be worth it. I wonder if he has an older brother?'

'I wonder how much Bill would pay to know his wife spent her entire lunch hour ogling a kid?'

Selena snorted as she placed her money on the table. 'I'm not ogling him for myself. I'm ogling him for you. It was, after all, your sex life we were discussing.'

'Well, my sex life is just hunky-dory, and not the business of the people in this restaurant.' Tossing her money on the table, Grace grabbed the last bite of cubed cheese and headed for the door.

'Don't get mad,' Selena said, following her out into the busy crowd of tourists and regulars thronging Jackson Square.

A lone saxophone played jazz above the cacophony of voices, horses, and car engines as a wave of Louisiana heat assaulted her.

Trying her best to ignore air so thick it could barely be inhaled, Grace wended her way through the crowd, and vendors' booths that were set in front of the wrought-iron fence surrounding Jackson Square.

'You know it's true,' Selena said as she caught up to her. 'I mean, goodness, Grace, it's been what? Two years?'

'Four,' she said absently. 'But who's counting?'

'Four years with no sex?' Selena repeated loudly in disbelief.

Several onlookers paused to look curiously from Selena to Grace.

Oblivious as usual to the attention they collected, Selena continued without pausing. 'Don't tell me that *you've* forgotten this is the Age of Electronics? I mean, really, do any of your patients know how long you've gone without sex?'

Grace swallowed her cheese and gave Selena a nasty glare. Did Selena intend to shout it out for every human, and every horse for that matter, in the Vieux Carré to hear?

'Keep your voice down,' she said, then added dryly, 'I don't think it's the business of my patients whether or not I'm a born-again virgin. And as for the Age of Electronics, I *really* don't want to get personal with something that comes with a warning label and batteries.'

Selena snorted. 'Yeah, well, to hear you talk, most men *should* come with warning labels.' She lifted her hands up to frame her next statement. *'Attention, please, Psycho Alert. Me, he-man, am prone to nasty mood swings, lengthy pouts, and possess the ability to tell a woman the truth about her weight without warning.'*

Grace laughed. She'd rattled off that spiel about men who needed warning labels countless times.

'Ah, I see, Dr. Sex,' Selena said with an imitation Dr. Ruth accent. 'You just sit there and listen to them spout off all the intimate details of their sexual encounters while you live like a lifetime member of the Teflon Panty Club.'

Dropping her accent, Selena added, 'I can't believe after all the stuff you've heard in your sessions that none of it has ever gotten your hormones revved.'

Grace gave Selena a droll look. 'Yeah, well, I *am* a sex therapist. It wouldn't do my patients much good for me to have *la petite mort* while they're in the middle of spewing out their problems. I mean really, Lanie, I'd lose my license.'

'Well, I don't see how you can advise them when you won't go anywhere near a man.'

Grimacing, Grace led the way back to the other side of the square, across from the Tourist Information Center where

Selena's tarot card and palm reading stand was set up.

When Grace reached the small card table draped with a dark purple cloth, she sighed. 'You know, I would date if I could ever find a man worth shaving my legs for. But most are such a waste of time that I'd rather sit at home and watch reruns of *Hee Haw*.'

Selena gave her an irritated smirk. 'What was wrong with Gerry?'

'Bad breath.'

'Jamie?'

'His fondness for mining nose gold. Especially during dinner.'

'Tony?'

Grace just looked at her.

Selena threw her hands up. 'Okay, so maybe he did have a little gambling problem. But then, everyone needs a hobby.'

Grace glared at her.

'Hey, Madam Selene, you back from lunch?' Sunshine asked from the next stand over where she hawked her sketches and pottery.

A few years younger than them, Sunshine had long, black hair and always wore clothes that reminded Grace of a fairy princess.

Her costume today was a wispy white skirt that would have been obscene if not for the pale pink leotard beneath it and a pretty peasant blouse.

'Yeah, I'm back,' Selena said as she knelt to unlock the doors on her metal wheeled cart that she secured every morning to the wrought-iron gate with a bicycle chain. 'Did I get any interest while I was gone?'

'A couple of guys took your business card and said they'd be back after they ate.'

'Thanks.' Selena placed her purse inside the cart, then pulled out the dark blue cigar box she used to hold her money, her tarot cards that she kept wrapped in a black silk scarf, and a thin, yet humongous, brown leather book Grace had never seen before.

Selena put her large-brimmed straw hat on her head, then turned and stood.

'Did you get all your pieces marked?' she asked Sunshine.

'Yes,' Sunshine said as she grabbed her purse. 'I still say it's bad luck. But at least if anyone wants to know the price for anything while I'm gone, it'll be there.'

A rough-looking biker pulled up to the curb. 'Hey, Sunshine,' he shouted, 'get your butt over here. I'm hungry.'

Sunshine waved her hand dismissively. 'Keep your chains on, Harry, and lay off or you'll be eating by yourself,' she said as she walked slowly toward him. She climbed up on the back of his motorcycle.

Grace shook her head at the two of them. Sunshine needed dating help a whole lot more than she did.

She watched as they drove past the Café du Monde. 'Ooo, I bet a beignet would be good for dessert.'

'Food is no substitute for sex,' Selena said as she placed the cards and book on her table. 'Isn't that what you keep telling—'

'All right, you've made your point. But really, Lanie, why are you suddenly so interested in *my* sex life? Or more importantly, the lack thereof?'

Selena handed her the book. 'Because I have an idea.'

Now that was something that chilled her to her bones, even in this wretched heat. And Grace didn't frighten easily. Well, not unless it involved Selena and one of her cocka-mamie ideas. 'Not another séance?'

'No, this is better.'

Inwardly, Grace cringed and wondered what she'd be

doing right now if she'd had a normal roommate her first year at Tulane instead of the flighty Gypsy wanna-be Selena. One thing was sure, she wouldn't be discussing her sex life in the middle of a crowded street.

In that instant, she became acutely aware of their differences. She stood in the humid heat wearing a thin, sleeveless Ralph Lauren creme silk dress, her dark hair pulled back into a sophisticated chignon while Selena wore a long flowing black broomstick skirt with a tight purple tank top that barely covered her ample chest.

Selena's shoulder-length frizzy brown hair was pulled up with a black leopard silk scarf and she had huge silver moon earrings hanging to her shoulders. Not to mention the silver mine she had strapped to both her wrists in the way of about a hundred and fifty silver bangles. Bangles that jingled every time she moved.

People had always remarked on their physical differences, but Grace knew Selena hid her astute mind and insecurity behind her 'exotic' attire. Inside, the two of them were far more alike than anyone would ever guess.

Except for Selena's bizarre belief in the occult.

And Selena's insatiable appetite for sex.

Moving to stand beside her, Selena forced the book into Grace's reluctant hands and thumbed through it. Grace did her best not to drop it.

Or roll her eyes.

'I found this the other day in that old bookstore by the Wax Museum. It was covered by a mountain of dust, and I was trying to find this book on psychometry when I came across it, and *voilà!*' Selena pointed triumphantly at the page.

Grace looked down at the picture, then gaped.

Never had she seen such a thing.

9

The man in the picture was riveting, and the picture absolutely shocking in its detail. If not for the deep impression marks on the page where it had been drawn, she would have sworn it was an actual photograph of some ancient Greek statue.

No, she corrected herself – a Greek god. Surely no mortal man could *ever* look that good.

Standing in *full* naked glory, the man oozed power, authority, and raw, animal sexuality. Even though his pose was a casual stance, he looked like some sleek predator ready to spring into action at a moment's notice.

His very veins stood out on a body made perfect with the promise of a hard, lean strength designed purely for feminine pleasure.

Her mouth dry, Grace trailed her gaze over his muscles, which bulged in perfect proportion to his height and weight. She followed the lean, hard muscles over the deep indentation that divided his pectorals, down the washboard stomach that just begged for a woman's touch.

To his navel.

And then to his …

Well, no one had bothered to put a fig leaf *there*. And why should they? Who in their right mind would want to cover up so *nice* a masculine package?

For that matter, who would need anything with batteries around with *that* in the house!

Licking her lips, Grace looked back at his face.

As she stared at the sharp, handsome features that held just a hint of a devilish smile, she had an image of a breeze tugging at sun-kissed, tawny locks that curled around a neck made for suckling. Of steely blue eyes piercing in their intensity as he raised an iron spear over his head and shouted.

She felt a sudden stirring in the thick, hot air around her, one that seemed to somehow caress her exposed skin.

She could almost hear the deep timbre of his voice, feel strong arms wrap about her and pull her back against a rock-hard chest while warm breath tickled her ear. Feel strong, competent hands roaming her body, giving her delight as they sought out her most private places.

A chill stole up her spine, and her body throbbed in areas she'd never known a body could throb. It was a fierce, demanding ache she'd never before known.

Blinking, she glanced up at Selena to see if she'd been affected the same way. If she had, she gave no clue.

Grace must be hallucinating. That was it! The spices from the red beans had finally seeped into her brain and turned it to mush.

'What do you think of him?' Selena asked, finally meeting her gaze.

Grace shrugged in an effort to subdue the slow burn of her body. Still, her eyes lingered on his perfect form. 'He looks like a client I signed up yesterday.'

Well, it wasn't exactly true – the guy she'd seen had been fairly attractive, but nothing like the man in the drawing.

She'd never seen anything like *him* in her life!

'Really?' Selena's eyes darkened in a way that warned her she was about to begin her long lecture on kismet and chance meetings.

'Yeah,' she said, cutting Selena off before she could start. 'He told me he was a lesbian trapped in a man's body.'

Selena's face fell. Grabbing the book from her and slamming it shut, Selena glared at her. 'You know the weirdest people.'

Grace cocked an eyebrow.

'Don't say it,' Selena said as she took her usual seat

behind her table. She placed the book down beside her. 'I'm telling you, *this* –' she tapped the center of the book twice '– is the answer for you.'

Grace stared at her friend, thinking how true to form Madam Selene, self-proclaimed Moon Mistress, looked sitting behind her tarot cards and purple table with the arcane book beneath her hand. At that moment, she could almost believe Selena *was* a mystical Gypsy.

If she believed in such things.

'Okay,' Grace said, giving in. 'Quit stalling and tell me what that book and picture have to do with my sex life.'

Selena's face became gravely earnest. 'That guy I showed you ... Julian ... is a Greek love-slave who is completely controlled by, and devoted to, whoever summons him.'

Grace laughed out loud. She knew it was rude, but she couldn't help it. How in the world could a Rhodes scholar with a Ph.D. in both ancient history and physics, even one with Selena's idiosyncrasies, believe in something so ludicrous?

'Don't laugh. I'm serious.'

'I know you are, that's what makes this so funny.' Clearing her throat, Grace sobered. 'Okay. What do I have to do? Strip off my clothes and dance by the Pontchartrain at midnight?' The corners of her mouth lifted even as Selena's eyes darkened in warning. 'You're right, I'd get sex all right, but I don't think it'd be from some gorgeous Greek love-slave.'

The book fell from the table.

Selena jumped with a shriek and scooted her chair back.

Grace gasped. 'You pushed that with your elbow, didn't you?'

Her eyes as round as saucers, Selena slowly shook her head no.

"Fess up, Lanie.'

'I didn't do it,' she said, her face deadly serious. 'I think you offended him.'

Shaking her head at that nonsense, Grace fished her sunglasses and keys out of her purse. Yeah, right, this was just like the time in college when Lanie had talked her into using a Ouija board and Lanie had made it say that Grace would marry a Greek god by the time she was thirty and have six kids by him.

To this day, Selena refused to admit that she'd been pushing the planchette.

And right now it was too hot under the August sun to argue. 'Look, I need to get back to the office. I have a two o'clock and I don't want to get caught in traffic.' She pulled her Ray-Bans on. 'Are you still coming over tonight?'

'Wouldn't miss it for the world. I'll bring the wine.'

'All right then, I'll see you at eight.' Grace paused long enough to say, 'Tell Bill I said hi and thanks for letting you come over for my birthday.'

Selena watched her walk off and smiled. 'Just wait until you see your birthday present,' she whispered, picking the book up from where it had fallen. She trailed her hand over the soft tooled leather, brushing away a few grains of dirt.

Opening it back up, Selena stared at the gorgeous picture, and at eyes that were drawn in black and yet somehow gave the impression of a deep, cobalt blue.

For once, her spell would work. She was sure of it.

'You'll like her, Julian,' Selena whispered to him as she traced her finger over his perfect body. 'But I should warn you, she'd try the patience of a saint. And getting inside her defenses will be as hard as breaching the walls of Troy. Still, I think if anyone can help her find herself, it's you.'

Underneath her hand, she felt the book grow warm and

13

instinctively she knew it was his way of agreeing with her.

Grace thought her crazy for her beliefs, but as the seventh daughter of a seventh daughter and with the blood of Gypsies flowing thick through her veins, Selena knew that there were certain things in life that defied explanation. Certain arcane energies that ebbed and flowed unchecked, just waiting for someone to channel them.

And tonight was a full moon.

Placing the book back into the safety of her cart where she locked it up tight, she was certain that kismet had placed the book in her hands. She had felt it calling to her as soon as she'd approached the bookstore shelf where it lay.

Since she had been happily married for the last two years, she knew the book wasn't meant for her. It was only using her to get where it needed to go.

To Grace.

Her smile grew wider. Imagine having such an incredibly handsome Greek love-slave at your beck and command for an entire month ...

Yep, this was definitely a birthday Grace would remember for the rest of her life.

Chapter Two

Hours later, Grace sighed as she opened the door to her two-story bungalow and stepped into her polished foyer. She tossed her handful of mail onto the antique drop-leaf table by her staircase before she shut and locked the door behind her, then dropped the keys next to the mail.

As she pulled off her black high heels, silence rang in her ears and a lump settled deep in her chest. Every night she followed the same innocuous routine. Come home to an empty house, drop her mail on the table, trudge upstairs to change, eat a small meal, sort the mail, read a book, call Selena, check with her answering service, then go to bed.

Selena was right, Grace's life was a short, boring study in monotony.

And at twenty-nine, Grace was tired of it.

Heck, even Jamie the nose-picker was starting to look good.

Well, maybe not Jamie, and most especially not Jamie's nose, but surely there was someone out there somewhere who wasn't a cretin.

15

Wasn't there?

As Grace headed up the stairs, she decided living by herself wasn't so terribly awful. At least she had plenty of time to devote to her hobbies.

Or to develop some hobbies, she thought as she walked down the hallway toward her bedroom. One day, she really was going to get herself a hobby.

She crossed her bedroom and dropped her shoes by the bed, then quickly changed.

She'd just finished pulling her hair into a ponytail when the doorbell rang.

Heading back downstairs, she went to let Selena in.

As soon as the door opened, Selena huffed, 'You're not wearing *that* tonight, are you?'

Grace looked down at the holes in her jeans and her over-sized T-shirt. 'Since when did you start caring about what *I* look like?'

Then she saw *it* in the huge wicker bag Selena used to carry her groceries. 'Ugh, not that book again.'

Looking a bit peeved, Selena said, 'You know what your problem is, Gracie?'

Grace looked up at the ceiling, seeking heavenly help. Unfortunately, none was forthcoming. 'What? That I don't go moon-crazy and toss my freckled, fat self at every guy I meet?'

'That you don't know just how adorable you really are.'

While Grace stood dumbfounded by such an unchar-acteristic remark, Selena took the book into her living room, and set it on the coffee table. Next, Selena removed the wine from her bag, and headed for the kitchen.

Grace didn't bother to follow after her. She'd called for pizza before she left work, and she knew Selena was just getting wine glasses.

As if pulled by an unseen hand, Grace felt herself drawn toward the coffee table and the book.

Unbidden, her hand reached out for it, and as she touched the soft leather, she could almost swear she felt something brush her cheek.

That was ridiculous.

You don't believe in this stuff.

Grace ran her hand over the smooth, perfect leather, noting that no lettering or title appeared anywhere on it. She opened the cover.

This was the strangest book she'd ever seen. The pages looked as if they'd once been some kind of scroll or something that had later been bound into book form.

The bleached parchment crinkled under her fingers as she turned to the first page and saw an intricate emblem of painted scrollwork that had three intersecting triangles and a beguiling image of three women united by swords.

Frowning, Grace vaguely recalled it as some sort of ancient Greek symbol.

Even more intrigued than before, she flipped through the book only to find it was completely empty except for the three pages ...

How weird.

It must have been some sort of sketchbook for an artist or a sculptor, she decided. That would be the only explanation for why the pages were left blank. Something must have happened before the artist had a chance to add anything more to the book.

But that didn't really explain why the pages looked a whole lot older than the binding ...

Flipping back to the drawing of the man, she studied the writing across the page from him but couldn't make any of it out. Unlike Selena, she'd avoided language classes in college like they were poison, and if not for Selena, she would never have passed that part of her core curriculum at all.

'It's definitely Greek to me,' she said under her breath, then she returned her attention to the man.

He was amazing. So very perfect and inviting.

So incredibly sexy.

Completely captivated by him, she wondered how long it would take to make a drawing so perfect. Someone must have spent years on it, because the guy literally looked as if he could step right off the page and into her house.

Selena paused in the doorway as she watched Grace staring at Julian. In all the years she'd known Grace, she'd never seen her so enthralled.

Good.

Maybe Julian could help her.

Four years was really too long.

But then Paul had been an inconsiderate, self-centered pig. His callousness for Grace's feelings had even made her cry the night he'd taken her virginity.

And no woman deserved to cry. Especially not while she was with someone who had told her he cared about her.

Julian would definitely be good for Grace. A month with him and Grace would forget all about Paul. And once Grace tasted what real, mutual sex was like, then she would be free of Paul's cruelty forever.

But first Selena had to get her stubborn chum to be a little more compliant.

'Did you order the pizza?' Selena asked, handing her a full glass of wine.

Grace absently took it. For some reason, she couldn't quite take her eyes off the picture.

'Gracie?'

Blinking, she forced herself to look up. 'Hmm?'

'Caught you looking,' Selena teased.

Grace cleared her throat. 'Oh, please, it's just a little black-and-white drawing.'

'Hon, there ain't nothing *little* in that drawing.'

'You're bad, Selena.'

'True enough. More wine?'

As if on cue, the doorbell rang. 'I'll get it,' Selena said, setting the wine down on the end table, then heading to the foyer.

A few minutes later Selena returned to the room. Grace let the wonderful aroma of a large pepperoni pizza drag her thoughts away from the book. And the man who seemed to have branded his image on her subconscious.

But it wasn't easy.

In fact, it seemed to get harder by the minute.

What the heck was wrong with her? She was the Ice Queen. Not even Brad Pitt or Brendan Fraser made her lustful. And they were in full, living color.

What was it about that drawing?

About *him*?

Grace took a careful bite of the pizza and defiantly moved to an armchair across the room. There. She'd show that book and Selena that *she* was in control.

Four pieces of pizza, two Hostess cupcakes, four glasses of wine, and a full movie later, she and Selena were lying on the floor draped over stacked sofa cushions while they laughed at *Sixteen Candles*.

'"You say it's your birthday,"' Selena started singing as she pounded the floor like a bongo drum. '"It's my birthday, too."'

Grace swiped her head with a cushion, then giggled as her head buzzed from the wine.

'Gracie?' Selena asked, her voice full of mirth. 'Are you tipsy?'

She giggled again. 'Maybe just comfortably toasty. Pop-Tart toasty.'

Selena laughed at Grace, and pulled the band from Grace's hair. 'Then are you willing to try a little experiment?'

'No!' Grace said emphatically, brushing her loose hair behind her ears. 'I don't want to Ouija, or do the pendulum thing, and I swear if I see one tarot card or rune stone I'll yack cupcake all over you.'

Biting her lower lip, Selena pulled the book off the table and flipped it open.

Five minutes to midnight.

She held the picture up for Grace's inspection and pointed to the incredible form. 'What about him?'

Grace looked at it and smiled. 'He *is* yummy, isn't he?'

Well, that was definitely progress. Selena couldn't remember the last time Grace had complimented a guy's looks. She waved the book teasingly before Grace's face.

'C'mon, Gracie. Admit it. You want this handsome guy.'

'If I said I wouldn't toss him out of my bed for eating crackers, would you leave me alone?'

'Maybe. What else wouldn't you toss him out of bed for?'

She rolled her eyes and laid her head down on the pillow. 'Eating greasy grimy gopher guts?'

'Now I think *I'm* going to yack.'

'Watch the movie.'

'Only if you'll try this *one* itty-bitty chant.'

Grace raised her head and sighed. She knew better than to argue with Selena – she had that *look*. And nothing short of a meteorite crashing through the house would make her stop until she got her way.

Besides, what was the harm? She'd learned years ago that nothing ever came of Selena's silly chants and spells. 'All right. If it'll ease your pain, I'll do it.'

'Yay!' Selena said, grabbing her arm and pulling her to her feet. 'We need to go out to the deck.'

'Fine, but I'm not ripping the head off a voodoo chicken or drinking anything disgusting.'

Feeling like a kid at a sleepover who had lost a truth-or-dare contest, Grace allowed Selena to pull her outside her sliding glass door. The damp air filled her lungs as crickets chirped, and a thousand stars twinkled above them. Grace supposed it was a beautiful night to summon a love-slave.

She snickered at the thought.

'What do you want me to do?' she asked Selena. 'Wish on some planet?'

Shaking her head, Selena moved her to stand in the circle of moonlight where it fell over the eaves of her roof. Selena handed her the opened book. 'Hold this to your breast.'

'Oh, baby,' Grace said in mock desire as she cuddled the book to her chest like a lover. 'You make me so hot and horny. I just can't wait to sink my teeth into that wonderful body of yours.'

Selena laughed. 'Stop it. This is serious!'

'Serious? Please. I'm standing out here on my twenty-ninth birthday, barefoot and in jeans my mother would burn, holding a stupid book to my chest in an effort to summon a Greek love-slave from the great beyond.' She looked at Selena. 'I only know one way to make this even more ridiculous ... '

Grace held the book in one hand, opened her arms wide, tipped her head back, and implored the dark sky above,

'Oh, take me, great gorgeous love-slave and have your wicked way with me. I command you to *rise*,' she said, wagging her eyebrows.

Selena snorted. 'That's not how you do it. You have to say his name three times.'

Grace straightened up. 'Love-slave, love-slave, love-slave.'

Her hands on her hips, Selena glared at her. 'Julian of Macedon.'

'Oh, sorry.' Grace hugged the book to her breast and closed her eyes. 'Come and ease my aching loins, O great Julian of Macedon, Julian of Macedon, Julian of Macedon.'

She looked back at Selena. 'You know, that's hard to say three times fast.'

But Selena wasn't paying a bit of attention to her. She was busy looking around for the appearance of a handsome Greek stranger.

Grace rolled her eyes again as a subtle wind swept across the yard and a faint scent of sandalwood wafted around them. Grace took a second to savor the pleasant smell before it evaporated and the breeze settled down to the hot, thick air that was so common on an August night.

All of a sudden, there was a faint sound in her backyard. A small rustle of leaves coming from the shrubs.

Cocking her brow, Grace looked to the bushes that were swaying.

Then, the imp in her took over. 'Oh, my God,' Grace breathed, pointing toward a bush in the backyard. 'Selena, look over there!'

Selena turned around in a hurry at her excited gesture. A tall shrub swayed as if someone were behind it.

'Julian?' Selena called.

Selena took a step closer.

The tree bent over. Suddenly, a hiss and a meow sounded an instant before two cats darted off across the backyard.

'Look, Lanie, it's Mr. Tomcat come to save me from my celibacy.' Cradling the book in one arm, Grace lifted the back of her hand to her brow in a feigned swoon. 'Oh, help me, Moon Mistress. Whatever am I to do with the attentions of such an unwanted suitor! Help me quick, before he kills me with my allergies.'

'Give me that book,' Selena snapped, snatching it from her chest. She headed back into the house while she flipped through its pages. 'Dammit, what did I do wrong?'

Grace slid open her door to let Selena back into the cool house. 'You didn't do anything wrong, hon. It's a farce. How many times do I have to tell you that some little old man sits in a back room somewhere making all this stuff up? I'll bet he's laughing his head off right now that we were dumb enough–'

'Maybe there was something else we needed to do. I'll bet there's something in the first few paragraphs that I can't read. That *must* be it.'

Grace locked the sliding glass door and begged for patience. *And Selena calls* me *stubborn.*

The phone rang. Answering it, Grace heard Bill's voice asking for Selena.

'It's for you,' she said, handing the phone over to her friend.

Selena took it. 'Yeah?' She paused for several minutes and Grace could hear his excited chatter. By the sudden pallor of Selena's features, she could tell something had happened.

'Okay, okay. I'll be right home. Are you sure you're all right? Okay, I love you. I'm on my way – don't try and do anything until I get there.'

A horrible stab of fear knotted Grace's stomach tight.

23

Over and over, she saw the policeman at her dorm room door, heard his dispassionate voice: *I'm sorry to inform you . . .*

'What is it?' Grace asked.

'Bill fell while they were playing basketball and broke his arm.'

She released her breath in relief. Thank God, it wasn't a car wreck. 'Is he all right?'

'He said so. His friends took him to a doc-in-the-box and had it X-rayed before they dropped him off. He told me not to worry, but I think I better get on home.'

'You want me to drive you?'

Selena shook her head. 'No, unlike me you've had one too many glasses of wine. Besides, I'm sure it's nothing serious. You know what a worrywart I am. You stay here and enjoy the rest of your movie. I'll call you tomorrow morning.'

'Okay. Let me know how he's doing.'

Selena gathered up her bag and dug out her keys. As she started out the door, she paused and handed the book back to Grace. 'What the hell. Keep it. It should give you a good laugh for the next few days while you remember what an idiot I am.'

'You're not an idiot. Just eccentric.'

'That's what they said about Mary Todd Lincoln. Until they locked her up.'

Laughing, Grace took the book and watched Selena walk out to her car. 'You be careful,' she shouted out the door. 'And thanks for the gift, and for coming over.'

Selena waved before getting into her bright red Jeep Cherokee and driving off.

With a tired sigh, Grace shut and locked the door, then tossed the book on the sofa. 'Now don't go anywhere, *love-slave*.'

Grace laughed at their silliness. Would Selena *ever* outgrow such nonsense?

She turned off the TV and took their dirty dishes to the kitchen sink. As she rinsed out the glasses, she saw a bright flash of light.

For a second, she thought it was lightning.

Until she realized it came from *inside* the house.

'What the ... ?'

She put the wine glasses aside and walked toward the living room. At first she didn't see anything. But as she came flush with the doorway, she *felt* a strange presence. One that made the hair on the back of her arms and neck rise.

Cautiously, she entered the room and saw a tall figure standing in front of the couch.

It was a man.

A handsome man.

A *naked* man!

Chapter Three

Grace did what most any woman would do while confronting a naked man in her living room. She screamed.

Then she ran for the front door.

Only she forgot about the cushions that were still on the floor where they'd piled them. Tripping over two, she went sprawling.

No! she silently cried as she landed in a painful heap. She had to do something to protect herself.

Terrified and shaking, she scrambled through the cushions, looking for a weapon. Feeling something, she pulled her hand up, only to find a pink bunny slipper.

Dammit! Out of the corner of her eye, she saw the wine bottle. Grace rolled toward it and grabbed it in her hand, then whirled to face her intruder.

Faster than she could react, he wrapped his warm hand around her wrist, tenderly immobilizing it. 'Are you hurt?' he asked.

Good gracious, but his deep masculine voice was rich, with a thick, lilting accent that could only be described as musical. Erotic. And downright yummy.

Her senses dulled, Grace looked up and . . .

Well . . .

Quite honestly, there was only one thing she saw, and *it* made her face hotter than Cajun gumbo. After all, how could she miss *it* since *it* was just an arm's reach away. And *it* was such a large *it*, too.

In the next instant, he knelt by her side and gently brushed her hair out of her eyes. He ran his hands over her scalp as if feeling for an injury.

Her gaze feasted on his chest. Unable to move or look past all that incredible skin, Grace fought the urge to moan at the intensely wicked sensation of his fingers in her hair. Her entire body burned from it.

'Did you hit your head?' he asked.

Again that strange, glorious accent that reverberated through her like a warm, soothing caress.

She stared at the wealth of golden, tawny skin that seemed to beckon her hand to reach out and touch it.

He practically glowed!

Compelled, she wanted to see his face, to see for herself if the whole of him was as incredible as his body.

As she looked up, past the sculpted muscles of his shoulders, her mouth dropped. The wine bottle slid from her numbed fingers.

It was *him*!

No! It couldn't be.

This couldn't be happening to her, and he couldn't be naked in her living room with his hands in her hair. Things like this just didn't happen in real life. Most especially not to average people like her.

And yet . . .

'Julian?' she asked breathlessly.

He had the sleek, powerful build of a finely toned gymnast. His muscles were hard, lean, and gorgeous, and well defined in places she didn't even know a man could get muscles. On top of his shoulders, his biceps and forearms. His chest and back. His neck to his legs.

You name it, it bulged with raw, masculine strength.

Even *it* had started to bulge.

His golden hair fell in haphazard waves around a clean-shaven face that looked as if it really had been carved from stone. Unbelievably handsome and captivating, his face was neither pretty nor feminine. But it was definitely breathtaking.

Full, sensuous lips curved into a halfhearted smile, displaying a set of dimples that cut deep moons into his tanned cheeks.

And those eyes.

Gracious!

They were the clear celestial blue of a perfect cloudless sky with a tiny band of dark blue highlighting the outer edges of his irises. His eyes were searing in their intensity and shining with intellect. She had a feeling his looks, really *could* kill.

Or at the very least, devastate.

And she was certainly devastated at the moment. Captivated by a man too perfect to be real.

Hesitantly, she reached out and placed a hand on his arm. She was amazed when his arm didn't evaporate, proving all this was just a drunken hallucination.

No, that arm was real. Real and hard and warm. The skin beneath her palm flexed into a powerful muscle that made her heart pound.

Stunned, Grace could do nothing but stare.

Julian arched a puzzled brow. Never before had a woman

run away from him. Nor discarded him after she'd spoken the summons's chant.

All the others had waited in expectation for his incarnation, then fallen instantly into his arms, demanding he pleasure them.

But not this one ...

She was different.

His lips itched to smile as he swept his gaze over her. Her thick, sable hair fell to the middle of her back, and her light gray eyes looked like the sea just before a storm. Gray eyes flecked with tiny bits of silver and green that shone with intelligence and warmth.

Her smooth, pale skin was covered with little light brown freckles. She was every bit as adorable as her smooth, accented voice.

Not that it would have mattered.

Regardless of her looks, he existed only to serve her sexually. To lose himself in the savoring of her body with his, and he fully intended to do just that.

'Here,' he said, taking her by her shoulders. 'Let me help you up.'

'You are naked,' she whispered, looking him up and down in astonishment as they came to their feet. 'You are *so* naked.'

He tucked the ends of her sable hair back behind her ears. 'I know.'

'*You are naked!*'

'We've established that.'

'You're *happy* and naked.'

Confused, Julian frowned. 'What?'

She looked down at his arousal. 'You are *happy*,' she said with a pointed glance. 'And you're naked.'

So, that was what they were calling it in this century. He would have to remember that.

29

'And this makes you uncomfortable?' he asked, amazed by the fact that a woman would mind his nudity when no one ever had before.

'Bingo!'

'Well, I know a cure,' Julian said, his voice dropping an octave as he stared at her shirt, and the hardened nipples that jutted out from the thin white material. Nipples he couldn't wait to see.

To taste.

He moved to touch her.

Grace stepped back, her heart hammering. This wasn't real. It couldn't be real. She was just drunk and delusional. Or she must have whacked her head on the coffee table and she was unconscious and bleeding to death.

Yes, that was it! That made sense.

At least it made a lot more sense than the deep humming throb that burned through her body. A throb that begged her to jump this guy's bones.

And they were such nice bones, too.

When you have a fantasy, girl, you definitely go all the way. You must've been working too hard lately. You're starting to take home your patients' dreams.

He reached out for her and cupped her cheeks in his strong hands. Grace couldn't move. All she could do was let him tilt her head up until she looked into those penetrating eyes she was sure could read her soul. They hypnotized her like those of a deadly predator lulling its prey.

She quivered in his embrace.

Then, hot, demanding lips covered her own. Grace moaned in response. She'd heard all her life about kisses that made women weak in their knees, but this was the first time she'd ever experienced one.

Oh, but he felt good, smelled good, and he tasted even better.

Of their own accord, her arms wrapped around his shoulders, broad and rock-hard. The heat of his chest seeped into hers, beckoning her with erotic, sensual promise of what was to come. And all the while, he ravished her mouth masterfully like a Viking marauder bent on total devastation.

Every inch of his magnificent body was pressed intimately against her own, rubbing hers in a manner meant to heighten her feminine awareness of him. And oh, baby, she was aware of him in a way she'd never been aware of any other man. She slid her hand down the sculpted muscles of his bare back and sighed as they bunched beneath her hand.

Grace decided right then and there that if this was a dream, she definitely didn't want the alarm to go off.

Or the phone to ring.

Or . . .

His hands roamed her back before cupping her buttocks and pressing her hips closer to his as his tongue danced with hers. The smell of sandalwood filled her senses.

Her body molten, Grace explored the taut, corded muscles of his naked back with her palms as his long hair swept against the back of her hands in an erotic caress.

Julian's head swam at her warm touch, at the pleasant feel of her arms wrapped tightly around him as he ran his hands over the bounty of her soft freckled skin.

How he loved the sounds she made as she responded so provocatively to him. Mmm, he couldn't wait to hear her scream out in release. To see her head thrown back while her body spasmed around his.

It had been so very long since he'd last felt a woman's touch. So long since he'd last had any human contact at all.

His body was white-hot with desire, and if this were anything but their first time, he'd devour her like a morsel of sweet chocolate. Lay her down and ravish her like a starving man at a banquet.

But that would have to wait until she was used to him.

He'd learned centuries ago that women always swooned from their first union. And he definitely didn't want this one to faint.

Not yet anyway.

Still, he couldn't wait another minute to have her.

Scooping her up in his arms, he headed for the stairs.

At first, Grace couldn't think past the incredible feel of strong arms surrounding her with heat – of a man actually picking her up and not groaning from the effort. But as they passed the large wooden pineapple at the base of her balustrade, she woke up with a start.

'Whoa, buster!' she snapped, grabbing on to the carved mahogany pineapple like a life preserver. 'Just where do you think you're taking me?'

He paused and looked down at her curiously. In that instant, she realized that as tall and powerful as he was, he could do anything in the world he wanted with her and she would be powerless to stop him.

A tremor of fear thrummed through her body.

Yet for all the danger, some part of her wasn't afraid. Something in her gut told her he wouldn't intentionally hurt her.

'I'm taking you to your bedroom where we can finish what we've started,' he said simply, as if he were discussing the weather.

'I don't think so.'

He shrugged those wonderfully broad shoulders. 'You would prefer the stairs, then? Or the couch perhaps?' He paused and looked about her house as if considering his choices. 'Not a bad thought, actually. It's been a long time since I took a woman on–'

'No, no, no! The only place you're going to *take* me is in your dreams. Now set me down before I really get mad.'

To her shock, he complied.

Feeling a little better once her feet were safely on the ground, she ascended two steps.

Now they were eye to eye, and on a little more equal footing – that was, if a person could ever *be* on equal footing with a man who possessed such innate power and authority.

Suddenly the full impact of his presence slammed into her.

He was real!

Dear heaven, she and Selena had actually conjured him to life!

His eyes bored into hers, his face stoic and completely unamused. 'I don't understand why I'm here. If you don't want me inside you, why did you call for me?'

She almost moaned at his words. Worse, the image of his golden, lean, and powerful body thrusting against hers flashed through her mind.

What would it feel like to have a man so incredibly scrumptious make love to her all night?

And he would be scrumptious in bed. There was no doubt. With the prowess and moves he'd shown her so far, there was no telling just how much better ...

Grace tensed at the thought. What was it about this man?

Never in her life had she felt sexual hunger like this. Never! She could literally lay him down on the floor and devour him.

It didn't make sense.

Over the years, she'd grown more than accustomed to sex being described in the most graphic of terms – some of her patients even purposely tried to shock or arouse her.

Never once had they elicited such a heated response from her.

But when it came to him, all she could think of was taking him into her arms and riding him into the ground.

That completely uncharacteristic thought sobered her.

Grace opened her mouth to respond to his question, then stopped. What was she going to do with this guy?

Other than *that*.

She shook her head in disbelief. 'What am I supposed to do with you?'

His eyes darkened with lust as he again reached for her.

Oh, yes, her body begged, *please touch me all over*.

'Stop that!' she snapped at both herself and him, refusing to let go of her control. Rational thought would reign here, not her hormones. She'd already made *that* mistake and she wasn't about to repeat it.

She jumped up another step and she stared at him. Holy guacamole, he was gorgeous. His wavy, tawny hair fell midway down his back where it was secured with a dark brown leather cord. All except for three thin braids that had beads attached to their ends – braids that swung in time with his movements.

Dark brown eyebrows slashed over eyes that were both beguiling and terrifying. Eyes that watched her with way too much heat.

And in that moment, she definitely wanted to kill Selena.

But not nearly as much as she wanted to crawl into bed with this man and sink her teeth into that golden tan.

Stop that!

'I don't understand what's going on,' she said at last. She had to think through this – figure out what to do. 'I need to sit down for a minute and you . . . ' She trailed her eyes over his perfect body. 'You need to cover up.'

The corners of Julian's mouth twitched. In the whole of his life, she was the first person to *ever* say that to him.

Indeed, all the women he'd known before the curse had done nothing except try and get him out of his clothes. As quickly as possible. And since the curse, his summoners had spent days staring at his nudity, running their hands over his body, savoring the sight of him.

'Stay here for a minute,' she said, before darting up the stairs.

He watched her hips sway with her steps, his body instantly growing hot and hard. Clenching his teeth in an effort to ignore the burning in his loins, he forced himself to look around. Distraction was definitely the key – at least until she gave in to him.

Which wouldn't be long. No woman could ever withhold herself from him for any length of time.

Smiling bitterly at the thought, he glanced about the house.

Just where and when was he?

He didn't know how long he'd been trapped. All he could remember were the sounds of voices over time, the subtle shifting and changing of accents and language dialects as the years passed.

Looking up at the light above his head, he frowned. No fire burned. What was that thing? His eyes watered in protest and he looked away.

That must be the lightbulb, he decided.

Hey, I need to change the lightbulb. Do me a favor and flip the switch by the door. 'Kay?

Remembering the shopkeeper's words, he looked to the door and saw what he assumed was the switch. Julian left the stairs and pulled down on the tiny lever. Immediately the lights went out. He switched them back on.

In spite of himself, he smiled again. What other marvels did this time hold?

'Here.'

Julian looked at Grace who stood on the bottom step. She tossed him a long rectangle of dark green fabric. He caught it against his chest as a wave of disbelief consumed him.

The woman had been serious about covering him up?

How very odd. His frown deepening, he wrapped the fabric around his hips.

Grace waited until he moved away from the door before she looked at him again. Thank goodness, he was finally covered. No wonder the Victorians insisted on fig leaves. Too bad she didn't have a few in her yard. The only thing out there was holly bushes and she doubted he'd appreciate that.

Grace headed to the living room and sat down on the couch. 'So help me, Lanie,' she breathed. 'I'm going to get you for this.'

And then he was there, sitting beside her, firing every hormone in her body with his presence.

Moving to the opposite end of the couch, Grace eyed him warily. 'So, how long are you here for?'

Oh, great question, Grace. Why not ask him for the weather or his sign while you're at it? Jeez!

'Until the next full moon.' His glacial eyes melted a degree. And as he ran it over her body, his gaze turned from ice to fire in the space of about two heartbeats.

He leaned toward her, reaching to touch her face.

Grace jumped to her feet and went to stand on the other side of the coffee table. 'Are you telling me that I'm stuck with you for the next month?'

'Yes.'

Stunned, Grace rubbed her hand over her eyes. She

36

couldn't entertain him for a month. A whole, solid month! She had responsibilities, obligations.

She had a new hobby to learn.

'Look,' she said. 'Believe it or not, I have a life. One that doesn't include you in it.'

She could tell by his face that he didn't care for her words. Not at all. 'If you think I'm thrilled by being here with you, you're sadly mistaken. I assure you I'm not here by choice.'

His words stung her.

'Well, not *all* of you feels that way.' She gave a pointed glare to the part of him that was still ramrod-stiff.

Looking down at his lap and the lump bulging under the towel, he sighed. 'Unfortunately, I don't have any more control over *that* than I do being here.'

'Well, there's the door,' she said, pointing toward it. 'Don't let it hit you on the rump on your way out.'

'Believe me, if I could leave, I would.'

Grace hesitated at his words, and their significance. 'Are you telling me that I can't wish you away? Or make you go back into the book?'

'I believe your word was *bingo*.'

She fell silent.

Rising slowly to his feet, Julian stared at her. In all the centuries he'd been damned, this was the first time this had come up. All his other summoners had known what he was, and they had been more than willing to spend the month in his arms, happily using his body for their pleasure.

He'd never in his life, either this one or his mortal one, found a woman who didn't want him physically.

It was ...

Odd.

Humbling.

Almost embarrassing.

Could it be that the curse was weakening? That maybe at last he might be free?

But even as the thought crossed his mind, he knew better. When the Greek gods handed down a punishment, they did it with style and with a vengeance that not even two millennia could mellow.

There had been a time once, long ago, when he had fought against his damnation. A time when he had believed he could be free. But over two thousand years of confinement and unrelenting torture had taught him one thing – resignation.

He had earned his hell, and like the soldier he'd once been, he accepted his punishment.

Swallowing the gall that stuck in his throat, Julian spread his arms out, and offered his body to her. 'You can do with me as you wish. Just tell me how to please you.'

'Then, I wish for you to leave.'

He dropped his arms to his side. 'Except for that.'

Frustrated, Grace started to pace. Her hormones finally whipped back under control and her head clearer, she yearned for a solution. But no matter how hard she tried, there didn't seem to be one.

A terrible ache began throbbing in her temples.

Whatever was she going to do for a month, a *solid month,* with him?

Again an image of him poised above her, his hair falling around them in a soft canopy while he plunged himself deep inside her body, tortured her.

'I need something . . .' Julian's voice trailed off.

She turned back to face him, her body still begging for his.

It would be so easy to give in to him. But that would be wrong. She refused to use him that way. Like . . .

No, she wouldn't think about *that.* She *refused* to think about that.

'What?' she asked.

'Food,' Julian repeated. 'If you're not going to use me right away, would you mind if I ate?' The sheepish, half-angry look on his face told her he didn't like asking for anything.

Then it dawned on her that as odd and difficult as this was for her, what on earth must it feel like for him? To be snatched from wherever it was he lived and thrown into her life like a slingshot? It must be terrible.

'Sure,' she said, motioning for him to follow her. 'The kitchen's in here.' She led him down the short hallway to the rear of the house.

She opened the fridge and let him look into it. 'What would you like?'

Instead of sticking his head in, he stayed about three feet back. 'Do you have any pizza left?'

'Pizza?' she repeated in shock. How did he know about pizza?

He shrugged. 'You seemed to really enjoy eating it.'

Her face flamed as she recalled her earlier play. Selena had made another comment about food substituting for sex, and she had faked an orgasm while savoring her last slice. 'You heard us?'

His face stoic, he spoke quietly. 'The *love-slave* hears everything said near the book.'

If her cheeks turned any hotter, they would explode. 'I don't have any pizza,' she said quickly, wanting to bury her head in the freezer to cool it off. 'I do have some leftover chicken and pasta.'

'And wine?'

She nodded.

'That's acceptable.'

His commanding tone really set her ire off. It was one of

39

those 'I'm the man, baby, get me some food' Tarzan tones that just set her blood to boil.

'Look, buster, I'm not your cooking wench. Mess with me and I'll feed you Alpo.'

He arched a brow. 'Alpo?'

'Never mind.' Still irritated, she pulled out her chicken primavera and prepared to nuke it.

He sat at her table with this oozing aura of male arrogance that just grated on her tolerance. Wishing she really had a can of Alpo, Grace forced herself to dump a heaped serving of pasta into a bowl.

'Just how long have you been in that book, anyway? Since the Dark Ages?' At least that's what he acted like.

He sat as still as a statue. No emotions, no nothing. If she didn't know better, she'd swear he was an android.

'The last time I was summoned, it was eighteen ninety-five.'

'Get out!' Grace gaped at him as she placed the bowl in the microwave. 'Eighteen ninety-five? Are you serious?'

He nodded.

'What year was it when you *first* got trapped?'

Rage flashed across his face with such high intensity that it startled her. 'One forty-nine B.C. by your calendar.'

Her eyes widened. 'One forty-nine B.C., as in one hundred forty-nine years before Christ? Holy guac. When I called Julian of Macedon, you really *are* of Macedon. Of *the* Macedon.'

He gave a curt nod.

Her thoughts whirled as she closed the door to the microwave and turned it on. This was impossible. It had to be impossible!

'How did you get trapped in the book? I mean, the ancient Greeks didn't have books, did they?'

'I was originally entombed in a scroll that was later bound to protect it,' he said darkly, his face still impassive. 'As for how I ended up cursed, I invaded Alexandria.'

Grace frowned. Now that didn't make a bit of sense, not that very much of *any* of this made sense to her. 'Why would invading a city get–'

'Alexandria wasn't a city, she was a Priapine virgin.'

She tensed at his words, and the implication of how invading a woman might get a man trapped for eternity. 'You raped a virgin?'

'I didn't rape her,' he said, meeting her gaze with a hard stare. 'It was by mutual consent, I assure you.'

Okay, there was a nerve there. Grace could see it clearly in his icy demeanor. The man didn't like talking about his past. She would have to be a little more subtle in her questioning.

Julian heard the strange bell toll before Grace pressed a bar and opened the black box where she'd placed his food.

She set the steaming bowl of food before him with a silver fork, knife, paper napkin, and glass goblet of wine. The warm aroma filled his head, making his stomach ache with need.

He supposed he should be shocked by the way and speed with which she'd cooked, but after hearing about things called a train, camera, automobile, phonograph, rockets, and computers, he doubted if anything could take him by surprise now.

In truth, there was nothing left for him to feel since, out of necessity, he'd banished his emotions long ago.

His existence was nothing more than snatches of days strung along centuries. His only purpose to serve his summoner's sexual needs.

And if he'd learned anything over the last two millennia,

it was to enjoy what few pleasures he could during each incarnation.

With that thought, he took a small bite of food and savored the delectable feel of the warm, creamy noodles on his tongue. It was pure bliss.

He let the smell of the chicken and spices fully invade his head. It had been an eternity since he'd last eaten anything. An eternity of unrelenting hunger.

Closing his eyes, he swallowed.

More used to starvation than nourishment, his stomach cramped viciously in reaction to the first bite of food. Julian clenched the knife and fork in his hands as he fought against the brutal pain.

But he didn't stop eating. Not while he had food.

He'd waited so long to finally quench his hunger that he wasn't about to stop now.

After a few more bites, the cramps eased, allowing him to actually enjoy the meal again.

And as the cramps lessened, it took all of his willpower to eat like a human and not shovel the food into his mouth by the handfuls in a desperate need to quench the gnawing hunger in his belly.

At times like this, it was hard to remember he was still a man and not some feral, rampaging beast that had been freed from its cage.

He'd lost most of his humanity centuries ago. What little was left, he intended to keep.

Grace leaned against the counter as she watched him eat, slowly, almost mechanically. She couldn't tell if he liked the food, but he kept eating it.

Yet what amazed her were the perfect European table manners he had. She'd never been able to successfully eat that way, and she wondered when he'd learned to use his knife to balance the pasta on the back of his fork and eat it.

'Did they have forks in ancient Macedonia?' she asked.

He paused. 'Excuse me?'

'I was just wondering when the fork was invented. Did they have them in ... '

You're rambling! her mind shouted at her.

Well, who wouldn't? Just look at the guy. How many times do you think someone has acted like an idiot and had a Greek statue come to life? Especially one who looks like that!

Not often.

'The fork was invented sometime in the fifteenth century, I believe.'

'Really?' she asked. 'Were you there?'

His features blank, he looked up and asked, 'What, for the invention of the fork, or the fifteenth century?'

'The fifteenth century, of course.' And then thinking better of it, she added, 'You weren't there when the fork was invented. Were you?'

'No.' He cleared his throat and wiped his mouth with the napkin. 'I was summoned four times during that century. Twice in Italy and once in England and France.'

'Really,' she said, trying to imagine what it must have been like back then. 'I bet you've seen all kinds of things over the centuries.'

'Not really.'

'Oh, come on. In two thousand years—'

'I've mostly seen bedrooms, beds, and closets.'

His flat tone gave her pause as he returned to eating. An image of Paul pierced her heart. She'd only known one selfish, uncaring jerk. It sounded as if Julian had known many more.

'So tell me, do you just lie in the book until someone calls you?'

He nodded.

'What do you do in the book to pass the time?'

He shrugged, and she homed in on the fact that he didn't possess a wide range of expressions.

Or words.

She moved forward and took a seat across the table from him. 'You know, according to you we have a month together, why not make it pleasurable and talk?'

Julian glanced up in surprise. He couldn't remember the last time anyone had actually conversed with him, except to issue encouragements or suggestions to help heighten the pleasure he was giving them.

Or to call him back to bed.

He'd learned very early in life that women only wanted one thing when it came to him – some part of his body buried deep between their legs.

With that thought in mind, he drifted his gaze slowly, leisurely, over her body, stopping at her breasts, which grew tight at his prolonged stare.

Indignantly, she crossed her arms over her chest and waited until he met her gaze.

Julian almost laughed. Almost.

'You know,' he said, using her words. 'There are far more entertaining things to do with a tongue than talk – like run it over your bare breasts and through the hollow of your throat.' His gaze dropped down to the table to the approximate area of her lap. 'Not to mention other places it can go.'

For an instant, Grace was dumbstruck. Then amused.

Then *very* horny.

As a therapist, she'd heard much more shocking things than that, she reminded herself.

Yeah, but not from a tongue that *she* wanted to do things with other than talk.

'You're right, there are other things to do with one, like cut it out,' she said, taking some satisfaction in the surprise that flickered in his eyes. 'But I'm a woman who likes talk and you are here to please *me, are you not?*'

There was only the subtlest of tenseness to his body as if he resisted his role. 'I am.'

'Then, tell me what you do while you're in the book.'

His gaze bored into hers with a heated intensity that she found unnerving, intriguing, and a bit frightening.

'It's like being trapped inside a sarcophagus,' he said quietly. 'I hear voices, but I can't see light or anything else. I just stand there, unable to move. Waiting. Listening.'

Grace cringed at the very idea. She remembered once, long ago, when she had accidentally locked herself in her father's toolshed. There had been no light, no way out. Terrified, she had felt her lungs seizing up, felt her head go light in panic. She had screamed and pounded on the door until she had bruised her entire hand.

Finally, her mother had heard her and let her out.

To this day, Grace was slightly claustrophobic from the experience. She couldn't imagine what it must be like to spend centuries in such a place.

'How horrible,' she breathed.

'You get used to it. In time.'

'Do you?' She didn't know, but for some reason she doubted it.

When her mother had released her from the toolshed, she found out she'd only been inside for half an hour, but to her it had seemed like an eternity. What would it be like to really spend eternity that way?

'Have you ever tried to escape?'

The look he gave her spoke loudly.

'What happened?' she asked.

45

'Obviously, I failed.'

She felt horrible for him. Two thousand years spent in a lightless crypt. It was a wonder he was still sane. That he was able to even sit here with her and speak at all.

No wonder he had wanted food. That kind of sensory deprivation was sheer, unrelenting torture.

In that moment, she knew she was going to help him. She didn't know how, but there had to be some way to break him out. 'What if we could find a way to get you free?'

'I assure you, there isn't one.'

'Fatalistic, aren't you?'

He cast a droll look at her. 'Being trapped for two thousand years does that to a person.'

Grace watched him eat, her thoughts whirling. The optimist in her refused to take his pessimism to heart, just like the therapist in her refused not to help him. She'd sworn an oath to relieve suffering when she could and Grace took her oaths most seriously.

Where there was a will, there was always a way.

And come heck or high water, she would find a way to get him free!

In the meantime, she decided she would do something for him she doubted anyone else ever had before – she was going to see to it that he enjoyed his reprieve in New Orleans. The other women might have kept him confined to their bedrooms or closets, but she wasn't about to put chains on anyone.

'Well, then, let's just say that this incarnation is for you, bud.'

He looked up from his food with sudden interest.

'I'm going to be *your* servant,' Grace continued. 'Whatever you want to do, we'll do. Whatever you want to see, you'll see.'

One corner of his mouth lifted in wry amusement as he took a drink of wine. 'Take off your shirt.'

'Excuse me?' she asked.

He set his glass of wine aside and pinned her with a hot, lustful stare. 'You said I can see what I want to see and do what I want to do. Well, I want to see your naked breasts, and then I want to run my tongue–'

'Whoa, big fellow, simmer down,' Grace said, her cheeks scalding, her body white-hot. 'I think there should be a few ground rules while you're here. Number one, there won't be *any* of *that*.'

'And why not?'

Yeah, her body demanded in a half begging, half angry inner voice. *Why not?*

'Because I'm not some alley cat with her tail up in the air waiting for the nearest Tom to come over, stick it in, and leave.'

Chapter Four

Julian cocked his brow at her wholly unexpected, wholly crude analogy. But even more surprising than her words was the amount of bitterness he heard in Grace's voice. She must have been badly used in the past. No wonder she was skittish of him.

An image of Penelope flashed through his mind, and he felt a stab of pain so ferocious in his chest that only his staunch military training kept him from wincing.

He had much to atone for. Sins so great that not even two thousand years could begin to compensate for them.

He hadn't just been born a bastard; because of a brutal life of desperation and betrayal, he had truly become one.

Closing his eyes, he forced those thoughts away. That was literally ancient history and this was the present. Grace was the present.

And he was here for her.

Now, he understood what Selena had meant when she'd spoken to him about Grace. That was why he was here. He was to show Grace that sex was enjoyable.

Never before had he encountered anything like this.

As he looked at Grace, a slow smile curved his lips. This would be the first time in his life he'd ever had to pursue a woman for his lover. No woman had ever turned his body down.

What with her wit and stubbornness he knew getting Grace into bed would prove to be every bit as challenging as outwitting the Roman army.

Yes, he would savor this.

Just as he would savor her. Every sweetly freckled inch of her.

Grace swallowed at the first true smile she'd seen from him. A smile that softened his features and made him even more devastating.

What on earth was he thinking?

For the umpteenth time, Grace felt her face flood with warmth as she thought about her crude words. She hadn't meant to let that slip out. It wasn't like her to betray her thoughts to anyone, especially a stranger.

But there was something so compelling about this man. Something that reached out to her in a most disturbing way. Maybe it was the thinly masked pain that flashed in those celestial blue eyes when she caught him off guard. Or maybe it was just her years of psychology training that couldn't stand the thought of having such a troubled soul in her home and not helping him.

She didn't know.

The grandfather clock in her upstairs hallway chimed one. 'Goodness,' she said, shocked that it had become so late. 'I've got to get up for work at six.'

'You're going to bed? To sleep?'

Had his mood not been so dour, the stunned look on his face would have made her laugh. 'I need to.'

His brow drew together in ...

Pain?

'Is something wrong?' she asked.

He shook his head.

'Well, then, I'll show you where you can sleep and–'

'I'm not sleepy.'

She started at his words. 'What?'

Julian looked up at her, unable to find the words to tell her what he felt. He'd been trapped in the book for so long that all he wanted to do was to run, or to jump. To do *anything* to celebrate his sudden freedom of movement.

He didn't want to go to bed. The thought of lying in darkness another minute ...

He struggled to breathe.

'I've been resting since eighteen ninety-five,' he explained. 'I'm not sure how long ago that was, but by the looks of things, it has been quite some time.'

'It's two thousand and two,' Grace supplied for his information. 'You've been "sleeping" for one hundred and seven years.' No, she corrected herself. He hadn't been asleep.

He'd told her that he could hear anything said around the book, which meant that he had been awake and locked up all this time. Isolated. Alone.

She was the first person in over a hundred years that he'd been able to talk to, or be with.

Her stomach tightened in sympathy. Even though her prison of shyness had never been tangible, she knew what it felt like to be somewhere listening to people and not be a part of them. To be on the outside looking in.

'I wish I could stay up,' she said, stifling a yawn. 'Really I do, but if I don't get enough sleep, my brain turns to Jell-O and I can't think for squat.'

50

'I understand. At least I think I get the gist of it, though I'm not sure what this Jell-O and squat is.'

Still, she could see his disappointment. 'You could watch TV.'

'TV?'

She picked up his empty bowl and rinsed it off before leading him back to the living room. Switching on her set, she showed him how to flip channels with the remote.

'Incredible,' he whispered as he surfed for the first time.

'Yeah, it is kind of nifty.'

Now, that should keep him busy. After all, men only needed three things to be happy – food, sex, and a remote. Two out three ought to satisfy him for a bit.

'Well,' she said, heading for the stairs. 'Good night.'

As she started past him, he touched her arm. Even though his hand was light, it sent a shock wave through her.

His face impassive, raw emotions flickered in his eyes. She saw his torment, his need, but most of all she saw his loneliness.

He didn't want her to leave.

Licking her suddenly dry lips, she said something she couldn't believe. 'I have another TV in my room. Why don't you watch that one while I sleep?'

He gave her a sheepish smile.

Julian followed her up the stairs, amazed that she had understood him without his speaking. That she would consider his need not to be alone while she had her own concerns.

It made him feel strange toward her. Put an odd feeling in his stomach.

Was it tenderness?

He didn't know for sure.

She led him into an enormous bedchamber with a large

51

four-poster bed set before the middle of the far wall. A medium-sized chest of drawers was set opposite the bed and on top of it was, what had she called it, a TV?

Grace watched as Julian walked around her room, looking at the pictures on her walls and dresser – pictures of her parents and grandparents, of Selena and her in college, and the one of the dog she'd owned as a child.

'You live alone?' he asked.

'Yes,' she said, moving to her Jenny Lind rocking chair by the bed where her nightgown was draped over the back. She picked it up and looked at him, and the green towel still wrapped around his lean hips. She couldn't very well let him join her in bed like that.

Sure you could.

No I can't.

Please?

Hush, self, let me think.

She still had her father's pajamas in her parents' bedroom where she kept all their possessions enshrined. Given the breadth of Julian's shoulders, she was sure the tops would never fit, but the bottoms had drawstrings and even if they didn't fit in length, they would at least stay up.

'Wait here,' she told him. 'I'll be right back.'

After she darted out the door, Julian walked over to the large windows and pulled back the white lace curtains. He watched strange boxlike things that must be automobiles move past her house, making strange droning noises that ebbed and flowed like a tide. Lights lit up the street and other buildings all over, much like torches had once done in his own homeland.

How strange this world was. So oddly similar to his and yet so very different.

He tried to associate the sights with all the words he'd

heard over the decades, words he didn't understand. Words like *TV* and *lightbulb*.

And for the first time since his childhood, he was afraid. He didn't like the changes he saw, the swiftness with which they had come to this world.

What would it be like the next time he was summoned?

How much more different *could* things become?

Or even more terrifying, what if he was never summoned again?

He swallowed at the thought. What would it be like to be trapped for eternity? Alone and alert. To feel the oppressive darkness closing in on him, squelching the breath from his lungs as it lacerated his body with pain.

To never again walk as a man? Never to speak or to touch?

These people had things now that were called computers. He'd heard the shop owner talk about them with a lot of customers. And one of those customers had said that they would one day, probably soon, completely replace books.

What would happen to him then?

Dressed in her pink dorm shirt, Grace paused in her parents' bedroom by the crystal dish on the dresser where she'd placed her mother's wedding rings the day after the funeral. She could see the faint sparkle of the half-carat marquis diamond.

Her throat constricting with pain, she fought against the tears that welled in her eyes.

Barely twenty-four at the time, she'd been arrogant enough to think she was grown, and capable of standing strong against anything life hurled at her. She had thought herself invincible. And in one split second, her life had come crumbling down around her.

Their deaths had robbed her of everything she'd ever had. Her security, her faith, her sense of justice, but most of all, she had lost their devoted love and emotional support.

In spite of her youthful vanity, she hadn't been prepared to be cast completely adrift without any family whatsoever.

And even though five years had passed, she still mourned them. Deeply. The old saying that it was better to have known love and lost it was a big fat crock. There was nothing worse than having someone to love and care for you, then losing them to a needless accident.

Unable to face their deaths, she'd sealed this room off the day after their funeral, and left everything in it just as it was.

Opening the drawer where her father had kept his pajamas, Grace swallowed. No one had touched these since the afternoon her mother had folded them, and they had brought the clothes up here and put them away.

Even now, she could remember her mother's laughter. The way her mother joked about her father's conservative taste in flannel PJs.

Worse, she remembered their love for each other.

What she wouldn't give to find a perfect partner like her parents had done. They'd been married twenty-five years before they died and they were every bit as in love then as they'd been the day they met.

She couldn't remember a time in her life when her mother hadn't been smiling, her father gently teasing. Everywhere they went, they held hands like teenagers and stole quick kisses when they thought no one was looking.

But she had seen.

She remembered.

She'd wanted that kind of love, too. But for some reason, she'd never found a man who made her breathless. One who made her heart pound and her senses reel.

A man she couldn't live without.

'Oh, Mama,' she breathed, wishing her parents hadn't died that night.

Wishing for ...

She didn't know. She just wanted something in her life that made her look forward to the future. Something that made her happy the way her father had always made her mother so happy.

Biting her lip, Grace balled her father's dark blue and white plaid pajama pants in her arms and ran from the room.

'Here,' she said, tossing them to Julian before she left him and ran to the bathroom in the middle of the hallway. She didn't want him to see her tears. She would never again show her vulnerability to a man.

Julian exchanged the cloth around his hips for the pants, then followed after Grace. She'd rushed to the next door down the hall and slammed it shut.

'Grace,' he said, gently nudging the door open.

He froze as he saw her weeping. She stood in a lavatory of some sort with two built-in sinks, and a white counter in front of her while she held a cloth to her mouth in an effort to muffle her wracking sobs.

In spite of his severe upbringing and aeons of control, a wave of pity washed over him. She cried as if her heart had been broken.

It made him uncomfortable. Uncertain.

Clenching his teeth, Julian forced his strange feelings away. One thing he'd learned early in his childhood, it didn't do any good to learn about people. To care for them. Every time he had made that mistake, he'd paid dearly for it.

Besides, his time here was short – way too short.

The less he entangled himself with her emotions and life,

the easier it would be to tolerate his next confinement.

It was then that her earlier words hit him square in the chest. She'd pegged him perfectly. He was nothing more than a tomcat who took his pleasure and left.

Julian clenched the cold doorknob at the thought. He wasn't an animal. He had feelings, too.

At least he used to.

Before he could reconsider his actions, he stepped into the room and drew her into a hug. Her arms encircled his waist and she held on to him like a lifeline as she buried her face into his bare chest and wept. Her entire body shook against his.

Something strange inside him unfurled. A deep longing for something he couldn't name.

Never in his life had he comforted a weeping woman. He'd had sex more times than he could count, but never once had he just held a woman like this. Not even after sex. Once he wore out his partner, he would get up and clean himself off, then go find something to occupy himself with until he was called again.

Even before the curse, he'd never shown anyone tenderness. Not even his wife.

As a soldier, he'd been trained from his first memory to be fierce, cold. Harsh.

'Return with your shield, or upon it.' That was what his stepmother had told him as she grabbed him by his hair and slung him out of her home to begin training for war at the tender age of seven.

His father had been even worse. A legendary Spartan commander, his father had tolerated no weakness. No emotion. The man had doled out Julian's childhood at the end of a braided leather whip, teaching him to hide his pain. To let no one see him suffer.

To this day Julian could feel the bite of the whip against his bare back, hear the sound it made as it cut through the air toward his skin. See the mocking sneer of contempt on his father's face.

'I'm sorry,' Grace whispered against his shoulder, dragging his thoughts back to the present.

She tilted her head to look up at him. Her gray eyes were bright and shiny, and they chipped at the edges of a heart frozen centuries before by necessity and by design.

Uncomfortable, he moved away from her. 'Feeling better?'

Grace wiped her tears away and cleared her throat. She didn't know what had made Julian come after her, but it had been a long time since anyone had comforted her when she cried. 'Yes,' she whispered. 'Thank you.'

He said nothing.

Instead of the tender man who had held her just an instant ago, he was back to being Mr. Statue, his entire body rigid and cold.

Drawing a ragged breath, she moved past him. 'I wouldn't have done that if I weren't *so* tired and still a little tipsy. I really do need to go to sleep.'

She knew he would follow, so she dutifully headed back to her room and climbed aboard her tall pineapple plantation bed where she snuggled beneath her thick comforter.

Sure enough, she felt the mattress dip under his weight an instant later.

Her heart quickened at the sudden warmth of his body next to hers. Worse, he instantly curled himself against her back, and draped one long, muscular arm over her waist.

'Julian!' she said with a warning note in her voice as she felt his erection against her hip. 'I think it might be best if you stay on your side of the bed, and I stay on mine.'

He didn't listen as he leaned his head down to hers and nibbled a small path along her hairline. 'I thought you wanted me to come ease your aching loins,' he whispered in her ear.

Her body on fire from his nearness and the scent of sandalwood that filled her head, Grace blushed as she remembered her words to Selena. 'My loins are just fine, and are quite happy as they are.'

'I promise you, I could make them much, much happier.'

Ooo, she didn't doubt it in the least. 'If you don't behave, I'm going to make you leave the room.'

She looked up at him and caught the disbelief in his eyes.

'I don't understand why you would send me away,' he said.

'Because I'm not going to use you like some nameless boy-toy who has no purpose except to serve me. Okay? I don't want to be intimate with a man I don't know.'

His blue eyes troubled, he finally withdrew from her and settled down beside her.

Grace took a deep breath as she tried to calm her racing heart and tame the fire in her blood. Goodness, he was a hard man to say no to.

Do you really think you're going to be able to sleep with this guy lying next to you? What, do you have rocks for brains?

Closing her eyes, she recited her boring litany. She *had* to go to sleep. There were no ifs, ands, or buts about it. Or even gorgeous Julians.

Julian propped the pillows up behind his back and looked over at Grace. This would be the first time in his exceptionally long life that he spent a night with a woman without making love to her.

It was inconceivable. No woman had ever pushed him away before.

She rolled over with another handset like the one she'd shown him downstairs. She pressed a button and turned on the TV, then lowered the sound of people talking.

'This is for the lights,' she said, pressing another button. Immediately, the lights turned off, leaving the TV to cast shadows on the wall behind him. 'I'm a pretty sound sleeper, so I don't think you'll wake me.'

She handed him the handset. 'Good night, Julian of Macedon.'

'Good night, Grace,' he whispered, watching the way her soft hair fanned out over the pillow as she snuggled down to sleep.

He put the handset aside and watched her for a long while as the light from the TV flickered across the relaxed planes of her face.

He could tell when she finally fell asleep by the evenness of her breathing. It was only then that he finally dared to touch her. Dared to trace the gentle outline of her soft cheek with the pad of his forefinger.

His body reacted with such violence that he bit his lip to keep from cursing. Fire streamed through his blood.

He'd known stabbing desires all his life – first a hunger in his belly for food, then a burning thirst for love and respect, and finally the demanding one in his loins for the wet sleekness of a woman's body. But never, never, had he experienced anything like this.

It was a hunger so strong, so raw, that it threatened his very sanity.

And all he could think of was spreading her creamy, silken thighs and planting himself deep inside her. Of sliding in and out of her body over and over until they both screamed out their release in unison.

Only that would never happen.

Julian moved farther away from her. To a safe distance in the bed where he could no longer smell her sweet feminine scent, feel the heat of her body beneath the covers.

He could give her pleasure for days on end without stopping, but for him there would never be peace.

'Damn you, Priapus,' he snarled, speaking the name of the god who had cursed him to this fate. 'I hope Hades is giving you your full due.'

His anger dulling, he sighed and realized that the Fates and Furies were certainly giving him his.

Grace came awake with a strange sense of warmth and security. It was a feeling she hadn't experienced in years.

Suddenly, she felt a tender kiss against her eyelids as if someone were brushing lips against her lashes. Warm, strong hands stroked her hair.

Julian!

She bolted up so quickly that she bumped heads with him. She heard his hiss of pain. Rubbing her forehead, she opened her eyes and saw him giving her a ferocious frown.

'Sorry,' she apologized, sitting up. 'You startled me.'

He opened his mouth and placed the pad of his thumb against his front teeth to check if she'd knocked them loose.

Worse, she couldn't miss the flick of his tongue as he tested his teeth with it. The sight of his incredibly white straight teeth that she would love to have nip her . . .

'What do you want for breakfast?' she asked, distracting herself from her thoughts.

His gaze shifted to the deep V of her dorm shirt. Following the line of his gaze, she realized that from the way she sat he could see all the way down to her embarrassingly pink Mickey Mouse underwear.

Before she could move, he pulled her across his body and claimed her lips.

Grace moaned her pleasure into his mouth as his tongue did the most wicked things to hers. Her head spun at the intense kiss, of his warm breath mingling with hers.

And to think, she'd never liked kissing.

She must have been crazy!

His arms tightened around her. A thousand flames fanned out over her body, burning her, inciting her, as they pooled into the molten zone between her thighs where she ached for him.

His lips left hers, and he trailed his tongue over her skin, searing a path to her throat where he made circles over her collarbone, her earlobe, her neck.

The man seemed to know every erogenous zone on a woman's body!

And better still, he knew how to use his tongue and hands to massage them all for maximum pleasure.

He breathed gently into her ear, sending waves of chills throughout her body, and when he stroked her inner ear with his tongue, she shook all over.

Her breasts tingled and swelled and tightened into hard nubs that begged for his kiss.

'Julian,' she moaned, unable to recognize her voice. Her mind wanted her to tell him to stop, but the words lodged themselves in her throat.

There was so much power in his touch. Such magic. It left her aching for more.

He rolled her over, pressing her back against the mattress. Even through his pajamas, she could feel his erection, hard and hot, against her hip as his hands cupped her buttocks and he breathed raggedly in her ear.

'You must stop,' she told him at last, her voice sounding weak.

'Stop what?' he asked. 'This?' His tongue swirled around and around her ear.

Grace hissed in pleasure. Chills shot all over her body like red embers, burning every inch of her. Her breasts swelled even tighter against his chest.

'Or this.' He moved one hand under the waistband of her panties to cup her where she craved him most.

Her toes actually curled in response to his hand between her legs as she arched her back against him. Oh, he was incredible!

He encircled the tender, throbbing flesh with one finger, making her burn from the inside out before he finally plunged two fingers deep inside her.

While his fingers circled and teased and stroked, he gently massaged her nub with his thumb.

'Ooo ...' Grace moaned, throwing her head back at the intensity of the pleasure.

She clung to him as his fingers and tongue continued their relentless assault of pleasure. Her control gone, she rubbed herself shamelessly against him, seeking even more of his heat, his touch.

Julian closed his eyes, savoring the scent of her body beneath his, the feel of her arms wrapped around him.

She was his. He could feel her quivering and pulsing around his hand as her body writhed to his caresses.

At any moment, she would climax.

With that thought foremost in his mind, he shoved her shirt up and dropped his head down to one taut peak where he gently suckled her areola, delighting in the feel of her puckered flesh teasing his tongue.

He couldn't remember a woman ever tasting this good. It was a taste that branded itself in his mind, one he knew he would never forget.

And she was ready for him. She was hot, wet, and tight – just the way he liked a woman's body.

He tore the thin piece of material away from her hips that impeded his access to the part of her he was dying to explore more fully.

And at much greater length.

Grace heard the rending of fabric, but she couldn't stop him. Her will was no longer her own. It had been swallowed up by sensations so intense that all she wanted was relief.

She had to have relief!

Reaching up, she buried her hands in his hair, not wanting him to leave her for even a second.

Julian kicked his pants off and spread her thighs wide.

Her body bursting into pure fire, Grace held her breath as he settled his long, hard body between her legs.

The tip of his manhood pressed against her core. She arched her hips toward him and clung to his broad shoulders, wanting him inside her with a desperation that defied belief.

Suddenly, the phone rang.

Grace jumped at the sound, her mind instantly slamming back into control.

'What is that noise?' he growled.

Grateful for the interruption, Grace struggled out from under him, her limbs trembling, her entire body burning. 'It's a phone,' she said, before leaning over to the nightstand and grabbing it.

Her hand actually shook as she brought the phone to her ear.

Cursing, Julian rolled to his side.

'Selena, thank goodness it's you,' Grace said as soon as she heard her voice.

Oh, how she was grateful for Selena's ability to know the *precise* moment to call!

'What is it?' Selena asked.

'Stop that,' Grace snapped at Julian as he licked his way down her bare buttocks. She pushed him back and put a little more distance between them.

'I'm not doing anything,' Selena said.

'Not you, Lanie.'

The other end fell as silent as the grave.

'Listen,' Grace said to Selena, her voice sharp with warning. 'I need you to get some of Bill's clothes and bring them over. Now.'

'It worked!' The piercing shriek almost splintered her eardrum. 'Oh, my God, it worked! Hallelujah, I can't believe it! I'm on my way!'

Grace turned the phone off just as Julian's tongue traced a path from her buttocks to her . . .

'Stop that!'

He pulled back and gave her a shocked frown. 'You don't like it when I do that?'

'That's not what I said,' she answered before she could stop herself.

He moved back to her . . .

Grace bolted from the bed. 'I *have* to get ready for work.'

He propped himself up on one arm and watched her while she picked up his discarded pants and tossed them at him. He caught them with one hand as his gaze wandered leisurely over her body. 'Why don't you call in sick?'

'Call in sick?' she repeated. 'How do you know what that is?'

He shrugged. 'I told you, I can hear during my confinement. It's what allows me to learn languages and understand changing syntax.'

Like a graceful panther coming out of a crouch, he pulled the blanket back and moved slowly from the bed. His pants forgotten. His body still fully erect.

Mesmerized, she couldn't move.

'We didn't finish,' he said, his voice low, deep. He reached for her.

'Oh, yes we did!' She ran for the safety of the bathroom and locked the door behind her.

Clenching his teeth, Julian had the sudden urge to put his head through the wall in frustration. Why was she being so stubborn?

He looked down at his stiffened body and cursed. 'And why won't *you* behave for five minutes!'

Grace took a long, cold shower. What was it about Julian that made her blood literally boil? Even now she could feel the heat of his body on hers.

His lips on her . . .

'Stop it, stop it, stop it!'

She was not some nymphomaniac who couldn't control herself. She was a Ph.D. with a brain – and *no* hormones.

Yet it would be so easy to just forget everything and spend the next month in bed with Julian.

'Fine,' she said to herself. 'Let's say you do crawl into bed with him for a month, then what?'

She soaped her body, her aggravation dispelling the last of her desire. 'I'll tell you what. He'll be gone and you, sister, will be left alone again.

'Remember what happened after Paul? Remember what it felt like to wander around the dorm, sick to your stomach because you let someone *use* you? Remember how humiliating it was?'

Worse, she could still hear Paul's mocking laughter as he bragged to his friends and collected his bet. How she wished she'd been a man long enough to kick open the door to his apartment, and beat him to smithereens.

No, she wouldn't let herself be used.

It had taken her years to get over Paul and his cruelty, and she wasn't about to undo all that on a whim. Not even a gorgeous whim!

Nope, nope, nope. The next time she gave herself to a man it would be to someone who was committed to her. Someone who cared for her.

Someone who wouldn't disregard her pain and continue to use her body for his pleasure as if she didn't matter, she thought, her repressed memories resurfacing with a vengeance. Paul had acted as if she weren't even there. As if she were nothing more than an emotionless doll designed only to serve his pleasure.

And she wasn't about to let anyone, especially Julian, treat her like that.

Never again.

Julian walked downstairs and marveled at the bright sunlight streaming through the windows. It was funny how people took such small things for granted. He remembered a time when he too had never noticed anything as simple as a sunny morning.

Now, every one was truly a gift from the gods. A gift he would savor for the next month until he was again forced to live in darkness.

His heart heavy, he headed into the kitchen and to the large cupboard where Grace stored her food. As he opened the door, the coldness inside amazed him. He spread his hand out, letting the rushing air wash over his skin. Incredible.

He picked up various containers, but couldn't read the writing on the labels.

'Don't eat anything you can't identify,' he reminded himself, remembering some of the disgusting things he'd seen people eat over the centuries.

Bending over, he searched until he found a ripe melon in a bottom drawer. After taking it to the island in the center of the kitchen, he picked a large knife out of a block where Grace kept a dozen of them, and cut it in half.

He sliced a piece of it off and placed it in his mouth.

Julian growled low in his throat as the delectable moisture washed over his tastebuds. The sweet pulp made his stomach rumble with a demanding need. His throat ached for more of its soothing wetness.

It was so good to have food again. To have something with which to quench his thirst and hunger.

Before he could stop himself, he set the knife aside and started grabbing at the melon, shoving pieces of it into his mouth as fast as he could.

Gods, but he was so hungry. So thirsty.

It wasn't until he found himself clawing at the rind that he became aware of his actions.

Julian froze as he stared at his hand covered with the melon's juices, his fingers curled against the side like the claw of some beast.

'Roll over, Julian, and face me. Now, be a good boy, and do what I tell you to. Touch me here. Mmm … yes, that's it. Good boy, good boy. Please me well, and I'll bring you some food in a little while.

Julian flinched at the unbidden memory from his last incarnation. No wonder he acted like an animal; he'd been treated like one for so long, he barely remembered being human.

At least Grace hadn't chained him to her bed.

Yet, anyway.

Disgusted, he glanced around the room, grateful Grace hadn't seen his lapse of self-control.

His breathing ragged, he grabbed the melon half and pitched it into the trash receptacle he had seen Grace use the night before. Then he moved to the sink to wash the sticky sweetness from his hands.

As soon as the cold water touched his skin, he sighed in pleasure. Water. Pure and cold. It was what he missed most during his confinements. What he craved hour after hour as his parched throat burned and ached.

He let the coldness slide over his skin before he captured it in his cupped hand, leaned down and drank the water from his palm, sucked it from his fingers. It was so soothing as it invaded his mouth and slid down his burning throat, slaking his thirst. He wanted nothing more than to be able to climb into the sink and feel the water slide all over his entire body.

To . . .

He heard a knock on the door followed by rushing foot-steps on the stairs. Turning off the water, Julian reached for the dry cloth next to the sink and wiped off his hands and face.

As he returned to the other half of the melon, he recognized Selena's voice. 'Where is he?'

Julian shook his head at her friend's enthusiasm. Now that was what he'd expected from Grace.

The two women entered the kitchen. He looked up from the melon and met brown eyes as wide as a Spartan shield.

'Holy green guacamole!' Selena gasped.

Grace folded her arms over her chest, her eyes twinkling in a cross between anger and amusement. 'Julian, meet Selena.'

'Holy green guacamole!' her friend repeated.

'Selena?' Grace waved her hand in front of Selena's face. Still Selena didn't blink.

'Holy gre–'

'Would you stop?' Grace chided.

Selena dropped the clothes in her hands straight to the floor and moved around the kitchen until she could see his entire body. Her gaze started at the top of his head and went all the way down to his bare feet.

Julian barely suppressed his ire over her actions. 'Would you like to examine my teeth next, or would you rather I drop my pants for your inspection?' he asked with more malice than he'd intended. She was, after all, technically on his side.

If only she'd close her mouth and quit looking at him *that* way. He'd never been able to stand such unnatural attention.

Selena hesitantly reached out her hand to touch his arm.

'Boo,' he snapped, making her jump a foot into the air.

Grace laughed.

Selena frowned and glared at both of them. 'All right, you two. Are you through making fun of me?'

'You deserved it.' Grace picked up a piece of melon that he'd just sliced and placed it into her mouth. 'Not to mention that *you* get to take him with you today.'

'What?' Julian and Selena asked in unison.

She swallowed her bite. 'Well, I can't very well take him to work with me, can I?'

Selena smiled wickedly. 'I bet Lisa and your female clients would love it.'

'And so would the *guy* I have coming in at eight. However, it wouldn't be productive.'

'Can't you cancel?' Selena asked.

Julian concurred. He had absolutely no desire to go anywhere public. The only part of his curse that he found

69

even remotely tolerable was the fact that most of his summoners kept him hidden in private rooms and gardens.

'You know better,' Grace said. 'I don't have a lawyer hubby who supports me. Besides, I don't think Julian wants to hang around the house by himself all day. I'm sure he would like to get out and see the city.'

'I'd rather stay here with you,' he said.

Because what he really wanted to do was see her writhing beneath him again, feel her slick body sliding down the length of his shaft as he made her scream out in ecstasy.

Grace met his gaze and he saw the hunger that flickered in the light gray depths of her eyes. In that instant, he knew her game. She was going in to work to avoid being around him.

Well, sooner or later she'd be back.

Then she would be his.

And once she surrendered to him, he was going to show her just what kind of stamina and passion a Spartan-trained Macedonian soldier was capable of.

Chapter Five

The morning seemed to drag by as Grace went through the usual round of clients. No matter how hard she tried to focus on them and their problems, she just couldn't quite succeed.

Over and over, she kept seeing deep, tawny skin and searing blue eyes.

And that smile ...

How she wished Julian had never smiled at her. His smile could definitely be her undoing.

' ... so then I said, Dave, look, if you want to borrow my clothes, fine. But leave off my expensive designer dresses 'cause when you look better in them than I do, then I just want to give them to the Salvation Army. So, was I right, Doc?'

Grace looked up from her pad where she was doodling pictures of stick men holding spears.

'What, Rachel?' she asked the patient who sat in the armchair across from her.

Rachel was an elegantly dressed photographer. 'Was I

right to tell Dave to leave off my clothes? I mean, damn, it's pretty bad when your boyfriend looks better in your clothes than you do, right?'

Grace nodded. 'Absolutely. They're your clothes and you shouldn't have to lock them up.'

'See, I knew it! That's what I told him. But does he listen? No. He can call himself Davida all he wants to, and tell me he's a woman in a man's body, but when it comes down to it all, he still listens to me like my ex-husband did. I swear ... '

Grace inadvertently checked her watch again. Her hour with Rachel was almost up.

'You know, Rachel,' she said, cutting her patient off before Rachel could begin her routine spiel about men and their annoying habits. 'Perhaps we should hold on to this until our Monday session with Dave?'

Rachel nodded. 'Will do. But remind me on Monday that I need to talk to you about Chico.'

'Chico?'

'The Chihuahua that lives next door. I swear that dog is giving me the eye.'

Grace frowned. Surely Rachel wasn't implying what she thought she was. 'The eye?'

'You know. *The eye*. He may look like a pooch, but that dog has sex on his mind. Every time I walk by, he looks up my skirt. And you don't want to know what he did to my running shoes. The dog is a pervert.'

'Okay,' Grace said, cutting her off again. She was beginning to suspect there was nothing she could do for Rachel and her obsession that all males in the world were dying to possess her. 'We will definitely cover the Chihuahua's infatuation with you.'

'Thanks, Doc. You're the best.' Rachel grabbed her bag

72

off the floor and headed out the door.

Grace rubbed her brow as Rachel's words rang in her head. A Chihuahua? Jeez!

Poor Rachel. Surely there was some way to help that poor woman.

Then again, it would be infinitely better to have a Chihuahua looking up her skirt with lust than a Greek love-slave.

'Oh, Lanie,' Grace breathed, 'how do I let you get me into these things?'

Before she could contemplate that further, her intercom buzzed.

'Yes, Lisa?'

'Your eleven o'clock canceled, and while you were seeing Ms. Thibideaux, your friend Selena Laurens called six dozen times, and I am neither exaggerating nor kidding. She left a stack of urgent messages for you to call her on her cell phone ASAP.'

'Thanks, Lisa.'

Picking up the phone, Grace called Selena.

'Oh, thank God.' Selena spoke before Grace could say a word. 'You have got to get your butt down here and take your boyfriend home. Now!'

'He's not my boyfriend, he's your–'

'Oh, you want to know what he is?' Selena asked with a note of hysteria in her voice. 'He's a friggin' estrogen magnet, that's what he is. I have women mobbing my stand even as we speak. Sunshine loves it, she's sold more pottery this morning than she ever has before. I tried to get him home earlier, but I can't even make a dent in this crowd. I swear, you'd think we had a celebrity out here. I've never seen anything like it in my life. Now get your butt down here and help me!'

73

The phone went dead.

Grace cursed her luck. Buzzing Lisa, she told her to cancel her appointments for the rest of the day.

As soon as she reached the square, Grace saw what Selena had meant. There had to be at least twenty women surrounding Julian, and dozens more gaping at him as they passed by.

The ones closest to him were elbowing and pushing each other, trying to gain his attention.

But the most unbelievable of all were the three women who had their arms draped over him while another one took a picture.

'Oh, thank you,' a woman in her mid-thirties purred to Julian as she snatched the camera out of the hands of the woman who had taken their picture.

She cradled the camera to her breast in a way meant to draw Julian's attention there, but he didn't seem the least bit interested.

'This is just so wonderful,' she continued to gush. 'I can't wait to get home and show this to my critique group. They'll never believe I found a real-life romance-novel cover model in the French Quarter.'

Something about the rigid way he stood made Grace suspect that Julian didn't care for the attention. But to his credit, he wasn't openly rude.

Still, his smile didn't reach his eyes and it was nothing like the one he'd given her last night.

'My pleasure,' he said to the women.

The giggles that erupted were deafening. Grace shook her head in disbelief. Women, get some dignity!

Then again, given Julian's face, body, and smile, she felt a little giddy every time he looked at her, too.

So who could really blame them for acting like prepubescent girls at a shopping-mall rock concert?

All of a sudden Julian looked past his sea of raging hormonal admirers to meet her gaze. Grace arched an amused brow at him.

Instantly, his smile vanished. His eyes focused on her like a hungry predator that had just found its next meal. 'If you'll excuse me,' he said, then waded through the women and headed directly toward her.

Grace gulped, noting the instant hostility of the women who frowned en masse in her direction.

But worse was the sudden, raw surge of desire that tore through her, making her heart pound out of control. And with every step he took, it increased tenfold.

'Greetings, *agapeemenee*,' Julian said, lifting her hand up to place a kiss on the backs of her knuckles.

A heated wave of electricity danced up her spine. And before she could move, he pulled her into his arms and gave her a hot, soul-wrenching kiss.

Instinctively, she closed her eyes and savored the warmth of his mouth, his breath. The feel of his arms holding her close to a rock-hard chest. Her head reeled from it.

Oh, but the man knew how to give a kiss! Julian had a way with his lips that defied explanation.

And his body ... Never had she felt anything like those lean, hard muscles flexing around her.

It was only the barely audible 'hussy' one of the women sneered that broke the spell.

'Julian, please,' she whispered. 'There are people watching us.'

'Do you think I care?'

'I do!'

He pulled his head away from hers with a low growl and

set her back on her feet. It was only then she realized she'd completely surrendered her weight to him, and he had supported it without effort.

Her cheeks scalding, Grace caught the envious stares of the women as they reluctantly dispersed.

His face showing the depth of his displeasure and reluctance, Julian let go of her and stepped back.

'Finally,' Selena said with a sigh. 'I can almost hear again.' She shook her head. 'If I'd known that would work, *I'd* have kissed him.'

Grace gave her a sideways smirk. 'Well, it's your own fault.'

'How do you figure?' Selena asked.

Grace indicated Julian's clothes with a wave of her hand. 'Look at how he's dressed. You don't bring a Greek god out into public wearing shorts and a tank top two sizes too small. Jeez, Selena, what were you thinking?'

'That it's one hundred and two degrees out, with one hundred and ten percent humidity. I didn't want him to die of heat stroke.'

'Ladies, please,' Julian said, placing himself between them. 'It's far too hot to stand out in the street fighting over something as trivial as my clothing.' He swept a hungry look over Grace, then smiled a smile that could make any woman melt. 'And I'm not a Greek god. I'm just a minor half-deity.'

Grace missed what he was saying for the fact that the sound of his voice captivated her. How did he do that? How did he make his voice so erotically charged?

Was it from his deep, rich accent?

No, there was more to it than that, but for her life she couldn't figure out what.

In truth, all she wanted to do was find a bed somewhere

and let him have his way with her. To feel his luscious skin beneath her hands.

She looked at Selena and caught the way Selena stared hungrily at Julian's bare legs and rump.

'You feel it, too, don't you?' Grace asked.

Blinking, Selena looked up. 'Feel what?'

'Him. It's like he's the Pied Piper and we're all mice enchanted by his music.' Grace turned about and noted the way women stared at him, some even craning their necks to get a better view of Julian.

'What is it about him that just pulls us against our wills?' Grace asked.

Julian arched one arrogant brow at her. 'Against your will?'

'Well, honestly, yes. I don't like feeling like this.'

'And how do you feel?' he asked.

'Sexual,' Grace said before she could stop herself.

'Like a goddess?' he asked, his voice dropping an octave.

'Yes,' she said as he took a single step toward her.

He didn't touch her, but then he didn't have to. His very presence overwhelmed her. Intoxicated her as he dipped that magnetic gaze to her lips, then to her neck. She swore she could already feel the sensation of his lips buried in the hollow of her throat.

And the man hadn't even moved.

'I can tell you what it is,' he all but purred.

'It's the spell, isn't it?'

He shook his head as he reached one hand out to gently drag his forefinger down her cheek. Grace shuttered her eyes as a wave of fierce desire scorched her. It was all she could do not to turn her head and capture that finger between her teeth.

Julian leaned closer and nuzzled her cheek with his. 'It's

77

the fact that I can appreciate you on a level the men of your age cannot.'

'It's the fact he has the tightest *gluteus rumpus* I've ever seen,' Sunshine said, interrupting them. 'Not to mention a voice and accent to die for. I really wish someone would tell me where I could get one of those.'

Grace burst out laughing at Sunshine's unexpected comments.

Looking less than pleased, Julian turned to face Sunshine.

'Look at him.' Sunshine gestured toward Julian with the pencil in her charcoal-covered hand. She also had a smear of charcoal across her right cheek. 'When was the last time you met a man so well toned that you could actually see the blood pumping through his veins? Your boyfriend is ... well, *way* buff. Monster buff.' Then with a serious face, she added, 'Lord, *king* buff.'

Sunshine turned her sketchbook around to where Grace could see her rendering of Julian. 'See the way the light brings out the golden color of his skin? It's almost as if he were really kissed by the sun.'

Grace frowned. There was some truth to that.

Julian leaned down at her, his blue eyes searing her with their heat. 'Come home with me, Grace,' he whispered in her ear. 'Now. Let me take you into my arms, strip your clothes from your body, and show you how the gods meant for a woman to know a man. I swear to you, you'll remember it for the rest of eternity.'

She closed her eyes as the scent of sandalwood filled her head. His breath tickled her neck while his cheek was so close to hers, she swore she could feel his whiskers touching her.

Every part of her wanted to surrender to him. Yes, please, yes.

Her gaze dropped down to his shoulder. To the hard sculpting of his muscles. To the hollow of his throat. Oh, how she longed to run her tongue over the golden bounty of his skin. To see if the rest of his body tasted as good as his mouth.

He would be splendid in bed. There was no doubt.

But she meant nothing to him. Nothing.

'I can't,' she breathed, taking a step back.

Disappointment filled his eyes. Then, his look turned hard, determined. 'You will,' he assured her.

Deep inside, she knew he probably spoke the truth. How long could a woman turn down a man like him?

Shaking off the thought, Grace glanced across the street to the Jackson Brewery. 'We need to go buy you some clothes that fit.'

'Can I help it if he's a head taller than Bill and twice as broad?' Selena asked. 'It was your bright idea for me to bring him along.'

Grace screwed up her face at Selena. 'Fine. We'll be in the Brewery if you need us.'

'Okay, but be careful.'

'Careful?' Grace asked.

Selena indicated Julian with her thumb. 'If women start to stampede, take my advice and get out of their way. I still don't have any feeling in my right foot from the last group.'

Laughing, Grace headed for the road, knowing Julian would follow her. In fact, she could feel him right behind her. His presence undeniable, he had an awful way of invading every thought and sense she possessed.

Neither one of them said a word as they crossed the busy street and headed into the first shop they reached.

Grace glanced around the department store, looking for Menswear. Spotting it, she made her way over to it.

'So, what's your style preference?' she asked Julian as she paused by a display of folded jeans.

'For what I have in mind, nudity works best.'

Grace rolled her eyes. 'You're trying to shock me, aren't you?'

'Perhaps. I have to admit I rather like the look of a blush on your face.'

He stepped toward her.

Grace retreated, placing the display of jeans between them. 'I think you'll need at least three pairs of jeans while you're here.'

He sighed as he gazed at the pants. 'Why bother, when I shall be gone in a few weeks?'

She glared at him. 'Jeez, Julian,' she snapped in aggravation. 'You act as if no one ever dressed you during your past incarnations.'

'They didn't.'

She froze at his hollow, empty tone. And the significance of his words.

Grace looked skeptically at him. 'Are you telling me that in the last two thousand years, no one has ever bothered to put clothes on you?'

'Just twice,' he said in that same flat tone. 'Once during a blizzard in the English Regency period, one of my summoners covered me in a frilly pink dressing gown before she shoved me onto her balcony to keep her husband from finding me in her bed. And the second time was far too embarrassing to mention.'

'You're not funny. And I know no woman would keep a man for a solid month and not put some clothes on him.'

'Look at me, Grace,' he said, spreading out his arms to show her his hard, delectable body. 'I'm a sex slave. No one before you ever thought I needed clothes to perform my duties.'

His heated gaze held hers enthralled, but what made her ache was the pain in those deep blue eyes that he tried so hard to conceal. A pain that touched her profoundly.

'I assure you,' he said quietly, 'once they had me inside them, they did everything they could to keep me there, including one summoner in the Middle Ages who bolted her bedroom door, and told everyone on the outside that she had the plague.'

Grace averted her gaze as his words singed her. The things he described were unbelievable, and yet by the look on his face, she could tell he wasn't exaggerating the tales.

She couldn't imagine the degradations he must have suffered over the centuries. Dear Lord, people treated animals better than what he was describing.

'They summoned you, yet none of them ever conversed with you or clothed you?'

'Every man's fantasy, is it not? To have a million women throwing themselves at him, wanting no commitments, no promises. Wanting nothing from him, other than his body, and the few weeks of pleasure he can give them?' His flippant words didn't quite mask the acid undertone.

That might be other men's fantasies, but she could tell it wasn't his.

'Well,' she said, returning to the jeans, 'I'm not like that and you're going to need something to wear when I take you out in public.'

Anger snapped so menacingly in his eyes that she took an involuntary step backward. 'I wasn't cursed to be viewed by the public, Grace. I am here for you, and you alone.'

How nice that sounded. Still, she wasn't about to fall for it. She couldn't use another human being the way Julian described. It was wrong, and she would never be able to live with herself if she did such a thing to him.

'Be that as it may,' she said in determination. 'I want to take you out in public. So you'll need clothes.' She started digging through the sizes.

He fell silent.

Grace looked up at him and caught the dark, angry look on his face. 'What?'

'What?' he shot back.

'Never mind. Let's see which of these fit best.' Grabbing several sizes, she handed the pants over to him. One would think she'd handed him a load of dog crap the way he reacted to the jeans.

Disregarding his appalled look, she had to practically shove him into a fitting room and close the partial door sharply behind him.

Julian entered the small cubicle and froze, assaulted simultaneously on three hostile fronts.

The first was the smallness of the space and the cold, fierce terror that washed over him from it. For a full minute, he couldn't breathe as he fought the urge to run from the tight, cramped space. He could barely move without bumping into the walls, door, or mirror.

But even worse than his claustrophobia was the face in the mirror. He hadn't seen his own reflection in centuries. And the face staring back at him looked so much like his father that he wanted to splinter it. He saw the same smoothly sculpted planes, the same contemptuous eyes.

The only thing missing was the deep, jagged scar that had run down his father's left cheek.

And for the first time in countless centuries, Julian saw the jarring sight of the three thin commander's braids that hung to his shoulder.

His hand shaking, he reached up and touched them as he did something he hadn't done in an exceptionally long time;

he remembered the day he had earned them.

It had been after the battle at Thebes when his commander had fallen and the Macedonian troops had started to panic and retreat. He had grabbed the commander's sword, regrouped them, and led them to victory against the Romans.

The day after the battle, the Macedonian queen herself had braided his hair, and placed her own personal beads on the ends.

Julian gripped the tiny glass beads in his fist.

Those braids had belonged to the once proud and mighty Macedonian commander who had led a conquering army so strong that he had forced the Romans to flee in cowering terror.

The sight haunted him.

He looked down at the ring on his right hand. A ring he had worn for so long that he had grown immune to its presence, and had long ago ceased to remember its significance.

But his braids . . .

He hadn't thought about them in a long, long time.

Touching them now, he remembered the man he'd been. He remembered the faces of his family. The people who had once rushed to serve his needs. Those who had respected and feared him.

A time when he had commanded his destiny, and the known world had been his for the taking.

And now he was . . .

His throat tight, Julian closed his eyes and removed the beads from the ends of his hair before he started unbraiding it.

As his fingers loosened the first braid, he looked down at the pants he had dropped on the floor.

Why was Grace doing this? Why did she have to treat him like a human being?

He'd grown so accustomed to being treated as an object that he found her kindness toward him unbearable. The other summoners' cold, impersonal distance had enabled him to tolerate his sentence, to not remember who and what he'd once been.

What he'd lost.

It enabled him to only focus on the here and now, and on the momentary, fleeting pleasures to be had.

But human beings didn't live that way. They had families, friends, futures, dreams.

Hopes.

Things that had been lost to him centuries ago. Things he would never know again.

'Damn you, Priapus,' he breathed as he viciously uncoiled the last braid. 'And damn me.'

Grace did a double-take as Julian finally left the dressing room wearing a pair of jeans that looked as if they had been made solely for him.

The tight tank top Selena had loaned him stopped just below his hard, narrow waist and the jeans rode low on his lean hips, leaving just a tiny peek of his hard, flat stomach and the small coffee-colored hairs that ran from his navel downward to disappear under the denim.

Grace had a strong desire to walk up to him and slide her hand down that inviting pathway and investigate where it led. And all too well, she remembered the sight of him standing naked in front of her.

Drawing her breath in sharply between her teeth, she had to admit he looked good in jeans. Even better than he'd looked in shorts – if such a thing were possible.

Sunshine was right, he had the best butt denim had ever cupped and all she could think of doing was running her hand over that rump and squeezing it tight.

The female salesclerk and woman beside her stopped talking and gaped.

'Are these acceptable?' Julian asked Grace.

'Oh, yeah, baby,' Grace said breathlessly before she could stop herself.

Julian gave her an amused grin that didn't quite reach his eyes.

Grace moved around him until she could see what size the pants were.

Oh, yeah, nice, nice *butt!*

Distracted by his shapely posterior, she inadvertently let her fingers brush against the skin of his back as she touched the tag. She felt Julian tense.

'You know,' Julian said, looking at her over his shoulder. 'That would feel a whole lot better if we were both naked. And in your bed.'

She heard the sharp intakes of breath from the salesclerk and customer.

Heat exploding over her face, Grace straightened up and glared at him. 'We really need to talk about what kind of comments are appropriate when we're in public.'

'If you took me home, you wouldn't have to worry about it.'

The man was relentless.

Shaking her head at him, Grace found two more pairs of jeans, a few shirts, a belt, a pair of sunglasses, socks, shoes, and several pairs of large, ugly boxers. No man could look good in boxers, she decided. And the last thing she wanted was for Julian to be any more appealing.

She made him change into a navy crew-neck shirt, his jeans, and running shoes before they left the department.

'Now you look almost human,' she said teasingly as he

came out of the dressing room.

He gave her a cold, dead look. 'Only on the outside,' he said in a voice so low she wasn't sure she heard it.

'What was that?' she asked.

'I'm only human on the outside,' he said louder.

She caught the anguish in his gaze. Her heart lurched.

'Julian,' she said, her tone chiding. 'You *are* human.'

He pressed his lips together, his gaze now shadowed and guarded. 'Am I? Is it human to live for two thousand years? To only be allowed to walk the earth a few weeks at a time?'

He looked around them at the women who were trying to sneak a peek at him over and around racks. Women who came to a complete stop as they caught their first glimpse of him.

He swept his hand out, indicating the spectacle around them. 'Do you see them doing that to anyone else?'

His face turned hard, dangerous, as his gaze delved into hers. 'No, Grace, I've never been human.'

Needing to comfort him, she reached up and placed her hand gently against his cheek. 'You are human, Julian.'

The doubt in his eyes wrung her heart.

Unsure of what she could say or do to make him feel better, she let the matter drop and started for the door. She was almost to it before she realized Julian wasn't with her.

Turning around, Grace spotted him easily enough. He'd gotten sidetracked in women's lingerie and stood next to a rack of *extremely* skimpy black negligees. Grace's face flamed. She swore she could hear the lecherous thoughts in his mind.

Worse, she had better go get him before one of the women offered to model it for him.

She quickly went up to him and cleared her throat. 'You ready?'

He gave her a slow, thorough once-over that let her know he had a vivid image in his mind of her wearing that gauzy thing. 'You would be breathtaking in this.'

Grace looked at it skeptically. The thing was so flimsy it was pretty much transparent. Unlike Julian, she didn't have a body that turned anyone's head, not unless they were extremely desperate. Or had been in prison for a couple of decades. 'I don't know about breathtaking, but I'd definitely be cold.'

'Not for long, you wouldn't.'

She sucked her breath in at his words, not doubting the truth of it for a minute. 'You are so bad.'

'Not in bed, I'm not.' He dipped his head toward hers. 'I'm actually very–'

'There you are!'

Grace jumped back at Selena's voice.

Julian said something to Selena in a strange language Grace didn't understand.

'Now, now,' Selena said with a chiding note in her voice. 'Gracie doesn't understand ancient Greek. She slept through the entire semester.'

Selena looked at Grace and clucked her tongue. 'See, I told you one day it would come in handy.'

'Oh, yeah,' Grace said with a laugh. 'Like I knew back then that one day you were going to conjure up a Greek love-sl . . .' Grace let her voice trail off as she realized what she'd almost said in front of Julian.

Embarrassed, she bit her lip.

'It's all right, Grace,' Julian said quietly.

Still, she knew it bothered him. There was no way it couldn't.

'I know what I am. You can't offend me with the truth of it. I'm actually more offended by the word *Greek* than I am *love-slave*. I was trained in Sparta, and fought for the Macedonians. I made it my habit to avoid Greece as much as possible before I was cursed.'

Grace cocked her head at what he'd said, or more to the point what he *hadn't* said. There was nothing about his childhood.

'Where were you born?' she asked.

A tic started in his jaw and his eyes darkened ominously. Wherever his birthplace had been, he didn't care for it. 'Very well, I'm half Greek, but I don't claim that half of my heritage.'

Okay, big nerve there. From now on, she would drop *Greek* from her vocabulary.

'Back to the black nightie,' Selena said. 'There's a red one over here that I'm thinking would look a whole lot better on her.'

'Selena!' Grace snapped.

She ignored her, and led Julian to where the red negligees were kept. Selena picked up a sheer red baby-doll number that was split down the front and only held together by two ribbons at the shoulders and one in the middle. Crotchless red panties and a lace garter belt completed the ensemble.

'What do you think?' Selena asked as she held it up in front of Julian.

He gave Grace a speculative glance.

If they kept this up, she was going to die of embarrassment. 'Would you two stop?' Grace asked. 'I'm not wearing that.'

'I'm buying it for you anyway,' Selena said in a firm voice. 'I'm relatively sure Julian can get you into it.'

Julian gave her a droll stare. 'I'd rather get her out of it.'

Grace covered her face with her hands and groaned.

'She'll come around,' Selena said conspiratorially.

'I will not,' Grace said from behind her hands.

'Yes, you will,' Julian said, as Selena went off to pay for the red negligee.

There was such arrogance and assuredness in his words. She could tell the man wasn't used to anyone defying him.

'Have you ever failed?' she asked.

The teasing in his eyes faded and she saw the veil come down over his face. He was hiding something with that look, she knew it. Something very painful, judging by the sudden tenseness of his body.

He didn't say another word until Selena returned and handed him the bag. 'Now,' she said. 'I'm thinking some candlelight, nice mood music, and–'

'Selena,' Grace said, cutting her off. 'I appreciate what you're trying to do, but instead of focusing on me for a minute, can we talk about Julian?'

Selena glanced at him. 'Sure. What about him?'

'Do you know how to get him out of the book? Permanently?'

'Absolutely clueless.' Selena turned her attention to Julian. 'Do you know?'

'I keep telling her, it's impossible.'

Selena nodded. 'She is stubborn. Never listens to a word said unless it's the word she wants to hear.'

'Stubborn or not,' Grace inserted, focusing on Julian, 'I can't imagine why you'd want to stay cursed in a book.'

He looked away.

'Grace, give the man a break.'

'That's what I'm trying to do.'

'Fine,' Selena said, finally giving in. 'Okay, Julian, what wretched awful act did you commit to get sucked into the book?'

'*Hubris.*'

'Ooo,' Selena said ominously, 'that's a baddie. Grace, he may be right. They used to do things like rip people to shreds over that. You should have paid attention in your Classics class. The Greek gods are really vicious when it comes to handing out punishments.'

Grace narrowed her eyes on both of them. 'I refuse to believe that there's no way to free him. Can't we destroy the book or summon one of your spirits or something to help?'

'Oh, so now you believe in my voodoo magick?'

'Not really, but you did manage to get him here. Can you manage to help?'

Selena chewed her thumbnail in thought. 'Julian, what god was most partial to you?'

He took a long, deep breath as if completely bored by their questions. 'In truth, none of them were overly fond of me. Being a soldier, I sacrificed mostly to Athena, but I had more direct contact with Eros.'

Selena flashed him a wicked grin. 'The god of lust and love, I can see why.'

'It's not for the reasons you think,' he said dryly.

Selena ignored him. 'So, have you ever tried to appeal to Eros?'

'We're not speaking to each other.'

Grace rolled her eyes at his flippant sarcasm.

'Why don't you try calling him?' Selena suggested.

Grace glared at her. 'You know, Selena, you could try to be a little more serious. I know I've mocked your beliefs over the years, but this is Julian's life we're talking about.'

'I am perfectly serious,' she said emphatically. 'The best way would be for Julian to summon him directly and see if he can help.'

What the hell? Grace thought. Last night, she would

never have believed anyone could conjure up Julian. Maybe Selena was right.

'Would you try it?' Grace asked him.

Julian gave a frustrated sigh, as if he were ready to shake both of them.

Looking greatly peeved, he leaned his head back and said quietly to the ceiling, 'Cupid, you worthless bastard, I summon you to human form.'

Grace threw her hands up. 'Gee, I can't imagine why he wouldn't respond to that.'

Selena laughed.

'Fine,' Grace said. 'I don't believe in this mumbo jumbo anyway. Let's go put this stuff in my car, get some lunch, and try to think up something a little more productive than "Cupid, you worthless bastard." Shall we?'

'Fine,' Selena said.

Grace handed Selena the bag that contained the clothes Selena had brought over. 'Here are Bill's things.'

Selena looked into the bag with a frown. 'Where's the white tank top?'

'I'll give it back later.'

Selena laughed again.

Julian trailed along behind them, listening to their bantering, as they made their way outside the store.

Luckily, Grace had found a rare parking place right outside the Brewery.

Julian watched as the women put the bags in the car. If he dared admit it, he actually liked the fact that Grace was so interested in helping him.

No one ever had before.

He had walked the whole of his life in solitude with only his strength and his wits to save him. Even before the curse, he'd been weary. Tired of the loneliness, tired of having no

91

one on earth, or beyond, who gave a damn about him.

It was a pity he hadn't met Grace before the curse. She would have definitely been a nice balm to soothe his restlessness. But then, the women of his time had been very different.

Grace saw him as an equal whereas the women in his day had seen him as a legend to be feared or placated.

What made Grace unique? What was it about her that allowed her to reach out to him when even his own family had turned their backs on him?

He didn't know for sure. She was just special. A pure heart in a world populated by selfish ones. He'd never thought to encounter anyone like her.

Uncomfortable with the direction of his thoughts, he glanced around the thronging crowd of people who didn't seem to mind the oppressive heat of the strange city.

His ears picked up on a couple arguing a few feet away, the wife angry over something the man had left behind. They had a small boy no older than three or four between them as they approached the sidewalk in front of him.

Julian smiled at them. He couldn't remember the last time he'd seen a family together, going about their routine business. It touched a part of him he barely remembered he had. His heart. And he wondered if they knew just what a gift they had in each other.

While the two parents continued to bicker, the child stopped, his attention focused on something across the street.

Julian held his breath as every instinct in his body told him what the little boy was about to do.

Grace closed the trunk to her car.

Out of the corner of her eye, she saw a blue blur headed for the street. It took her a full second to realize it was

Julian running across the lot. She frowned at his actions, until she saw the small boy who was stepping off the curb into traffic.

'Oh, my God,' Grace gasped as she heard car brakes squealing.

'Steven!' a woman shouted.

With a move straight out of Hollywood, Julian jumped over the low parking lot wall, plucked the child up from the road, and, holding the boy against his chest, he ran up onto the fender of the braking car, then turned a side flip, up, over, and away from the car.

They landed safely in the other lane a spilt second before a second car jerked around the first and plowed straight into them.

Horrified, Grace watched as Julian slammed into the hood of an old Chevy. He slid up it, into the windshield, and was then flung forward onto the street where he rolled for several yards before finally coming to a stop.

He lay on his side, unmoving.

Total chaos broke out everywhere as people screamed and shouted, and crowded around the accident.

Terrified, Grace trembled all over as she pushed her way through the crowd, trying to reach Julian. 'Please be okay, please be okay,' she whispered, over and over, praying both of them had survived being hit.

As she finally broke through the people around him, she realized he hadn't let go of the child. The boy was still carefully cradled in his arms.

Unable to believe the sight, Grace paused, her heart hammering.

Were they alive?

'Never saw nothing like that in my life,' a man said beside her.

His sentiment was echoed everywhere.

Slowly, fearfully, Grace approached Julian as he started to move.

'Are you all right?' she heard him ask the child.

The small toddler answered with a screaming wail.

Oblivious to the piercing sound, Julian rose carefully with the boy in his arms.

Relieved they were alive, Grace couldn't believe her eyes. How in the world could he move?

How had he managed to keep his hold on the boy through all that?

He staggered back a step, then quickly caught his balance, all the while maintaining his grip on the child.

Grace steadied him with a hand against his spine. 'You shouldn't stand,' she told Julian as she saw the blood that coated his left arm.

Julian didn't seem to hear her.

His eyes were dark and strange looking. 'Sh, little one,' he said, holding the boy with one arm while he cupped the child's face with the other.

Moving only his upper body, he gently rocked the boy in the soothing, confident pattern only a parent would use. His gaze haunted, Julian laid his cheek against the top of the boy's head. 'Sh, I've got you,' he murmured. 'You're safe now.'

His actions startled her. It was apparent this was a man who had soothed children before.

But when would a Greek soldier have been around children ... ?

Unless he'd been a father.

Grace's mind whirled at the possibility as Julian carefully handed the sobbing boy to his hysterical mother who wailed even louder than the toddler.

Dear Lord, was it possible that Julian could be a father?

If so, where were his children?

What had happened to them?

'Steven,' his mother wept as she held the boy against her chest. 'How many times have I told you to stay by my side?'

'Are you okay?' the father and the driver asked Julian.

Grimacing, Julian ran his hand over his left bicep as if testing the arm. 'I'm fine,' he said, but Grace noted the way he still favored his right leg where the car had hit him.

'You need a doctor,' she said as Selena joined them.

'I'm fine. Really.' Julian gave her a halfhearted smile, then lowered his voice so that only she could hear it. 'But I have to say, chariots hurt a lot less than cars when they slam into you.'

Grace was aghast at his misplaced humor. 'How can you make a joke? I thought you were dead.'

He shrugged.

As the man continued to thank him profusely for saving his son, Grace glanced at the blood on Julian's arm just above his elbow. Blood that evaporated from his skin like some weird science fiction movie effect.

Suddenly, Julian put his full weight back on his injured leg, and the pain crimping his brow vanished.

She exchanged a wide-eyed stare with Selena, who had also seen it. What the hell was *that*?

Was Julian human or not?

'I can't thank you enough,' the father said again. 'I thought he was dead.'

'I'm just glad I saw him,' Julian whispered. He reached a hand out toward the boy's head.

His fingers were about to brush the light brown curls when he paused. Grace watched emotions war on Julian's face before he recovered his stoicism and dropped his hand back to his side.

Without a word, he headed to the curb.

'Julian?' she asked, rushing to catch up to him. 'Are you really okay?'

'Don't worry about me, Grace. I don't break and I seldom bleed.' This time, there was no mistaking the bitterness in his voice. 'It's a gift of the curse. The Fates forbid I should actually *die* and escape my punishment.'

She flinched at the anguish she saw in his eyes.

But his survival wasn't the only question she had. She wanted to ask him about the child, about the way he had looked at the boy as if reliving some horrible nightmare. But the words lodged themselves in her throat.

'Man, he deserves a hero cookie,' Selena said as she joined them. 'Upstairs to the Praline Factory!'

'Selena, I don't think—'

'What's a praline?' Julian asked.

'It's Cajun ambrosia,' Selena explained, 'something that should be right up your alley.'

Against Grace's best arguments, Selena led them inside, to the escalator.

Selena took the first stair, then turned back to look at Julian, who stood between them. 'How did you do that thing where you flipped over the car? It was awesome!'

Julian shrugged.

'Oh, man, don't be modest. You looked like Keanu Reeves in *The Matrix*. Gracie, did you see that move he did?'

'I saw it,' she said softly, noting just how uncomfortable Selena's praise was making Julian.

She also noted the way the women around them gawked.

Julian was right. It wasn't normal. But then, how often did a man like him appear in the flesh? A man who oozed such raw sexual attraction?

96

The man was a walking pheromone.

And now a hero.

But most of all, he was a great mystery to her. There was a lot about him she was dying to know. And one way or another over the next month, she was going to learn it.

When they reached the Praline Factory on the top floor, Grace bought two fudge-pecan pralines and a Coke.

Without thinking twice, she held a praline up for Julian. Instead of taking it from her hand, he leaned forward and took a bite while she held it.

He savored the sugary confection in a way that drove heat through her body, while those searing blue eyes stared at her as if he were wishing she were what he feasted on.

'You were right,' he said in that low tone that sent shivers over her. 'It is delicious.'

'Wow,' the female clerk said from across the counter. 'That's some accent you got there. You must not be from around these parts.'

'No,' Julian said. 'I'm not.'

'So where you from?'

'Macedonia.'

'Is that out in California?' the girl asked. 'You look like one of those surfer types who hang out on the beach.'

He frowned. 'California?'

'He's from Greece,' Selena supplied for the girl.

'Ah!' the girl said.

Julian arched a censoring brow at her. 'Macedonia isn't–'

'Buddy,' Selena said around her mouthful of praline, 'around here you'd be lucky to find anyone who would know the difference.'

Before Grace could respond to Selena's harsh words, Julian placed his hands on her waist and brought her right up against his steely chest.

97

He leaned down and caught her bottom lip between his teeth, then gently stroked her lip with his tongue.

Her head swam from the tender embrace.

He deepened his kiss an instant before releasing her and stepping back.

'You had sugar on your bottom lip,' he explained with a devilish smile that displayed his dimples to perfection.

Grace blinked, amazed at how hot and cold his touch made her. 'You could have just said something.'

'True, but my way was far more enjoyable.'

She couldn't argue that.

Quickly, she stepped away from him and tried to ignore Selena's knowing smile.

'Why are you so afraid of me?' Julian asked unexpectedly as he fell in by her side.

'I'm not afraid of you.'

'No? Then what scares you so? Every time I come near you, you cringe.'

'I'm not cringing,' Grace insisted. *Damn, was there an echo?*

He reached out to put his arm around her. Grace quickly sidestepped him.

'You're cringing,' he said pointedly as they got back on the escalator.

Even though she was on the step below, he braced his arms on each side of her, then leaned his head close to her own. His presence surrounded her, enveloped her, and made her strangely giddy and warm.

She stared at the strength of his tense, tanned hands on the belt behind hers. The way the veins stood out to emphasize the power and beauty of them. Like the rest of him, his hands and arms were gorgeous.

'You've never had an orgasm, have you?' he whispered in her ear.

Grace choked on her praline. 'This is not the place to talk about it.'

'That's it, isn't it?' he asked. 'That's why–'

'That's not it,' she interrupted him. 'As a matter of fact, I have.'

Okay, it was a lie, but he didn't have to know that.

'With a man?'

'Julian!' she snapped. 'What is it with you and Selena that you think you can discuss my personal life out in public?'

He dipped his head lower, down to her neck so close that she could feel his breath falling against her skin, smell the warm, clean scent of him. 'You know, Grace. I can give you pleasure the likes of which you can't imagine.'

A shiver went over her. She could easily believe that.

It would be so easy to let him prove those words.

But she couldn't. It would be wrong, and no matter what he said, it would bother her. And deep down, she suspected it bothered him, as well.

She leaned back ever so slightly and met his gaze. 'Has it ever occurred to you that I don't want it?'

He looked shocked by her words. 'How can that be?'

'I told you. The next time I get intimate with a man, I want more than just his necessary parts involved. I want his heart.'

Julian stared hungrily at her lips. 'I can assure you, you wouldn't miss it.'

'Yes I would.'

Flinching from her as if she'd slapped him, he straightened.

Grace knew she'd struck another nerve. Wanting to discover more about him, she turned to look up at him. 'Why is it so important to you that I give in? Does something happen to you if I don't comply?'

He laughed bitterly. 'As if anything could be worse.'

'Then why can't you just enjoy your time here with me without any–' she lowered her voice '–sex?'

His eyes flared. 'Enjoy what? Enjoy getting to know people whose faces will haunt me for eternity? Do you think I enjoy looking around here knowing that in a few days I'll be pulled back into a blank, empty hole where I can hear, but I can't see, can't taste, feel, or smell, where my stomach churns constantly from hunger and my throat burns with an unquenchable thirst? You are the only thing I'm permitted to enjoy. And you would deny me that.'

Tears pricked the backs of her eyes at his words. She didn't want to hurt him. Truly, she didn't.

But it had been a very similar ploy for sympathy that Paul had used to get her into bed, and that event had torn her heart out.

After the death of her parents, Paul had claimed to care about her. He had been there to comfort her and hold her. And then when she had finally trusted him with her body, he had hurt her so badly, so cruelly, that even now it cut her all the way to her soul.

'I am so sorry, Julian. Really, I am. But I can't do this.' She left the escalator and headed back through the mall.

'Why?' Julian asked as he and Selena caught up to her.

How could she explain it to him? Paul had hurt her so badly that night. He had had no regard for her feelings. She had begged him to stop but he had persisted.

'Look, it's supposed to hurt the first time.' Paul had said. *'Jeez, just stop crying. I'll be finished in a minute and then you can leave.'*

By the time he was finished, she was so humiliated and hurt that she had cried for days.

'Grace?' Julian's voice broke through her whirling thoughts. 'What is it?'

It took all her strength to hold her tears back. But she wouldn't cry. Not out in public. Not like this. She would not be pitied.

'It's nothing,' she said.

Needing a breath of fresh air, even if it was hotter and thicker than steam, she headed out the side door of the Brewery toward the Moonwalk.

Julian and Selena followed.

'Grace, what made you cry?' Julian asked.

'It's Paul,' she heard Selena whisper to Julian.

Grace glared at Selena as she forced herself to calm down. Drawing a ragged breath, she turned back to Julian. 'I wish I could just fling myself into bed with you, but I can't. I don't want to be used that way, and I don't want to use you! Can't you understand that?'

His jaw tense, he looked away.

Grace followed his gaze and saw a group of six rough-looking bikers headed in their direction. Their leather outfits had to be stifling in the heat, but they didn't seem to notice as they ribbed each other and laughed.

It was then Grace saw the woman with them. A woman whose slow, seductive walk was the female equivalent to Julian's graceful, loose-limbed saunter. The woman also possessed the kind of rare beauty that would best any actress or model.

Tall and blond, the woman wore a skimpy leather halter and tight short-shorts that hugged a figure Grace would kill to possess.

And the woman was slowing down, falling behind the men as she slid her black sunglasses down the bridge of her nose to stare straight at Julian.

101

Inwardly, Grace cringed.

Oh, good Lord, this could get ugly fast. None of the scruffy, tough-as-nails bikers looked like the type who would tolerate their girlfriend looking at another guy. And the last thing she wanted was a fight on the Moonwalk.

Grace grabbed Julian's hand to pull him in the other direction.

He refused to move.

'C'mon, Julian,' she said urgently. 'We need to get back inside.'

Still, he didn't budge.

He glared at the bikers as if he wanted to kill them. Then, before she could blink, he shrugged off her hold, and rushed forward. He grabbed one of the men by his shirt.

Dumbfounded, Grace watched as Julian punched the man in the jaw.

Chapter Six

'You worthless piece of ... ' Julian let out a string of curses that would make a sailor blush.

Grace's eyes widened. She didn't know what startled her most, Julian assaulting the unknown biker or the language he used.

As he pummeled the biker, the man fought back, but his fighting skills were nowhere near Julian's.

Forgetting Selena, Grace ran toward them, her heart hammering as she tried to think of what she should do. There was no way she could get between the two men. Not at the rate they were trying to kill each other.

'Julian, stop it before you hurt him!' the biker woman cried.

Grace froze at the words.

How did she know Julian's name?

The woman danced around as if trying to help the biker thwart Julian. 'Honey, watch out, he's going to ... ouch, that had to hurt!' The woman cringed in sympathetic pain after Julian hit the biker in the nose. 'Julian, stop hitting him like that! You're going to make his nose swell. Ew, baby, duck!'

The biker didn't duck, and Julian caught him one hard blow to the chin that made him stagger backward.

Totally befuddled, Grace looked back and forth between the woman and Julian.

How could they possibly know each other?

'Eros, baby. No!' the woman shouted again, waving her hands around her face like a bird about to take flight.

Selena moved to stand beside Grace.

'Is that the Eros Julian was trying to summon?' Grace asked.

Selena shrugged. 'Maybe, but I never thought of Cupid as a biker.'

'Where's Priapus?' Julian demanded as he grabbed Eros and forced him back against the wooden railing above the water.

'I don't know,' Eros said as he struggled to loosen Julian's two hands from his black T-shirt.

'Don't you *dare* lie to me,' Julian growled.

'I don't know!'

Julian tightened his grip as two thousand years of pain and rage swept through him. His hands shook while he held Eros in his fists. But worse than his desire to kill was the unrelenting questions that screamed through him.

Why had no one ever answered his summons before?

Why had Eros betrayed him?

And how could they have done this to him, then walk away and leave him to suffer?

'Where is he?' Julian asked again.

'Eating, belching, hell, I don't know. I haven't seen him in forever and a day.'

Julian pulled Eros away from the railing. All the wrath of

hell was branded into his face as he released him.

'I have to find him,' Julian said between clenched teeth. 'Now.'

A muscle in Eros's jaw twitched as he brushed his hands down the front of his T-shirt to straighten it. 'Well, shaking the shit out of me isn't going to get his attention.'

'Then maybe killing you will.' Julian reached for him again.

Suddenly, the other bikers started for Julian.

As the men closed in, Eros ducked Julian's blow and whirled to stop his friends.

'Leave him alone, guys,' Eros said, grabbing the one closest to him by the arms and pushing him backward. 'You don't want to fight him. Trust me. He could rip your heart out and feed it to you before you hit the ground dead.'

Julian scanned the bikers with a glare that dared any of them to approach him. The cold, lethal look terrified Grace and she held no doubt he could do just what Eros said.

'What are you, crazy?' the tallest one asked as he raked a disbelieving stare over Julian. 'He don't look like much to me.'

Eros wiped the blood from the corner of his mouth and gave a half-grin as he saw the blood on his thumb. 'Yeah, well, take my word for it. The man has fists like a sledge-hammer and the ability to move a hell of a lot faster than you can dodge.'

In spite of his dusty black leather pants and torn T-shirt, Eros was incredibly handsome, and lacked the worn-out look of his companions. His youthful face would have been very pretty if not for the dark brown goatee surrounded by a three-day growth of whiskers, and the military cut of his hair.

'Besides, it's just a little family squabble,' Eros said with a strange glint in his eyes. He patted the biker on the arm and laughed. 'My kid brother always did have a nasty temper on him.'

Grace exchanged a stunned, disbelieving gape with Selena.

'Did I hear that?' she asked Selena. 'Surely he can't be a brother of Julian's. Can he?'

'How would I know?'

Julian said something to Eros in ancient Greek. Selena's eyes bulged and the smile faded instantly from Eros's face.

'If you weren't my brother, I'd kill you for that.'

Julian's gaze shot daggers. 'If I didn't need you, you'd already be dead.'

Instead of becoming angry, Eros laughed.

'Don't you dare laugh,' the woman said angrily to Eros. 'You better remember he's one of the few people capable of carrying out that threat.'

Eros nodded, then turned to the other four bikers. 'Go on,' he said to his friends. 'I'll catch up later.'

'You sure?' the tall one asked, sliding a nervous look to Julian. 'We can hang if you need us to.'

'Nah, it's all right,' Eros said with a dismissive wave. 'Remember, I told you I had to meet someone here? My brother's just pissed at me, but he'll get over it.'

Grace stepped back as the bikers walked past her. All of them except for the stunning woman. She folded her arms across her leather-clad, amply endowed chest and eyed the two men warily.

Oblivious to her, Selena, and the woman, Eros walked a slow circle around Julian, looking him up and down.

'Keeping company with mortals?' Julian asked as he raked an equally cold sneer over Eros. 'My, Cupid, has Tartarus frozen over while I was away?'

106

Eros disregarded his angry words. 'Damn, boy,' he said in disbelief, 'you haven't changed a bit. I thought you were mortal.'

'I was supposed to be, you ...' Julian went off again into a cursing frenzy.

Eros's eyes flashed. 'With a mouth like that, you ought to hang out with Ares. Sheesh, little brother, I didn't think you knew the meaning of all that.'

Julian grabbed his brother by the shirt. But before he could do anything more to Eros, the woman threw her arm out and held up her hand.

Julian froze as still as a statue. By the look on his face, Grace could tell he wasn't pleased.

'Let go of me, Psyche,' Julian growled.

Grace's jaw dropped.

Psyche? Could it be?

'Only if you promise not to hit him anymore,' Psyche said. 'I know the two of you haven't been on the best of terms, but respect the fact that I rather like his face as it is and I won't stand for you damaging it any further.'

'Let ... me ... go,' Julian said again, stressing each word.

'You better do it, Psych,' Eros said. 'He's being nice to you right now, but he can break your hold even more easily than I can, thanks to Mom. And if he does, you *will* get hurt.'

Psyche lowered her hand.

Julian released his brother. 'I don't find you amusing, Cupid. I don't find anything about this funny. Now, where is Priapus?'

'Hell, I don't know. Last I heard, he was living it up in southern France.'

Grace's head buzzed from her newfound knowledge. She looked back and forth between Cupid and Psyche. Could it be? Could they really, truly, be *Cupid and Psyche*?

And could they really be related to Julian? Was such a thing possible?

Then again, she supposed it was as likely as two drunk women conjuring a Greek love-slave out of an ancient book.

She caught Selena's delighted, eager look.

'Who's Priapus?' Grace asked Selena.

'A phallic fertility god who was always portrayed as walking around with a hard-on,' she whispered.

'Why does Julian need him?'

Selena shrugged. 'Maybe he's the one who cursed him? But here's the fun fact. Priapus is Eros's brother, so if Julian is related to one, there's a darn good chance he's related to the other.'

Cursed into an eternity of slavery by his own brother? The very thought made Grace ill.

'Summon him,' Julian said darkly to Eros.

'You summon him. He's p.o'd at me.'

'P.o.'d?'

Cupid responded in Greek.

Her mind overwhelmed by it all, Grace decided to interrupt them and get a few answers.

'Excuse me, but what is going on here?' she asked Julian. 'Why did you hit him?'

Julian gave her a droll look. 'Because it gave me a great deal of pleasure.'

'Nice,' Cupid said slowly to Julian, never once looking Grace's way. 'You haven't seen me in what, two thousand years? So, instead of a friendly, brotherly hug, I get slugged.'

Cupid smirked at Psyche. 'And Mom wonders why I'm not closer to my siblings.'

'I'm in no mood for your sarcasm, Cupid,' Julian said between clenched teeth.

Cupid snorted. 'Would you stop calling me that god-awful name? I never could stand it, and I can't believe you would use it, given how much you hated the Romans.'

Julian smiled coldly. 'I use it only because I know how much you despise it, *Cupid*.'

Cupid clenched his teeth and Grace could tell he barely restrained himself from striking out at Julian. 'Tell me, did you summon me just so you could beat the crap out of me? Or is there a more productive reason for why I'm here?'

'Honestly, I didn't think you'd bother coming since you ignored me the last three thousand times I called.'

'That's because I knew you were going to beat me.' Cupid pointed to his swollen cheek. 'Which you did.'

'Then, why did you bother coming now?' Julian asked.

'Honestly,' he said, repeating Julian's words. 'I assumed by now you'd be dead, and that it was some other mortal who just happened to sound like you.'

Grace watched as all emotions left Julian. It was almost as if Cupid's hurtful words had killed something inside of him.

The words also seemed to take some of the steam out of Cupid as well.

'Look,' he said to Julian, 'I know you blame me, but what happened to Penelope wasn't my fault. I had no way of knowing what Priapus was going to do when he found out.'

Julian winced as if Cupid had slugged him. Raw, tormented agony glowed in his eyes and on the lines of his face. Grace had no idea who Penelope was, but it was obvious she had meant quite a bit to Julian.

'Didn't you?' Julian asked, his voice hoarse.

'I swear to you, little brother,' Cupid said softly. He glanced to Psyche, then back at Julian. 'I never meant for her to get hurt, and I never meant to betray you.'

'Right,' Julian sneered. 'You expect me to believe that? I know you too well, Cupid. You delight in wreaking havoc on mortal lives.'

'But he didn't do it to *you*, Julian,' Psyche said, her tone pleading. 'If you won't believe him, then believe me. No one ever intended that Penelope should die that way. Your mother still mourns their deaths.'

Julian's glare hardened. 'How can *you* even stand to speak of her? Aphrodite was so jealous of you that she tried first to marry you off to a hideous man, then kill you to keep you from marrying Cupid. For the Goddess of Love, she certainly has very little of it in her for anyone other than herself.'

Psyche looked away.

'Don't you talk about her that way,' Cupid snapped. 'She's our mother and deserving of your respect.'

The grim anger on Julian's face would have scared the devil himself and Cupid shrank before it. 'Don't you *ever* defend her to me.'

It was only then Cupid noticed Grace and Selena. He did a double-take as if they had just popped into the group. 'Who are they?'

'Friends,' Julian said to Grace's surprise.

Cupid's face turned harsh, cold. 'You don't have any friends.'

Julian said nothing in response, but the strained expression on his face touched Grace deeply.

Seemingly unaware of how biting his words had been, Cupid casually moved to stand beside Psyche. 'You still haven't told me why it's so important that you get a hold of Priapus.'

Julian's jaw ticked. 'Because Priapus cursed me into an eternity of slavery, and I can't break out of it. I want him here long enough to start pulling off parts of him that don't grow back.'

Cupid's face blanched. 'Man, he had balls to do that. Mom would've killed him had she known.'

'Do you honestly expect me to believe he did this without her knowledge? I'm not that stupid, Eros. That woman couldn't care less what happens to me.'

Cupid shook his head. 'Don't start on that. When I offered you her gifts, you told me to shove them straight up my back orifice. Remember?'

'I wonder why?' Julian asked sarcastically. 'Zeus cast me out of Olympus just hours after my birth, and Aphrodite never bothered to argue. The only time any of you ever came near me was to heap some form of torture on my head.'

Julian leveled a killing glare at Cupid. 'There's only so many times you can kick a dog before it turns vicious.'

'Okay, granted, some of us could have been a little nicer to you, but—'

'But nothing, Cupid. None of you ever gave a damn about me. Especially not *her*.'

'That's not true. Mom never got over you turning your back on her. You were her favorite.'

Julian scoffed. 'Which is why I've been trapped in a book for the last two thousand years?'

Grace ached for him. How could Cupid just stand there, listening to this and not do everything within his power to save his brother from a fate worse than death?

No wonder Julian cursed them.

Suddenly, Julian grabbed the knife from Cupid's belt and slashed his own wrist.

Grace gasped in horror, but before she even finished making the noise, Julian's wound healed up without so much as a tiny bead of blood.

Cupid's eyes widened. 'Holy shit,' he breathed. 'That's one of Hephaestus's daggers.'

'I know.' Julian handed the dagger back to Cupid. 'Even you can be killed by one, but I can't. I have been completely damned by Priapus.'

Grace saw the terror in Cupid's eyes as he realized the full depth of Julian's sentence. 'I knew he hated you, but I never thought he'd stoop this low. Man, what was he thinking?'

'I don't care what he was thinking. I just want out.'

Cupid nodded. For the first time, she saw sympathy and concern on Cupid's face. 'All right, little brother. First things first. Hang tight and let me go find Mom and see what she has to say.'

'If she loves me as much as you say, why not summon her here and let me speak directly with her?'

Cupid gave him a duh-stare. 'Because the last time I mentioned your name, she cried for a century. You really hurt her feelings.'

Though Julian's stance and face were rigid and cool, in her heart, Grace suspected Julian must have surely suffered just as much as his mother.

If not more.

'I'll consult with her and be with you shortly,' Cupid said, draping an arm over Psyche. 'Okay?'

Julian reached out and grabbed the necklace from Cupid's neck. He jerked it off with one hard tug.

'Hey!' Cupid shouted. 'Careful with that.'

Julian balled the chain up in his fist and left the small bow to dangle out of his hand. 'This way, I know you'll come back.'

Looking greatly peeved, Cupid rubbed his neck. 'Just take care of it. That bow is dangerous in the wrong hands.'

112

'Have no fear. I well remember the bite of it.'

The two of them exchanged a look of wary understanding.

'Later.' Cupid clapped his hands, then he and Psyche vanished in a puff of golden smoke.

Grace took a step back, her mind whirling. She couldn't believe what she'd just heard and seen.

'I have to be dreaming,' she whispered. 'Either that or I've watched one too many episodes of *Xena*.'

Grace stood still as she struggled to digest all she had seen and heard. 'That couldn't have been real. It had to have been some sort of hallucination.'

Julian sighed wearily. 'I wish I had the option of believing that.'

'My God, that was Cupid!' Selena said excitedly. 'Cupid. The real thing. The cute little cherub who hands out hearts.'

Julian scoffed. 'Cupid is anything but cute. As for handing out hearts, he's more likely to rip them out.'

'But he can make people fall in love.'

'No,' he said, tightening his grip on the necklace. 'What he offers is an illusion. No power from above can make one human love another. Love comes from within the heart.' There was a haunting quality to his voice.

Grace met his gaze. 'You say that as if you know.'

'I do.'

She could feel his pain as if it were her own. She reached out to touch him lightly on the arm. 'Is that what happened to Penelope?' Grace asked quietly.

His eyes tortured, Julian looked away from her. 'Is there some place I can get my hair cut?' he asked unexpectedly.

'What?' Grace asked, knowing he was changing the subject to keep from answering her question. 'Why?'

'I want nothing to remind me of *them*.' The grief and

113

hatred on his face was tangible.

Reluctantly, she nodded. 'There's a place in the Brewery.'

'Please take me there.'

Grace did. She led him and Selena back into the Brewery to the salon.

No one spoke again until after the beautician had him firmly planted in the chair.

'You sure you want me to cut this off?' the woman asked as she raked adoring hands through the long, golden locks. 'It sure is gorgeous. Most men look like crap with long hair, but it really becomes you, and it's so healthy and soft! I'd love to know what you use to condition this.'

Julian's face was impassive. 'Cut it.'

The petite brunette looked over her shoulder at Grace. 'You know, if I had this to run my hand through at night, I think I'd be a little ticked that he wants to whack it off.'

Grace smiled to herself. If the woman only knew. 'It's his hair.'

'Okay,' she said with a wistful sigh. She cut it to his shoulders.

'Shorter,' Julian said as she pulled back.

The beautician looked skeptical. 'You sure?'

He nodded.

Grace watched silently as the beautician cut his hair into a becoming style that curled around his face, reminding her of Michelangelo's *David*.

If it were at all possible, he was even more dazzling than before.

'How's that?' the woman asked him at long last.

'It's fine,' Julian said. 'Thank you.'

Grace tipped the woman, then paid for the cut.

Looking up at Julian, she smiled. 'Now, you look like you belong here.'

He snapped his head to the left as if she'd slapped him.

'Did that offend you?' she asked, concerned that she had inadvertently hurt him somehow. Heaven knew, that was the last thing he needed.

'No.'

But inside, she knew better. Something about her innocent comment had wounded him. Deeply.

'So,' Selena said slowly as they headed back into the crowd in the Brewery. 'You're the son of Aphrodite?'

He cut a sideways glare at her. 'I'm no one's son. My mother abandoned me, my father disowned me, and I was raised on a Spartan battlefield under the fist of whoever was around.'

His words cut straight into Grace's heart. No wonder he was so tough. So strong.

She wondered if anyone had ever held him lovingly in their arms. Just once, without demanding he please them first.

He walked on ahead of them. Grace watched the sinuous way he moved. Like a deadly, sleek predator. He had his thumbs tucked into the front pockets of his jeans, and seemed oblivious of the women who gawked and sighed as he passed.

In her mind, she could just imagine what he must have looked like in his day, wearing battle armor.

Given his arrogance and moves, he must have been a fierce fighter.

'Selena,' Grace said quietly. 'Didn't I read in college that the Spartans beat their sons every day just to see how much pain they could endure?'

Julian answered for her. 'They did. And once a year, they held contests to see who could endure the harshest beating before crying out.'

'And a number of them died from the contests,' Selena

115

added. 'Either during the actual beating, or later from the wounds.'

It all came together for Grace. His earlier words about being trained in Sparta and his hatred for the Greeks.

Selena passed a sad look to Grace before she spoke to Julian. 'Being the son of a goddess, I imagine you can take quite a beating.'

'Yes, I can,' he said simply, his voice devoid of emotions.

Grace had never wanted to reach out and hold anyone as much as she wanted to hold Julian right then.

But she knew he wouldn't welcome it.

'You know,' Selena said, and by the look in her eyes, Grace could tell she was trying to lighten their moods. 'I'm kind of hungry. Why don't we grab a burger at the Hard Rock?'

Julian drew his brows into a deep V. 'Why do I constantly feel as if all of you are speaking a foreign language? What is "grabbing a burger at the Hard Rock" supposed to mean?'

Grace laughed. 'The Hard Rock Cafe is a restaurant.'

He looked aghast. 'You eat at a place that advertises its food is hard as a rock?'

She laughed harder. Why had she never thought of that? 'It's really good. C'mon, I'll show you.'

They left the Brewery and headed across the parking lot to the Hard Rock Cafe.

Luckily, they didn't have to wait long before the hostess called them to be seated.

'Hey!' a guy said as they neared the hostess. 'We were here first.'

The hostess gave the man a cutting glare. '*Your* table's not ready yet.' Then, she turned a pair of goo-goo eyes at Julian and smiled widely. 'If you'll please follow me ... '

The woman swung her hips like nobody's business.

Grace looked drolly at Selena as she silently indicated the girl's actions.

'Don't knock it,' Selena said. 'It got us in here in front of ten other people.'

The hostess showed them to a back booth. 'Now you just stay right here,' she said, touching Julian lightly on his arm, 'and I'll make sure your server comes right over to you.'

'What are we, invisible?' Grace asked as the hostess left them.

'I'm beginning to think so,' Selena said as she took the booth facing the back wall.

Grace slid into the opposite seat. As expected, Julian sat next to her.

She handed him a menu.

'I can't read this,' he said before giving it back to her.

'Oh,' Grace said, embarrassed that she hadn't thought of that. 'I guess they didn't teach ancient soldiers to read.'

He stroked his chin with his hand and looked a bit peeved by her comment. 'Actually, they did. The problem is, they taught me to read and write ancient Greek, Latin, Sanskrit, Egyptian hieroglyphics and other long-dead languages. In your own words, that menu is Greek to me.'

Grace cringed. 'You're not going to let me forget the fact that you heard everything I said about you before you appeared, are you?'

'Most likely not.'

He laid his arm across on the table.

Selena looked down from her menu and gasped. 'Is that what I think it is?' She reached for his hand.

To Grace's amazement, Julian let Selena lift his right hand into hers and look at the ring on his finger.

'Gracie, have you seen this?'

Grace sat forward to where she could see it. 'Not really. I've been a bit distracted.'

A bit distracted, yeah, right. That would be like calling Mount Everest a bump in the road.

Even in the dim light, the gold shone. The top of it was flat and had a sword surrounded by laurel leaves engraved into it and inlaid with what appeared to be rubies and emeralds.

'It's beautiful,' Grace said.

'It's a friggin' general's ring, isn't it?' Selena asked. 'You weren't just a run-of-the-mill soldier. You were a friggin' general!'

Julian nodded grimly. 'The terms are equivalent.'

Selena let out an awed breath. 'Gracie, you have no idea! To have a ring like that, Julian was someone of major importance in his time. They didn't just hand those out to everyone.' Selena shook her head. 'I am impressed.'

'Don't be,' Julian said.

For the first time ever, Grace envied Selena her Ph.D. in ancient history. Lanie knew so much more about Julian and his world than she could ever hope to.

But she didn't need that degree to understand how terrible it must have been for Julian to go from being a commander of men to being enslaved by women.

'I bet you were a great general,' Grace said.

Julian turned his attention to Grace and the raw sincerity he'd heard in her voice when she'd said that. For some unfathomable reason, her compliment warmed him.

'I held my own.'

'I bet you kicked major butt,' she said.

Julian smiled. He hadn't thought about his victories in centuries. 'I did put a major hurt on a couple of Romans.'

Grace laughed at his use of her slang. 'You're a fast learner.'

'Hey,' Selena said, interrupting them. 'Can I see Cupid's bow?'

118

'Oh, yeah,' Grace said. 'Can we?'

Julian took it out of his pocket and set it on the table. 'Careful,' he warned Selena as she reached for it. 'The golden arrow is loaded. One prick and you'll fall in love with the next person you see.'

She pulled her hand away.

Grace picked up her fork and used it to drag the bow over to her. 'Is it supposed to be that small?'

Julian smiled. 'Didn't you ever hear the phrase "size doesn't matter"?'

She rolled her eyes at him. 'I don't want to hear it from a man as large as you.'

'Gracie!' Selena gasped. 'I've never heard you speak that way before.'

'That was extremely mild considering what the two of you have said to me the last few days.'

Julian brushed her hair back over her shoulder. She didn't flinch this time.

He was making progress.

'So, how does Cupid use this thing?' Grace asked.

Julian let his fingers slide lightly through the silken strands of her hair. Even in the dim light, it shimmered. He longed to feel it draped over his bare chest. To bury his face in it and let it caress his cheeks.

Shuttering his gaze, he imagined the feel of her body surrounding his. The sound of her breathing in his ear.

'Julian?' she asked, shaking him out of his reverie. 'How does Cupid use this?'

'He can either shrink down to the size of the bow or he can make it bigger to suit his purpose.'

'Really?' Selena asked. 'I didn't know that.'

Their waitress came running over to them, pulling out her pad and ogling Julian as if he were the daily special.

Inconspicuously, Julian slid the bow off the table and returned it to his pocket.

'I'm so sorry I made you wait. Had I known you hadn't been helped, you better believe I would have been here the minute you sat down.'

Grace frowned at the young woman. Damn, couldn't Julian have five seconds without some female throwing herself at him?

Does that include you?

She paused at the thought. She was just like all the others. Staring at his butt, drooling over his body. It was a wonder he could stand being anywhere near her.

Scooting over in the booth, Grace promised herself that she wouldn't treat him that way.

He wasn't a piece of meat. He was a person and he deserved to be treated with respect and dignity.

She ordered for the three of them, and when the waitress returned with their drinks, she also brought out an order of buffalo wings.

'We didn't order these,' Selena said.

'Oh, I know,' the girl responded. She smiled at Julian. 'We're backed up in the kitchen, so it'll take a few extra minutes to get the food out. I thought you might be hungry, so I nabbed these. If you don't like them, I can get you something else. But don't worry about it, they're on the house. So, would you prefer something else?'

Oh, the double entendre was thick and made Grace want to wrench the strawberry-blond hair out by its roots.

'These are fine, thank you,' Julian said.

'Oh, my God, could you say something else to me?' the girl asked, practically swooning. 'Oh, say my name! It's Mary.'

'Thank you, Mary.'

'Ooo,' the girl crooned. 'That gives me chills.' With one

last hungry look at Julian, the girl left them.

'I can't believe this,' Grace said. 'Do women always do this to you?'

'Yes,' Julian said, his tone edged by ire. 'That's why I hate going into public places.'

'Don't knock it,' Selena said as she reached for a buffalo wing. 'It definitely comes in handy. In fact, I say we take him out more often.'

Grace scoffed. 'Yeah, well, if that little critter scribbles her name and number on the bill before she hands it over, I might have to hurt her.'

Selena burst out laughing.

Before Grace could ask anything else, Cupid sauntered into the restaurant and approached their booth.

The left side of his face had a light bruise where Julian had struck him. Cupid tried to appear casual, yet she sensed his tension, as if he were ready to flee at a moment's notice. He quirked a brow at Julian's short hair, but said nothing as he sat down next to Selena.

'Well?' Julian asked.

Cupid let out a long sigh. 'You want the bad news, or the *really* bad news?'

'Oh, let's see ... how about we make my day special, and start with the worst, then work our way up?'

Cupid nodded. 'All right. At worst, the curse will most likely never be broken.'

Julian took the news better than she did. He merely nodded in acceptance.

Grace narrowed her eyes at Cupid. 'How can you do this to him? Good Lord, my parents would have moved heaven and earth to help me, and yet here you sit without even an *I'm sorry* for him. What kind of brother are you?'

121

'Grace,' Julian said with an edge to his voice. 'Don't challenge him. There's no telling what consequences it might bring.'

'That's right, mort–'

'You touch her,' Julian said to Cupid, interrupting him, 'and I *will* take that dagger at your side and cut your heart out with it.'

Cupid slid farther away from Julian. 'By the way, you left out some really important details.'

Julian gave him a shuttered glare. 'Such as?'

'Such as the little fact you slept with one of Priapus's virgins. Man, what were you thinking? You didn't even bother to remove his robe from her when you took her. You knew better than that. Why would you have done such a thing?'

'If you recall, I was rather angry with him at the time,' he said bitterly.

'Then you should have picked one of Mom's followers. That's what they were there for.'

'She wasn't the one who killed my wife. Priapus was.'

Grace felt her lungs seize at his words. Was he serious?

Cupid ignored his hostility. 'Well, Priapus is still raw over it. He seems to view it as the last insult where you're concerned.'

'Oh, I see,' Julian growled. 'Big brother's mad at me for daring to sleep with one of his consecrated virgins while I was supposed to just sit back and let him murder my family on a whim?' The fury in Julian's tone sent a shiver up her spine. 'Did you bother to ask Priapus why he went after them?'

Cupid rubbed a hand over his eyes as he let out a ragged breath. 'Yeah, remember when you routed and defeated Livius outside of Conjara? Livius called out for vengeance against you right before you beheaded him.'

'It was war.'

'And you know how much Priapus always hated you. He was looking for an opening to go after you without fear of retribution, and you gave it to him.'

Grace looked to Julian, but no emotions whatsoever showed on his face.

'Did you tell Priapus I wanted to see him?' Julian asked.

'What are you, crazed? Hell, no. I mentioned your name and he about blew a gasket. Said you could rot in Tartarus forever. Believe me, you don't want to be near him.'

'Oh, trust me, I do.'

Cupid nodded. 'Yeah, but if you kill him, you'll have Zeus, Tisiphone, and Nemesis to deal with.'

'Do you think they scare me?'

'I know they don't, but I really don't want to see you die that way. And if you'd stop being pig-headed for three seconds, you'd realize it yourself. C'mon, do you really want to pull down the wrath of the big man?'

By the look on Julian's face, Grace would say he really didn't care one way or the other.

'But,' Cupid continued, 'Mom pointed out that there is a way to break the curse.'

Grace held her breath as hope flitted across Julian's face. They both waited for Cupid to elaborate.

Instead, Cupid trailed his gaze over the dark interior of the restaurant. 'Do you believe people eat this sh–'

Julian snapped his fingers in front of Cupid's face. 'How do I break the curse?'

Cupid leaned back in the booth. 'You know everything in the universe is cyclical. As it began, so shall it end. Since Alexandria caused the curse, you have to be summoned by another woman of Alexander. One who also needs you. You must make a sacrifice for her and–' Cupid broke off into laughter.

Until Julian reached across the table and seized his shirt in his fist. 'And?'

Cupid knocked his grip away and sobered. 'Well ... ' Cupid's gaze slid to Grace and Selena. 'Would you excuse us for a minute?'

'I'm a sex therapist,' Grace told him. 'There's nothing you can say that will shock me.'

'And I ain't about to leave this booth until I hear the juicy tidbits,' Selena said.

'All right, then.' He looked back at Julian. 'When the woman of Alexander summons you, you can't put your spoon in her jelly jar until the last day of your incarnation. Then, the two of you must unite carnally before midnight and you must keep your bodies joined until the sun rises. If you withdraw from her at any point, for any reason, you will immediately return to the book, and the curse continues.'

Julian cursed and looked away.

'Exactly,' Cupid said. 'You know how strong Priapus's curse is. There's no way in hell you'll ever make it thirty days without boinking your summoner.'

'That's not the problem,' Julian said between clenched teeth. 'The problem is finding a woman of Alexander to summon me.'

Her heart hammering nervously, Grace sat forward. 'What does that mean? A woman of Alexander?'

Cupid shrugged. 'Well, she has to have Alexander in her name.'

'Like a surname?' she asked.

'Yes.'

Grace looked up and caught Julian's tortured gaze. 'Julian, my name is Grace Alexander.'

Chapter Seven

Julian stared at Grace, his mind whirling as her words rang in his head.

Could it be? Dare he believe it?

Dare he even hope after all this time ...

'Your surname is Alexander?' he repeated in disbelief.

'Yes,' she said, a slow, encouraging smile breaking across her face.

Cupid looked sharply at him. 'Have you two made friendly with the privates yet?'

'No,' Julian said. 'We haven't.' And to think he had been angry over that.

Grace had saved him from making the third biggest mistake of his life. At that moment, he could have kissed her.

A smile split Cupid's face. 'Well, I'll be damned. Or you'll be undamned, I should say. I never knew a woman who could be around you more than ten minutes who didn't drop her–'

'Cupid,' Julian snapped, cutting him off before he gave a

lengthy discourse on the number of women Julian had slept with. 'Do you have anything else informative to say?'

'Just this. Mom's curse-breaker is contingent on Priapus's not finding out. If he does, he could circumvent the whole thing with one of his nasty whammies.'

Julian clenched his fists as he remembered quite clearly some of his half-brother's more evil actions.

For some reason he'd never fully understood, Priapus had hated him since the moment of his birth. And over the years, Priapus had given sibling rivalry a whole new meaning.

Julian took a sip of his drink. 'He won't find out unless you tell him.'

'Don't look at me,' Cupid said. 'I don't run with his crowd. You have me confused with cousin Dion. And on that note, I need to go meet up with my boys. We plan to do a major tribute to old Bacchus later tonight.' Cupid held his hand out, palm upward. 'My bow, if you please.'

Careful lest it prick him, Julian fished it out of his pocket and returned to him.

It was then he caught a rare, honest look of affection from his older brother. 'I'll be around if you need me. Just call my name – the one *not* Cupid. And please lay off the "worthless bastard" stuff. Sheez.' He raked him with a smirk. 'I should have known it was you.'

Julian said nothing as he remembered what had happened the last time he took his brother up on that offer.

Cupid scooted out of the booth, looked at Grace and Selena, then smiled at Julian. 'Good luck with earning your freedom. May the strength of Ares and wisdom of Athena see you through.'

'And may Hades roast your hoary soul.'

Cupid laughed. 'Too late. He did that in the third century and it wasn't so bad. Later, little brother.'

Julian didn't speak as Cupid made his way out of the restaurant like an almost normal human being.

The waitress brought their food to them.

Julian picked at the strange meat on bread, but he didn't feel like eating it. He'd lost his appetite.

Grace poured something red to cover the meat, then placed the bread together and took a bite while Selena ate a salad drenched with white sauce.

Looking up, Grace caught Julian's frown as he watched her eat. His face even more troubled than before, he had a hardness to his jaw that said he was clenching his teeth. 'What's the matter?' she asked.

He narrowed his eyes suspiciously. 'Are you really willing to do what Eros said?'

Grace set her burger down and wiped her mouth with her napkin. In truth, she didn't like the thought of Julian using her body to gain his freedom. A one-night stand with no commitments, no promises.

Julian would be gone as soon as he finished with her. She had no doubt about that.

Why would a man like him ever want to stay with her when he could have any woman on the planet eating out of his hand?

Still, she couldn't condemn him to live out eternity in a book. Not when she could free him.

'Tell me something,' she said quietly. 'I want to know the whole story of how you got into that book. And what happened to your wife.'

She wouldn't have thought it possible, but his jaw got even tenser. He was trying to hide again.

But Grace refused to let him run. It was time he understood exactly why the thought of sleeping with him bothered her. 'Julian, you're asking a lot of me. I haven't had much experience with men in social situations.'

He frowned. 'You are a virgin?'

'I wish,' she breathed.

Julian saw the pain in her eyes as she whispered the words. She dropped her shamed gaze to the floor.

No, his mind roared. Surely she hadn't been through what he suspected. As the very idea went through his mind, an unexpected rage coiled through him. 'Were you raped?'

'No,' she whispered. 'Not ... exactly.'

His confusion dispelled his anger. 'Then what?'

'I was young and stupid,' she said softly.

'The pig took advantage of the fact she was grieving over the death of her parents,' Selena said, her voice filled with acrimony. 'He was one of those "I just want to take care of you" lying creeps who use you, and then leave you the minute he has what he's after.'

'He hurt you?' Julian asked.

Grace nodded.

Another wave of peculiar anger ripped through him. He didn't know why it mattered to him what had happened to her, but for some reason he couldn't fathom, it did.

And he wanted vengeance on her behalf.

He saw her hand shaking. Covering it with his, he gently stroked the backs of her knuckles with his thumb.

'I only slept with him once,' she said quietly. 'I know there's supposed to be pain the first time, but not like that. And as much as it hurt physically, the worst pain was from the fact that he didn't seem to care. It felt like I was just there to serve him, that I wasn't even a person to him.'

Julian's stomach knotted. He knew that feeling all too well.

'Later that week,' Grace continued, 'when he didn't call or answer his phone, I went by his apartment to see him. It

128

was spring and he had his window open. As I walked by I … ' She choked on a sob.

'He and his roommate had a bet going to see who could deflower the most virgins for the year,' Selena said. 'She overheard them laughing about her.'

Rage, dark and deadly, descended on him. He'd known such men, personally. And he never could stand them. Indeed, he had taken great pleasure in purging the earth of their fetid presence.

'I felt so used, so stupid,' Grace whispered. She looked up at him. The agony in her eyes seared him. 'I don't ever want to feel that way again.' She covered her face with one hand, but not before he saw the humiliation in her eyes.

'I'm sorry, Grace,' he whispered, pulling her against him.

So, that was it. That was the source of her demons. Julian held her tightly, and leaned his cheek against the top of her hair. The soft, feminine scent of flowers surrounded him.

How he longed to soothe her. And how guilty he felt. No doubt Penelope had felt just as used by him. The gods knew he had done her far more harm in the end.

He should be damned, he thought bitterly.

He had more than earned it, and he wouldn't hurt Grace anymore. She was a good woman with a good heart, and he refused to take advantage of it.

'It's all right, Grace,' he said softly, wrapping his arm around her head to cradle it. He kissed her lightly on the top of her head. 'I would never ask you to do this for me.'

Grace looked up at him in stunned surprise. She couldn't believe he would say such a thing. 'I can't *not* do it.'

'Yes you can. You just walk away.'

There was such a haunted note to his voice. It was strange and foreign, and spoke volumes about the man he had once been. 'Do you really think I could do that?'

129

'Why not? Every member of my family did it to me. You don't even know me.' His gaze turned dull as he released her.

'Julian—'

'Take my word for it, Grace. I'm not worth it.' He swallowed hard before he spoke again. 'As a general, I was relentless in battle. I can still see the horror-stricken eyes of a thousand men who perished under my sword as I hacked them to pieces without the tiniest bit of remorse.'

He met Grace's gaze. 'Now why would you *ever* want to save someone like me?'

In her mind's eye, she saw the way he had cuddled the boy in his arms, heard the way he had threatened Cupid should his brother harm her, and she knew why. He might have done those things in the past, but he wasn't pure evil.

He could have raped her at any time. Instead, the man who had so seldom known kindness had only held her.

No, in spite of his past crimes, there was goodness in him.

Julian had merely been a man of his time. A general in an ancient world forged by battles. A man who had been raised on a battlefield under brutal conditions she couldn't even imagine.

'And your wife?' Grace asked.

A tic began in his jaw. 'I lied to her, betrayed and tricked her, and in the end I killed her.'

Grace tensed at his unexpected words. '*You* killed her?'

'I may not have been the one who took her life, but I killed her just the same. Had I not ...' His voice trailed off as he clenched his eyes shut.

'What?' she asked. 'What happened?'

'I tampered with my destiny and hers, and in the end the Fates punished me for it.'

Grace wouldn't let it go at that. 'How did she die?'

'She went mad when she learned what I'd done to her. What Eros had done ... ' Julian buried his face in his hands as memories tore through him. 'I was a fool to ever believe Eros could make someone love me.'

Grace reached up and brushed a gentle hand across his face. He stared at her. She was so beautiful sitting there. The tenderness in her gaze amazed him. No woman had ever looked at him that way.

Not even Penelope. There had always been something missing when his wife looked at him. Something missing from her touch.

Her heart, he realized with a start. Grace had been right. There was a difference when someone's heart wasn't involved. It was subtle, but he had always felt the hollowness of Penelope's caresses, heard the emptiness in her words, and it had burned him all the way to his blackened soul.

Suddenly, Cupid materialized next to Selena, and gave him a sheepish look. 'I forgot something.'

Julian let out a long, acerbated breath. 'It seems to me, one of you is always forgetting something, and usually, it's the most important something. What did you forget *this* time?'

Cupid refused to meet his gaze. 'As you well know, you're doomed to feel compelled, shall we say, to pleasure the woman who summons you.'

Julian glanced to Grace and his groin tightened viciously in response. 'I'm very much aware of that fact.'

'But are you aware of the fact that every day that passes without your having her, more of your sanity will slip away? By the end of the month, you'll be a stark raving loon from sex deprivation and the only way to cure it is to give in. If you don't, you, my brother, are going to be in so much physical pain that it will make Prometheus's punishment

131

look like he spent eternity in the Elysian Fields.'

Selena gasped.

'Isn't Prometheus the god who supposedly gave fire to mankind?' Grace asked.

'Yes,' Cupid said.

Grace glanced nervously at Julian. 'The one who was chained to a rock and had a buzzard eat his innards every day?'

'And every night he grew a new set for the bird to eat,' Julian finished for her. The gods certainly knew how to punish those who displeased them.

Bitter anger coursed through his veins as he glared at Cupid. 'I hate all of you.'

Cupid nodded. 'I know you do. I just wish I had never done what you asked. I am sorry for it. Whether you believe it or not, Mom and I both are.'

His emotions churning, Julian could say nothing as desolation rushed through him. He saw Penelope's face in his mind and winced.

It was one thing for his family to punish him, but they should never have gone after the innocent.

Cupid placed a small box on the table in front of him. 'If you're to have any hope for freedom, you'll more than likely need those.'

'Beware of Greeks bearing gifts,' Julian said bitterly as he opened the box to find two pairs of large silver shackles and a set of small keys resting in a bed of dark blue satin. Instantly, he recognized his stepfather's intricate work. 'Hephaestus?'

Cupid nodded. 'Not even Zeus can break them. When you feel your control slipping, I would advise you to fasten yourself to something really solid and keep . . .–' he directed a glare at Grace '–*her* at a distance.'

Julian took a deep, ragged breath. He would have laughed at the irony, but he couldn't quite muster it. One way or another during his incarnations, he always seemed to find himself chained to something.

'It's inhuman,' Grace gasped.

Cupid gave her a fierce stare. 'Baby, believe me, if you don't chain him down, you *will* regret it.'

'How much time do I have?' Julian asked.

He shrugged. 'I don't know. It largely depends on you and how much self-control you have.' Cupid snorted. 'Then again, given it's you, you might be able to slide by without using them at all.'

Julian closed the box. He was strong, but he wasn't as optimistic as Eros. His optimism had died a slow, painful death long ago.

Eros clapped him on the back. 'Good luck.'

Julian didn't speak as Eros left them. He stared at the box while Cupid's words sifted through his mind. If he had learned anything over the centuries, it was to let the Fates have their way.

It was stupid to even think he had a chance to break free. This was his lot and he would accept it. He was a slave, and a slave he would remain.

'Julian?' Grace asked. 'What is it?'

'We can't do this. Just take me home, Grace. Take me home, and let me make love to you. Let's just get it over with before someone, most likely you, gets hurt.'

'But this is your chance for freedom. It could very well be the only shot you have at it. Have you ever before been summoned by a woman with Alexander in her name?'

'No.'

'Then we have to do this.'

'You don't understand,' he said between clenched teeth.

'If what Eros said is true, by the time that last night arrives, I won't be me.'

'Who will you be?'

'I'll be a monster.'

She looked skeptical. 'I don't think you could ever be a monster.'

He glared at her. 'You have no idea what I'm capable of. And when the gods' madness comes upon you, you are beyond all help. All hope.'

A knot settled tight in his stomach.

'You should have never summoned me, Grace.' Julian reached for his drink.

'Did you ever think that maybe this was what was meant to be?' she asked suddenly. 'Maybe I summoned you because I was meant to free you.'

He looked across the table at Selena. 'You summoned me because Selena tricked you. All she wanted was for you to have a few nights of pleasure so that you could go off and find a decent man without fear of him hurting you.'

'But maybe—'

'No buts, Grace. It's not meant to be.'

Grace's gaze fell down to his wrist. She reached out and touched the Greek writing that ran from his inner wrist halfway up his arm.

'How beautiful,' she said. 'Is it a tattoo?'

'No.'

'What is it?' Grace persisted.

'Priapus burned it there,' he said, avoiding the answer.

Selena sat forward and looked at it. 'It says "damned for eternity and beyond."'

Grace closed her hand over the writing and met his gaze. 'I can't imagine what you must have suffered all this time. Any more than I can understand why your own brother would do such a thing to you.'

'As Cupid said, I knew better than to touch one of Priapus's virgins.'

'So, why did you do it?'

'I was stupid.'

Grace ground her teeth, wanting to strangle him. Why couldn't he just answer her questions? 'What would make you—'

'I have no wish to discuss it,' he snapped.

She released his arm. 'Have you ever let anyone close to you, Julian? I bet you've always been one of those men who trusted no one near your heart. One of those guys who would rather have his tongue cut out than actually let anyone know you're anything but impervious. Were you like that with Penelope?'

Julian looked away as memories poured through him. Memories of a childhood spent in hunger and deprivation. Memories of nights spent in agony of . . .

'Yes,' he said simply. 'I was always alone.'

Grace felt for him. But she couldn't let him give up. Somehow she would find a way to reach him. To make him want to try and break the curse.

Surely there had to be some way to make him fight this. And she vowed to find it.

Chapter Eight

Julian and Grace helped Selena close down her stand and get to her Jeep before they headed home through Friday evening traffic.

'You've been quiet,' Grace said as she stopped for a red light.

She watched the way his gaze followed the path of the other cars on the road. He looked so lost, like someone caught between dreams and reality.

'I don't know what to say,' he responded after a brief pause.

'Tell me how you feel.'

'About what?'

Grace laughed. 'You are definitely a man,' she said. 'You know, the guys give me the hardest time during my sessions. They come in, spend one hundred and twenty-five dollars an hour to basically say nothing. I'll never figure it out.'

His gaze dropped to his lap and she saw the way he rubbed his general's ring idly with his thumb. 'You said you were a sex therapist. What exactly is that?'

She started back into traffic. 'You and I are sort of in the same business. I help people who have relationship troubles. Women who are afraid to be intimate with men, or women who love men a little too zealously.'

'Nymphomaniacs?'

She nodded.

'I've known a few of those,' he said with a sigh.

'I bet you have.'

'And the men?' he asked.

'They're not so easy. Like I said, they don't talk as much. I have a few cases of men who have performance anxiety–'

'What's that?'

'Something I'm sure you'll never have,' she said, thinking of the arrogant way he constantly pursued her.

Clearing her throat, she explained. 'They're men who are afraid their partners will laugh at them while they're in bed.'

'Oh.'

'I also have a couple who are verbally abusive to their spouses and girlfriends. A couple who want to have their sex changed–'

'Can they do that?' Julian asked in a shocked tone.

'Oh, yeah,' she said with a wave of her hand. 'You'd be amazed what the doctors today are capable of.'

She turned toward her house.

Julian was quiet for so long that she was about to show him the radio when all of a sudden he asked, 'Why do you want to help these people?'

'I don't know,' she answered honestly. 'I guess it goes back to my childhood when I was very insecure. My parents loved me, but I didn't know how to relate to other kids. My father was a history professor, and my mother a house-wife–'

'She married a house?'

Grace laughed. 'No, she just stayed at home and did mom things. They never treated me like a child, really, and so when I got around other children I didn't know what to do. What to say. I would get so scared, I would tremble. Finally, my father started taking me to counseling and after a while, I got a lot better.'

'Except around men.'

'That's a whole 'nother story,' she said with a sigh. 'I was an awkward teenager and the guys in my school never came around unless they wanted to mock me.'

'Mock you how?'

Grace shrugged nonchalantly. At least now, those old memories had ceased to bother her. She'd come to terms with it long ago. 'Because I have no boobs. My ears stand out, and I have freckles all over me.'

'Boobs?'

'Breasts.'

She swore she could feel his hot, prolonged stare on her chest.

Glancing sideways, she was able to confirm it. In fact, he looked at her as if he had her shirt off and was in the midst of–

'You have very nice breasts.'

'Thanks,' she said awkwardly, and yet somehow the un-orthodox compliment warmed her. 'What about you?'

'I have no breasts.'

He said it in such a serious deadpan tone that she burst out laughing. 'That's not what I mean, and you know it. What were you like as a teenager?'

'I already told you.'

She gave him a menacing glance. 'Seriously.'

'Seriously, I fought, ate, drank, had sex, and bathed. Usually in that order.'

138

'We're still having this whole intimacy issue, aren't we?' she asked rhetorically.

Then, falling into her role as a counselor, she moved on to something that was hopefully a little easier for him to talk about. 'Why don't you tell me how you felt the first time you went into battle.'

'I felt nothing.'

'You weren't scared?'

'Of what?'

'Of dying or being maimed?'

'No.'

The sincerity of that single word baffled her. 'How could you not be afraid?'

'You can't fear dying when you have no reason to live.'

Haunted by his words, Grace pulled into her driveway.

Deciding it was best to leave off so serious a discussion for the time being, she left the car and opened the trunk. Julian gathered the bags before following her into the house.

They went upstairs and Grace reached into her top dresser drawer to get her comfortable jeans. Then, she made room for his clothes in her chest of drawers.

'So,' she said, grabbing the empty bags and tossing them into the wicker trash can by her closet. 'It's Friday night. What would you like to do? Quiet night in or would you like to go out on the town?'

His hungry gaze ran down the length of her body, making her hot instantaneously. 'You know the answer to that.'

'Okay, one vote for jumping the doctor's bones, and one vote not to jump the doctor's bones. Can I hear another option?'

'How about just a nice quiet evening at home, then?'

'Okay,' she said, heading to her phone on the nightstand.

'Let me check my messages, then we can start dinner.'

Julian finished putting his clothes away while she called her answering service and talked to them.

He had just tucked away the last item when he heard an alarmed note in Grace's voice.

'Did he say what he needed?'

Julian turned to look at her. Her eyes were slightly dilated and she had a firm, tense grip on the phone.

'Why did you give him this number?' she asked angrily. 'My patients are never to receive my home number. Do you have a supervisor I can talk to?'

Julian went to stand beside her. 'Is something wrong?'

She held her hand up to tell him to be quiet as she listened to the other person.

'All right,' she said after a long pause. 'I'll just have to get my number changed again. Thanks.' She turned the phone off and set it down. Worry knitted her brow.

'What happened?' he asked.

She let out an irritated breath as she rubbed at her neck. 'The answering service hired this new girl who slipped up and gave out my home number to one of my patients who called in today.'

She talked so fast, he could barely follow her.

'Well, he's not really one of *my* patients,' she continued without pausing. 'I would never have taken such a man on as a patient, but Luanne, Dr. Jenkins, isn't so picky. And she rushed out of town last week, on some personal emergency. So Beth and I had to divvy up her patients who had to have counseling while she's gone. Still, I didn't want this creepy guy, but Beth doesn't work on Fridays, and he has to have Wednesdays and Fridays because of his release program.'

She looked up at him with panic in her light gray eyes. 'I still didn't want him, but his case worker swore to me there

140

wouldn't be any problems. He said the man wasn't a threat to anyone.'

Julian's head ached from all the information she unloaded, and the words she used that didn't make sense to him. 'Is that a problem?'

'Just a little scary,' she said, her hand shaking. 'He's a stalker who was released from the mental ward.'

'Stalker from a mental ward? What is that?'

As she explained it to him, he actually gaped. 'You let these people loose on your society?'

'Well, yes. The idea is to help them.'

Julian was aghast. What kind of world was this that the men in it refused to protect their women and children from such? 'Where I come from, we didn't let people like that near our families. And we damn sure didn't let them loose on our streets.'

'Welcome to the twenty-first century,' she said bitterly. 'Here, we do things a little differently.'

Julian shook his head as he thought about all the things in this time that were so alien to him. He just couldn't comprehend these people and the way they lived. 'I really don't belong here,' he said under his breath.

'Julian ... '

He pulled away as she reached for him. 'Grace, you know it's true. Let's say we break the curse; what good does it do me? What am I supposed to do here? I can't read your language. I can't drive your car, or work. There's so much I don't comprehend. I'm lost here.'

Grace flinched at the underlying anguish he was trying so hard to conceal. 'You're just overwhelmed by it all. But we'll take it in tiny steps. I can teach you to drive and read. As for work ... I know there are things you can do.'

'Such as?'

'I don't know. Other than be a soldier, what else did you do in Macedonia?'

'I was a commander, Grace. All I know how to do is lead an ancient army into battle. That's it.'

She cupped her hands around his face, and gave him a hard stare. 'Don't you dare give up on this. You said you weren't afraid in battle, then how can you be afraid of this?'

'I just am.'

Something strange happened then as Grace realized he had let her inside him. Not very deep, but she could tell by his face that he had made himself vulnerable to her by admitting that. She knew in her heart that he wasn't the kind of man who often made such admissions. 'I will help you.'

The doubt in those blue eyes twisted her gut. 'Why?'

'We're friends,' she said gently as she brushed his cheek with her thumb. 'Isn't that what you told Cupid?'

'And you heard his response. I don't have any friends.'

'You do now.'

He leaned down and kissed her forehead, then pulled her against him into a tight hug. The warm scent of sandalwood filled her head as she listened to his heart beating fiercely under her cheek while his tanned biceps flexed next to her face. His tender embrace went deeper than just a momentary physical gesture, it touched her profoundly.

'All right, Grace,' he said quietly. 'We'll try this. But just promise me that you won't let me hurt you.'

She frowned up at him.

'I'm serious. Once I'm shackled, don't release me for any reason. Swear it.'

'But–'

'Swear it!' he insisted sternly.

'All right. If you can't control yourself, I won't let you go. But I want you to make a promise to me.'

He pulled back and looked at her skeptically, but left his soothing arms around her. 'What?'

Grace braced her hands against the strength of his biceps. She felt chills spread over his arms the instant her palms made contact with his flesh. He glanced down at her hands with one of the tenderest expressions she'd ever seen.

'Promise me that you won't give up on being free,' she said. 'I want you to try to beat this curse.'

He gave an odd half-smile. 'Very well. I shall try.'

'And you will succeed.'

He laughed at that. 'You have the optimism of a child.'

She returned his smile. 'Peter Pan all the way.'

'Peter who?'

Reluctantly, she withdrew from his arms. Taking his hand, she led him toward the bedroom door. 'Come with me, my Macedonian love-slave, and I will tell you of Peter Pan and his Lost Boys.'

'So, this boy never grew up?' Julian asked as they made dinner.

Grace was actually amazed he hadn't complained when she asked him to make a salad. He seemed to like using knives on food.

Unwilling to investigate that little idiosyncrasy, she concentrated on her spaghetti sauce. 'Nope. He went back to the island with Tinker Bell.'

'Interesting.'

Grace dipped a spoon into the sauce. Cupping her hand under it, she blew across the top of it, then took it over to Julian. 'Tell me what you think.'

He bent down and opened his mouth.

Grace fed it to him and watched the way he savored it. 'It's delicious.'

'Not too much salt?'

'Perfect.'

She beamed.

'Here,' Julian said, holding a piece of cubed cheese for her.

Grace opened her mouth for it, but he didn't give her the cheese. He took advantage of her open mouth to kiss the daylights out of her.

Goodness, but someone ought to be able to bronze a tongue that could move like his, or do something to preserve it. Such a treasure should never be lost.

And those lips ...

Mmm, she didn't want to think about those delectable lips and what they were capable of.

He splayed his fingers against her lower back and pressed her against his hips where he bulged in his jeans. Mercy, the man was heavily endowed, and she trembled at the thought of having all his sexual powers unleashed on her.

Would she even be able to survive it?

She felt his body tense as his breathing changed. He was seriously getting into this and she was seriously beginning to fear that if she didn't stop it, neither one of them would be able to pull away.

As much as she hated to leave his hot embrace, she stepped back.

'Julian, behave.'

His breathing ragged, she saw him fighting with himself as he dragged a hungry look over her body. 'It would be a lot easier to behave if you didn't look so damn good.'

His words shocked her so much that she actually laughed at them.

'I'm sorry,' she said as she saw the irritated look on his face. 'You have to remember that, unlike you, I'm not used to people saying things like that to me. The biggest compliment I've ever gotten from a guy was from Rick Glysdale when he came to pick me up for the prom. He took one look at me and said, "Damn, you cleaned up better than I thought you would."'

Julian scowled. 'I worry about the men of your time, Grace. They all seem to be great fools.'

Laughing again, she kissed him lightly on the cheek, then went to get their pasta off the stove before it overboiled.

As she dumped the noodles into the sieve, she remembered the bread. 'Can you check the rolls?'

Julian moved to the oven and leaned over, gifting her with one luscious view of his rear. Grace bit her bottom lip as she forced herself not to go over there, and run her hand across that tight, firm butt.

'They're about to burn.'

'Oh, shoot! Can you pull them out?' she asked, trying not to spill the boiling water.

'Sure.' Julian grabbed the dish towel from the counter, and started to pull them out. All of a sudden, he shouted an expletive that caught her attention.

Turning, she saw the cloth had caught fire.

'Over here!' she said, moving out of the way. 'Drop it in the sink.'

He did, but not before part of it caught her on the hand. Grace hissed.

'Did I get you?' he asked.

'A little toasted.'

Julian grimaced as he took her hand in his and examined the burn. 'I'm sorry,' he said an instant before he placed her fingertip in his mouth.

Stunned, she couldn't move as he ran his tongue around the sensitive flesh of her finger. In spite of the burning sensation, it felt good. Really, really good.

'You're not helping my burn,' she whispered.

With her finger still in his mouth, he smiled wickedly, then reached behind his back to turn on the cold water. He twirled his tongue one last time around her finger before opening his mouth and moving her hand under the cool stream.

While he held her finger there with one hand, he reached to her potted plant in the windowsill and broke a piece off her aloe plant with the other.

'How do you know about aloe?' she asked.

'Its curative powers were known even before I was born,' he said.

Chills swept up her spine and coiled around her stomach as he rubbed the gooey gel over her finger. 'Better?'

She nodded.

His gaze warm, he stared longingly at her lips as if he could already taste them. 'I think I'll let you handle the oven from now on,' he said.

'Probably for the best.'

She moved past him and took the bread out just before it was too cooked to eat.

Grace made them plates, then led Julian into the living room to eat on the floor by the sofa while they watched *The Matrix*.

'I love this movie,' she said as it began.

Julian set his plate on the coffee table, then sat next to her. 'Do you always eat on the floor?' he asked, before placing a piece of bread in his mouth.

Fascinated by the symphony of movement of his body, she watched the way his jaw flexed as he chewed.

Was there any part of his body not mouth-wateringly gorgeous? She was beginning to understand why his other summoners had treated him the way they had.

The idea of keeping him locked in a bedroom for a month was seriously starting to appeal to her.

And they did have those handcuffs ...

'Well,' she said, forcing her thoughts away from what all that glorious golden skin would look like if he were indeed spread out naked on her mattress. 'I have the dining room table, but since it's just me most nights, I pretty much do a cup of soup on the couch.'

He twirled his fork expertly in the bowl of his spoon until the noodles were wrapped around the tines. 'You need someone to take care of you,' he said before he bit into it.

Grace shrugged. 'I have myself for that.'

'It's not the same.'

She frowned at him. There was an underlying note to his voice that told her he wasn't taking a shot at her being a woman. He was speaking from his heart and experience.

'I guess we all need someone to take care of us, don't we?' she whispered.

He looked back toward the TV, but not before she caught the flash of longing in his eyes.

Grace watched him watch the movie for several minutes. Even while distracted, he had the most impeccable table manners she'd ever seen.

She had spaghetti sauce flying everywhere while he never splashed one single drop. 'Show me how you do that,' she said.

He looked at her curiously. 'Do what?'

'That whole spoon thing you're doing. It's making me crazy. I can never get my noodles to stick to the tines of my fork. They flop all around and make a giant mess.'

'Well, we certainly can't have giant noodles flopping around making a mess, now can we?'

Grace laughed at his words, knowing he wasn't talking about the spaghetti. 'Anyway, how do you do that?'

He took a drink of wine, then set it aside. 'Here, it'll be easier for me to show you this way.'

He squeezed himself in between her and the couch.

'Julian . . . ' she said in warning.

'I'm just showing you what you wanted to know.'

'Um-hum,' she said doubtfully.

Still, she couldn't help but feel him all the way to her bones, to her very soul. The warmth of his chest invaded her back as he surrounded her with his marvelous arms.

He had his legs bent on each side of her. And as he leaned forward, she felt his erection against the back of her hip. For once it didn't shock her. Oddly enough, she was growing accustomed to it.

As his lithe, toned body moved around her, she felt his power, his strength. It left her breathless and unsure.

Unfamiliar feelings washed over her with an intensity she had never known before. What was it about Julian that made her feel so happy and safe?

If this was the curse, then it should be renamed, because there was nothing malevolent about the sensations spiraling through her.

'Okay,' he breathed in her ear, sending electric waves through her. He picked her hands up in his and, together, they held her silverware.

Julian closed his eyes as he inhaled the sweet, pleasant floral scent of her hair. It took every ounce of his willpower to focus on the task and not on how badly he wanted to make love to her.

Her fingers slid provocatively between his, heightening his awareness of her warm, soft skin. A new kind of desperation seized him. One he couldn't name. He knew what he wanted from her, and it wasn't just her body.

But he dared not think those thoughts.

Dared not hope.

She was beyond his grasp. He knew it in his heart, and in his soul. And all the longing in the world would never change the one basic fact that he wasn't worthy of a woman like this.

He had never been worthy . . .

Opening his eyes, Julian showed her how to use the spoon as a bowl for the fork to tuck the noodles together.

'See,' he whispered, bringing the fork to her lips. 'It's simple.'

She opened her mouth and he gently placed the noodles on her tongue. As they slid the fork slowly back out, between her lips, he felt as though he had been spread out on a torture rack.

His heart pounded in a wild, frenzied rhythm as his common sense told him to move away from her.

But he couldn't. He'd been so long without a companion. So long without a friend . . .

He couldn't let go right now. He didn't know how.

So, he continued to feed her.

Grace leaned back into the shelter of his arms. She dropped her hands from his and just let him take control. As she swallowed the next bite, she reached for the bread and fed a piece of it to Julian. He nipped her fingers with his teeth as she placed it in his mouth.

Smiling, she ran her hand down the line of his jaw as he chewed. Oh, the way that muscle flexed beneath her hand. She just loved the way his body moved, the way it rippled with every activity no matter how large or small.

A woman would never get tired of watching this man.

149

While she took a drink of wine, Julian snuck a bite of her spaghetti.

'Hey, now,' she said teasingly. 'That's mine.'

His celestial blue eyes glowed as he smiled, then fed her another bite.

While she chewed, she gave him a drink of her wine.

Unfortunately, she misjudged her timing and pulled back too soon, spilling a bit down his chin and the front of his shirt. 'I'm sorry!' she said, wiping his chin with her fingers. His whiskers scraped gently against her flesh. 'Jeez, I stink at this.'

He didn't seem to mind. Taking her hand in his, he sucked the wine from her fingertips.

Grace moaned low in her throat. A million ribbons of pleasure spread through her body as his tongue slid the entire length of her fingers while his teeth gently nipped her flesh.

One by one, he slowly cleaned them all. And when he was done, he tilted her chin up and captured her lips with his.

But this wasn't the fiercely demanding kiss she was used to from him. The one he used to seduce and devour her.

This one was gentle, quiet. Soft. His lips were feather-light and questing.

He pulled back. 'Still hungry?' he asked.

'Yes,' she breathed, not really talking about the food, but more about the aching of her body for his.

He fed her another bite of spaghetti.

And the next time she sought to quench his thirst, he covered her hand with his while his eyes teased her.

They stayed like that, gently feeding each other and just reveling in one another's company, until the end of the movie, when Julian became suddenly interested in the final fight scenes.

'Your guns are fascinating,' he said as he watched it.

'I guess a general would think so.'

He glanced at her, then back to the movie. 'What do you like most about this play?'

'The allegories.'

He nodded. 'I see a lot of Plato in it.'

'You know of Plato?' she asked in surprise.

'I studied him when I was young.'

'Really?'

He looked less than amused. 'They did manage to teach us a few things while they were knocking us around.'

'You're being flippant.'

'Somewhat.'

After the movie ended, Julian helped her clean up.

While she was loading the dishwasher, the phone rang. 'I'll be back in a sec,' she said, dashing to the living room to pick up the phone.

'Grace, is that you?'

Grace froze at the sound of Rodney Carmichael's voice. 'Hello, Mr. Carmichael,' she said coldly.

At that moment, she could have killed Luanne for going out of town.

She'd only had the one session with Rodney that past Wednesday, but it had been enough to make her want to hire an investigator to find Luanne and bring her home.

The man gave her the creeps.

'Where were you today, Grace? You're not sick, are you? I could bring you some–'

'Didn't Lisa reschedule your appointment?'

'She did, but I was thinking we could–'

'Look, Mr. Carmichael, I don't see patients in my home. I'll see you at your appointment time. Okay?'

The line went dead.

'Grace?'

151

She jumped and screamed at Julian's voice behind her.

He stared at her with a curious look that would have been funny had she not been terrified.

'Are you all right?' he asked.

'Yeah, I'm sorry.' She set the phone down. 'It was just that patient I told you about. Rodney Carmichael. He weirds me out.'

'Weirds?'

'Makes me nervous.' For the first time, she was more than grateful for Julian's presence. Otherwise, she'd be headed over to Selena and Bill's to impose herself on their hospitality for the rest of the weekend.

'C'mon,' she said, turning off the kitchen light. 'Why don't we go upstairs, and I can start teaching you to read English?'

He shook his head. 'You don't give up, do you?'

'Nope.'

'All right,' he said, falling in behind her. 'I'll let you teach me, but only if you put on your red night–'

'No, no, no.' She paused on the stairs and turned around to look at him. 'I don't think so.'

He reached up and brushed her hair from her shoulder. 'Don't you know I need a Muse to inspire me to learn? And what better Muse than you in–'

She stopped his words by placing her fingers over his lips. 'If I put that on, I seriously doubt you'll learn anything you don't already know.'

He nipped her fingers with his teeth. 'I promise to behave.'

Knowing it was a very bad idea, she let him talk her into it.

'You better behave,' she said over her shoulder as she continued up the stairs and to her bedroom.

Grace entered her large, walk-in closet that her father had

turned into a small library years ago, and dug around the bookshelves until she found her ancient copy of *Peter Pan*.

Julian dug in her dresser until he found that wretched outfit.

They exchanged items in the center of the room. Grace ran to the bathroom and changed clothes, but as soon as she saw herself in the gauzy red nightie, she froze. Ugh! If Julian caught sight of her in this, he'd run screaming from the room.

Unable to bear the humiliation of seeing his disappointment in her body, she changed out of the nightie and into her modest pink dorm shirt, then wrapped herself in her thick, terry-cloth robe before returning to her room.

Julian shook his head at her. 'Why are you wearing that?'

'Look, I'm not an idiot. I don't have the kind of body that makes men drool.'

'What are you trying to tell me? You're a man?'

She frowned at his logic. 'No.'

'Then how do you know what men want to ogle?'

'Because they never do. Okay? Men don't drool over me the way women drool over you. Heck, I'm lucky if they even realize I'm female.'

'Grace,' he breathed, moving from the bed. He went to stand at the foot of it.

'Come here,' he commanded.

She obeyed.

He stood her directly in front of her full-length mirror. 'Tell me what you see?' he asked.

'You.'

He smiled at her reflection.

Leaning down, he rested his chin on her shoulder. 'What do you see when you look at you?'

'Someone who needs to lose fifteen to twenty pounds and

153

buy stock in Porcelana fade cream for my freckles.'

He didn't look amused.

He reached his hands around her waist, to the front of the robe where her belt tied it closed.

'Let me tell you what I see.' He all but purred in her ear as he placed his hands on the belt without opening it. 'I see beautiful hair as dark as night. Soft and thick. You have the kind of hair that a man loves to feel cascading over his bare stomach. Hair a man wants to bury his face in so that he can smell you.'

She shivered.

'You have the heart-shaped face of a mischievous imp with full, sensuous lips that beg for kisses. As for your freckles, they are beguiling. They add a youthful charm to your body that is uniquely you, and utterly irresistible.'

It didn't sound so bad when he put it that way.

He tugged open her robe and grimaced at the sight of her pink dorm shirt.

He parted the robe wider.

'What have we here?' he breathed, his eyes devouring her.

Before she could think to protest, he pulled the robe from her shoulders and let it fall in a pool at her feet. He returned to rest his chin on her shoulder as his gaze captured hers in the mirror.

He lifted the hem of her dorm shirt.

'Julian,' she said, catching his hand.

They locked gazes in the mirror. Grace froze, unable to move as his hot, tender look held her enthralled.

'I want to see you, Grace,' he said in a tone that let her know he would not be denied.

Before she could gather her thoughts, he removed her shirt from her, then skimmed his hand over the bare skin of her stomach.

'Your breasts are not small,' he whispered, straightening to tower over her. 'They're the perfect size for a man's hand.' To prove his point, he reached up and cupped them in both his hands.

'Julian,' she half moaned, her body on fire. 'Remember your promise.'

'I'm behaving myself,' he said, his voice hoarse.

Leaning her head back against his hard pecs, Grace breathlessly watched him in the mirror as he released her breasts and ran his hands over her ribs, down to her hips, then under the waistband of her panties.

'You have a beautiful body, Grace,' he said as he brushed his hand over her mound.

For the first time in her life, she actually believed it. He nuzzled her neck as his hand played in the short, dark curls.

'Julian,' she cried, knowing if she didn't stop him now, she would never be able to stop him later.

'Sh,' he breathed in her ear. 'I've got you.'

And then he separated the tender folds of her body and touched her core.

Grace moaned as heat tore through her. Julian captured her lips with his own and kissed her deeply and fully.

Instinctively, she turned in his arms to taste him better.

He picked her up then, never leaving her lips as he carried her to the bed. Somehow, he even managed to lay her back and join her on the mattress, all the while maintaining his kiss.

The man was seriously talented.

And oh, her body was hot. Afire from his touch. His wickedly erotic smell. With the feeling of his body lying against hers. Grace trembled all over as he separated her thighs with his knees and placed his fully clothed body against her.

His weight was wonderful. His body hard and virile as he ground his lean hips against hers. Even through his jeans, she could feel his erection pressing against the center of her body. As if magnetized, her hips rose to meet his.

'That's it, Grace,' he whispered against her lips as he continued to grind his swollen groin against her in a masterful way that told her she would already be climaxing if he were inside her. 'Feel me touching you. Feel my desire for you and you alone. Don't fight it.'

She moaned again as he left her lips and trailed hot, searing kisses down her throat, to her breasts which he suckled gently.

She was delirious from pleasure as she buried her hands in his soft, tawny locks.

He tormented her breast with his tongue, and was relentless in his tasting of her.

Julian's entire body trembled from the amount of force he was using to keep his clothes on his body. He wanted to be inside her so badly that it was slowly shredding his sanity.

With every thrust of his hips against hers, he wanted to cry out from the agony of unspent lust. It was the most bittersweet torture he had ever experienced.

Worse, he felt her hands roaming over his back before she slid them into his back pockets and squeezed him tightly.

He shuddered from it.

'Yes, oh yes,' she murmured as he quickened his strokes.

Julian's head spun. He had to get inside her. And if he couldn't do it one way, then by all the temples in Athens, he would get in another way.

Tearing away from her, he moved lower, trailing his lips over her belly to her hip as he pulled her underwear from her.

Grace's entire body shook from his unyielding power.

'Please,' she murmured, unable to take any more.

He nudged her legs farther apart. Grace obliged. He placed his hands under her, then lifted her hips up to let her legs fall over his shoulders.

Her eyes flew wide the instant he took her into his mouth.

Burying her hands in his hair, Grace threw her head back and hissed in pleasure as his pulsating tongue stroked her intimately. Never had she felt anything like it. Over and over, in and out, he delved and licked and tormented, making her breathless. Weak.

Julian closed his eyes and growled low in his throat as he tasted her for the very first time. And he reveled in it. The sound of her murmured pleasure echoed in his ears. He could feel her body respond to every careful, sensual lick he delivered to her. Indeed, he felt the quivering in her thighs and buttocks against his cheeks and shoulders.

She writhed sensuously in response to him.

His breathing ragged, he wanted to show her exactly what she had been missing. When she left this room tonight, she would never again flinch from his touch.

Grace moaned as he moved his hand slightly and dipped his thumb inside her while he continued to tease her with his tongue.

'Julian!' she gasped as her body involuntarily shook and shivered.

He moved his thumb and tongue even faster, deeper. Swirling and swirling, delving and caressing. Her head swam at the feel of his whiskers gently scraping between her thighs, rubbing her between her legs.

And just when she thought she could take no more of it, her release came so fiercely that she threw her head back and screamed from the deep, cascading waves of pleasure that rippled through her.

And still he continued, driving her pleasure on until she climaxed again, hard on the heels of the first one.

When he did it to her a third time, she thought she might very well perish from it.

Weak and more than spent, she rolled her head back and forth against the pillow as he continued his relentless pace. 'Please, Julian, please,' she begged as her body continued to spasm from his touch. 'I can't take any more.'

Only then did he withdraw.

Her breathing ragged, she throbbed from the top of her head, all the way down to the very tips of her toes. She'd never in her life known such intense pleasure.

He kissed a slow path back up her body, before he buried his lips against her throat.

'Tell me the truth, Grace,' he breathed in her ear. 'Have you ever felt that before?'

'No,' she whispered honestly, doubting few, if any, women had ever experienced anything like what he'd just done to her. 'I had no idea.'

His eyes hungry, he stared at her as if he still wanted to devour her.

Grace felt his erection against her hip and realized he hadn't released himself. He had kept his word to her.

Her heart hammering at the knowledge, she wanted to help him experience what she had. Or at least a close proximity of it.

Reaching down, she started to unbutton his pants.

He caught her hand, then moved it to his lips where he kissed her palm sweetly. 'It's a nice thought, but don't bother.'

'Julian,' she said chidingly. 'I know it gets really painful for men if they don't–'

'I can't,' he insisted, interrupting her.

She frowned. 'Can't what?'

'I can't orgasm.'

Her jaw dropped at his words. Surely he wasn't serious? And yet his eyes were deadly earnest.

'It's part of the curse,' he said. 'I can give you pleasure, but if you touch me right now, you'll only make me hurt more.'

Aching for him, she reached out and placed her hand against his cheek. 'Then why did you do—'

'Because I wanted to.'

She didn't believe it. Not for a minute. She dropped her hand away from him and looked away. 'You had to, you mean. It's part of the curse, too, isn't it?'

He caught her chin in his hand and forced her to look up at him. 'No. I'm fighting the curse, otherwise I'd be inside you right now.'

'I don't understand.'

'Neither do I,' he said, his gaze searching hers as if she held the answer. 'Just lie with me,' he whispered. 'Please.'

Grace winced at the pain she heard behind that simple request. Her poor Julian. What had they done to him?

How could anyone do such a thing to someone like him?

He picked up the book from the bed and placed it in her hands. 'Read to me.'

She opened the book while Julian piled the pillows up against the headboard.

He lay back, then leaned her against his side. Without a word, he covered them with a blanket, and cradled her tenderly with his arm.

The smell of sandalwood filled her head as she started reading to him of Wendy and Peter Pan.

They lay like that for over an hour.

'I love the sound of your voice. The way you speak,' he said as she paused to turn another page.

159

Grace smiled. 'I have to say the same of you. You have the most killer accent I've ever heard.'

He took the book from her hands and placed it on the nightstand. Grace looked up at him. Molten desire filled his eyes as he stared at her face with a hunger that stole her breath.

Then, to her amazement, he kissed her lightly on the tip of her nose.

He reached over and grabbed her remote, then dimmed the lights to their lowest setting. Grace didn't know what to say as he snuggled up against her back and just held her close.

He brushed her hair back from her face and laid his head above hers. 'I love the way you smell,' he whispered, his arms tightening around her.

'Thank you,' she whispered.

She wasn't sure, but she thought he might be smiling at her.

Grace snuggled even closer to his warmth, but his jeans rubbed against her bare legs. 'Are you comfortable in your clothes? Shouldn't you change?'

'No,' he said quietly. 'This way I know my spoon will stay away from your–'

'Don't you say it!' she said with a laugh. 'No offense, your brother is disgusting.'

'I knew I liked you for a reason.'

Grace took the remote from his hand. 'Good night, Julian.'

'Good night, my sweet.'

She switched off the light.

Instantly, she felt Julian tense around her, heard his breathing change into short, sharp intakes. He pulled away from her.

'Julian?'

He didn't respond.

Worried, she turned the lights back on to see him, leaning on his arms, braced and locked, to support his upper body. His forehead damp from perspiration, his eyes were wild and panicked as he struggled to breathe.

'Julian?'

He looked around the bedroom as if he had awakened from some terrifying nightmare. She watched as he lifted one hand and placed it against the wall above the headboard as if to assure himself it was real and not a hallucination.

Licking his lips, he rubbed his hand over his chest and swallowed hard.

It was then, she knew.

It was the darkness. That was why he had only dimmed the lights.

'I'm so sorry, Julian. I didn't think.'

He didn't speak.

Grace pulled him into her arms, amazed at the way a man as strong as this one held on to her as if he couldn't let go. Julian laid his head against her breasts.

Clenching her teeth, she felt tears sting her eyes. And in that moment, she knew she could never let him go back into that book. Never.

Somehow, they would beat this curse. And when it was over, she hoped Julian got his own revenge against the ones responsible.

Chapter Nine

Grace remained still for hours, listening to Julian breathe, calmly, peacefully, as he slept behind her. He had one thigh nestled snugly between her legs and one arm draped over her waist.

The feel of his body around hers made her throb with longing.

And his scent ...

It was all she could do not to turn over and bury her nose in the warm, spicy scent of his skin. No one had ever made her feel like this. So wanted, so secure.

So desirable.

And she wondered how that could be, given the fact that they barely knew each other. Julian touched something inside her on a level that went beyond the physical.

He was so strong, so commanding. And funny. He made her laugh and he wrung her heart.

She reached out and ran her fingers lightly over his hand that lay in front of her, just below her chin. He had such beautiful hands. Long and tapered. Even when they were relaxed in sleep, the power of them was undeniable. And the magic they could work on her body . . .

It was nothing short of miraculous.

She ran her thumb over his general's ring and wondered what Julian had been like back then. Unless the curse had altered his physical age, he didn't appear very old. Certainly, not much more than thirty.

How had he ever led an army at such a young age? But then, Alexander the Great had barely been old enough to shave when he'd started his campaigns.

Julian must have been fabulous on the battlefield. Closing her eyes, she tried to imagine him on his horse, riding out against his enemies. She had a vivid image of him in his armor, his sword raised as he fought hand to hand against the Romans.

'Iason?'

She tensed as she heard him whisper in his sleep.

Rolling over, she looked at him. 'Julian?'

He tensed behind her and started speaking in a jumbled mixture of English and ancient Greek. 'Don't! *Okhee*! *Okhee*! No!'

He sat straight up in bed. She couldn't tell if he was awake or asleep.

Instinctively, she touched his arm.

With a curse, he grabbed her and pulled her over his body. He threw her back against the mattress. His eyes were wild as he held her down, his lips curled.

'Damn you!' he snarled.

'Julian,' she gasped as his grip on her arm tightened and she tried to make him let her go. 'It's me, Grace!'

'Grace?' he repeated, his brows drawing together into a deep frown as he focused on her face.

Blinking, he pulled back from her. He lifted his hands and

163

stared at them as if they were alien appendages he'd never seen before.

He looked at her. 'Did I hurt you?'

'No, I'm fine. Are you all right?'

He didn't move.

'Julian?' She reached for him.

He pulled back from her as if she were poisonous. 'I'm fine. It was just a bad dream.'

'A bad dream or a bad memory?'

'A bad memory that always haunts my dreams,' he whispered, his voice laden with grief. He got out of bed. 'I should sleep somewhere else.'

Grace caught his arm before he could leave, and pulled him back toward the bed. 'Is that what you've always done in the past?'

He nodded.

'Have you ever told anyone about the dream?'

Julian stared aghast at her. What did she take him for? Some sniveling child that needed its mother?

He'd always borne his anguish inside. As he'd been taught. It was only when he slept that the memories were able to sneak past his defenses. Only when he slept that he was weak.

In the book, there was no one to hurt when his nightmare came upon him. But once released from his prison, he knew better than to sleep at the side of someone he might inadvertently grab while in the throes of it.

He could have accidentally killed her.

That thought terrified him.

'No,' he whispered. 'I've never told anyone.'

'Then tell me.'

'No,' he said firmly. 'I don't want to relive it.'

'If you're reliving it every time you dream, then what's the

164

difference? Let me in, Julian. Let me see if I can help.'

Dare he even hope that she could?

You know better.

And yet ...

He wanted to purge the demons. He wanted to sleep one night in peaceful slumber, free of torment.

'Tell me,' she gently insisted.

Grace sensed his reluctance as he rejoined her in bed. He remained seated on the side, his head in his hands. 'You asked me earlier how I became damned. I was cursed because I betrayed the only brother I ever knew. The only family I ever had.'

His anguish reached deep inside her. She wanted desperately to run her hand over his back in a comforting manner, but didn't dare touch him lest it make him withdraw again. 'What did you do?'

He ran his hand through his hair, then balled his fist in it. His jaw more rigid than steel, he stared at the carpet. 'I allowed envy to poison me.'

'How?'

He paused for a long minute before he spoke again. 'I met Iason not long after my stepmother sent me to live in the barracks.'

She vaguely remembered Selena telling her about the Spartan barracks where sons were forced to live away from their homes and families. She'd always thought of them as a kind of boarding school. 'How old were you?'

'Seven.'

Unable to imagine being forced from her parents at that age, Grace gasped.

'There was nothing unusual about it,' he said without looking at her. 'And I was big for my age. Besides, life at the barracks was infinitely preferable to living with my stepmother.'

She heard the venom in his voice and wondered what the woman had been like. 'I take it Iason lived in the barracks with you?'

'Yes,' he whispered. 'Each barracks was divided up into groups where we chose the boy we wanted to lead us. Iason was the leader of my group.'

'What did these groups do?'

'We functioned like a military unit. We studied, performed chores, but most of all, we banded together to survive.'

She started at such a harsh word. 'Survive what?'

'The Spartan lifestyle,' he said, his voice laced with acrimony. 'I don't know how much you know about my father's people, but they didn't have the luxuries of the other Greeks.

'The Spartans only wanted one thing from their sons. They wanted us to grow into the strongest fighting force of the ancient world. To prepare us for our future, we were taught how to survive with only the barest of necessities. We were given one tunic to last us the year, and if it became damaged or lost or we outgrew it, we had to go without one. We were only permitted a bed provided we made it ourselves. And once we reached puberty, we were no longer allowed shoes for our feet.'

He laughed bitterly. 'I can still remember how badly my feet would ache in the winter. We were forbidden a fire or blanket to keep us warm, so we tied rags around our feet at night to keep them from frostbite. Then, in the morning, we would carry away the bodies of the boys who had died of exposure in their sleep.'

Grace cringed at the world he was describing. She tried to imagine what it must have been like to live in it. Worse, she remembered the fit she'd pitched at age thirteen for a pair of eighty-dollar shoes her mother had said were too mature for her, while at the same age, Julian would have been scrounging for rags. The injustice of it cut her. 'You were just children.'

'I was never a child,' he said simply. 'But worst of all, we were never given much food to eat, so we were forced to steal or to starve.'

'And parents allowed this?'

He cast a sardonic look to her over his shoulder. 'They considered it their civic duty. And since my father was the Spartan *stratgoi,* most of the boys and teachers despised me the instant they saw me, and I was given even less food than the others.'

'Your father was what?' she asked, not understanding the Greek term he used.

'The top general, if you will.' He took a deep breath and continued. 'Because of his position and reputation for cruelty, I was a pariah to my group. While they would band together to steal, I was left on my own to survive as best I could. Then one day, Iason was caught stealing bread. When we returned to the barracks, they were going to punish him for being caught. So I stepped forward, and took the blame.'

'Why?'

He shrugged as if the matter were of little importance. 'He was so weak from his earlier beating that I didn't think he could survive another one.'

'Why had they beaten him earlier that day?'

'That's the way we always started our day. As soon as we were dragged from our beds, we were severely beaten.'

Grace winced. 'Then why would you take the beating for him, if you were sore, too?'

'Being born of a goddess, I can take quite a beating.'

Grace closed her eyes as he repeated Selena's words from

167

that afternoon. This time, she couldn't resist reaching out to him. She placed her hand against his biceps.

He didn't pull away.

Instead, he covered her hand with his own and gave a light squeeze. 'From that day forward, Iason called me his brother, and made the other boys accept me. Though both my mother and father had other sons, I had never had a brother before.'

She smiled. 'What happened after that?'

He flexed the muscle beneath her hand. 'We decided to join forces to get what we needed. He would distract and I would steal so that if we were caught, I would be the one who suffered for it.'

Why? was on the tip of her tongue, but she bit it back. In her heart, she knew the answer already. Julian was protecting his brother.

'As time went by,' he continued, 'I started noticing that his father would sneak to watch him in the village. The love and pride on his father's face was indescribable. His mother was the same way. We were supposed to be scrounging for food on our own, and yet every other day, he'd find something one of his parents had left for him. Fresh bread, roasted lamb, a flagon of milk. Sometimes money.'

'That's sweet.'

'Yes, it was, but every time I saw what they did for him, it cut through me. I wanted my parents to feel like that about me. I would gladly have given up my life to have my father, just once, look at me without contempt in his eyes. Or to have my mother care enough to come see me at all. The closest I could ever get to her was to visit her temple at Thymaria. I used to spend hours staring at her statue, and wondering if that was really what she looked like. Wondering if she ever gave me a passing thought.'

Grace sat up and leaned against his back, then hugged him about the waist. She rested her chin on his shoulder. 'You never saw your mother as a child?'

He encircled her arms with his own, and leaned his head back against her shoulder blade. She smiled at the gesture. Even though he was tense and stressed, he was trusting her with things she knew he'd never shared with anyone else.

It made her feel incredibly close to him.

'I haven't seen her to this day,' he said quietly. 'She would send others to me, but she, herself, would never come. No matter how much I implored her, she refused to come to me. After a time, I ceased to ask. Finally, I quit going to her temples altogether.'

Grace placed a tender kiss on his shoulder. How could his mother have ignored him so? How could any mother not answer the plea of her child to come visit him?

She thought of her own parents. Of the love and kindness they had lavished on her. And for the first time, she realized her feelings about their deaths were wrong. All these years, she'd told herself that it would have been better to never have known their love than to have it taken away so cruelly.

But it wasn't. Even though the memories of her parents and childhood were bittersweet, they comforted her.

Julian had never had the warmth of a loving embrace. The security of knowing that no matter what he did, his parents would be there for him.

She couldn't imagine growing up the way Julian had.

'But you had Iason,' she whispered, wondering if that had been enough for him.

'I did. After my father died when I was fourteen, Iason was even kind enough to let me go home with him on furlough. It was on one of those visits that I first saw Penelope.'

Grace felt a tiny stab of jealousy at the mention of his wife's name.

'She was so beautiful,' Julian whispered, 'and promised to Iason.'

She went still at his words.

Oh, this wasn't good.

'Even worse,' he said, lightly stroking her arm, 'she was in love with him. Every time we visited, she'd be there to throw herself into his arms and kiss him. Tell him how much he meant to her. When we'd leave, she'd quietly beg him to be careful. Then, she too started leaving things for him to find.'

Julian paused as he remembered the way Iason would look when he returned to the barracks with Penelope's gifts.

'You may marry one day, Julian,' Iason would say as he flaunted her tokens, 'but you'll never have a wife like her warming your bed.'

Though Iason didn't say it, Julian knew all too well the reason why. No noble father would ever consent to give his daughter to a baseborn, disinherited man who had absolutely no family that would acknowledge him.

Every time Iason had uttered those words, they had cut him to pieces. There had been times when he suspected Iason salted the wound out of jealousy because of the way Penelope would let her gaze linger too long on him when she didn't think Iason was looking. Iason may have held her heart, but like other women, Penelope had ogled Julian whenever he came near.

It was for that reason that Iason stopped asking him to visit altogether. And it had torn him apart to be banned from the only safe home he'd ever known.

'I should have let them marry,' Julian said as he cupped Grace's head with his arm, and buried his face against her neck to inhale the sweet comfort of her scent. 'I knew it even then. But I couldn't stand it. Year after year, I would see her love him. I watched his family dote upon him, while I didn't even have a home to go to.'

'Why?' she asked. 'You said you had brothers, wouldn't they let you stay with them?'

He shook his head. 'My father's sons hated me passionately. Their mother would have let me in, but I refused to pay the price she asked for it. I didn't have much in those days, but I still had my dignity.'

'You have dignity now, too,' she whispered, tightening her hold on his waist. 'I've seen enough of it to know.'

Releasing her, he looked away at her words, his jaw tense.

'What happened to Iason?' she asked, seeking to keep him talking while he was in the mood for it. 'Did he die in battle?'

He laughed bitterly. 'No. When we were old enough to join the army, I kept him safe on the battlefield. I'd promised Penelope and his family that I wouldn't let anything happen to him.'

Grace felt his heart pounding fiercely against her arms.

'As the years went by, it was my name people whispered in awe and fear. My legend and victories recounted over and over again. And when I returned to Thymaria, I ended up sleeping in the streets, or in the bed of whatever woman opened her door to me for the night, just biding my time until I could return to battle.'

Tears stung her eyes at the pain she heard in his voice. How could anyone have treated him that way?

'What happened to change it?' she asked.

He sighed. 'One night, while I was looking for a place to sleep, I stumbled across the two of them in a lovers' embrace. I quickly apologized, but as I left, I overheard Iason talking to Penelope.'

His entire body went rigid in her arms as his heartbeat raced even faster.

'What did he say?' Grace prompted.

The light in his eyes faded. 'Penelope asked him why I never went to my brothers' homes. Iason laughed and said, "No one wants Julian. He's the son of Aphrodite, the Goddess of Love, and not even she can stand to be near him."'

Grace couldn't breathe as he repeated the cruel words, and she could only imagine what he must have felt when he heard them.

Julian drew a ragged breath. 'I had guarded him more times than I could count. Had taken numerous wounds in battle to protect him, including a spear straight through my side, and there he was mocking me to her. I couldn't stand the injustice of it. I had thought we were brothers. And I guess in the end, we really were since he treated me the way the rest of my family had. I had never been anything more than a bastard stepchild. Alone and unwanted. I couldn't understand why he had so many people to love him when I only wanted one.

'Angry and hurt by his words, I did what I'd never done before. I called out to Eros.'

Grace could easily guess what happened after that. 'He made Penelope fall in love with you.'

He nodded. 'He shot Iason with a lead arrow to kill his love for Penelope, and Penelope was given the golden arrow to make her love me. That was supposed to be the end of it ...'

Rocking him gently in her arms, she waited for him to find his next words.

'It took two years before I finally convinced her father to let her marry a disinherited bastard without family influence.

By then, my legend had grown, and I'd been promoted. I'd finally accumulated enough wealth to house her like royalty. And I spared no expense when it came to her. We had gardens, slaves, everything she wanted. I gave her freedom and latitude that no other woman of her time enjoyed.'

'It wasn't enough?'

He shook his head. 'There was still something missing and I knew she wasn't quite right. Even before Eros interfered, she was always overly emotional. She would cling to Iason in a manner forbidden of Spartan women, and one time when he'd been wounded, she had shorn her hair completely off in grief.

'Then, after Eros shot her with his arrow, she would have long periods of great depression or rage. I did the best I could for her and I tried so hard to make her happy.'

Grace brushed his hair back as she listened.

'She told me she loved me, but I knew she didn't care for me the way she'd cared for Iason. She gave herself willingly to me, and yet there was no real passion in her touch. I knew from the very first time I kissed her.

'I tried to tell myself that it didn't matter. Very few men in those days had love in their marriages. Besides, I was gone for months, even years, as I led my army. But in the end, I guess I had too much of my mother in me, because I wanted more.'

Grace ached for him.

'And then the day came when Eros, too, betrayed me.'

'Betrayed you how?' she asked anxiously, knowing this was the source of his curse.

'He and Priapus were drinking the night after I killed Livius. Eros drunkenly told him what he'd done for me. As soon as Priapus heard the story, he knew how to take revenge.

173

'He went to the Underworld and filled a cup with water from the Pool of Memory, then gave the cup to Iason for him to drink. As soon as the water touched his lips, Iason remembered their love. Priapus told him what I'd done, then gave him more water for Penelope.'

Julian felt his lips moving, but he wasn't conscious of the words anymore. Instead, he closed his eyes and relived that wretched day.

He'd just come in from the stables and had happened upon Penelope and Iason in the atrium. Kissing.

Stunned, he'd stopped mid-stride as a wave of trepidation washed over him while he watched the heated way they embraced.

Until Iason looked up and saw him in the doorway.

The instant their eyes met, Iason curled his lip. 'You worthless thief! Priapus told me of your treachery. How could you?'

Her face contorted by hatred, Penelope rushed at Julian, then slapped him. 'You filthy bastard, I could kill you for what you've done.'

'And I *will* kill you for it.' Iason unsheathed his sword.

Julian tried to push Penelope out of the way, but she refused.

'Dear gods, I bore your children,' she said, trying to claw his face.

Julian held her wrists. 'Penelope, I–'

'Don't you touch me,' she snarled, wringing her arms from his grasp. 'It makes my flesh crawl. Do you honestly think any decent woman would ever want you in the light of day? You are vile. Repulsive.'

She shoved him toward Iason. 'Cut his heart out. I want to bathe in his blood until I can no longer smell his touch on me.'

Iason swung his sword.

Julian jumped back, out of the blade's arc.

Instinctively, he reached for his own sword, but stopped. The last thing he wanted was to draw Iason's blood. 'I don't want to fight you.'

'Don't you? You violated my woman and sired children on her that should have been mine! I welcomed you into my home. I gave you a bed when no one else would have you near them, and this is how you repay me?'

Julian stared in disbelief. 'Repaid *you*? Have you any idea the number of times I've saved your life in battle? How many beatings did I take for you? Can you even count them all? And yet you dared mock me.'

Iason laughed cruelly. 'Everyone except Kyrian mocks you, you fool. In fact, he defends you so strongly that it makes me wonder what the two of you do when you wander off alone.'

Squelching the rage that would leave him vulnerable to Iason's blade, Julian barely ducked the next attack. 'Stop it, Iason. Don't make me do something we'll both regret.'

'The only thing I regret is that I let a thief into my house,' Iason bellowed with rage, and swung again.

Julian tried to duck, but Penelope ran at him from behind and pushed him forward.

Iason's blade caught him across the ribs.

Hissing in pain, Julian drew his own sword, then deflected a blow that would have left him headless had it made contact.

Iason tried to engage him, but Julian did nothing more than defend himself while trying to keep Penelope out of the thick of the fight.

'Don't do this, Iason. You know your skills are inferior to mine.'

Iason pressed his attack. 'There's no way I'm going to let you keep her.'

The next few seconds had happened so fast, and yet Julian saw them unfold in sharp, crisp clarity.

Penelope caught Julian's free arm at the same time Iason swung his sword. The blade narrowly missed Julian as she slung him about. Unbalanced, Julian tried to extract himself from her, but with Penelope in the way, he staggered forward at the same time Iason did.

The instant they collided, he felt his sword sink deep into Iason's body.

'No!' Julian shouted, drawing his sword out of Iason's stomach as Penelope let out a scream of pure, tormented anguish.

Slowly, Iason fell to the ground.

Dropping to his knees, Julian tossed his sword aside, and pulled his friend into his arms. 'Dear gods, what have you done?'

Coughing up blood, Iason stared accusingly at him. 'I did nothing. It was you who betrayed me. We were brothers and you stole my heart.'

Iason swallowed painfully as his pale eyes bored into Julian. 'You never had anything in your life you didn't steal from someone else.'

Julian trembled as guilt and agony washed over him. He'd never meant for this to happen. Never meant to hurt anyone, least of all Iason. He'd only wanted someone to love him. Only wanted a home where he was welcome.

But Iason was right. It was all his fault. All of it.

Penelope's screams echoed in his ears. She grabbed him by the hair and pulled it as hard as she could. Her eyes wild, she wrenched the dagger from his waist.

'I want you dead! Dead!'

She plunged the dagger into his arm, then pulled back to strike again. Julian grabbed her hand.

With a feral shriek, she wrenched herself away.

'No,' she said, her eyes crazed. 'I want you to suffer. You took from me what I loved most. Now I will take the same from you.' She ran from the room.

Overwhelmed by his grief and anger, Julian couldn't move as he watched the life drain out of Iason's body.

Until Penelope's words sank into his dazed mind.

'No!' he roared, rising to his feet. 'Don't!'

He reached the door to her chambers in time to hear the children screaming. His heart shredded, he tried to open it, but she'd bolted it from the inside.

By the time he broke into her rooms, it was too late.

Too late . . .

Julian pressed his hands against his eyes as the horror of that day washed over him anew, and he felt Grace's soothing touch on his skin.

He would never be able to purge the sight of them, the fear in his heart. The absolute agony.

The only thing in life he'd ever loved had been his children.

And they alone had loved him.

Why? Why had they had to suffer for his actions? Why couldn't Priapus have tortured him without hurting them?

And how could Aphrodite have let it happen? It was one thing for her to turn a blind eye to him, but to let his children die . . .

That was why he'd gone to her temple that day. He'd planned to kill Priapus. To cleave his head from his shoulders and mount it on a pike.

'What happened?' Grace asked, dragging his thoughts back to the present.

'By the time I got there, it was too late,' he said, his throat aching as raw grief tore through him. 'Our children were dead, killed by their own mother. Penelope had already slashed her wrists and lay dying by their side. I called for a physician and tried to staunch the blood.' He paused. 'With her dying breath, she spat in my face.'

Grace closed her eyes as his pain washed over her. It was even worse than she had imagined.

Dear Lord, how had he survived it?

Over the years, she'd heard numerous horror stories, but none could compete with what he'd been through. And he'd suffered it all alone, with no one to help him. No one to care.

'I am so sorry,' she whispered, rubbing her hands over his chest to comfort him.

'I still can't believe they're gone,' he whispered, his voice laden with grief. 'You asked me what I do while I'm in the book. I just stand there, and remember my son's and daughter's faces. I remember what it felt like when their tiny arms wrapped around me. The way they ran out to meet me when I came home from campaigns. And I relive every moment of that day, wishing I could have done something to save them.'

Grace blinked back her tears. No wonder he'd never spoken of it.

Julian drew a deep, tormented breath. 'The gods won't even grant me insanity to escape those memories. I'm not allowed even that much comfort.'

After that, he spoke no more of it, or of anything else. He merely lay quietly in her arms.

Amazed by the strength of him, Grace sat for hours, just holding him. She didn't know what else to do.

For the first time in years, her therapist's training failed her completely.

*

Grace came awake to bright sunlight streaming in through her windows. It took her a full minute before she remembered the night before.

Sitting up, she reached over for Julian and found nothing but an empty bed.

'Julian?' she asked.

No one answered.

Throwing back the covers, she got up and quickly dressed.

'Julian?' she called as she went down the stairs.

Nothing. Not a single sound, other than her heart beating fiercely in her ears.

Panic began to set in. Had something happened to him?

Grace rushed into the living room where the book was lying on the coffee table. Flipping through it, she saw the blank page where Julian had been. Relieved he hadn't somehow returned to the book, she continued searching the house.

Where was he?

She went to the kitchen and noticed the back door slightly ajar. Her frown deepening, she opened it wider and walked out onto the deck.

Grace looked about the yard until she saw the neighbors' children sitting on the grass between her house and theirs. But what stunned her most was Julian sitting with them as he showed them a game with rocks and sticks.

The two boys and one of the girls were sitting next to him, listening attentively while their two-year-old sister toddled between them.

Grace smiled at the tranquil sight. Warmth flooded her, and she wondered if that was what Julian had looked like with his own children.

Leaving the deck, she walked toward them.

Bobby was the eldest of the children at nine, then his brother Tommy was a year younger and Katie was barely six. Their parents had moved in almost ten years ago as newlyweds and though they were friendly enough, they had never been much more than passing acquaintances.

'So, then what happened?' Bobby asked as Julian took a turn.

'Well, the army was trapped,' Julian said, moving one of the rocks over a stick. 'Betrayed by one of their own. A young hoplite who had sold out his comrades because he wanted to be a Roman centurion.'

'They were the best,' Bobby interrupted.

Julian scoffed. 'They were nothing compared to the Spartans.'

'Go, Spartans!' Tommy shouted. 'That's our school mascot.'

Bobby shoved his brother, knocking him over. 'You're interrupting the story.'

'You should never hit your brother,' Julian said, his voice both stern, and yet strangely gentle. 'Brothers are supposed to protect one another, not hurt each other.'

The irony of his words wrenched her heart. It was a pity no one had ever taught his brothers that lesson.

'Sorry,' Bobby said. 'So what happened after that?'

Before Julian could answer, the baby fell and scattered the rocks and sticks. The boys shouted at her, but Julian calmed them while lifting Allison up and setting her back on her feet.

He touched the baby lightly on the nose, making her laugh. Then he set the game up again.

As Bobby took his turn with a rock, Julian began the story where he'd left off. 'The Macedonian commander looked around the hills where the Romans had his army cornered. There was no way to outflank them, nowhere to retreat.'

'Did they surrender?' Bobby asked.

'Never,' Julian said with conviction. 'Death always before dishonor.'

Julian paused as the words echoed in his mind. Those words had been engraved on his shield. As a commander, he had lived by them.

As a slave, he'd long forgotten them.

The boys moved closer.

'Did they die?' Katie asked.

'Some did,' Julian said, trying to banish the memories that surged through him. Memories of a man who had once known no master save himself. 'But not before they set the Romans back on their heels.'

'How?' the boys asked anxiously.

This time, Julian caught the baby before she interrupted their game.

'Well,' Julian said, giving Allison her small red ball. She sat on his bent knee and he held her in place with one hand around her waist. 'As the Romans were riding down upon them, the Macedonian commander knew the Romans would expect him to pull his forces together into a phalanx, making them easy prey for the Roman cavalry and archers above. Instead, the commander ordered his men to disband, to aim their spears toward the horses, and break apart the Roman cavalry lines.'

'Did it work?' Tommy asked.

Even Grace was getting interested in the story.

Julian nodded. 'The Romans hadn't expected such a tactic from a civilized army. Completely unprepared for the move, their troops scattered.'

'And the Macedonian commander?'

'He gave a mighty battle cry as he rode his horse, Mania, across the field, and up the hillock where the Roman commanders were retreating. They turned to attack him, but it did them no good. With fury in his heart over the betrayal, the commander cut through them, leaving only one survivor.'

'Why?' Bobby asked.

'He wanted him to deliver a message.'

'What?' Tommy asked.

Julian smiled at their eager questions. 'The commander ripped the Roman standard to shreds, then used the cloth of it to help the Roman staunch the bleeding of his wounds. With a lethal grin, he looked at the Roman and said, "Roma delenda est." Rome must be destroyed. Then he sent the Roman general home in chains to deliver the message to the Roman Senate.'

'Wow!' Bobby said in awe. 'I wish you were my teacher in school. I might actually pass history if you were.'

Julian ruffled the boy's black hair. 'If it makes you feel any better, I didn't care for the subject either at your age. All I wanted to do was get into mischief.'

'Hi, Miss Grace!' Tommy said as he finally caught sight of her. 'Did you hear Mr. Julian's story? He said the Romans were bad men.'

Julian looked up to see Grace standing a few feet away.

Grace smiled. 'I'm sure he would know.'

'Can you fix my doll?' Katie asked, handing it to Julian.

Julian let go of the baby and took the doll. He popped its arm back in place.

'Thank you,' Katie said as she threw her arms around Julian and hugged his neck.

The longing on Julian's face stung her heart. Grace knew it was the face of his own daughter he saw when he looked at Katie.

182

'You're very welcome, little one,' he said hoarsely, pulling away from her.

'Katie, Tommy, Bobby? What are you doing over there?' Grace looked up as Emily rounded the side of the house. 'You're not bothering Miss Grace, are you?'

'No, they're not bothering me,' Grace said to her.

Emily didn't seem to hear her as she continued fussing at the children. 'And what's the baby doing out here? You're supposed to stay in the backyard.'

'Hey, Mom,' Bobby yelled as he ran to her. 'Do you know how to play Parcelon? Mr. Julian showed us.'

Grace laughed as the five of them returned to the front yard, while Bobby's excited chatter echoed around them.

Julian had his eyes closed and looked as if he were savoring the sound of the children's voices.

'You're quite a storyteller,' she said after he moved to join her.

'Not really.'

'Really,' she said emphatically. 'You know, it got me to thinking. Bobby's right. You would make a great teacher.'

He smirked at her. 'Commander to teacher. Why not call me Cato the Elder, and really insult me while you're at it?'

She laughed. 'You're not as offended as you pretend.'

'How do you know?'

'I can tell by the look on your face, and the light in your eyes.' She took his arm and led him back toward the deck. 'You really should think about it. Selena got her Ph.D. from Tulane and she knows the faculty there. Who better to teach ancient civilization than someone who actually lived it?'

He didn't respond. Instead, she noticed the way he shifted his bare feet against the ground.

'What are you doing?' she asked.

'I'm enjoying the feel of grass,' he whispered. 'The way the blades tickle my toes.'

She smiled at the childlike action. 'That's why you came outside?'

He nodded. 'I love to feel the sunshine on my face.'

And in her heart, she knew he'd had way too little of it to feel. 'C'mon, I'll make us some cereal and we can eat it on the deck.'

She led him back up the five stairs to the deck, and left him sitting in her wicker rocker as she went inside and poured the cereal.

When she returned, he had his head lying back and his eyes serenely closed.

Not wanting to disturb him, she stepped back.

'Do you know, I can feel your presence all over my body? With every sense I possess?' he asked, then opened his eyes to pin her with a hot stare.

'No,' she said nervously, handing him his bowl.

He took the bowl, but didn't elaborate on his words. He just sat there quietly eating his breakfast.

Absorbing the warm sunshine, Julian listened to the soft breeze as he felt Grace's calming presence beside him.

He had awakened at dawn to watch the sunrise through her bedroom windows, and had spent an hour just letting Grace's body soothe his.

She tempted him in a way he'd never before known. For a minute, he allowed himself to think of staying in this time.

But then what?

He only had one 'skill' he could use in this modern world, and he wasn't the kind of man who could live off a woman's charity and like it.

Not after . . .

He ground his teeth as the memory burned him.

At fourteen, he'd traded his virginity for a bowl of cold porridge and a cup of soured milk. Even now, after all this time, he could feel the woman's hands on his body, removing his clothes, grabbing feverishly at his skin as she showed him how to pleasure her.

'Ooo,' she'd cooed, 'you are a pretty one, aren't you? If you ever need more porridge, you just come back and see me any time my husband's not home.'

He'd felt so dirty afterward. So used.

Over the next few years, he'd spent more nights sleeping in shadows than in warm beds merely because he wasn't willing to pay that price again for a meal and temporary comfort.

And should he ever get his freedom again, he didn't want to . . .

Julian clenched his eyes shut. He just couldn't see himself in this world. It was too different. Too strange.

'Finished?'

He looked up to see Grace standing by his side with her hand outstretched for his bowl. 'Yes, thank you,' he said, handing it to her.

'I'm going to take a quick shower. I'll be back in a few minutes.'

He watched her leave, his gaze lingering on her bare legs. Already, he could taste her skin on his tongue. Smell the sweet scent of her body.

The woman haunted him. It wasn't just the curse. There was something more. Something he'd never encountered.

For the first time in over two thousand years he felt like a man again, and with that feeling came a longing so profound that it sliced through his heart.

He wanted her. Body and soul.

And he wanted her love.

The thought jolted him.

But it was the truth. Not since his childhood had he felt such a gut-wrenching ache for someone to hold him tenderly. Someone who would tell him that she loved him and mean it from her heart and not because of a spell.

Leaning his head back, he cursed. When would he learn?

He had been born to suffer. The Delphi Oracle had told him as much.

'*You will suffer as no man has ever suffered.*'

'But will I be loved?'

'Not in this lifetime.'

He had walked away crushed by her prophecy. Little had he known then exactly how much suffering lay before him.

'*He's the son of the Goddess of Love and not even she can stand to be near him.*'

He winced at the truth. Grace would never love him. No one would. His destiny wasn't to be released from his suffering. And even worse, his destiny had a tragic way of bleeding over onto those around him.

Pain lacerated his chest as he thought about something happening to Grace.

He couldn't allow that. He had to protect her at any cost. Even if it meant losing his freedom.

With that thought on his mind, he went to find her.

Grace wiped the soap from her eyes. Opening them, she jumped as she caught sight of Julian watching her through the small parting of the shower curtains.

'You scared the be-jesus out of me!' she snapped.

'Sorry.'

He stood outside of her extra-large, claw-foot tub, wearing nothing but boxers and leaning back against the wall in the same pose he'd had in the book. His broad shoulders were thrown back to support him and his long arms were casually at his sides.

She licked her lips at the sight of the hard, sculpted muscles of his chest and torso. Unbidden, her gaze fell lower to the red and yellow boxers.

Well, so much for thinking no man could look good in those. Because he did. There were truly no words to describe exactly how good he looked in them.

And that devilish, half-taunting smile on his face could melt the heart of even the most frigid of women.

The man was hot.

Nervously, she realized she was standing completely naked. 'Do you need something?' she asked, covering her breasts with the washcloth.

To her dismay, he removed his boxers, then stepped into the tub with her.

Her mind turned to mush as he overwhelmed her with his powerful, masculine presence. That incredible, dimpled smile hovered at the edges of his lips, making her heart race. Her body tremble.

'I just wanted to watch you,' he said, his voice low and tender. 'Do you have any idea what it does to me when you run your hands over your bare breasts?'

Judging from the size of his erection, she could give a good guess.

'Julian ... '

'Hmmm?'

She forgot what she was going to say as he dipped his head down to her neck. Chills rippled through her as his tongue scorched her flesh.

Grace moaned at the sensory overload of his hands and the hot water running over her body. She only vaguely felt him pull the cloth from her breasts before he took one in his mouth.

She hissed in pleasure as his tongue swirled around the taut peak, flicking across her flesh and making her burn.

He lowered her down in the tub, to lean against the sloping back. The contrast of the cool porcelain at her back and his warm body in front of her while the water poured down over the two of them titillated her in a way she'd never imagined.

Never before had she truly appreciated the size of the huge antique tub, but at the moment, she wouldn't have traded it for anything.

'Touch me, Grace,' he said hoarsely, taking her hand into his and leading it to his swollen shaft. 'I want to feel your hands on me.'

He shuddered as she stroked the velvety hardness of him.

Julian closed his eyes at the feelings swirling through him. Her touch wasn't just physical, it touched him on a level that was undefinable. Unbelievable.

He wanted more of her. He wanted *all* of her.

'I love your hands on me,' he breathed as she cupped him. Oh, gods, how he ached for her. How he wished for just one moment she was really making love to *him*.

Making love to him with her heart.

Pain sliced through his chest. No matter how many times he had sex, the end result was the same. It always hurt. If not his body, then deep in his soul.

No decent woman would ever have you in the light of day.

It was true and he knew it.

Grace felt him tense. 'Did I hurt you?' she asked, pulling her hand away.

He shook his head, then placed his hands on each side of her neck and kissed her deeply. Suddenly, his kiss intensified as if he were trying to prove something to both of them.

He slid his hand down her arm to capture her hand in his. He laced his fingers through hers, then moved his hand to cup her between her legs.

Grace moaned as he stroked her with their hands entwined. It was the most erotic thing she had ever experienced.

She shook all over as he quickened the rhythm of their joined fingers against her. And when he plunged their fingers inside her, she cried out in pleasure.

'That's it,' he breathed in her ear. 'Feel us joined.'

Breathless, Grace clutched at his shoulders with her other arm, her body on fire. Oh, he was an incredible lover!

Suddenly, he moved their hands away, then lifted one of her legs to curl about his waist.

Grace followed his lead, until she realized what he meant to do. He was preparing to drive himself into her.

'No!' she gasped, shoving at him. 'Julian, you can't.'

His eyes burned her with his need, his raw hunger. 'I want at least this much of you, Grace. Now, let me have it.'

She almost did.

Until something strange happened to his eyes. They turned a full shade darker, the pupils dilating.

Julian froze. His breathing labored, he closed his eyes as if struggling against an unseen attacker.

With a curse, he turned away from her. 'Run!' he said.

She didn't hesitate.

Grace pulled herself out from under him, grabbed the towel and ran for the door. But she couldn't leave him.

Pausing at the door, she looked back and watched as he went down on all fours and writhed as if he were being tortured.

She heard him strike the tub with his fist as he growled in pain.

Her heart pounded as he struggled. If only she knew what to do.

Finally, he collapsed in the tub.

Terrified and shaking, she took three tentative steps back into the bathroom, ready to run if he reached for her.

He rested on his side with his eyes closed. His breathing ragged, he looked weak and drained while the water pelted him, plastering his dark gold hair against his face.

She turned the water off.

Still, he didn't move.

'Julian?'

He opened his eyes. 'Did I scare you?'

'A little,' she answered honestly.

He took a deep, tortured breath, then sat up slowly. He didn't look at her. His gaze was focused somewhere past her shoulder.

'I'm not going to be able to fight that,' he said after a long pause. He looked at her. 'We're fooling ourselves, Grace. Let me take you now while I'm calm.'

'Is that really what you want?'

Julian ground his teeth at her question. No, it wasn't what he wanted. But what he wanted was beyond his ability to claim.

He wanted things the gods had never meant for him to have. Things he dared not name, because the naming of them made their absence all the more unbearable.

'I just wish I could die.'

Grace flinched at the heartfelt words. How she wished she could soothe him. Take away his pain.

'I know,' she said, her voice thick with unshed tears for him. She wrapped her arms around his sleek, strong shoulders and held him tight against her.

To her amazement, he laid his cheek against hers.

Neither said a word as they held each other.

Finally, Julian withdrew. 'We'd better stop before ... '

He didn't finish the sentence, but then he didn't have to. Grace had already seen the consequences and had no wish for a repeat.

She left him in the bathroom and went to dress.

Julian rose slowly from the tub, then toweled himself dry. He heard Grace in her room, opening the door to her second closet, and in his mind an image of her naked body scorched him.

A crippling wave of desire crashed through him with such force, that it almost sent him back to the floor.

He braced his arms against the vanity as he fought with himself. 'I can't live like this anymore,' he breathed. 'I am not an animal.'

He looked up and saw his father in the mirror. He glared at his reflection, hating it.

He could feel the sting of the whip as his father beat him until he could barely stand. *'Don't you dare cry, Pretty-boy. Not one whimper. You might be born of a goddess, but it's this world you live in, and here we don't coddle pretty little boys like you.'*

In the back of his mind, he could see the look of hatred on his father's face as he knocked him to the ground, and grabbed him in a choking headlock. Julian had kicked and fought, but at fourteen, he'd been too young, too inexperienced, to loosen the commander's hold.

His face contorted by a contemptuous sneer, his father had dragged his dagger down Julian's cheek, laying it open to the bone. And all because his father had caught his wife staring at Julian while they ate.

'Let's see if she'll lust for you now.'

The throbbing pain of the cut had been unbearable and

the blood had poured down his face the rest of the day. By the next morning, the wound had vanished without a trace.

His father's wrath had been immeasurable.

'Julian?'

Startled, he jerked at the sound of a voice he hadn't heard in over two thousand years.

He looked around the room, but didn't see anything.

Unsure if he'd heard the voice, he spoke quietly. 'Athena?'

She materialized before him, just inside the doorway. Though her clothes were modern, she wore her hair in a Grecian style piled high on her head with black ringlets falling down around her shoulders. Her pale blue eyes were gentle as she smiled. 'I've come on behalf of your mother.'

'She still can't face me?'

Athena looked away.

Julian felt a sudden urge to laugh. Why did he even bother to hope his mother might want to see him?

He should be used to it.

Athena fingered one of her dark ringlets as she watched him with an odd half-sad look on her face. 'You have to know I would have helped you had I known about this. You were my favorite general.'

All of a sudden, he understood what had happened to him all those centuries ago. 'You played me against Priapus, didn't you?'

He saw the guilt an instant before she shielded it. 'What's done is done.'

His lips curling with anger, he glared at her. 'Is it? Why did you send me to that battle when you knew Priapus hated me?'

'Because I knew you could win, and I hated the Romans. You were the only general I had who could have vanquished Livius, and you did. I was never prouder of you than I was

192

the moment you took his head.'

Bitterness roiled through him. He couldn't believe his ears. 'Now, you tell me you're proud?'

She disregarded his words. 'Your mother and I have spoken to Clotho on your behalf.'

Julian paused at her words. Clotho was the Fate in charge of lives. The spinner of destinies. 'And?'

'If you can beat the curse, we can return you to Macedonia, back to the same day you were pulled into the scroll.'

'I can go back?' he repeated in numbed disbelief.

'But you won't be able to fight anymore. If you do, you will change history. If we send you back, you must swear to retire to your villa.'

There was always a catch. He should have known better than to think for even an instant that they would really help him. 'To what purpose?'

'You will be in your own time. In a world you know.' She looked around the room. 'Or you could stay here, if you prefer. The choice is yours.'

Julian snorted. 'Some choice.'

'Some is better than none.'

Was it? He wasn't sure any longer.

'And my children?' he asked, wanting, no, needing his family to restore the only two people in life who had ever meant anything to him.

'You know we can't undo that.'

He cursed her. The gods could only take from him. Never once had they given.

Athena reached out and touched him lightly on the cheek. 'Choose wisely,' she whispered, then vanished.

'Julian? Who are you talking to?'

He blinked as Grace paused in the hallway.

'No one,' he said. 'Just myself.'

'Oh,' she said, accepting his lie without question. 'I was thinking of taking you back to the Quarter this afternoon. We could visit the aquarium. What do you think?'

'Sure,' he said, leaving the bathroom.

She frowned, but said nothing more as she headed for the stairs.

Julian went to the bedroom to change. As he was pulling on his pants, he caught sight of Grace's photographs on the dresser. She looked so happy in her childhood. So free. He particularly liked the picture where her mother had her arms wrapped protectively around Grace's neck while the two of them laughed.

In that moment, he knew the truth. No matter how much he might want otherwise, he could never stay here with Grace. She had said it herself the night he appeared.

She had her own life. One that didn't include him in it.

No, she didn't need someone like him. Someone who would only bring the unwanted attention of the gods down upon her head.

He would beat the curse, and then he would take Athena up on her offer.

He didn't belong here. He belonged in ancient Macedonia. Alone.

Chapter Ten

Something was wrong. Grace could feel it in her bones as she drove them into the Quarter. Julian sat beside her, staring out the window.

She'd tried several times to get him to talk, but he remained tight-lipped. All she could figure was that he was depressed by what had happened in the bathroom. It must be hard for a man used to being in control of himself to lose it that way.

Pulling into the public lot, she parked the car.

'Ooo, it's hot,' she said as she got out, and was immediately assaulted by the thick, heavy air.

She looked over at Julian who was truly dazzling in the dark sunglasses she'd bought for him. He'd already started to sweat.

'Is it too hot out here for you?' she asked, thinking of how awful it must be for him in jeans and a knit shirt.

'I'm not going to die from it, if that's what you mean,' he said sardonically.

'Just a little testy, are we?'

'I'm sorry,' he said as he joined her. 'I'm taking things out on you that aren't your fault.'

'It's all right. I'm used to being a scapegoat. In fact, I've made a profession of it.'

Since she couldn't see his eyes, she couldn't tell if he was amused by her words or not.

'Is that what your patients do?'

She nodded. 'It can get really hairy some days. I don't mind the women yelling at me so much as the men.'

'Have they ever hurt you?' The protectiveness in his voice startled her. And it felt strangely wonderful. She'd missed having someone to be protective of her.

'No, they haven't,' she said, trying to dispel the tenseness of his body. And she hoped it stayed that way, but after Rodney's call, she wasn't so sure that he might be the one exception who ended up hurting her.

You're being ridiculous. Just because he's creepy doesn't mean he's dangerous.

Julian's face was stern and harsh. 'I think you should find a new occupation.'

'Maybe,' she said dismissively. She had no intention of giving up her job. 'So, where would you like to go first?'

He shrugged nonchalantly. 'Makes little difference to me.'

'Then let's go to the aquarium. At least it's air-conditioned.'

Taking his arm, she led him across the lot, and down the Moonwalk toward the aquarium.

Julian remained silent as she paid their admission, and then led him inside. He didn't speak again until they walked through the manmade water tunnel that allowed them to watch all the different species of sea creatures in their natural habitat.

'Incredible,' he breathed as a huge stingray swam over his head. The look on his face reminded her of a child. An inner light sparkled in his eyes, warming her heart.

Suddenly, her pager went off. Grace cursed, until she saw the number.

Someone was calling her from the office on a Saturday? How weird.

She dug her cell phone out of her purse and called.

'Hey, Grace,' Beth said as soon as she answered. 'Listen, I'm down here in my office. We were broken into last night.'

'No! Who would do such a thing?'

Grace caught the curious look Julian directed at her. She offered him a tentative smile as she listened to Beth Livingston, the psychiatrist who shared office space with her and Luanne.

'I have no idea. They've got a crime scene unit down here taking prints. As far as I can tell, though, nothing important was taken. Did you have anything valuable in your office?'

'Just my computer.'

'It's still here. Anything else? Money or anything?'

'No. I never leave valuables there.'

'Hang on, the officer wants to talk to you.'

Grace waited until she heard a man's voice. 'Dr. Alexander?'

'Yes.'

'I'm Officer Allred. It looks like someone took your Rolodex and a few files. Any idea who would want them?'

'No, I don't. Do you need me to come down there?'

'I don't think so. Basically, we're just pulling prints, but if you can think of anything else, please give us a call.' He handed the phone back to Beth.

'Do you need me?' Grace asked.

'Nah. There's really nothing you can do. It's actually pretty boring.'

'Okay, buzz me if you need something.'

'Will do.'

Grace hung up the phone and returned it to her purse.

'Is something wrong?' Julian asked.

'Someone broke into my office last night.'

He frowned. 'Why?'

'I have no idea.' Grace duplicated his frown as she thought the matter over. 'I can't figure out why anyone would want my Rolodex. Since I bought my Palm Pilot last spring, I haven't even used it. It's just odd.'

'Do we need to leave?'

She shook her head. 'Nope.'

Julian allowed Grace to lead him around the various tanks as she read the foreign writing to him that explained the different breeds and habitats.

Gods, how he loved the sound of her voice when she read to him. There was something so comforting in it. He draped an arm over her shoulders as they walked. She placed her arm around his waist, curling one finger in his belt loop.

The gesture warmed him. And it was then he realized he lived for the feel of her body close to his. And he'd like it a whole lot more if they were both naked.

When she smiled up at him, he felt his heart pound out of control. What was it about this woman that touched him in a way no one ever had before?

But then he knew. She was the first woman to see *him*. Not his looks, not his body, not his warrior's prowess. She saw inside his soul.

He'd never known such a person existed.

Grace treated him like a friend. And she was genuinely interested in helping him. Or at least she seemed to be.

It's part of her job.

Or was it?

Could a woman as wonderful and kind as her ever really care for a man like him?

She stopped at another plaque. Julian stood directly behind her and wrapped his arms around her shoulders. She idly stroked his forearms as she read.

His body on fire for her, he leaned his chin down to rest on top of her head as he listened to her voice and watched the fish swim. The smell of her skin invaded his head as he longed to be back at her house where he could strip her clothes from her.

He couldn't remember the last time he'd wanted a woman as badly as he wanted Grace. In fact, he didn't think he'd ever wanted one the way he did her. He wanted to lose himself inside her. To feel her nails scoring his back as he made her scream in release.

May the Fates have mercy on him, but she was under his skin.

That's what truly scared him. For she held a place inside him that could hurt him in a way he'd never been hurt before.

She, alone, could finally break him.

It was almost one before they left the aquarium. Grace cringed as soon as they went back outside where the heat assailed her. On days like this, she wondered how anyone had survived before air-conditioning.

She looked over at Julian and smiled. Now he was someone who could finally answer that question for her. 'Tell me, what did you guys do to survive days that were this hot?'

He arched an arrogant brow. 'This isn't hot. If you want hot, try marching an army across a desert, wearing armor with only half a bladder of water to sustain you.'

She cringed for him. 'Now that sounds hot.'

He didn't respond.

Grace glanced over to the square, which was packed with people. 'Do you want to see Selena while we're out and about? She should be at her stand. Saturday is usually a big day for her.'

'I'm just following you.'

Taking his hand, Grace led him down the street, over to Jackson Square. Sure enough, Selena was at her stand with a client. Grace started to walk past without interrupting them, when Selena waved her over.

'Hey, Gracie, you remember Ben? Or rather Dr. Lewis from school?'

Grace hesitated as she recognized the portly man in his mid-forties.

Remember him? He'd given her a D, and brought down her entire average. Not to mention he had an ego the size of Alaska, and loved to embarrass students in class. In fact, she remembered one poor girl crying when he handed out his sadistic final exam to them. The man had actually laughed at the girl's reaction.

'Hi,' Grace said, trying not to let her distaste show. She supposed the man couldn't help being obnoxious. A Harvard Ph.D., he thought the world revolved around him.

'Miss Alexander,' he said in that same snide tone she remembered and loathed so much.

'Actually, it's *Dr*. Alexander,' she corrected, delighting in the way he widened his eyes in surprise.

'Forgive me,' he said in a voice that was anything other than apologetic.

'Ben and I were talking about ancient Greece,' Selena said, casting a devilish grin at Julian. 'I'm of the opinion that Aphrodite was the daughter of Uranus.'

Ben rolled his eyes. 'I keep telling you that the accepted

opinion is that she was born of Zeus and Dione. When are you going to give in, and join the rest of us?'

Selena ignored him. 'So tell me, Julian, who's right?'

'You are,' he said to Selena.

Ben raked a haughty look over Julian. Grace knew he saw nothing in Julian, except a very handsome man, who most likely knew only beer commercials and cars. 'Young man, have you *ever* read Homer? Do you even know who he is?'

Grace stifled her laughter at the question. She couldn't wait to hear Julian's response.

Julian laughed out loud. 'I've read Homer extensively. The tales attributed to him are an amalgam of legends told and retold until the true facts are lost to antiquity, whereas Hesiod wrote the *Theogony* with the direct aid of Clio.'

Dr. Lewis said something in ancient Greek.

'It's more than just an opinion, Doctor,' Julian responded in English. 'It happens to be fact.'

Ben took another look at Julian, but she could still tell he wasn't quite ready to believe someone who looked like Julian would have a clue about his chosen field. 'And how would you know?'

Julian answered in Greek.

For the first time since she'd met the man a decade before, Grace saw the doctor look amazed. 'My God,' he gasped. 'You speak as if you were born to it.'

Julian cast an amused smile to Grace.

'I told you,' Selena said. 'He knows the Greek gods and goddesses better than anyone on earth.'

Dr. Lewis noticed the ring on Julian's hand. 'Is that what I think it is?' he asked. 'Is that a general's ring?'

Julian nodded. 'It is.'

'Would you mind if I looked at it?'

Julian slid it from his finger and handed it to him.

Dr. Lewis sucked his breath in sharply. 'Macedonian? Second century B.C., I would presume.'

'Very good.'

'It's an incredible reproduction,' Ben said, handing it back.

Julian returned it to his hand. 'It's not a reproduction.'

'No!' Ben gasped in disbelief. 'It can't be an original. It's far too pristine.'

'It was held by a private collector,' Selena inserted.

Ben looked back and forth between them. 'How did you get it?' he asked Julian.

Julian paused as he remembered the day it had been awarded to him. He and Kyrian of Thrace had been promoted together after they had single-handedly saved Themopoly from the Romans.

It had been a long, brutal, and bloody fight.

Their army had broken and left the two of them alone to defend the town. Julian had expected Kyrian to abandon him as well, but the young fool had just smiled at him, grabbed a sword for each hand, and said, 'It's a beautiful day to die. What say we slay as many of these bastards as we can before we pay Charon?'

A complete and utter lunatic, Kyrian had always had more guts than brains.

Afterward, they had drunk each other under the table in celebration. And in the morning, they had awakened and been promoted.

Gods, of all the people Julian had known in Macedonia, he missed Kyrian most. Kyrian was the only man who had ever stood at his back and defended it.

'It was a gift,' Julian said.

Ben glanced at Julian's hand, his gaze filled with covetous awe. 'Would you consider selling it? I'd be willing to pay quite a bit for it.'

202

'Never,' Julian said as he thought over the wounds he had received during the battle for Themopoly. 'You've no idea what I had to go through to get this.'

Ben shook his head. 'I wish someone would give me a gift like that. Have you any idea how much it's worth?'

'My weight in gold, last I checked.'

Ben laughed out loud, and smacked his hand against Selena's card table. 'Good one. That was the ransom to get back captured generals, wasn't it?'

'For those too cowardly to die fighting, it was.'

A new respect shone in Ben's eyes as he regarded Julian. 'Any idea who it belonged to?'

Selena answered for Julian. 'Julian of Macedon. Ever heard of him, Ben?'

Ben's jaw dropped. His eyes widened. 'Are you serious? Do *you* know who that was?'

Selena made a strange face.

Assuming she didn't, Ben continued speaking. 'Tesius wrote that Julian was going to be the next Alexander the Great. Julian was the son of Diokles of Sparta, also known as Diokles the Butcher. That man made the Marquis de Sade look like Ronald McDonald.

'Rumor had it, Julian was born of a union between Aphrodite and the general, after Diokles had saved one of her temples from desecration. The modern accepted opinion, of course, is that his mother was actually one of Aphrodite's priestesses.'

'Really?' Grace asked.

Julian rolled his eyes. 'No one cares who Julian was. That man died a long time ago.'

Ben ignored him as he continued to flaunt his knowledge. 'Known to the Romans as Augustus Julius Punitor ... ' He glanced to Grace and added for her benefit, 'Julian the

203

Great Punisher. He and Kyrian of Thrace cut a trail of slaughter through the Mediterranean during the Fourth Macedonian War against Rome. Julian despised Rome, and vowed he'd see the city fall to his army. He and Kyrian damn near succeeded in bringing Rome to her knees.'

Julian's jaw flexed. 'Do you know what happened to Kyrian of Thrace?'

Ben let out a low whistle. 'His wasn't a pretty end. He was captured and crucified by the Romans in one forty-seven B.C.'

Julian flinched at the words. His eyes troubled, he toyed with his ring. 'That man was probably one of the best warriors who ever lived. He loved battle like no one I've ever known.' He shook his head. 'I remember Kyrian once drove his chariot up and over a shield wall where he broke the backbone of the Romans. It allowed his soldiers to defeat them with only a handful of losses.' He frowned. 'I can't believe they ever captured him.'

Ben shrugged nonchalantly. 'Well, once Julian disappeared, Kyrian was the only Macedonian general worthy of leading an army, so the Romans went after him with everything they had.'

'What happened to Julian?' Grace asked, wondering what the historians had to say about the matter.

Julian glared at her.

'No one knows,' Ben said. 'It's one of the greatest mysteries of the ancient world. Here you have this general who can't be defeated in arms by anyone, and then poof, at age thirty-two, he vanishes without a trace.'

Ben tapped his hand against Selena's table. 'The last anyone saw of Julian was at the battle of Conjara. In a brilliant move, he tricked Livius into giving up his impregnable position. It was one of the worst defeats in Roman history.'

'Who cares?' Julian groused.

Ben ignored his interruption. 'After the battle, Julian was reputed to have sent word to Scipio the Younger that he was coming for him in the name of vengeance for Scipio's defeat of the Macedonians. Terrified, Scipio gave up his military service in Macedonia and volunteered to fight in Spain instead.'

Ben shook his head. 'But before Julian could carry out the threat, he vanished. His family was found slaughtered in their home. And that's where it gets interesting.' Ben looked at Selena. 'The Macedonian accounts say he was mortally wounded by Livius during the battle, and in incredible pain he rode home to kill his family to keep them from being taken as slaves by his enemies. Roman accounts claim Scipio sent several of his soldiers to attack Julian in the middle of the night. Supposedly, they killed him with his family, then cut up his body and hid the pieces.'

Julian scoffed at that. 'Scipio was a coward and a bully. He would never have dared to attack m–'

'So,' Grace said, interrupting Julian before he could give himself away. 'Nice weather, eh?'

'Scipio was not a coward,' Ben said to Julian. 'No one can argue his successes in Spain.'

She saw hatred flash across Julian's eyes.

Ben didn't seem to notice. 'Young man, that ring of yours is absolutely priceless. I would *love* to know how someone got a hold of it. For that matter, I'd kill to know what happened to its original owner.'

Grace exchanged an uncomfortable look with Selena.

Julian smirked wryly at Ben. 'Julian of Macedon incurred the wrath of the gods and was punished for his arrogance.'

'That's another explanation, I suppose.' His watch alarm went off. 'Damn, I have to go pick up my wife.'

He got up and held his hand out to Julian. 'We didn't meet properly, I'm Ben Lewis.'

'Julian,' he said, shaking his hand.

Ben laughed. Until he realized Julian wasn't joking. 'Really?'

'Named for your Macedonian general, you might say.'

'Your father must have been like mine. In love with all things Greek.'

'His allegiance was actually to Sparta.'

Ben laughed even harder. He glanced back at Selena. 'Why don't you bring him to our next Socrates club meeting? I'd love for the guys to meet him. It's not often I find someone who knows Greek history almost as well as I do.' He turned his attention back to Julian. 'It's been a pleasure.

'Later,' Ben said, waving to Selena.

'Well,' Selena said to Julian once Ben had vanished into the crowd. 'You, my friend, have accomplished the impossible. You have just impressed one of the leading ancient Greek scholars in this country.'

Julian didn't seem to care, but Grace did. 'Lanie, do you think it's possible that Julian could be a professor once he breaks the curse? I was thinking he'd–'

'Don't, Grace,' Julian said, interrupting her.

'Don't what? You're going to need something–'

'I'm not staying here.'

The cold, emotionless gaze was the same one he had worn the first night she'd conjured him. And it sliced through her.

'What do you mean?' Grace asked.

He averted his gaze. 'Athena has offered me a way to return home. Once the curse is broken, she'll send me back to Macedonia.'

Grace struggled to breathe. 'I see,' she said, even though

206

inside she was dying. 'You'll just use my body, then leave.' Her throat constricted. 'At least I won't need Selena to drive me home afterward.'

Julian flinched as if she'd slapped him. 'What do you want from me, Grace? Why would you want me to stay here?'

She didn't know the answer to that. All she knew was that she didn't want him to leave. She wanted him to stay.

But not if he didn't want to.

'You know what,' she said, growing angry at the thought of his leaving her. 'I don't want you to stay here. In fact, why don't you go home with Selena for a few days?' She looked at Selena. 'Would you mind?'

Selena's mouth opened and closed like a fish gulping for air.

Julian reached for her. 'Grace–'

'Don't touch me,' she said, wringing her arm away from him. 'It makes my skin crawl.'

'Grace!' Selena snapped. 'I can't believe you–'

'It's all right,' Julian said, his voice empty and cold. 'At least she didn't spit in my face with her dying breath.'

She'd hurt him. Grace could see it in his eyes, but then he had hurt her, too. Terribly.

'I'll see you later,' she said to Selena, then left Julian standing there.

Selena let out a long, slow breath as she looked up at Julian while he watched Grace walk away from them. His entire body was rigidly still, and she saw the fierce tic in his jaw.

'They shoot, they score. A direct hit straight through the heart and into the raw nerves.'

Julian pinned her with a hostile glare. 'Tell me, Oracle. What should I have said?'

Selena shuffled her cards. 'I don't know,' she said wistfully. 'I guess you can never go wrong with honesty.'

Julian rubbed his eyes as he sat down in the chair before Selena's table. He hadn't meant to hurt Grace.

And he would never forget the look on her face as she spat those words at him. *'Don't touch me. It makes my skin crawl.'*

He struggled to breathe through the agony in his chest. The Fates were still mocking him.

It must be a boring day for them up on Olympus.

'You want me to do a reading for you?' Selena asked, dragging his thoughts away from the past.

'Sure,' he said. 'Why not?' She couldn't tell him anything he didn't already know.

'What's your question?'

'Will I ever ... ' Julian paused before he asked her the same question he'd once asked the Oracle at Delphi.

'Will I ever break the curse?' he asked quietly.

Selena shuffled her cards, then laid three of them out. Her eyes widened.

He didn't need her to read them. He could see for himself, a card with a tower being struck by lightning, a card of three swords piercing a heart, and a demon holding the chains of two people.

'It's all right,' he said to Selena. 'I never really thought it would come to pass.'

'That's not what they say,' she whispered. 'But you have one hell of a battle to come.'

He laughed bitterly. 'Battles I can handle.' It was the ache in his heart that was going to kill him.

Grace wiped the tears from her face as she pulled into the driveway. She clenched her teeth as she got out and slammed the door shut.

To hell with Julian. He could just stay trapped in that book for eternity. She wasn't some piece of meat to serve his needs.

How could he–

She fumbled with the key to her door.

'How could he not?' she whispered as she found the right key and opened the door.

Her anger drained out of her. She was being unreasonable, and she knew it. It wasn't Julian's fault Paul had been a selfish pig. And it wasn't his fault that she had a fear of being used.

She was blaming Julian for something he had no part in, and yet . . .

She just wanted someone who loved her. Someone who wanted to stay with her.

She'd hoped that by helping Julian, he would stay around and . . .

Closing the door, she shook her head. No matter how much she wanted it to be different, it wasn't meant to be. She'd heard what Ben had said about Julian's life. The story Julian, himself, had told the children about his battle.

She remembered the way he had darted across the street and saved that child's life.

Julian had been born and bred to lead armies. He didn't belong in her world.

He belonged in his own.

It was selfish of her to try and keep him like some pet she'd rescued.

Grace trudged up the stairs, her heart heavy. She would just have to guard herself from him. That was all she could do. Because deep inside she knew the more she learned about him, the more she cared for him. And if Julian had no intention of staying, then she would end up getting hurt.

209

She was halfway up the stairs when someone knocked on her front door. For an instant, her spirits lifted as she thought it might be Julian – Until she got to the front door and saw the outline of a small man on her porch.

She cracked open the door, then gaped.

It was Rodney Carmichael.

He wore a dark brown suit with a yellow shirt and red tie. His short, black hair was slicked back and he offered her a beaming smile. 'Hi, Grace.'

'Mr. Carmichael,' she said coldly, even though her heart was pounding. There was something indefinably creepy about this little, wiry man. 'What are you doing here?'

'I just wanted to stop by and say hi. I thought we could–'

'You need to leave.'

He frowned at her. 'Why? I just want to talk to you.'

'Because I don't see patients in my home.'

'Yeah, but I'm not–'

'Mr. Carmichael,' she said sternly. 'I really need you to leave. If you don't, I'm calling the police.'

Unaffected by the anger in her voice, he nodded with saintly patience. 'Oh, so you must be busy. I can relate. I have a lot of stuff to do, too. How 'bout I come by later? We could have dinner tonight.'

Dumbfounded, she stared at him. 'No.'

He smiled at that. 'C'mon, Grace. Don't be that way. You know we're meant for each other. If you'd just let me–'

'Leave!'

'Okay, but I'll be back. We have a lot of things to talk about.' He turned around and headed across her porch.

Her heart hammering, Grace shut and locked the door.

'I'm going to kill you, Luanne,' she said as she made her way to the kitchen. As she passed through the living room, a shape in her window caught her attention.

It was Rodney.

Aghast, Grace picked up the phone and called the police.

It was almost an hour later before they came. Rodney stayed outside the entire time, moving from window to window to watch her through the closed slits of her blinds, and it wasn't until he saw the police car pulling into the driveway that he ran across her backyard and vanished.

Grace took a deep breath to calm her raw nerves, then went to let the officers in.

They stayed only long enough to tell her there was nothing they could do to keep Rodney permanently away from her. The best she could do would be to swear out a restraining order, but since she was required to treat Rodney until Luanne returned, that was useless.

'I'm sorry,' the officer said in the doorway as she showed them out. 'But he didn't break any laws that would allow us to really get him out of your hair. You could swear out a warrant for trespassing, but unless he has priors, there's not a whole lot they're going to do to him.'

The young officer gave her a sympathetic look. 'I know it's not much comfort. We can try to patrol the area a little more, but the summer is a really busy time of year for us. Personally, I'd advise you to stay with a friend for a while.'

'All right, thanks.' As soon as they were gone, she rushed through the house making sure all the doors and windows were locked tight.

Apprehensive, Grace looked around the house, half expecting Rodney to enter through a crack in the wall like a cockroach.

If only she knew whether or not Rodney was dangerous. His report from the state hospital mentioned his routine deviant behavior of butting into women's lives, but he'd never harmed anyone physically. He'd just terrified his victims with his blind persistence, which was why he'd been sent to the hospital for evaluation to begin with.

The psychologist in Grace said there was nothing particularly dangerous about Rodney, but the woman in her was scared anyway.

The last thing she wanted was to become a statistic.

No, she couldn't stay here waiting for him to come back and find her alone.

Rushing upstairs, she went to pack.

Chapter Eleven

Selena watched as Julian paced back and forth in front of her stand while she gave a reading to a tourist. Ooo boy, she could watch that man walk all day long. He had such an eye-popping gait that it made her yearn to rush home to Bill and do some wicked things to him.

Over and over, women approached Julian, and he kept sending them away. It was actually funny to watch women strut around him while he remained oblivious to their machinations. She'd never known such a man existed.

But then, even she could get sick of chocolate if she ate too much of it.

Judging by the way women responded to Julian, she was sure he had quite a bellyache from overindulgence. Worse, he looked terribly troubled.

And she felt awful for what she had done to both of them. Her idea had seemed flawless at first. If only she'd thought it through a little more.

How was she to know who Julian had been? If only his name had rung a bell. But her specialty was Bronze Age

Greece which had been ancient history even in Julian's time.

Even worse, she hadn't really thought about the man in the book as being a real person. She'd thought he was some kind of genie-like creature without a past or feelings.

Boy, when she screwed up, she always managed to do it in a big way.

Shaking her head, Selena watched while he turned down yet another offer from an attractive redhead. The man was a serious estrogen magnet.

She finished the reading.

Julian waited a few minutes before heading back to her table. 'Take me to Grace.'

It wasn't a request. He said it in a tone of voice she was sure he'd once used to order his troops into battle formation. 'She said–'

'I don't care what she said. I need to see her.'

Selena wrapped her cards in her black silk scarf. What the hell? She didn't need a best friend anyway. 'It's your funeral.'

'I wish,' he said in a tone so low she wasn't sure she heard it correctly.

He helped her close up her stand and wheel her cart to the small shed she rented to house it.

In no time, they were headed to Grace's.

They pulled into the drive at the same time Grace was packing her car.

'Hey, Gracie,' Selena called. 'Where you going?'

Grace glared at Julian. 'Away for a few days.'

'Where?' Selena asked.

She didn't answer.

Julian left the car and headed straight for Grace. He was going to set this right, no matter what it took.

She tossed a bag in the trunk of the car and started away from him.

Julian grabbed her arm. 'You didn't answer her question.'

Grace shrugged his hand off. 'What are you going to do, manhandle me if I don't answer?' Her eyes narrowed on him.

He winced at her rancor. 'And you wonder why I want to leave?'

Then he saw it, the tears she was trying so hard to hide. Her eyes were bright and shiny.

Pain cut him deeply. 'I'm sorry, Grace,' he whispered, cupping her cheek in his hand. 'I didn't mean to hurt you.'

Grace watched the regret and longing war on his face. His touch was so warm and gentle. For a moment, she could almost believe he did care for her.

'I'm sorry, too,' she whispered. 'I know it's not your fault.'

He gave a bitter half-laugh. 'Actually, everything about this is my fault.'

'Hey? Are you two kosher?' Selena asked.

Julian's gaze burned into Grace's, making her tremble from its intensity.

'Do you want me to leave?' he asked.

No, she didn't. That was the whole problem. She never wanted him to leave her again. Ever.

She took his hands into hers, then lowered them from her face. 'It's okay, Selena.'

'In that case, I'll be heading home. Later.'

Grace barely heard her drive away. Julian commanded all her attention.

'Now, where were you going?' he asked.

For the first time since the police had left, she actually felt as if she could breathe again. With Julian's presence, all her fear had evaporated like mist under sunlight.

She truly felt safe. 'Remember I told you about Rodney Carmichael?'

He nodded.

'He came by a little while ago. He ... he worries me.'

The hard, cold rage on his face stunned her. 'Where is he now?'

'I don't know. The police came and he vanished. That's why I was leaving. I was going to stay in a hotel.'

'Do you still want to leave?'

She shook her head. With him here, she felt completely protected.

'I'll get your bag,' he said.

He pulled it out of her car, then closed the trunk.

Grace led the way back into the house.

They spent the rest of the day in quiet solitude. That evening, they were lying on the floor in front of the couch, supported by cushions.

Grace lay with her head on Julian's hard stomach as she read him the rest of *Peter Pan*, and did her best not to notice just how wonderful he smelled. And how wonderful he felt.

It took all her willpower not to roll over and explore his taut, muscled chest with her mouth.

He brushed his hand slowly through her hair as he watched her. Oh, how his touch burned her. How it made her wish she could strip those clothes off his body and taste every single inch of him.

'The end,' she said, closing the book.

The heated look on his face took her breath.

Grace stretched, arching her back ever so slightly against him. 'Want me to read something else?'

'Please. Your voice soothes me.'

She stared at him for a long minute, then smiled. She couldn't remember the last compliment that touched her as profoundly as that one.

'I keep most of my books in my room,' she said, getting up. 'Come on, and I'll show you my special treasure trove and we'll find something else.'

He followed her upstairs. Grace didn't miss the hot, longing gaze he gave the bed, then her.

Choosing to ignore it, Grace opened the door to her large walk-in closet. She turned on the light and brushed her hand lovingly over the homemade shelves her father had built years ago.

He'd been so funny when he and his best friend assembled the bookshelves. Both of them scholars, they'd made a terrible mess and ended up blackening two of her father's fingernails before the project was completed. Her mother had teased her father endlessly by calling him a Keystone Carpenter. But her father hadn't minded, and the look on his face when he had proudly finished and placed her books on the shelves was indelibly imprinted in her heart.

How she adored this room. It was here she truly felt her parents' love. Here she went to escape any trouble or pain that plagued her.

Every book in the closet was a special memory, and they all meant the world to her. To her left she glanced at *Shanna*, which had started her addiction to romance novels. *The Wolfling*, which had introduced her to science fiction. And her prized *Bimbos of the Death Sun*, which had been her very first mystery novel.

Her father and mother's old novels were in here, too, as well as three copies of the textbooks her father had written before she was born.

This was her special sanctuary and Julian was the first

person, other than her parents, she had ever let inside it.

'You've been collecting books for quite some time,' Julian said as he glanced around the crowded shelves.

She nodded. 'They were my best friends growing up. I think the love of reading is probably the greatest gift my parents ever gave me.' She held up *Peter Pan*. 'This one was my father's when he was a boy. It's my most prized possession.'

She put it back on a shelf and picked up a copy of *Black Beauty*. 'This was the one my mother read over and over to me.'

Grace gave him a quick tour of her books. '*The Outsiders*,' she breathed reverently. 'This was my favorite book in junior high school. Oh, and this one, *Can You Sue Your Parents for Malpractice?*'

Julian laughed. 'I can tell how much they mean to you. Your entire face is glowing.'

Something in his eyes made her think that he was contemplating a way he could make her glow, as well.

Swallowing at the thought, she turned and rummaged through the shelf on her right where she kept her classics while Julian looked at the books to her left.

'How about this one?' he asked, handing her one of her historical romance novels.

Grace laughed nervously at the half-dressed couple entwined on the cover. 'Oh, I don't think so.'

He looked at the cover with one highly arched brow.

'Okay,' she said, taking it from his hand. 'You've discovered my guilty secret. I'm an awful addict when it comes to historical romances, but the last thing you need is for me to read a steamy love scene out loud, thank you very much.'

His gaze focused on her lips. 'I would much rather create a steamy love scene,' he breathed, moving to stand in front of her.

Grace trembled. With her back to the bookshelf, she couldn't retreat. He braced an arm above her head as he pressed his body against her, then lowered his mouth to hers.

Closing her eyes, all she could taste or smell was Julian. He surrounded her in a most disturbing way.

For once, he kept his hands to himself and touched only her lips with his. It didn't matter.

Her head still swam.

How could his wife ever have chosen another man over Julian? How could any woman in her right mind not want this man? He was heaven.

Julian deepened his kiss, exploring her mouth with his tongue. She felt his heart pounding as he pressed her back, felt his muscles flexing all around her.

Never before had she been so aware of another human being. He set her on edge, made her feel sensations she'd never known existed.

He pulled back and pressed his cheek against hers. His breath stirred her hair and sent chills all over her.

'I want to be inside you so badly, Grace,' he whispered. 'I want to feel your legs wrapped around me, feel your breasts against my chest, hear you moaning as I make slow, sweet love to you. I want your smell on my body, your breath on my skin.'

His entire body went rigid before he pushed himself away from her.

'But then, I'm used to wanting things I can't have,' he whispered.

She reached out and touched his arm. He captured her hand with his, then lifted it to his lips where he lightly kissed her knuckles.

The longing on his handsome face made her ache. 'Find

us a book, and I shall behave.'

Grace swallowed as he left her. It was then her gaze fell to her old copy of *The Iliad*. She smiled. He would like that, she was sure of it.

Grabbing it, she went back downstairs.

Julian sat in front of the couch.

'Guess what I found!' she said excitedly.

'I have no idea.'

She held it up and grinned. '*The Iliad!*'

His mood instantly lifted as he flashed those dimples at her. 'Sing to me, O goddess.'

'Very good,' she said as she sat down beside him. 'And you'll like this even more. It's got both the original Greek and the English translation.'

She handed it to him.

He looked as if she had just handed him a king's treasure. He opened the book.

Immediately his eyes danced across the pages as he ran his hand reverently over the ancient Greek writing.

Julian couldn't believe it as he saw his language again after all this time. It had been so long since he'd last seen it anywhere other than on his arm.

He'd always loved *The Iliad* and *The Odyssey*. As a boy, he'd spent hours hidden behind the barracks, reading scrolls over and over again, or sneaking out to hear the bards in the town square.

He well understood how Grace felt about her books. He'd been the same way in his youth. Every chance he'd gotten, he had escaped into the world of fantasy where heroes always triumphed. Where demons and villains were vanquished. Where mothers and fathers loved their children.

In the stories, there was no hunger, no pain. There was

freedom and hope. It was through such stories that he learned of compassion and kindness. Of honor and integrity.

Grace knelt beside him. 'You miss your home, don't you?'

Julian looked away. The only thing he missed was his children.

Unlike Kyrian, he had never cared for battle. The stench of death and blood, the moans of the dying. He'd fought only because it was expected of him. And he'd led because, as Plato said, everyone by nature was suited to a particular activity, which ideally they would pursue. By his nature, Julian had always been a leader and not one to follow others.

No, he didn't really miss it, but ...

'It was all I knew.'

She touched his shoulder, yet it was the concern in her light gray eyes that undid him.

'Did you want your son to be a soldier?'

He shook his head. 'I never wanted him to be cut down in his youth like so many of my soldiers had been,' he said, his voice hoarse. 'Rather ironic, isn't it? I wouldn't even allow him to keep the play-sword Kyrian had given him as a birthday gift, or to touch mine when I was home.'

She placed her hand against his neck, then pulled him to her. Her touch was so incredibly soothing. So warm. It filled him with aching loneliness.

'What was his name?'

Julian swallowed. He hadn't uttered his children's names aloud since the day they'd died. He hadn't dared, and yet he wanted to share that with her. 'Atolycus. My daughter was Callista.'

Her smile was edged by sadness as if she shared his pain at their loss. 'They had beautiful names.'

'They were beautiful children.'

'If they were anything like you, I can believe that.'

That was the kindest thing anyone had ever said to him.

Julian ran his hand under her hair and let the silken strands fill his palm. Closing his eyes, he wanted to stay like this forever.

Fear of letting her go ripped through him. He'd never liked the idea of being sucked into his empty hell, but now the thought of never seeing her again, of never again smelling her sweet skin, of never again laying his palm against the warm blush of her cheek ...

It was more than he could bear.

Gods, and he had thought himself cursed before.

She pulled back and kissed him lightly on the lips, then picked up the book.

Julian swallowed. She wanted to save him, and for the first time in centuries, he wanted to be saved.

He slid down lower on the floor to where she could return to lying against him. He loved feeling her there. Feeling her hair spilling across his arms, his chest.

They lay on the floor until the wee hours of the morning while Julian listened to her read of Odysseus and Achilles.

He watched as she grew tired, but she continued to read. The clock above struck three as she yawned and turned a page.

She tried to blink her eyes open, but her exhaustion was too much. Finally, she closed her eyes and fell asleep.

Julian smiled as he took the book from her hand and set it aside. He cupped her cheek while he watched her.

He wasn't sleepy. He didn't want to miss a single second of being with her. Watching her, touching her. Absorbing her. He would treasure it forever.

Never had he spent an evening like this, just lying

comfortably with a woman without her groping his body, demanding that he touch and fill her.

In his day, men and women didn't spend much time together. During the times he was at home, Penelope had seldom spoken to him. In fact, she hadn't shown much interest in him at all.

On the nights when he sought her out, she hadn't refused him. But she was never eager for his touch, either. He'd always been able to coax a heated response from her body, but never one from her heart.

He brushed his hand through Grace's sable hair, delighting in the way it wrapped around his hand. His gaze dropped to his ring. It glinted dully in the light.

In his mind's eye he could see it coated in blood. Feel the way it bit into his finger as he wielded his sword in battle. That ring had meant everything to him, and it hadn't come easy. He'd earned it through the sweat of his brow and at the price of stinging attacks on his flesh. It had been costly, but it had been well worth it.

There for a time, if not loved, he had been respected. In his mortal life, that had meant everything to him.

Sighing, he leaned his head back against the sofa cushion behind him and closed his eyes.

As he finally drifted to sleep, it wasn't the faces of the past that haunted his dreams, it was the vision of light gray eyes laughing with him, and of dark hair spilling over his chest as a warm, soft voice read words that were familiar and yet somehow foreign.

Grace stretched languidly as she came awake. Opening her eyes, she was surprised to find her head lying on Julian's stomach. His right hand was buried in her hair and by the deep even breaths she knew he was still asleep.

She looked up at him. His face relaxed, he looked almost childlike.

And it was then she realized his nightmare hadn't come. He had slept through the night.

Smiling, she rose slowly, trying not to wake him.

It didn't work. The instant she withdrew, his eyes flew open, searing her with their heat.

'Grace,' he breathed.

'I didn't mean to wake you.'

'It's all right.'

Grace motioned to the stairs with her thumb. 'I was going upstairs to shower. Should I lock the door?'

He raked a searing look over her. 'No, I think I can behave.'

She smiled. 'It seems I've heard that one before.'

He didn't respond.

Grace went above and took a quick shower.

When she finished, she went to her bedroom and found Julian lying on the bed, flipping through her copy of *The Iliad*.

He did a double-take as he looked up to see her wearing nothing but a towel. Those dimples flashed lecherously and sent heat dancing all over her body.

'I'll just get my clothes, and–'

'No,' he said in a commanding tone.

'No?' she asked in disbelief.

His face softened. 'I'd rather you dress in here.'

'Julian–'

'Please.'

Grace squirmed uneasily at his request. She'd never done anything like that in her life.

'Pretty please,' he asked again with just a hint of a smile.

What woman could say no to that look?

224

She looked askance at him. 'Don't you dare laugh,' she said as she hesitantly opened the towel.

He dropped a hungry look to her breasts. 'You can rest assured laughter is the farthest thing from my mind.'

Then he left the bed. He moved like a graceful predator as he opened the drawer where she kept her underwear. A strange shiver went over her as she watched his hand moving through her panties until he found the black silk ones Selena had given her as a gag gift.

Pulling them out, he knelt on the floor before her to put them on her. Breathless and hot, she looked down at the top of his golden head. She lifted her foot and let him dress her.

As his hands slid the silk up her leg and his lips kissed a trail behind them, she trembled. He splayed his hands against her flesh for maximum devastation to her senses. Worse, once he had them in place, he caressed her lightly between her legs before moving away.

Next, he pulled out the matching black bra.

Like a doll with no will of its own, she let him put it on her. His hands brushed her nipples as he closed the front catch, then he slid his hand between the satin and her skin and gave a hot caress that sent chills all over her.

Julian bent his head down to capture her lips with his. Even now he felt the fire coursing through him, demanding he take her. Demanding he ease the pain in his groin if only for an instant.

Grace moaned as he deepened his kiss. Her will gone, she felt him lift her to the bed where he set her before him. Instinctively, she wrapped her legs around his waist and hissed at the feeling of those steely abs pressing against the center of her body.

Julian ran his hands over her back. The image of her wet, naked body was branded in his mind. He was almost to the point of no return when a bright light flashed through the room.

His eyes aching from it, Julian pulled away from her.

'Was that you?' she asked breathlessly, looking up at him with adoring eyes.

Amused, Julian shook his head. 'I wish I could take credit for it, but I'm quite sure it had another source.'

Looking around the room, his gaze fell to the bed. He blinked.

It couldn't be ...

'What is that?' Grace asked, turning to look at the bed.

'It's my shield,' he said, still unable to believe his eyes.

He hadn't seen his shield in centuries. Stunned, he stared at it where it rested in the center of the mattress, glinting dimly in the light.

He knew every dent and scratch on it, remembered the blows that had made each mark.

Afraid he was dreaming, he reached his hand out to the bronze relief of Athena and her owl.

'And your sword, too?'

He grabbed Grace's hand before she touched it. 'That's the Sword of Cronus. Never touch it. If anyone handles it who doesn't have his blood in them, it burns their skin forever.'

'Really?' she asked, sliding off the bed, away from it.

'Really.'

She looked back at the bed with a stern frown. 'Why are they here?'

'I don't know.'

'Who sent them?'

'I don't know.'

'Well, that's not really helpful.'

Julian didn't seem to hear her sarcasm. Instead, Grace watched as he stared at his shield. He ran his hand over it

226

like an adoring father who had found a long-lost child.

He pulled the sword from the mattress, then slid it far beneath the bed. 'Don't forget it's under here,' he said sternly. 'Make sure you never touch it.'

His frown deepened as he straightened up and looked at the shield. 'My mother must have sent them to me. Only she or one of her sons could have done it.'

'Why would she do that?'

Julian narrowed his eyes as he remembered the rest of the sword's legend. 'I'm sure she sent it in the event I have to face Priapus. The Sword of Cronus is also called the Sword of Justice. It won't kill him, but it will cause him to take my place in the book.'

'Are you serious?'

He nodded.

'May I touch the shield?'

'Sure.'

Grace ran her hand over the gold and black inlays that formed the image of Athena and her owl. 'It's beautiful,' she said in awe.

'Kyrian had it made as a gift for me when I became a full commander.'

She touched the engraving below Athena. 'What do the words say?'

'"Death before dishonor,"' he said, the words catching in his throat.

Julian smiled wistfully as he remembered Kyrian standing at his side during their battles together. 'Kyrian's shield read, "Spoils to the Victor." He used to look at me before battle and say, "You take the honor, *adelphos,* and leave the booty for me."'

Grace paused at the odd note in his voice. Trying to imagine what he must have looked like holding his shield, she pulled it closer. 'Kyrian? The man who was crucified?'

'Yes.'

'You liked him a lot, didn't you?'

He smiled sadly. 'It took a while for him to grow on me. When I was twenty-three, his uncle assigned him to my command with the strictest warning of what would happen to me should I let *His Highness* get hurt.'

'He was a prince?'

Julian nodded. 'And he was truly fearless. Barely twenty, he would charge into battle or fights half-cocked, daring anyone to hurt him. It seemed every time I turned around, I was hauling him out of some bizarre mishap. But he was a hard man to hate. In spite of his hot-headed ways, he had a great sense of humor and was loyal to a fault.'

He ran his hand over his shield. 'I just wish I'd been there to save him from the Romans.'

Grace rubbed his arm in sympathy. 'I'm sure the two of you could have battled your way out of anything.'

A spark came to his eyes at her words. 'When we marched our armies together, we were invincible.' His jaw flexed as he looked at her. 'It was just a matter of time before Rome would have been ours.'

'Why did the two of you want Rome so badly?'

'I vowed to destroy Rome after they took Prymaria. Kyrian and I had been sent for, but by the time we arrived, it was too late. The Romans had cold-bloodedly rounded up and murdered every woman and child in the city. I'd never seen such carnage.' His eyes darkened. 'While we were trying to bury the dead, the Romans ambushed us.'

Grace went cold at the words. 'What happened?'

'I had Livius routed and was about to kill him when Priapus intervened. He sent a lightning bolt into my horse and I was thrown to the Romans. I was sure I was dead;

then out of nowhere Kyrian appeared. He drove Livius back until I was able to regain my feet. Livius called for a retreat and vanished before we could kill him.'

Grace realized Julian stood directly behind her, his body so close to hers that she could feel his body heat. He placed his arms on each side of her, braced against the mattress, before he pressed his chest against her back.

Grace clenched her teeth at the ferocity of the desire that swept through her. He didn't hold her, but the devastation to her senses was just as profound. He bent his head down and nuzzled her neck.

His tongue on her skin fired every hormone in her body. Grace arched her back as her breasts tingled. If she didn't stop him ...

'Julian,' she breathed, but her voice was far from carrying the warning note she intended.

'I know,' he whispered. 'I'm on my way to take a cold shower.' As he left the room, she heard him snarl an angry word under his breath. 'Alone.'

After they had breakfast, Grace decided to teach Julian to drive.

'This is ridiculous,' he said as she pulled into the high school's parking lot.

'Oh, come on,' she teased, 'aren't you curious?'

'No.'

'No?'

He sighed. 'Okay, a little.'

'Well, then, just imagine the stories you can tell your men when you get back to Macedonia about the great steel beast you drove ... around a parking lot.'

He gave her a puzzled stare. 'Does this mean you're okay with my leaving?'

No, she wanted to shout. But instead she sighed. In her heart, she knew she could never ask him to give up all he'd been to stay here with her.

Julian of Macedon was a hero. A legend.

He would never be a mild-mannered twenty-first-century man.

'I know I can't keep you. You're not some lost puppy who followed me home.'

Julian tensed at her words. How true to form they were. It was what made leaving her so damn difficult. How could he give up the only person who had ever seen him as a man?

He didn't know why she wanted to teach him to drive, but then, sharing her world with him seemed to please her. And for some reason that didn't bear thinking about, he liked making her happy. 'All right, then, show me how to tame this beast.'

Grace parked the car and they traded seats.

As soon as Julian got in, she cringed at the sight of a six-foot-three man wedged into a space meant to accommodate a five-two woman. 'I forgot to move the seat back. Sorry.'

'I can neither breathe nor move, but that's okay.'

She laughed. 'There's a lever under the seat. Pull it out and you can move the seat back.'

He tried, but he was crammed in so tightly that he couldn't reach it.

'Here,' Grace said. 'I got it.'

Julian threw his head back as she leaned over his thigh, pressing her breasts to his leg while she reached between his knees. His body snapped to attention, instantly hot and hard.

When she put her cheek against his groin as she struggled with the release, he thought he would die from it.

'You know, you're in the perfect position to–'

230

'Julian!' she snapped. She pulled back and saw the bulge in his jeans. Her face turned bright red. 'Sorry.'

'Me, too,' he breathed.

Unfortunately, she had yet to move the seat, so he was forced to endure the position one more time.

Grinding his teeth, Julian reached one arm over his head to grab the headrest and clench it tightly. It was all he could do not to yield to the fiery lust inside his body.

'You okay?' she asked once she released the seat and returned to her own.

'Oh, yeah,' he said sarcastically. 'I'm just fine considering the fact I've walked through burning fires that hurt less than my groin does right now.'

'I said I was sorry.'

He just looked at her.

She patted his arm tenderly. 'Okay, can you reach the pedals?'

'I'd like to reach your pedals . . . '

'Julian!' Grace snapped again. The man was truly lecherous. 'Would you concentrate?'

'All right, I'm concentrating.'

'I don't mean on my breasts.'

He dropped his hungry gaze to her lap.

'Or there, either.'

To her amazement, he playfully poked his bottom lip out like a pouting child. The look was so uncharacteristic of him that she laughed again.

'Okay,' she said. 'The pedal on the far left is your clutch, the middle is the brake and the one on the far right is the gas. You remember what I told you about them?'

'I remember.'

'Good. Now the first thing you do is press in the clutch and slide the gear into reverse.' She placed his hand on the gear shift in the center of her car, and showed him how to move it up and down.

'You know, you really shouldn't fondle that in front of me, Grace. It's cruel.'

'Julian! Do you mind? I'm only trying to show you how to shift my gears.'

He snorted. 'I wish you'd shift my gear like that.'

Grace growled at him.

With a devilish gleam in his eyes, he looked totally unrepentant.

Then he attempted to back up, but he released the clutch too soon and stalled the car.

'It's not supposed to do that, is it?' he asked.

'Not unless you want to have a wreck.'

He sighed and tried again.

An hour later, after Julian still hadn't managed to drive around the parking lot without hitting a curb or stalling the car, Grace conceded failure.

'It's a good thing you were a better general than you are a driver.'

'Ha, ha,' he said sarcastically, but there was a glint in his eye that let her know he wasn't truly offended. 'All I have to say in my defense is that my first car was a war chariot.'

Grace smiled at him. 'Well, we're not at war on these streets.'

Looking skeptical, he retorted, 'I wouldn't say that. You forget, I've seen your late-night news.'

Julian turned the engine off. 'I think I'll let you drive for a while.'

'Probably wise. I can't really afford a new car right now anyway.'

She got out to exchange sides with him again. But as they crossed paths at the trunk, Julian grabbed her for a hot kiss that made her dizzy. He took her hands in his and held them tightly against his lean hips as he nibbled her lips.

Goodness, a woman could get used to this. Really, really used to it.

Julian pulled back. 'Want to take me home and let me nibble on other things?'

Yes, she did, which was why she didn't dare. In fact, she was so delirious from that one kiss that she couldn't even speak.

Julian smiled at the dazed, hungry look on her face. She stared at his lips as if she were still tasting them. In that moment, he wanted her more than he ever had before. Most of all, he wanted to take the band from her ponytail and let her hair spill over his chest.

How he wished they were back at her house where he could peel the short set from her and listen to her sweet murmurs of pleasure as he ...

'The car,' she said, blinking her eyes as if awaking from a dream. 'We were getting into the car.'

Julian kissed her lightly on the cheek.

After they both got in, and were buckled up, Grace looked sideways at him. 'You know, it seems to me there are two things in New Orleans that you have yet to experience.'

'Number one, I have yet to take you on a–'

'Would you stop!'

He cleared his throat. 'Okay, what's your list?'

'Bourbon Street and modern music. One of which I can take care of right now.' Grace switched on the radio.

She laughed as she recognized 'Hot Blooded' by Foreigner. How apropos, given her passenger.

Julian listened, but didn't appear impressed.

Grace changed the station.

Julian frowned at her actions. 'What did you do?'

'I changed to another station. All you have to do is press these buttons.'

He toyed with it for several minutes until he found a station playing 'Love Hurts' by Nazareth. 'Your music is interesting.'

'Does it make you miss your own?'

'Since most of the music I heard was pipers and drummers leading us into battle, no. I think I can appreciate this.'

'Appreciate what?' she asked flippantly. 'The music or the fact that love hurts?'

The humor fled his face. 'Since I've never known love, I wouldn't know whether or not it hurts. But I can't imagine how being loved could possibly hurt as much as not.'

Her chest tightened at his words.

'So,' she asked, wanting to change the subject, 'what do you plan to do as soon as you get home?'

'I don't know.'

'You'll probably go kick Scipio's butt, right?'

He laughed at that. 'I would like to.'

'Why? What did he ever do to you?'

'He got in my way.'

Okay, not what she expected to hear. 'You don't like anyone to get in your way, do you?'

'Do you?'

She thought about it. 'I guess not.'

By the time they reached Bourbon Street, the Sunday afternoon crowd was swarming. Grace fanned her face as she fought the oppressive heat.

She looked up at Julian who even sweated attractively. His damp hair hung in becoming curls around his face, and with those sunglasses on ... ooo, baby!

Of course, the look was helped by the white T-shirt that emphasized the breadth of his shoulders, and his lean, flat six-pack of abs. As she trailed her gaze over the button-fly jeans, she wished she had opted for a baggier pair.

But then given his confident, seductive walk, she doubted if even baggy jeans could hide such raw, overt sexiness.

Julian paused as they passed by a strip club. To his credit, he didn't gape at the scantily clad women in the window, but Grace sensed his shock plainly enough.

Staring at Julian as if she'd like to devour him, the exotic dancer bit her full bottom lip, then ran her tongue around her lips suggestively as she groped at her breasts. She crooked her finger for him.

Julian turned away.

'Never seen anything like it, have you?' Grace asked, trying to mask her discomfort at the woman's actions and relief at Julian's reaction.

'Rome,' he said plainly.

She laughed. 'They weren't that decadent, were they?'

'You'd be amazed. At least no one's having an orgy on the ... ' He broke off as he walked past a couple making out on the corner. 'Never mind.'

Grace laughed.

'Ooo, baby,' a prostitute called to Julian as they passed another club. 'Come inside, and I'll do *you* for free.'

He shook his head without breaking his stride.

Grace grabbed his hand and pulled him to a stop. 'Were women like this before the curse?'

He nodded. 'It's the reason Kyrian was my only friend. The men around me couldn't stand the attention I received, and women followed me everywhere I went, trying to shove their hands under my armor.'

She thought about that for a minute. 'And you're sure

235

none of these women loved you?'

He looked at her drolly. 'Love and lust are not the same thing. How can you love someone you don't know?'

'I guess you're right.'

They headed down the street. 'So, tell me about this friend of yours. Why didn't he mind the way women gawked at you?'

Julian flashed his dimples. 'Kyrian was deeply in love with his wife, and couldn't have cared less about any other woman. He never saw me as competition.'

'Did you ever meet his wife?'

He shook his head. 'Even though we never discussed it, I think we both knew it would be a very bad idea.'

Grace watched him as his face changed. He was remembering Kyrian, she was sure of it. 'You're blaming yourself for what happened to him, aren't you?'

Julian clenched his teeth as he thought about what Kyrian must have felt when the Romans captured him. Considering how badly the Romans had wanted the two of them, there was no telling what else they'd done to Kyrian before they took his life.

'Yes,' he said quietly. 'I know it's my fault. Had I not angered Priapus, I would have been there to help Kyrian fight them.'

And there was little doubt in his mind that half of Kyrian's fate had come from the fact that Kyrian had been foolish enough to befriend him.

Julian sighed. 'What a waste of a brilliant life. Had he ever learned to master his recklessness, I know Kyrian would have made a fine ruler one day.' He took her hand in his and gave a light squeeze.

They walked in silence while Grace tried to think of some way to cheer him.

As they passed Marie Laveau's House of Voodoo, Grace stopped, then dragged him inside.

She explained the origins of voodoo to him as they toured the miniature museum.

'Ooo,' she said, picking up a male voodoo doll from a display. 'Want to dress him up like Priapus and stick little pins in him?'

Julian laughed. 'Want to pretend it's Rodney Carmichael?'

Grace suppressed a smile. 'Now that would be unprofessional of me, wouldn't it? But it is tempting.'

Grace set the doll down as her gaze fell to the glass display case that held assorted amulets and jewelry. In the middle of the case was a necklace of black, blue, and hunter green threads braided so intricately that it looked like a thin black wire.

'It brings good luck to the wearer,' the saleswoman told her as she noticed her interest. 'Would you like to see it?'

Grace nodded. 'Does it work?'

'Oh, yes. The thread pattern is strong magic.'

Grace didn't know if she believed that, but then, a week ago she would never have believed two drunk women could conjure a Macedonian general to life, either.

She paid the woman for it, then turned to Julian.

'Lean down,' she told him.

He looked skeptical.

'C'mon,' she teased. 'Humor me.'

The saleswoman laughed at them as Grace fastened it around his neck. 'That boy don't need no luck charm, chère, he be needing a spell to thwart the attention of those women staring at his rear while he's stooped over.'

Grace looked past him to see the three women who were indeed ogling his butt. For the first time, she felt a vicious stab of jealousy.

The feeling evaporated as Julian kissed her cheek tenderly before straightening. His look devilish, he draped a possessive arm over her shoulders.

As they passed the women, Grace couldn't suppress her own mischievous impulse. She paused by the women. 'By the way, he looks even better naked.'

'You would certainly know, my sweet,' Julian said as he put his sunglasses on, then draped his arm back over her shoulders.

Grace slid her hand around his waist and into his front pocket as he hugged her against his side.

'You know,' Julian whispered to her. 'If you want to move that hand a little lower in my pocket, I wouldn't mind a bit.'

She squeezed him, but kept her hand where it was.

The women's envious stares followed them all the way down the street.

For dinner, Grace took him to Mike Anderson's Seafood to eat. She cringed as they brought out Julian's oysters and placed them on the table.

'Ew,' she said as he ate one.

Offended, he scowled at her. 'They're delicious.'

'I don't think so.'

'That's only because you don't know how to eat them.'

'Sure I do. You open your mouth and let the slimy thing slide down your throat.'

He took a swig of beer. 'That's one way of doing it.'

'That's how *you* just did it.'

'True, but would you like to try another way?'

She bit her lip in indecision. Something in his demeanor warned her it could be most dangerous to take him up on this challenge. 'I don't know.'

'Trust me?'

'Hardly,' she scoffed.

He shrugged and took another swig of beer. 'Your loss.'

'Oh, all right,' she relented, too curious by now to continue declining. 'But if I gag, remember I warned you.'

Julian hooked his heels around her chair legs, and pulled her so close to him that their thighs were pressed together. He wiped his hands on his jeans, then picked up the smallest oyster on his plate.

'All right, then,' he murmured in her ear. He draped his arm over her shoulders. 'Tilt your head back.'

She did. He stroked her throat with his fingers, causing chills to erupt all over her body. She swallowed, amazed by the tenderness of his touch. Amazed at just how good he felt by her side.

'Open your mouth,' he breathed as he nuzzled her neck with his nose.

She obeyed.

He tilted the oyster to slide into her mouth. As the oyster slid down her throat, he ran his tongue up her neck in the opposite direction.

Grace shuddered at the unexpected sensations. Her breasts tingled and a thousand chills went through her. It was incredible! And for once, she didn't mind the taste of the oyster at all.

Her face flamed as she remembered where they were. Opening her eyes, she was immediately grateful that they were seated in a dark corner.

'Did you like it?' he asked playfully.

She couldn't resist smiling. 'You are incorrigible.'

'I endeavor to be, anyway.'

'And you succeed admirably.'

Before he could respond, her cell phone rang.

239

'Ugh!' she said, pulling it out. Whoever it was, it had better be darn important.

She answered it.

'Grace?'

She cringed as she heard Rodney's voice. 'Mr. Carmichael, how did you get this number?'

'It was in your Rolodex. I came by to see you again, but you're not home.' He sighed. 'I was so looking forward to being with you today. We still need to have that talk. But that's okay. I can come to you. Are you down in the Quarter again visiting your psychic friend?'

Fear cut through her. 'How do you know about my friend?'

'I know lots of things about you, Grace. Hmmm,' he breathed into the phone. 'You scent your underwear with rose potpourri.'

Grace froze as her terror swelled to titanic proportions. Her hands started shaking. 'Are you in my house?'

She could hear drawers opening and closing on the other end of the line. Suddenly, he let out a curse. 'You slut!' he snarled. 'Who is he? Who the hell have you been sleeping with?'

'Now that's–'

The line went dead.

Grace shook so badly, she could barely turn the phone off.

'What is it?' Julian asked, his brow knitted with concern.

'Rodney's at my house,' she said, her voice quaking. She immediately dialed the police to notify them.

'We'll meet you there,' the officer told her. 'Whatever you do, don't go inside until we get there.'

'Don't worry.'

Julian covered her hands with his. 'You're shaking.'

240

'You think? I only have a psycho in my house sniffing my lingerie and calling me names. Why should I be shaking?'

His deep blue eyes soothed her with their protectiveness. He tightened his grip on her hands. 'You know I won't let him hurt you.'

'I appreciate the thought, Julian, but this man is—'

'Dead if he comes near you. You know I won't leave you.'

'Not until the next full moon anyway.'

He looked away then, and she saw the truth of it. 'It's okay,' she said bravely. 'I can handle this, really. I've been on my own for years now. He's not the first client to harass me. I doubt he'll be the last.'

Julian's eyes snapped blue fire as he met her gaze. 'Just how many of these people harass you?'

'It's not your problem. It's mine.'

He looked as if he were ready to strangle her.

Chapter Twelve

Grace reached her house at the same time the police arrived.

The young, heavy-set officer cast a suspicious glare at Julian. 'Who's he?'

'A friend,' she said.

The officer held his hand out to her. 'All right, give me the keys, and let me search the place. Officer Reynolds will stay out here with you until I finish.'

Grace dutifully handed over her house keys.

She chewed her thumbnail as she watched him enter. *Please let Rodney be in there.*

He wasn't. The police officer came out a short time later, shaking his head.

'Damn,' she breathed.

Officer Reynolds walked her to her house with Julian one step behind. 'We need you to come in, and take a look around, see if anything's missing.'

'Did he make a mess?' Grace asked.

'Only in the bedrooms.'

Heartsick, Grace walked into the house and up the stairs to her room.

Julian trailed behind, and watched the way she held herself rigidly cool. Her face was so pale that it made her freckles all the more apparent. He could kill the man responsible for this. No woman should ever be this afraid, especially not in her own home.

When they reached the top of the stairs, he saw the door at the end of the hallway ajar. Grace ran to it.

'No!' she gasped.

Julian rushed in behind her.

The grief on her face made him see red. He felt her pain in his heart as if it were his own.

Tears streamed down her face as her gaze darted over the shambles. The bed had been torn apart and drawers over-turned as if Zephyros had come through on a tirade.

Julian put his hand on her shoulder to comfort her.

'How could he do this to their room?' she asked.

'Whose room?' Officer Reynolds asked. 'I thought you lived alone.'

'I do. This was my parents' room before they died.' Grace looked around in disbelief. It was one thing to go after her, but why would he have done *this*?

She looked about at the scattered clothes, clothes that reminded her of so many wonderful moments. Her father's shirts that he'd worn every day to work. Her mother's favorite sweater that Grace used to beg to borrow. The earrings her father had given her mother the anniversary before they died. All of it was now tossed about as if it were worthless.

But it wasn't worthless to her. It was all she had left of them. The hurt stabbed deeply into her heart.

'How could he do this?' she asked as rage tore through her.

243

Julian pulled her into his arms and held her tight. 'It's okay, Grace,' he breathed against her hair.

But it wasn't okay. Grace doubted if it would ever be okay again. She couldn't stand the thought of that animal running his hands through her mother's clothes. Of him stripping the sheets off their bed. How dare he!

Julian looked at the police officer.

'Don't worry,' the man said, 'we'll find the guy.'

'And then what?' Julian asked.

'That's for the courts to decide.'

Julian raked him with a disgusted sneer. Courts. He had no use for modern courts that could turn such an animal loose.

'I know this is hard,' the officer said. 'But we really need you to keep looking around, Dr. Alexander, to see if he took anything.'

She nodded.

Her courage amazed Julian as she withdrew from his embrace, and brushed the tears from her cheeks. She started looking through the debris. Julian knelt by her side, wanting to be close should she need him again.

After a thorough search, Grace crossed her arms over her chest and looked at the officer. 'Nothing's missing,' she said, then went to her own bedroom.

Grace stepped tentatively inside. A quick perusal showed the same kind of damage in here. Both her and Julian's clothes had been thoroughly searched. Underwear was scattered all about, and her bed had been stripped and the mattress was askew.

How she wished the beast had found Julian's sword beneath the bed and made the mistake of touching it. Now that would truly have been justice.

But Rodney hadn't found it. In fact, Julian's shield was

still where he'd left it, propped against the wall beside the bed.

Looking around at her scattered clothing, Grace felt so violated, as if Rodney's creepy hands had touched her body.

Grace saw the door to her book closet slightly ajar. Her heart stopped beating as she walked to it, and opened the door wider. In that moment, she truly felt as if Rodney had ripped her heart out and stomped on it.

'My books,' she whispered.

Julian crossed the room to see what she was looking at. His breath caught in his throat as he stood behind her.

Every single book she owned had been torn to pieces.

'Not my books,' she said, falling to her knees.

Grace's hand shook as she touched the pages of the books her father had written. They were irreplaceable. Never again would she be able to open them up and hear his voice speaking to her from the past. Nor would she be able to open up *Black Beauty* and hear the faint memory of her mother reading it to her.

It was all gone.

In one move, Rodney Carmichael had killed her parents all over again.

And then her gaze fell to the shredded pieces of *The Iliad*. Tears filled her eyes as she remembered the way Julian had looked when he'd seen it. The hours they had spent with each other as she read.

Those hours had been so special. So magical as they lay in front of the couch lost in the words of the story. It was their own little realm. Their own special heaven.

'He decimated all of them,' she whispered. 'Oh, God, he must have been here for hours.'

'Ma'am, they're just–'

Julian grabbed Officer Reynolds by the arm, and pulled

him back into the bedroom. 'They're not just books to her,' he said between clenched teeth. 'Don't mock her pain.'

'Oh,' he said sheepishly. 'Sorry.'

Julian returned to Grace inside the closet.

She was sobbing uncontrollably as she ran her hand over the shredded pages. 'Why would he do this?'

Julian picked her up and carried her out of the closet, then laid her on the bed. She held on to him so tightly that he could barely breathe, and she sobbed as if her heart were splintering.

In that moment, Julian wanted to kill the man who'd done this to her.

The phone rang.

Grace screamed and struggled to get up.

'Sh,' Julian said, wiping her tears with his hand while holding her steady. 'It's all right. I'm here. I've got you.'

Officer Reynolds handed her the phone. 'Answer it in case it's him.'

Julian glared at the man. How could he be so insensitive as to ask her to talk to that rabid mongrel?

'Hi, Selena,' Grace said, then she burst into tears again as she told Selena what had happened.

Julian's thoughts whirled as he considered the man who had invaded her home and wounded her so deeply. What concerned him most was the fact that the man knew what to go after. He knew Grace. Knew what was important to her.

And that made him far more dangerous than the police realized.

Grace hung up the phone. 'I'm sorry for the outburst,' she said, wiping her tears away. 'It's been a long day.'

'Yes, ma'am, we understand.'

Julian watched as she pulled herself together with a

strength of will he had known few men to possess.

She led the police through the rest of her house.

'He must not have seen this book,' one of the officers said as he handed Julian's book to her.

Julian took it from Grace's hands. Unlike the officer, he wasn't so sure. If the bastard had tried to tear it up, then he had been in for one nasty surprise.

The book could never be destroyed. Over the centuries, he had tried to do it himself, countless times. Not even fire could mar it. But the book served to remind him of just how true Grace's earlier words were.

In a few days, he would be gone and she would have no one to protect her.

That thought made him ill.

The police were finally leaving as Selena pulled into the driveway. She got out of her Jeep with a tall, dark-haired man who had his arm bound in a cast, and came running to the door.

'Are you okay?' she asked Grace as she hugged her.

'I'm fine,' Grace said, then looking over Selena's shoulder, she greeted the man. 'Hi, Bill.'

'Hi, Grace. We came to help.'

Grace introduced him to Julian, then the four of them went inside.

Julian stopped Selena as soon as they entered, and pulled her aside. 'Can you keep her downstairs for a bit?'

'Why?'

'I have something I need to take care of.'

Selena frowned. 'Sure, okay.'

Julian waited until Selena and Bill sat Grace down on the couch. Then he went to the kitchen, grabbed a couple of trash bags, and headed upstairs to the closet.

As quickly as he could, he started cleaning up the mess so Grace wouldn't have to see it again. But with every piece of paper he touched, his rage grew.

Over and over, he saw the tender look on her face as she had looked through her collection, searching for a book to read. Closing his eyes, he could see her hair falling over his chest as she read to him.

And in that moment, he wanted blood.

'Jeez,' Bill said from the doorway. 'He do all this?'

'Yes.'

'Man, what a psycho.'

Julian didn't say anything as he continued to shove papers into the bag. All he could focus on was the scream in his soul that demanded vengeance. It made a mockery of the one that called out for Priapus.

It was one thing to wound him. But to hurt Grace ...

The Fates had better have mercy on the man, because Julian wouldn't.

'So, you been dating Grace long?'

'No.'

'Didn't think so. Selena hasn't mentioned you, but come to think of it, she hasn't been so worried over Grace being alone since her birthday, either. You must have met her then.'

'Yes.'

'Yes, no, yes. You're not much on talking, are you?'

'No.'

'Well, I can take a hint. See ya later.'

Julian paused as his hand brushed the cover to *Peter Pan*. He picked it up and ground his teeth. Pain assailed him. She'd loved this book most of all.

He clenched it tight in his hand, then added it to the bag, as well.

*

248

Grace didn't know how long she sat on the couch unmoving. All she knew was how much she hurt. Rodney had struck deeply in his violation of her.

Selena brought her a cup of hot chocolate.

Grace tried to drink it, but her hands still shook so badly that she was afraid she'd spill it. She set it aside. 'I guess I need to go clean up.'

'Julian already did that,' Bill said from her armchair as he flipped channels on the TV.

Grace frowned. 'What? When?'

'He was up there a little while ago, cleaning out the closet.'

Gaping at the news, Grace went to find him.

Julian was in her parents' room. She watched him from the doorway as he straightened the last of the mess. He folded her father's pants in a way that would have made Martha Stewart cringe, then placed them in the drawer and slid it shut.

Tenderness flooded her at the sight of a once legendary general cleaning up her house to keep her from having to do it. His kindness touched her all the way to her heart.

He looked up and met her gaze. The warm concern in those deep blue eyes warmed her deeply.

'Thank you,' she said.

He shrugged. 'Didn't have anything else to do.' Though he'd said the words casually, there was a note in his voice that belied his nonchalance.

'I'm still grateful.' She walked into the room, looking around at all his hard work. Her throat tight, she placed her hand on the mahogany footboard. 'This was my grandmother's bed,' she told him. 'I can still hear my mother telling me how my grandfather made it for her. He was a carpenter.'

His jaw rigid, he stared at her hand. 'It's hard, isn't it?'

'What?'

'Letting go of the ones you love.'

She knew he spoke from his heart. From the heart of a father who missed his children.

Though he no longer thrashed about at night, she still heard him whisper their names, and she wondered if he knew how often he dreamed of them.

And she wondered how many times a day he must think of them and ache for the loss.

'Yes,' she said quietly, 'but then, you know that better than I do, don't you?'

He didn't speak.

Grace let her gaze drift around the room. 'I guess it's time I move on, but I swear I can still hear them, feel them.'

'It's their love you feel. It still warms you.'

'You know, I think you're right.'

'Hey,' Selena said from the doorway, interrupting them. 'Bill's calling for a pizza. You feel up to eating?'

'I think so,' Grace said.

'What about you?' Selena asked Julian.

Julian cast a knowing smile to Grace. 'I'd love some pizza.'

Grace actually laughed as she remembered him asking for it the night she'd conjured him.

'Okay,' Selena said, 'pizza it is.'

Julian handed Grace her mother's wedding rings. 'I found those on the floor.'

Grace started to put them back on the dresser, but she couldn't. Instead, she placed them on her right hand, and for the first time in years, she felt comforted by them.

As they left the room, Julian started to close the door.

'No,' Grace said softly. 'Leave it open.'

'You sure?'

She nodded.

As she entered her bedroom, she realized he'd cleaned it as well. But when she saw the empty shelves where her books had once been, her heart broke again.

This time, when Julian closed the door, she didn't argue.

Hours later, after they had eaten, Grace finally convinced Bill and Selena to leave.

'I'm fine, really,' she assured them for the umpteenth time at the door. Reaching out, she placed her hand on Julian's arm, grateful for the strength of his presence. 'Besides, I have Julian.'

Selena gave her a stern look. 'You call if you need anything.'

'I will.'

Still unable to feel completely at ease, she locked the door and led Julian upstairs to her room.

She lay in bed with Julian at her side.

'I just feel so vulnerable,' she whispered.

He stroked her hair. 'I know. Just close your eyes and know that I'm here. I'll keep you safe.'

He wrapped his arms around her. Grace sighed at the comfort he gave. No one else had ever soothed her the way he did.

They lay for hours before she finally fell into an exhausted sleep.

Grace came awake with a scream lodged in her throat.

'I'm right here, Grace.'

She heard Julian's voice beside her and instantly calmed. 'Thank God, it's you,' she whispered. 'I had a bad dream.'

He kissed her lightly on the shoulder. 'I understand.'

She gave his hand a squeeze before leaving the bed to get ready for work.

As she tried to dress, her hands shook so badly she couldn't even button her shirt.

'Here,' Julian said, moving her hands away so that he could button it for her. 'You don't have to be scared, Grace. I won't let him hurt you.'

'I know. I know the police will get him and it'll be over.'

He said nothing as he helped her dress.

Once they were ready, she drove them to her downtown office. Her stomach was so knotted that she could barely breathe. But she had to do this. She wasn't about to let Rodney control her life. She was in charge and no one would take that away from her. Not without a fight.

Still, she was glad for Julian's presence. It comforted her in a way she didn't want to think about.

'What is this called?' Julian asked as she led him into the huge antique elevator in her turn-of-the-century office building.

Grace showed him how to pull the door closed and noted his immediate discomfort as they were sealed inside it.

'It's an elevator,' she explained. 'You press these buttons to reach whatever floor you want. I'm on the top one, which is eight.' She pressed the old knob-style button.

Julian tensed even more as the elevator moved. 'Is it safe?'

She arched a curious brow at him. 'Surely the man who fearlessly faced down Roman armies isn't scared of an elevator?'

He gave her a peeved glare. 'Romans I understand, this thing I don't.'

She wrapped her arm around his. 'There's not much to it.' She pointed up at the trap door. 'Outside that door are cables that lift it up and down, and there's a phone.' She pointed to the call box below the buttons. 'If you get stuck

252

in the elevator all you have to do is pick up the phone and you're connected directly to an emergency staff.'

His eyes darkened. 'Does the elevator get stuck a lot?'

'Not really. I've had my office here for four years and so far it's never once gotten stuck.'

'If you weren't on it, how would you know if it got stuck or not?'

'Elevators let out this piercing alarm when they stop. Trust me, if it got stuck, someone would know.'

He swept his gaze around the wide space of the elevator, and by the light in his eyes, she could tell naughty things were on his mind. 'Could you make it stop on purpose?'

She laughed. 'Yes, but I really don't want to be caught *flagrante delicto* at work.'

He dipped his head down and kissed her lightly on the cheek. 'But being caught *flagrante delicto* at work could be a whole lot of fun.'

Grace hugged him close. What was it about him that made her feel better? No matter what, he always seemed to make things more fun. Brighter. 'You are bad,' she said, reluctantly letting go of him.

'True, but you love that about me.'

She laughed again. 'You're right. I do.'

The doors opened, and Grace led him the short distance to her office.

Lisa looked up as they entered and widened her eyes. A smile spread across her face as she gave Julian a thorough once-over. 'Dr. Grace,' she teased, toying with a strand of her blond hair. 'You got a hot boyfriend.'

Shaking her head, Grace introduced them, then she showed Julian her office. Julian stood by the windows as she turned on her computer and placed her purse in her desk drawer.

She paused as she caught him staring at her. 'You're really going to spend all day hanging around my office?'

He shrugged. 'I have nothing better to do.'

'You'll be bored.'

'I assure you, I'm used to be being bored.'

The bad thing was, Grace knew just how much experience he had in that department. She placed her hand against his cheek as she thought of him inside the book, alone, and encased in darkness.

Rising up on her tiptoes, she gave him a gentle kiss. 'Thank you for coming with me today. I don't think I could be here without you.'

He nibbled her lips. 'My pleasure.'

Lisa buzzed her. 'Dr. Grace, your eight o'clock is here.'

'I'll wait outside,' Julian said.

Grace gave his hand a squeeze before she let him leave.

For the next hour, she barely paid attention. Her thoughts were on the man outside and how much he meant to her.

And how much she hated the thought of him leaving.

As soon as she finished her session, she walked her patient out.

Lisa was showing Julian how to play solitaire on her computer. 'Hey, Dr. Grace,' she said. 'Did you know Julian never played solitaire before?'

Grace exchanged an amused smile with Julian. 'Really?'

Lisa scooted away from Julian to look at her appointment book. 'By the way, your three o'clock canceled. And your nine o'clock called and said he'd be a few minutes late.'

'Okay.' Grace gestured to the door with her thumb. 'While you two play, I'm going to make a dash out to my car to get my Palm Pilot.'

Julian looked up. 'I'll go.'

Grace shook her head. 'I can do it.'

Without pausing, he came around Lisa's desk and held his hand out for her keys. 'I'll go,' he said in a voice that let her know he wasn't about to concede.

Not willing to argue, she handed her keys over. 'It's under the driver's seat.'

'Okay, I'll be right back.'

Grace gave him a military salute.

Unamused, Julian left her office and headed toward the elevator at the end of the hallway.

He reached for the button, then paused. Gods, how he hated that tight, square thing.

And the thought of being in it alone . . .

Looking around, he saw a flight of stairs. Without a second's hesitation, he headed for them instead.

Grace was trying to find Rachel's file in her briefcase when she remembered she'd left a couple of folders in her backseat.

'Where is my mind?' she snapped at herself. But then, she knew. Her thoughts were scattered between the two men who had completely altered her life.

Aggravated at herself for not being able to focus, she took her briefcase and followed after Julian.

'Where are you going, Dr. Grace?' Lisa asked.

'I left a couple of files in my car, too. I'll be right back.'

Lisa nodded.

Grace went to the elevator. She was still rummaging through her briefcase in search of the missing files when the doors opened.

Without looking up, she stepped inside, and automatically pushed the lobby button.

It wasn't until the doors closed that she realized she wasn't alone.

Rodney Carmichael stood on the opposite side, staring at her.

'So, who is he?'

Grace froze as waves of fear and rage tore through her. She wanted to tear him to pieces! But even though he was small for a man, he was still a head taller than her.

And very unstable.

Hiding her rising panic, she spoke calmly. 'What are you doing here?'

He curled his lip at her. 'You didn't answer my question. I want to know whose clothes were in your house.'

'That's none of your business.'

'Bullshit,' he shrieked. He was teetering on the brink of insanity, and the last thing she needed was for him to fall over it while they were trapped in the elevator. 'Everything that concerns you is my business.'

Grace tried to take control of the situation. 'Now listen to me, Mr. Carmichael, I don't know you and you don't know me. I can't imagine why you're fixated on me, but I want it to stop.'

He pushed the button to stall the elevator. 'Now *you* listen to me, Grace. We're perfect for each other. You know it as well as I do. We were meant to be together.'

'Okay,' she said, trying to calm him down. 'Let's discuss this in my office.' She pressed the button to start the elevator.

He stopped it again. 'We'll talk here.'

Grace took a deep breath as her hands started shaking. She had to get out of here without making him any angrier. 'We'd be more comfortable in my office.'

This time when she reached for the button, he grabbed her hand.

'Why won't you just talk to me?' he asked.

'We are talking.' Grace inched toward the call box.

'I bet you talk with him, don't you? I bet you spend hours laughing and doing God only knows what with him. Now, tell me who he is.'

'Mr. Carmichael–'

'Rodney!' he shouted. 'Dammit, my name is Rodney.'

'Okay, Rodney. Let's–'

'I bet he's had his filthy hands all over you, hasn't he?' He cornered her by the buttons. 'How many times have you slept with him since you met me, huh?'

Grace trembled at the feral look in his beady eyes. He was slipping. She reached behind her to pick up the phone, but before she could get it to her ear, he grabbed it.

'What the hell are you doing?' he asked.

'You need help.'

He smashed the phone against the buttons. 'I don't need help. I just need you to talk to me. Do you hear me? I just need you to talk to me!' He punctuated each word by bashing the phone into the control panel.

Terrified, Grace watched as the phone splintered. Then, he started pulling at his hair.

'He's kissed you, I know he has.' He repeated the words over and over again as he wrenched his hair out by the handfuls.

Oh, God! She was trapped with a lunatic.

And there was no way out.

Julian returned to Grace's office with her Palm Pilot. 'Where's Grace?' he asked Lisa when he didn't find Grace at her desk.

'Didn't you see her? She went down to the car a few minutes after you left.'

He frowned. 'Are you sure?'

'Yeah. She said she left some files or something.'

Before he could ask anything else, an attractive African-American woman walked into the office dressed in a conservative black suit and holding a briefcase.

She paused inside the doorway to kick off a shoe and rub her heel. 'It's definitely a Monday,' she said to Lisa. 'I just had to walk up eight flights of stairs because the elevator is stuck between floors. Now what wonderful news do you have for me?'

'Hi, Dr. Beth,' Lisa said cheerfully, running her hand down the book on her desk. 'Your nine o'clock is with Rodney Carmichael.'

Julian went cold.

'Oh, no, wait,' Lisa said, 'that's Dr. Grace. Yours–'

'Did you say Rodney Carmichael?' he asked.

'Yeah. He called to reschedule.'

Julian didn't wait for her to finish. He tossed the Palm Pilot on Lisa's desk, then ran out of the office toward the elevator. His heart hammering, all he think of was getting to Grace as fast as he could.

It was then he realized the buzzing he'd been hearing was an alarm bell ringing.

A cold shiver went down his spine as every instinct he possessed told him what had happened. Rodney had stopped the elevator with Grace inside. He was sure of it.

Suddenly, a muffled scream sounded from behind the closed elevator doors.

His vision clouding with anger and fear, he wrenched open the door to the shaft.

Julian froze.

He couldn't see the car. All he could see was the black cavern. And it looked just like the book. Worse, going down it would feel like being sucked into his hell. Of darkness. Cramped. Tight.

He struggled to breathe as terror washed over him.

In his heart, he knew Grace was down there. Alone with a madman and with no one to help her.

Grinding his teeth, he stepped back and jumped to the cables.

Pushing violently, Grace forced Rodney off her.

'I'm not going to share you!' he snarled, grabbing her arms again. 'You are mine.'

'I don't belong to anyone except me.' Grace kneed him in the groin.

He sank to the floor.

Desperate, Grace tried to climb up the side rails to reach the trapdoor above her head. If she could get to that . . .

Rodney grabbed her about the waist and slung her back into the corner.

His face contorted with rage, he braced his arms on each side of her. 'Tell me the name of the man who has been inside you, Grace! Tell me so I will know who I have to kill.'

His eyes empty and terrifying, he started clawing at his face and neck so fiercely that he made bloody welts. 'Don't you know, you're my woman? We are going to be together. I know how to take care of you. What you need. I am so much better than *him*!'

Grace ducked away from Rodney, then kicked her high heels off and grabbed them in her hands. They weren't the best weapons, but they were better than nothing.

'I want to know who you've been with!' he shrieked.

At the same moment Rodney took a step forward, the trapdoor above her head opened. Grace looked up.

Julian dropped through the hole and landed in a deadly crouch like some sleek predator. An aura of dangerous calm surrounded him, but it was his eyes that were terrifying.

Snapping fire and hell-wrath, they focused on Rodney with murderous intent.

Then, slowly, methodically, Julian rose to his full height.

Rodney stopped dead in his tracks as he took in the size of Julian. 'Who the hell are you?'

'I'm the man she's been with.'

Rodney's jaw dropped.

Julian passed a quick glance over Grace to assure himself she was safe and whole, and then he turned on Rodney with a roar.

He slung Rodney against the wall with such force, she was amazed it didn't leave a dent in the wooden panels.

Julian grabbed him by the shirt and held him against the wall.

When Julian spoke, the coldness of his voice sent a shiver over her. 'It's a pity you're not big enough for me to kill, because I want you dead.' He tightened his fist. 'But little or not, if I ever find you near Grace again, if you ever cause her to shed another tear, there is no power on this earth or beyond that will keep me from crushing you. Do you understand?'

Rodney fought uselessly against his hold. 'She's mine! I'll kill you if you come between us.'

Julian cocked his head as if he couldn't believe his ears. 'Are you insane?'

Rodney kicked Julian viciously in the stomach.

His eyes darkening, Julian slugged him hard against the jaw. Rodney crumpled to the floor.

As Julian knelt down by Rodney's side, Grace shook in relief. It was over.

'You better stay unconscious,' Julian said ominously to Rodney.

Rising to his feet, Julian pulled her to him in a crushing embrace. 'Are you okay, Grace?'

She couldn't breathe, but at the moment, she didn't care. 'I'm fine, and you?'

'Better now that I know you're all right.'

It was a few minutes later when the police finally pried open the door of the elevator, and Grace saw they were trapped between floors.

Julian lifted her from her waist as Grace took the policeman's extended hand and let him pull her up to the floor above them.

Once she was out of the elevator, she frowned at the three officers who were helping Julian with Rodney's unconscious body. 'How did you know to be here?'

The older policeman stood back as the other two officers lifted Rodney's unconscious body out. 'The emergency phone operator called us. She said it sounded like a war was going on in the elevator.'

'It was,' she said nervously.

'So, who do we handcuff?'

'The unconscious one.'

While Grace waited for Julian to rejoin her, she noticed the darkness of the elevator shaft he had climbed down to reach her. The smallness of the space.

And she remembered the look on Julian's face the night she'd turned off the lights. The nervous look he'd had earlier when they rode the elevator up to her office.

Still, he had come for her.

Overwhelmed, she felt tears sting her eyes. *He went through it to protect me.*

As soon as he was out of the elevator car, she wrapped her arms around him and held him tight.

Julian trembled from the force of his emotions. He was so grateful she was alive and unhurt. Picking her up, he kissed her.

261

'No!'

Julian released her at the same moment Rodney kicked the policeman away from him. The handcuffs dangled off one of his wrists as he grabbed the policeman's gun and aimed.

His reactions honed by battle, Julian grabbed Grace and forced her to the left as the gun went off.

Rodney's shot missed them, but was followed by two more as the older officer opened fire on Rodney.

Grace tried to pull away. Julian refused to let her.

He kept her face against his chest as he saw Rodney die. 'Don't look, Grace,' he whispered. 'There are some memories you don't need.'

Chapter Thirteen

'Yes, Selena,' Grace said into the phone as she dressed for work. 'It's been a week. I'm fine.'

'You don't sound fine,' Selena said skeptically. 'You still sound a little shaken.'

Truthfully, she was. But she was safe thanks to Julian. And she hadn't seen poor Rodney afterward.

Once the police had statements from them, Julian had taken her home and she'd done her best not to dwell on it. 'Really. I'm okay.'

Julian came into the bedroom. 'You're running late.' He took the phone from her and handed her a Danish. 'Finish dressing,' he said to her, then he turned his attention to Selena.

Grace frowned as he walked out of the room and she couldn't hear him talking.

As she dressed, it dawned on her just how comfortable she'd become with Julian. She absolutely loved having him around. She loved taking care of him and having him take care of her. The mutualness of their relationship was wonderful.

'Grace,' he said as he stuck his head back into the bedroom. 'You're still running late.'

She laughed as she slid her high heels on. 'I'm going, I'm going.'

When they got to the front door, she realized he didn't have his shoes on. 'You're not coming today?'

'Do you need me to?'

Grace hesitated. She actually liked being able to have lunch with him and tease him between sessions. But then, she was sure it was boring for him to sit up there hour after hour, waiting for her. 'No.'

He gave her a hungry kiss. 'I'll see you tonight.'

Reluctantly, she let go and hurried out the door to her car.

It was one of the longest days in history. Grace sat at her desk, counting the seconds until she could get her patient out the door.

When five o'clock came, she gave poor Rachel the bum's rush for the door, then quickly gathered up her things and went home.

It didn't take her long to get there. She frowned as she saw Selena waiting for her on the front porch.

'Something wrong?' Grace asked as she joined her.

'Not hardly. But I'll give you a word of advice, break that curse. Julian is a major keeper.'

Grace frowned even more as Selena left her and headed to her Jeep. Bemused, she opened the door.

'Julian?' she called.

'I'm in the bedroom.'

Grace headed up the stairs. She found him lying in a most yummy way on the bed with his head propped up on one arm, and a single red rose lying on the mattress before him.

He was so incredibly gorgeous and inviting. Especially with those dimples flashing, and with a light in his celestial blue eyes that could only be called impish.

'You look like the cat that ate the canary,' she said quietly. 'What did the two of you do today?'

'Nothing.'

'Nothing,' she repeated doubtfully. Now why didn't she believe that? *Because he looks just a little too mischievous.*

Her gaze fell to the rose. 'For me?'

'Yes.'

She smiled at his clipped, short answers, and dropped her shoes by the bed before pulling off her hose.

Looking up, she caught Julian's very interested stare as he craned his neck to watch her. He smiled again.

Grace picked up the rose and smelled its sweet fragrance. 'It's a nice surprise,' she said, kissing Julian on the cheek for it. 'Thank you.'

'I'm glad you like it,' he whispered, running his hand along her jawbone.

Reluctantly, Grace withdrew and crossed the room to place the rose on the dresser and open the top drawer.

She froze. Lying on top of her clothes was a small hardcover copy of *Peter Pan* with a big red ribbon tied around it.

Gasping, she took it in her hands and untied the ribbon. As she flipped to the first page, her heart skipped a beat. 'Oh, my God, it's a signed first edition!'

'Do you like it?'

'Like it?' she said, her eyes misting. 'Oh, Julian!'

She launched herself at him and rained kisses all over his face. 'You are so wonderful! Thank you!'

For the first time, she saw him look embarrassed.

'This is just ... ' Her voice trailed off as she glanced to her closet. The door was slightly ajar, and the light inside was on.

Surely, he hadn't . . .

Slowly, Grace approached it. She opened the door wider, and looked inside.

Joyous tears filled her eyes as warmth spread through her. Her shelves were again covered in books. Her hand shook as she reached out and ran it over the spines of her new collection.

'Am I dreaming?' she whispered.

She felt Julian behind her. He wasn't touching her, yet she could feel him with every pore, every sense of her body. It wasn't physical, but it was earth-shattering. And it left her breathless.

'We couldn't find all of them, especially your paperbacks, but Selena said we got the most important ones.'

A single tear fell down her cheek as she saw copies of her father's books. How had they managed to find them?

Her heart pounded as she glanced at all her favorite titles: *The Three Musketeers, Beowulf, The Scarlet Letter, The Wolf and the Dove, Master of Desire, Fallen, The Lawman Who Loved Her,* on and on it went until it made her dizzy.

Overwhelmed and giddy, she let the tears fall down her cheeks.

She turned about and threw her arms around Julian. 'Thank you,' she wept. 'But how? How did you do this?'

He shrugged, then reached up to wipe away her tears. It was then she noticed his hand.

And what was missing from it.

'Not your ring,' she whispered, seeing the light skin on one of the fingers of his right hand where the ring had been. 'Tell me you didn't?'

'It was just a ring, Grace.'

No it wasn't. She remembered the look on his face when Dr. Lewis had asked to buy it.

'*Never,*' *Julian had said.* '*You've no idea what I had to go through to get this.*'

But after hearing his stories of his past, she had a good idea. And he had sold it for *her*.

Trembling, she stood up on her tiptoes and kissed him fiercely.

Julian froze in shock as her lips touched his. She'd never before reached out to him in such a manner. Closing his eyes, he clenched his hand in her hair, letting it spill down his forearm as he moaned into her mouth.

His head spun from the taste of her. From the feel of her. From the way she kissed him as he'd never been kissed before–

With the whole of her heart.

It shook him all the way to his cursed soul.

In that moment, he truly wanted time to stand still. He didn't want to live another second without her in it. Couldn't imagine a day when he didn't have her by his side.

He felt his control slipping. The pain of madness sliced across his head and his groin simultaneously.

Not yet! his mind shouted. He didn't want it to end. Not right now. Not when he was so close.

So close . . .

But he had no choice.

Reluctantly, he pulled back from her. 'I take it you like that, as well?'

She laughed at him. 'Of course I do, you crazy man.' She wrapped her arms around his waist and laid her head against his chest.

Julian quivered as unfamiliar emotions tore through him. He enveloped her with his arms, feeling her heart beating in rapid time with his.

If he could, he'd stay like this, holding on to her forever.

But he couldn't.

He stepped back from her.

She looked up, her brow wrinkled.

He smoothed the frown away with his hand. 'I'm not rejecting you, my sweet,' he whispered. 'I'm just not feeling like myself at the moment.'

'The curse?'

He nodded.

'Is there anything I can do?'

'Just give me a minute to fight it.'

Grace bit her lip as he moved stiffly to the bed. It was the only time she hadn't seen absolute, fluid grace in his movements. He looked as if he could barely breathe, as if he had a terrible ache in the pit of his stomach. He wrapped his hand around the bedpost so tightly that she could see his knuckles protrude.

Pain sliced through her at the sight and she wanted to comfort him. More than ever, she wanted to help him.

In fact, she wanted him ...

She wanted *him*. Period.

Grace's jaw dropped as the full impact of her thoughts swept over her.

She loved him.

She truly, deeply, and most profoundly loved him.

How could she not?

Her heart hammering, Grace swept her gaze over the books in her closet. Memories assailed her. Julian the night he'd appeared and offered himself to her, Julian loving her in the shower, Julian comforting her, making her laugh, Julian coming through the top of the elevator to save her, and Julian lying on the bed with the rose as he watched her find his gifts.

Selena was right. He was a major keeper and she never wanted to let him go.

It was on the tip of her tongue to tell him, but she caught herself. Now wasn't the time. Not when he was in such obvious agony. Not when he was vulnerable.

He would want to know.

Or would he?

Grace considered the repercussions of telling him. He didn't like it here in her time. She knew that. He wanted to go home. If she told him how she felt, he might stay for no other reason, and if he had no reason of his own to stay, he might grow to resent her for keeping him away from all he'd once known. All he'd been.

Or worse, what if it didn't work out?

As a psychologist, she knew better than anyone all the problems that could crop up in a relationship and destroy it.

One of the biggest reasons for breakups was the lack of common ground to build on between two people who shared nothing but physical attraction.

She and Julian were about as different as two people could ever be. She was a plain, twenty-first-century psychologist and he was a gorgeous second-century B.C. Macedonian general. Talk about a fish and a bird trying to find a place where they could both live!

Two more different people had never been born and forced together.

Right now, they were both basking in the newness of the relationship. But they didn't really know each other *that* well. What if in a year's time they weren't really in love?

For that matter, what if he changed once the curse was lifted?

Julian had told her that he'd been a different man back in Macedonia. What if part of his current charm or his attraction to her was from the curse? According to Cupid, the curse made Julian feel compelled toward her.

What if they broke the curse and he became someone else entirely? Someone who no longer wanted her?

What then?

Once he gave up his chance to go home, she was sure he'd never have another one.

Grace struggled to breathe as she realized she couldn't even say to him, 'Let's try and see what happens.' Because once he made his decision, there would be *no* second chances.

Grace swallowed, wishing she could see into the future like Selena did. But then, even Selena was wrong at times. For Julian's sake, Grace couldn't afford to be wrong.

No, there would only be one acceptable reason for him to stay. He would have to love her as much as she loved him.

And that was about as likely as the sky falling in on her head in the next ten minutes.

Closing her eyes, Grace winced at the truth. He could never be hers. One way or another, she would have to let him go.

And it was going to kill her.

Julian drew a ragged breath and released the bed. He gave her a tenuous smile. 'That hurt,' he said.

'I can tell.' She reached to touch him, but he stepped back from her like a man who was about to come into contact with a snake.

Grace dropped her hand. 'I'll go fix dinner.'

Julian watched her leave the room. He wanted to go after her so badly that he could barely refrain. But he didn't dare.

He needed a little more time to compose himself. More time to quell the fire coursing through him, threatening to overwhelm him.

He shook his head. How could her touch give him such strength, and yet at the same time make him so incredibly weak?

Grace had just finished making canned soup and sandwiches when Julian joined her in the kitchen.

'Feeling better?'

'Yes,' he said, sitting down at the table.

Grace circled her spoon around her bowl while she watched him eat. The fading sunlight caught in his hair, highlighting it. He sat perfectly straight up in the chair and every time he moved, a surge of desire tore through her. She could watch him all day and never grow tired of it.

Worse, what she really wanted to do was get up, go over to him, and sit in his lap. Then run her hands through those golden waves as she kissed the daylights out of him.

Stop it! If she didn't get hold of herself, she would succumb to that urge!

'You know,' she said hesitantly. 'I've been thinking. What if you did stay here? Would it be so bad to live in my time?'

The look he gave her quelled her. 'We've already had this discussion. I don't belong here. I don't understand your world, your customs. I feel awkward and I hate that.'

Grace cleared her throat. Fine, she wouldn't mention it again.

Sighing, she picked up her sandwich and ate it, even though what she really wanted to do was argue.

After they finished dinner, Julian helped her clean the kitchen.

'You want me to read to you?' she asked.

'Sure,' he said, but she could tell there was something wrong. He was guarded with her, almost cold.

She hadn't seen him like this since he'd first appeared.

Grace went upstairs and got her new copy of *Peter Pan*, then came back downstairs. Julian was already on the floor, piling the cushions for them.

She took her seat, lying perpendicular to him and propping her head against the side of his stomach. After turning to the first page, she began to read.

Julian listened to Grace's smooth, lilting voice, all the while staring at her. As she read the words, he watched her eyes dance across the page.

He'd promised himself he wouldn't touch her, but against his will, he found himself reaching to stroke her hair. The contact of it against his skin made him burn, made his groin tighten even more as he ached to possess her.

While the silken sable strands of her hair caressed his fingers, he let her voice take him far away from here. To a place that was so comforting, it almost felt like the elusive home he had searched eternity for.

A place where only the two of them existed. There were no gods here, no curses.

Just them.

And it felt wonderful.

Grace arched a brow as she felt Julian's hand leave her hair and reach for the top button on her shirt. She held her breath in hopeful expectation, yet she also hesitated.

'What are you–'

'Keep reading,' he said as he worked the button through the hole.

Her body growing hot, she read the next paragraph. He undid the next button.

'Julian–'

'Read.'

She read another paragraph as his hand moved to the next button down. His actions were making her crazy as her breath quickened, her heart pounded.

She looked over to see the hungry look in his eyes. 'What is this? A strip reading session? I read a paragraph, you open a button?'

He answered her question by running his warm hand over her bra, cupping her breast gently in his palm. Grace moaned in pleasure as he massaged her through the satin. The warmth of his hand on her skin sent chills up her arms.

'Read,' he commanded again.

'Oh, yeah, like I can do that while you're ... '

He released the front catch on her bra, then cupped her breast tenderly in his hand.

'Julian!'

'Read to me, Grace. Please.'

As if that were possible!

But the underlying plea in his tone tugged at her heart. Forcing herself, she turned her attention to the book as Julian glided his hand over her bare skin.

His touch was so soothing, so gentle. Sublime. This wasn't the fiery caress he used to seduce and inflame her, it was something else entirely. It went beyond the depth of her flesh. It went all the way to her heart.

After a time, she grew used to the small circles he drew around her breasts and nipples, down her belly. She lost herself to the moment, to the feeling of closeness she shared with him.

By the time she finished the book, it was almost ten. Julian ran the backs of his knuckles across her hardened nipple as she set the book aside.

'You have such beautiful breasts.'

'I'm glad you think so.' She heard his stomach rumble under her ear. 'Sounds like you're hungry.'

'What I'm hungry for, food won't sate.'

Her face flooded with heat.

He ran his hand from her belly button, up to her throat, then down the line of her jaw to her hair. He traced the outline of her lips with his thumb.

'How odd,' he said. 'It's your kiss that sends me over the brink.'

'I beg your pardon?'

He dropped his hand back to her stomach. 'I love the way your skin feels against me. The softness of your flesh under my hand,' he said quietly. 'But it's only when our lips touch that I feel my sanity slipping. Why do you think that is?'

'I don't know.'

The phone rang.

Julian cursed. 'I really hate those things.'

'I'm beginning to, too.'

He moved his hand away from her so she could rise. Grace captured his hand and moved it back to her breasts. 'Let it ring.'

He smiled at that, then dipped his head toward hers. Their lips were so close, she could feel his breath on her face. Suddenly, he pulled back sharply.

She saw the agony, the longing in his eyes an instant before he closed them, and clenched his teeth as if struggling to restrain himself.

'Go answer your phone,' he whispered, releasing her.

Grace stood on shaky legs and crossed the room to her cordless phone as she clutched her shirt closed over her breasts.

'Hi, Selena.'

Julian listened to her talk, his heart heavy as he fought down the fire tearing through him.

The last thing he wanted was to leave this haven. He'd never enjoyed much of anything in his life until he'd met

Grace. Now, he was covetous of every second of her time.

'Hang on, let me ask.' Grace came back to his side. 'Selena and Bill want to know if we want to go out with them Saturday?'

'It's up to you,' he said, hoping she would decline.

She smiled and put the phone back to her ear. 'That sounds great, Selena. It'll be a lot of fun ... Okay, see you then.'

She set the phone aside. 'I'm going to take a quick shower before bed. Okay?'

Julian nodded. He watched her walk up the stairs. More than ever before, he wished himself mortal again.

He would give anything to be able to follow her up the stairs, lay her down on the bed, and bury himself deep inside her body.

Closing his eyes, he swore he could feel the wet heat of her surrounding him.

He clenched his fist in his hair. How many more days could he stand the torture?

And yet, he wanted to fight it. He refused to surrender his sanity even one second sooner than the Fates decreed.

Grace felt Julian's presence. Turning around, she saw him outside the shower, completely naked.

Her gaze feasted on every inch of that golden body, but it was his warm, charming smile that absolutely stole her heart and made her breathless.

Without a word, he stepped inside.

'You know,' he said with a casualness that astounded her. 'I found something interesting this morning.'

She watched the water fall over him, slicking his hair back until it fell in short, wet ringlets about his face.

'Did you?' she asked, resisting her impulse to reach up

and capture one of those locks between her fingertips. Or better yet, her teeth.

'Mmm,' he said, running his hand up the long cord of the shower until he took the shower head from its cradle. He turned the dial to a soft massage. 'Turn around.'

Grace hesitated before she obeyed.

Julian ran his gaze over her sleek, wet back. In all his life, he'd never seen a woman more inviting.

She was everything he'd ever dreamed of having and yet he dared not hope. Dared not dream.

He lowered his gaze down her voluptuous curves. Her legs were slightly parted as she stood. An image of spreading them wider and plunging himself into her tore through him.

Struggling to breathe, he aimed the shower head at her shoulders.

'That feels so good,' she whispered.

Julian couldn't speak. He clenched his jaw to keep himself from yielding to his body's ravenous demand for hers. His need to touch her was so profound that it made a mockery of the one he felt for food and water while trapped in the book.

Grace turned to him, her face glowing. She reached around him and picked up the washcloth and soaped it. Julian didn't move as she bathed him. Her hands slid over his chest and abdomen, firing his hunger for her even more.

He held his breath in eager anticipation as her hand moved lower and lower.

Grace bit her lip as she touched the rigid muscles of his stomach. She looked up to watch Julian watch her. His eyes were half-closed, and he appeared to be savoring every stroke of her hands on his skin.

Wanting to please him, she ran the cloth over the coffee-colored curls at the center of his body. He sucked his breath in sharply as she reached between his legs to cup him gently in her hand. She smiled again as she felt a shudder run through him.

The look of pleasure on his face delighted her. Her heart pounding, she moved her hand up to gently massage his swollen shaft.

She heard the shower head hit the side of the tub an instant before he enveloped her in his arms and buried his lips against her neck.

Grace trembled from the sensations as their wet bodies entwined. The love she felt for him swelled through her, begging for a miracle that would let them have a life together.

In that instant, she wished she could feel him inside her. Feel him take possession of her body the way he had her heart.

As his lips tortured her with pleasure, he brought his thigh up between her legs. The tiny hairs on his leg teased her in a way that melted her will.

Feverishly, Grace rubbed herself against his wet, sleek thigh, relishing the feel of his strong muscles contracting between her legs as he continued to suckle her throat. Oh, how she loved this man. How she longed to hear him tell her that she meant as much to him as he did to her.

He ran his hands over her back, then her front.

His gaze scorched her as he lowered her to the bottom of the tub.

'What are you ... ' Her words ended in a gasp as he plunged his tongue into her ear.

She felt his arm flex as he reached for the shower head and brought it back to pummel her body with its pulsating heat. He moved it in slow, sensuous circles over her breasts, her stomach. On fire from the stimulation of the water and his body, she struggled to breathe.

Julian shook all over in desperate need. He wanted to please her in a way he'd never wanted to please anyone. He longed to see her writhing beneath him. Hear her screaming out her release.

Nudging her thighs farther apart, he moved the shower head to spray between her legs.

Grace choked as an indescribable pleasure ripped through her. 'Julian?' she gasped as her body quivered from the feel of his fingers inside her, filling her, teasing her while the water heightened his moves.

Never, never had she experienced anything like it. He rotated his wrist, circling the pulsating water around her until she couldn't stand it.

When her climax came a second later, she screamed from it.

Julian smiled while he held his body rigidly still to keep from filling her. Even so, he wasn't through with her. He would never be through with her.

With his hands, his tongue, and the shower, he brought her to climax five more times.

'Please, Julian,' she begged after the last one. 'Have mercy. I can't take any more.'

Deciding he had tortured the two of them enough, Julian reached behind him and turned off the water.

Grace couldn't move. Any sensation, no matter how small, rocked her. She watched him stand up between her legs, staring at her with a hint of a smile on his face.

'You've killed me,' she breathed. 'Now you have to hide the body.'

He laughed at that. He stepped out of the tub, then reached over and picked her up.

She savored the feel of his bare skin against hers as he carried her to the bed, then dried her off with the towel.

Slowly, carefully, he used the terry cloth in a way she was sure no one had ever meant for terry cloth to be used. He slid it sensuously over her arms, her breasts, then down her stomach in slow, torturous swirls.

'Open your legs for me, Grace.'

Her will gone, she obeyed.

Grace moaned at the feel of the cloth stroking the tender, throbbing flesh between her thighs. Then the cloth was gone, replaced by his fingers.

'Julian, please. I don't think I can do it again.'

He didn't listen. Neither did her body. To her amazement, she came again.

Julian leaned over her then and whispered in her ear, 'I could make you do that all night.'

She looked up into his eyes, and it was then she realized the full extent of his curse. His body was still fully erect, his brow covered in sweat.

How could he stand to watch her climax again and again, knowing he, himself, couldn't?

Her only thought her love for him, she sat up and kissed him.

Julian pulled away violently. He sank to the floor, writhing as if he were being beaten.

Terrified of what she'd done, Grace slid off the bed. 'I'm sorry,' she said, reaching out to him. 'I forgot.'

He whirled on her then, his eyes that strange, horrible dark color.

Julian trembled as he fought his madness down. It was the fear in her face that finally succeeded in calming him.

He moved away from her as if she were poisonous.

Grace watched as he used the steps to her bed to push himself to his feet.

'It's getting worse,' he said, his voice shaky.

Grace couldn't speak. She couldn't stand seeing him in pain. And she hated herself for pushing him over the edge.

Without looking back at her, Julian gathered his clothes and left the room.

It was several heartbeats before Grace could move again. When she finally found the ability to stand, she went to dress. She opened the top drawer and her eyes fell to the box that contained the handcuffs.

How many more days would they have before she lost him forever?

Chapter Fourteen

The next few days were the best of Grace's life. Once she got used to Julian's rule of no kissing and hot, intimate touches, they fell into an easy relationship that amazed and delighted her.

She spent her days at work, often meeting Julian and Selena for lunch, and her nights lying in Julian's scrumptious arms.

But with every day that passed, the knowledge that he was going to leave at the end of the month cut her all the more.

How would she be able to bear it?

Though the subject was never far from her mind, she refused to bring it up again. She would just live for the moment, and worry about tomorrow when it arrived.

Saturday night, they met Selena and Bill at Tip's in the Quarter. Though more touristy than the original Tippitina's, it was Zydeco Night and she wanted Julian to hear the music New Orleans had made famous.

'Hey!' Selena said as they approached the tables in the

back. 'I was beginning to wonder if you were no-shows.'

Grace felt her face flame as she remembered what had kept them. One day, she was going to learn to lock the bathroom door when she bathed.

'Hi, Julian, Grace,' Bill greeted.

Grace smiled at Bill's plaster cast, which Selena had painted with fluorescent colors.

Julian inclined his head to Bill as he held a chair out for Grace, then took a seat beside her. As soon as a waiter came over, they ordered beer and nachos while Selena kept the beat on the table with her hands.

'Come on, Lane,' Bill said, his voice testy. 'We'd better dance before I kill you over that incessant noise.'

A little envious, Grace watched them walk off.

'Would you like to dance?' Julian asked.

She loved to dance, but she didn't want to embarrass Julian. There was no doubt in her mind that he had no idea how to do a modern dance. Still, it was incredibly sweet of him to offer. 'That's okay.'

He didn't listen. He rose to his feet and held his hand out to her. 'Yes, you do.'

As soon as they reached the dance floor, Grace realized the man could dance as good as he looked.

Julian knew every step as if he'd been born to it. In fact, he had perfect moves, graceful, yet incredibly masculine and sexy. Grace had never seen anything like it. And judging by the envious glares the women around them were directing at her, she figured none of them ever had either.

By the time the band ended the song, she was breathless and hot. 'How did you—'

'It was a gift from Terpsichore,' Julian said as he dropped his arm over her shoulders and held her tightly against his side.

'Who?'

'The Muse of dance.'

Grace smiled. 'Remind me to send her a thank-you note.'

When the next song started, Julian did a double-take as he looked to his left.

He frowned.

'Is something wrong?' Grace asked as she followed the line of his gaze.

He shook his head and rubbed a hand over his eyes. 'I must be seeing things.'

'Seeing what?'

Julian looked back through the crowd, searching for the tall blond man he'd seen out of the corner of his eye. Though he'd barely caught a glimpse of the man, he would have sworn it was Kyrian of Thrace.

Standing an easy six foot five, Kyrian had always been a hard man to miss in a crowd, and he'd owned a very distinctive and deadly swagger.

But Kyrian here, in this time, was impossible. It must be the madness returning to him – it was making him see things.

'Nothing,' he said.

Putting the matter out of his mind, he smiled at her.

The next song was slow. Julian pulled her into his arms and held her close as they swayed gently to the beat. Grace wrapped her arms around his neck and laid her head on his chest where she just breathed in the warm, sandalwood scent of his body. She didn't know what it was about his smell that literally turned her inside out, but it made her mouth water for him.

With his cheek against the top of her head, he stroked her hair as she listened to his heart pounding. She could have stayed like that forever.

But all too soon, the song ended. And after two more fast

ones, Grace had to sit down. She just didn't have Julian's stamina.

As they headed to the table, she realized Julian wasn't even breathing heavily, but his brow was damp from sweat.

Julian held the chair for her. Sitting close beside her, he reached for his beer and took a deep drink.

'Julian!' Selena said with a laugh. 'I had no idea you had moves on you like that.'

Bill rolled his eyes. 'Lusting again, Lane?'

Selena punched her husband in the belly. 'You know better than that. You're the only boy-toy I want.'

Bill cast a skeptical look to Julian. 'Yeah, right.'

Grace saw the shadow fall over Julian's face. 'You okay?' she asked.

He smiled those dimples at her and she forgot her question.

They sat in silence, listening to the band while she and Julian fed each other nachos.

As Grace pulled her hand away from his lips, Julian captured it, then brought it back to his mouth to lick a bit of cheese from her fingertips. His tongue brushed against her skin, setting fire to her entire body.

Grace laughed as desire spread through her. How she really wished they had stayed home. She would love to strip Julian's clothes off his body and lick cheese from it for the rest of the night!

She was definitely going to add Cheez Whiz to her grocery list.

His eyes glowing, Julian moved her hand to his lap, and nuzzled her neck just a bit before pulling back and taking another drink of beer.

'Here, Selena,' Bill said, drawing Grace's attention back to them. He handed her a napkin. 'You might want to wipe the drool off your chin.'

Selena rolled her eyes at him. 'Hey, Gracie, I need a bathroom break. C'mon.'

Julian leaned back to let her rise. He watched Grace vanish into the crowd, then almost on cue, women started moving in.

His stomach drew tight. Why did they always have to gravitate toward him? Just once, he'd like to be able to sit in peace, and not have to fend off the hands of women who didn't even bother to learn his name before they started groping.

'Hey, baby,' an attractive blonde cooed as she stepped up first. 'I like the way you dance. Why don't–'

'I'm here with someone,' Julian said, narrowing his eyes on her in warning.

'You and *her*?' the woman laughed while indicating the direction Grace had vanished with her thumb. 'C'mon. I thought you'd lost a bet or something.'

'I thought she was his pity date,' another woman said as she and a black-haired friend joined them.

Two men appeared out of the crowd. 'What are the three of you doing back here?' the men asked their dates.

The women passed a regretful look to Julian.

'Nothing,' the blonde purred as she cast one last glance at Julian, then turned around and left.

The men glared at Julian.

He arched a taunting brow at them as he took a casual drink of beer. They must have realized the stupidity of fighting him, because they gathered their women and left.

Julian sighed in disgust. No matter the time period, some things never changed.

'Hey,' Bill said, leaning forward over the table. 'I know you've been spending a lot of time with my wife lately, you better not be moving in on my territory. You hear me?'

Julian took a long, deep breath. Not him, too. 'In case you haven't noticed, my only interest is in Grace.'

'Yeah, right,' Bill sneered. 'Don't get me wrong, I like Grace a lot, but I'm not an idiot. I can't believe you're the kind of guy who goes for a cheeseburger when there are so many filet mignons waiting for you.'

'I personally don't give a damn what you believe.'

Grace hesitated as she and Selena rejoined Julian and Bill. The tension around Julian was tangible. His grip on the beer bottle so tight, she wasn't sure how he kept from shattering the glass.

'Hey, Bill,' Selena said as she draped her arms over her husband's neck. 'You wouldn't mind if I had a dance with Julian, would you?'

'Hell, yes, I'd mind.'

Immediately, Julian excused himself and went to the bar. Grace quickly followed.

He ordered another beer as she came up behind him.

'You okay?' she asked.

'Fine.'

He didn't sound fine. He definitely didn't look fine. 'You know, I can tell you're not being honest with me. Now, 'fess up, Julian. What's wrong?'

'We should leave.'

'Why?'

He cast a glance over to Selena and Bill. 'I just think it would be wise.'

'Why?'

He growled low in his throat.

Before Julian could respond, three men came up beside him, and by the looks on their faces, Grace could tell they weren't happy.

Worse, Julian appeared to be the source of their ire.

The biggest was a body-builder monstrosity who was about three inches shorter than Julian, but quite a bit thicker and wider. He curled his lip as he ran his gaze over Julian's back. And it wasn't until that instant that Grace recognized him.

Paul.

Her heart hammered. Physically, he'd changed a lot over the years. His face was broader, with premature wrinkles around his eyes, and he'd lost a great deal of hair. But he still had the same sneer.

'He was the one messing with Amber,' one of his flunkies said.

A deadly calm fell over Julian, and it sent a shiver down her spine. There was no telling what Julian might do, and judging by what she saw, Paul hadn't changed nearly as much inside as he had outside. A frat-boy poster-child, Paul had always traveled with an entourage. He believed in making a show of power in everything he did. That macho ego of his wouldn't let him leave until he pushed Julian into a fight.

She only hoped her general had more sense than to fall for such a stunt.

'Do you need something?' Julian asked without looking at Paul or his friends.

Paul laughed and slapped one of his friends across the chest. 'What kind of faggot accent is that? I thought you told me Pretty-boy here was after my girl. From the look and sound of him, I'd say he was after one of you.'

Julian turned and cut a glare to Paul that would have made anyone with sense back away.

Paul, of course, had no sense. He'd never had.

'What's the matter, Pretty-boy?' Paul mocked. 'Did I

287

offend you?' He looked at his friends and shook his head. 'Just what I thought, he ain't nothing but a pretty, faggoty coward.'

Julian laughed, but the tone of it was more evil than happy.

'C'mon, Julian,' Grace said, taking his arm before things got any worse. 'Let's leave.'

Paul turned that sneer on her, until he recognized her. 'Well, well, Grace Alexander. It's been a while.' He clapped the short, dark-haired man next to him on the back. 'Hey, Tom, you remember Grace from college, don't you? Her little white panties put me over the top of our bet.'

Julian froze at the words.

Grace could feel the old pain swell, but she refused to show it. She would never again give Paul that power over her.

'No wonder he was after Amber,' Paul continued. 'He probably wanted to try a woman who doesn't cry all over him when he screws her.'

Julian whirled on Paul so fast that she could barely follow the motion. Paul swung. Julian ducked and sent a fist into Paul's ribs that knocked him five feet into the crowd.

Cursing, he ran back at Julian.

Julian moved to the side, tripped Paul and flipped him into the air.

Paul landed on his back.

Before he could move, Julian placed his foot on Paul's throat, and smiled a cold, small smile that chilled her all the way to her toes.

Paul grabbed Julian's shoe in both hands and tried to remove it. He shook from the effort of it, but still Julian kept his foot where it was.

'Did you know,' Julian asked in a casual tone that was

truly terrifying, 'that it only takes five pounds to completely collapse your esophagus?'

Paul's eyes and arms bulged as Julian increased the weight on his neck.

'Please, man,' Paul begged as he tried to push Julian's shoe off his throat. 'Please don't hurt me, okay?'

Grace held her breath in terror as Julian applied even more pressure.

Tom took a step forward.

'Do it,' Julian said in warning, 'and I'll rip your heart out and feed it to your friend.'

Grace froze at the deadly look on Julian's face. This wasn't the tender man who made love to her at night. This was the face of the general who had once laid waste to Rome's finest.

There was no doubt in her mind that Julian could, and would, carry out that threat. Judging by the pallor of Tom's face as he stepped back, she could tell he knew it, too.

'Please,' Paul begged again as tears fell down his face. 'Please don't hurt me.'

Grace swallowed as those haunting words tore through her. They were the same ones she had once cried in Paul's bed.

It was then Julian met her gaze. She saw the fury in Julian's eyes, as well as his desire to kill Paul for her.

'Let him go, Julian,' she said softly. 'His entire body isn't worth one molecule of yours.'

Julian looked down at Paul and narrowed his eyes. 'Where I come from, we butchered worthless cowards like you just for practice.'

Just as she was sure Julian was going to kill Paul, he stepped back. 'Get up.'

Rubbing his throat, Paul rose slowly to his feet.

Julian's cold, dead look actually made Paul flinch. 'You owe my lady an apology.'

Paul wiped his nose on the back of his hand. 'I'm sorry.'

'Say it like you mean it,' Julian said quietly.

'I'm sorry, Grace. Really. I'm very, very sorry.'

Before Grace could respond, Julian draped a possessive arm over her shoulders and walked her out of the club.

They didn't speak until they reached her car, but Grace could sense something was profoundly wrong with Julian. His entire body was tense, like a spring coiled way too tight.

'I wish you had let me kill him,' Julian said as she fumbled in her jeans pocket for her keys.

'Julian—'

'You have no idea how much it hurt for me to walk away from him. I am not the kind of man who just walks away.' He slammed his hand onto the top of her car, then spun around and growled like a cornered lion. 'Dammit, Grace. I once fed on the entrails of men like him. And I went from that to . . . '

Julian hesitated as two thousand years of repressed memories flooded through him. He saw himself as the respected leader he'd been. The hero of Macedonia. The man who had once made entire legions of Romans surrender as soon as they recognized his standard.

And then he saw himself as what he had become. An empty shell. A coveted pet, performing at the beck and call of his summoner.

For two thousand years he had lived without emotions, lived without speaking more than a handful of words.

He had gone into survival mode. And he had lost himself to it.

Until Grace had reached out and found the human side of him . . .

Grace watched a myriad of emotions cross Julian's face. Anger, confusion, horror, and finally agony. She walked to his side of the car, but he refused to let her touch him.

'Don't you see?' he said, his tone raw from his emotions. 'I don't know who I am anymore. I knew who I was in Macedonia, and then I became this.' He held his arm up so that she could see the words Priapus had burned into his forearm. 'And then you changed that,' he said, looking at her.

The anguish in his eyes tore through her. 'Why did you have to change me, Grace? Why couldn't you have left me as I was? I'd taught myself to feel nothing anymore. I just came, did what I was told, and left. I no longer wanted anything. And now ...' He looked around him like a man caught in the middle of a nightmare he couldn't escape.

She reached for him. 'Julian–'

Shaking his head, he stepped away from her grasp. 'No!' He raked his hand through his hair. 'I don't know where I belong anymore. You don't understand.'

'Then tell me,' she begged.

'How can I tell you what it's like to walk between two worlds? To be despised by both? I am neither man nor god, I am a hybrid abomination. You have no idea how I grew up. My mother passed me off to my father who passed me off to his wife who passed me around to anyone who could get me out of her sight. And for the last twenty centuries, I have been bartered and sold. I have spent my entire life searching for someplace to call home. Someone who would want *me*, and not my face, or my body.' The tormented look in his eyes burned her.

'I want you, Julian.'

'No you don't. How could you?'

She gaped at his question. 'How could I not? My God,

I've never in my life wanted to be with anyone as much as I want to be with you.'

'It's lust you feel.'

Now, that made her angry. How dare he dismiss her feelings as something so trivial. Her feelings for him ran much deeper than mere lust, they reached all the way to her soul. 'Don't tell me what I feel. I'm not a child.'

Julian shook his head, unable to believe her words. It was the curse. It had to be. No one could love him. No one ever had; not since the moment he'd been born.

For Grace to love him . . .

It would be a miracle. It would be . . .

Pure bliss. And he had not been born to feel bliss.

You will suffer as no man ever has.

This was just another trick of the gods. Another cruel hoax sent to punish him.

He was tired now. Weary and exhausted from the fight. He just wanted peace from the pain. A haven from the frightening feelings he felt every time he looked at her.

Grace clenched her teeth at the denial she saw in Julian's eyes. But then, who could blame him?

He had been hurt so many times. But somehow, some way, she was going to prove to him just how much he meant to her.

She had to. Because losing him would kill her.

Chapter Fifteen

Julian kept a distance between them for the rest of the weekend. No matter what Grace tried to do to break through the intangible wall around him, he pushed her away.

He wouldn't even let her read to him.

Disheartened, she went to work on Monday morning, but she shouldn't have bothered. She couldn't focus on anything except celestial blue eyes filled with unshared turmoil.

'Grace Alexander?'

Grace looked up from her desk to see an incredibly beautiful blond woman in her early twenties standing in the doorway. Looking as if she'd just stepped off a fashion runway in Europe, the statuesque beauty was dressed in a red silk Armani suit with matching hose and shoes.

'I'm sorry,' Grace said to the woman. 'I'm closed. If you want to call tomorrow–'

'Do I look like I need a sex therapist?'

Offhand, no. But then, Grace had learned a long time ago not to make snap judgments about people's problems.

Uninvited, the woman sauntered into her office with a graceful, arrogant stride that seemed oddly familiar. She walked over to the wall where Grace's certificates and degrees were hung.

'Impressive,' she said, but her tone implied otherwise.

She turned to give Grace a thorough once-over, and by the sneer on her lovely face, Grace could tell the woman found her seriously lacking. 'You're not pretty enough for him, you know. Too short, too wide. And wherever did you find *that* dress?'

Completely offended, Grace went rigid. 'I beg your pardon?'

The woman ignored her question. 'Tell me, doesn't it just pain you to be around a man who looks like Julian, knowing if he had a choice, he'd never want to be with *you*? He's so lean and graceful. Strong and fierce. I know you've never had a man like him want you, and you never will again.'

Stunned, Grace couldn't speak.

She didn't have to; the woman continued without pausing. 'His father was like that, too. Imagine Julian with black hair. A little shorter and stockier, and not nearly as refined. Still, that man had a way with his hands that was ... mmm ... '

Aphrodite smiled reflectively, her eyes unfocused. 'Of course, Diokles was scarred abysmally from his battles. He had this one horrible mark that ran the whole length of his left cheek.'

Her gaze narrowed in anger. 'I'll never forget the day he took a dagger to Julian's face, trying to scar it like his. I would say Diokles lived to regret that transgression, but I made certain he didn't. Julian is physical perfection, and I shall never let anyone mar the beauty I gave him.'

294

The cold, calculating look Aphrodite delivered to her chilled Grace all the way to her bones.

'I *won't* share my son with you.'

The possessiveness of Aphrodite's words ignited Grace's anger. How dare she show up now and say such a thing. 'If Julian means so much to you, then why did you abandon him?'

Aphrodite glared at her. 'Do you think I had a choice? Zeus refused ambrosia to him, and no mortal can live on Olympus. Before I could even protest, Hermes swept him out of my arms and took him to his father.'

Grace saw the horror on Aphrodite's face as she relived that moment.

'My grief at his loss was beyond human measure. Inconsolable, I locked myself away, and when I was finally able to emerge, fourteen years had passed on earth. I barely recognized the baby I had suckled. And he *hated* me.'

Aphrodite's eyes turned shiny as if she were fighting back tears. 'You have no idea what it's like to be a mother, and have the child you carried in your womb curse your very name.'

Grace sympathized with her grief, but it was Julian she loved, and Julian's pain that concerned her most. 'Did you ever try to tell him how you feel?'

'Of course I did,' Aphrodite snapped. 'I sent Eros to him, offering him my gifts. He sent them back with words no son should ever utter about his mother.'

'He was hurt.'

'So was I,' Aphrodite shrieked. Her entire body shook with her rage.

Apprehensive and more than a bit scared of what an angry goddess could do to her, Grace watched as Aphrodite closed her eyes, took a deep breath and calmed herself.

When Aphrodite spoke again, her tone and body were rigid and sharp. 'Even so, I sent Eros back with more offerings for Julian. He spurned every one. I was forced to watch as Julian vindictively swore his loyalty and service to Athena.' She spat the name as if she despised it.

'It was in *her* name he conquered cities with the birth gifts I had bestowed upon him; the might of Ares, the temperance of Apollo, the blessings of the Muses and Graces. I even dipped him in the river Styx to make sure no mortal weapon could ever kill or scar him, and unlike Thetis with Achilles, I coated his ankles so that he would have absolutely no vulnerable spots.'

Aphrodite shook her head as if she still couldn't believe what he'd done. 'I did everything in my power for that boy, and he showed no gratitude to me. No respect. Finally, I gave up trying. Since he refused my love, I made sure no one would *ever* love him.'

Grace's heart stopped at the selfish words. 'What did you do?'

Aphrodite lifted her chin haughtily like a queen who was proud of her cold-blooded war. 'I cursed him the way he cursed me. I made sure no mortal woman can look at him without wanting his body, and no mortal man can be around him without feeling his heart swell in envy.'

Grace couldn't believe her ears. How could a mother be so cruel?

And as soon as that thought finished, another, even more horrible one ripped through her. 'You're the reason Penelope died, aren't you?'

'No, Julian did that one himself. Granted, I was enraged when Eros told me what he had done for his brother, that Julian had gone to him and not me.

'Since I couldn't undo Eros's love arrow, I decided to dull

its effects. What Julian had with Penelope was empty, and he knew it.'

Aphrodite moved to the window to stare out onto the city. 'Had Julian ever come to me, I would have lifted it from her. But he didn't. I watched him go to her night after night, taking her over and over again, and I felt his restlessness, his anguish over the fact she didn't truly love him. Still, he denied and cursed me.

'It was my tears over his betrayal that first set Priapus against him. Priapus has always been the most loyal of my sons. As soon as I saw Priapus was out for Julian's blood, I should have stopped it. But I didn't. I was hoping Priapus's anger would make Julian seek me out. Ask for my help.'

She clenched her teeth. 'But he never did.'

Grace felt for her, but it didn't change what she'd done to her own son. 'How did Julian get cursed?'

Aphrodite swallowed. 'It started the night Athena told Priapus that he had no man as courageous and strong as Julian. She dared him to pit his best general against hers. Two days later, I watched Julian ride into battle, and knew he wouldn't lose. When he beat the Romans back, Priapus became enraged. Once Eros let slip to him what he'd done, Priapus immediately went after Iason and Penelope. I had no idea what the repercussions of that event would be.'

Aphrodite wrapped her trembling arms around herself. 'I never meant for the children to die. You can't imagine how many times a day I ache over what I let happen.'

'There was no way you could have stopped it?'

Aphrodite shook her head sadly. 'Even my powers are limited by the Fates. When Julian started for my temple after their deaths, I held my breath, thinking that finally he would turn to me. Then, he saw that slut wearing Priapus's robes. She threw herself at him and begged him to take her

297

virginity before the ceremony where Priapus would claim her. Even then, Julian tried to get past her, but she wouldn't let him. Had he been thinking clearly, I know he would have denied her.'

Aphrodite's face darkened in rage. 'If not for Alexandria, I would have had my son that day. I know he would have called on me. But it was too late. The moment he released himself in her, it was too late.'

'And still you refused to help Julian?'

'How could I choose one son over another?'

Grace was aghast at her question. 'Isn't that what you did the minute you let Julian be placed inside a scroll?'

Aphrodite's eyes flared with such malice, Grace took a step back. 'Julian was the one who refused *me*. All he had to do was call for my help and I would have given it to him.'

Grace couldn't believe what she was hearing. For a goddess, Aphrodite was incredibly selfish and short-sighted. 'All this tragedy because the two of you refuse to acknowledge each other. I can't believe you'd make Julian strong, and then curse him for the strength you gave him. Instead of waiting for him, sending others on your behalf, did it never occur to you to go yourself?'

Aphrodite raked her with an indignant glare. 'I am the Goddess of Love and you would have me crawl? Have you any idea what an embarrassment it is to be me and have my own son hate me?'

'An embarrassment for you? You had the entire world to love you. Julian had no one.'

Aphrodite took an angry step forward. 'Stay away from him. I'm warning you.'

'Why? Why would you warn me and not Penelope?'

'Because he didn't love *her*.'

Grace froze at the words. 'Are you saying–'

Aphrodite vanished.

'Oh, come on!' Grace shouted at the ceiling. 'You can't just poof out in the middle of a conversation!'

'Grace?'

She jumped at Beth's voice. Whirling around, she saw her peeping in through the door.

'Who are you talking to?' Beth asked.

Grace gestured around the room, then thought better of telling Beth the truth. 'Myself.'

Beth looked skeptically at her. 'You always yell at yourself?'

'Sometimes.'

Beth arched one dark brow. 'Sounds like we need to have a session,' she said as she walked off.

Disregarding her, Grace wasted no time gathering her things. She wanted to get home to Julian.

As soon as she opened the door to her house, Grace knew something was wrong. Julian wasn't there to greet her.

'Julian?' she called.

'Upstairs.'

She dropped her keys and mail on the table and ascended the steps two at a time.

'You're not going to believe who stopped by ... ' Her voice trailed off as she reached the door of her bedroom and saw Julian with one hand cuffed to her bed. He was lying in the middle of the mattress, shirtless, with his brow damp.

'What are you doing?' she asked as dread consumed her.

'I can't fight it anymore, Grace,' he said, his breathing labored.

'You have to.'

He shook his head. 'I need you to shackle my other hand. I can't reach to do it.'

'Julian–'

He cut her words off with a bitter, harsh laugh. 'How ironic is this? You, I have to beg to chain me, while the others did it freely within hours of my incarnation.'

His gaze bored into hers. 'Do it, Grace. I couldn't live with myself if I hurt you.'

Her throat tight, she crossed the room to where he lay.

When she was close enough, he reached out and cupped her cheek with his free hand. He pulled her to his lips and kissed her so thoroughly she thought she might pass out from it.

It was fierce, demanding, a kiss of longing. And one of promise.

He nipped her lips with his teeth as he pulled away. 'Do it.'

She ran the silver cuff around her bolster.

It was only then Julian relaxed. Until that moment, she hadn't realized just how tense he'd been the past week. He laid his head back on her pillows and took a deep, ragged breath.

Grace reached out and touched his damp brow. 'Good Lord,' she breathed. He was so hot it practically singed her skin. 'Can I do anything?'

'No, but thanks for asking.'

Grace moved to her dresser to get her clothes. As she started unbuttoning her blouse, Julian stopped her. 'Please don't do that in front of me. If I see your breasts ... ' He threw his head back as if someone had stuck a hot brand to him.

Grace realized just how comfortable she had become with him. 'I'm sorry,' she said.

She went to the bathroom to change, then made a cold compress.

She returned to the bedroom to bathe his fevered brow. She brushed her hand through his sweat-dampened hair. 'You're on fire.'

'I know. It feels like I'm lying on a bed of coals.'

He hissed as she drew the cool cloth over his skin.

'You haven't told me about your day,' he said breathlessly.

Grace choked on the happiness and love that filled her. Every day, he asked her that. Every day, she looked forward to coming home to be with him.

She had no idea what she would do when he was gone.

Forcing herself not to think about it, she focused her attention on taking care of him.

'Not much to tell,' she whispered. She didn't want to burden him with what his mother had said. Not while he was like this. He'd been hurt enough in his life; she had no desire to make it any worse.

'Are you hungry?' she asked.

'No.'

Grace settled down by his side. She spent the night alternating between reading to him and bathing his feverish skin.

Julian didn't sleep that night. He couldn't. All he could feel was Grace's skin on his, smell her sweet floral scent. It invaded his head and made his senses reel. Every nerve in his body screamed for her.

Grinding his teeth, he clenched the silver chains in his fists and fought down the swirling darkness that tried to claim him. He didn't want to surrender to it.

He didn't want to close his eyes and miss a minute of being with Grace while he was still sane and whole. If he let the darkness take him, he might not wake up from it until he was in the book. Alone.

'I can't lose her,' he whispered. The very thought of it shredded what little of his heart he still possessed.

The clock in the hallway struck three. Grace had fallen asleep a short time ago. She lay with her head and hand on his belly, her breath falling gently across his stomach.

He could feel her hair tickle his skin, her warmth seeping into his soul.

What he wouldn't give to be able to touch her.

Closing his eyes, he laid his head back and allowed himself to dream for the first time in centuries. He dreamed of nights spent with Grace. Of days laughing by her side.

He dreamed of a day when he could love her as she deserved to be loved. A day when he would be free to give himself to her. He dreamed of having a home with her.

Most of all, he dreamed of children with happy, gray eyes and sweet, impish smiles.

Julian was still dreaming of those things when the morning light broke and the clock struck six and Grace woke up.

She rubbed her face against his chest, nuzzling him in a way that was sheer torture.

'Good morning,' she said, smiling.

'Good morning.'

She bit her lips as she ran her gaze over his body, her brow wrinkled by concern. 'Are you sure we have to do this? Can I not let you up for a little bit?'

'No!' he said emphatically.

She picked up her phone and dialed Beth. 'I'm not going to be in for a few days, can you take some of my clients?'

Julian frowned at her words. 'You're not going to work?' he asked as soon as she hung up.

Grace couldn't believe he'd ask her such a question. 'And leave you here like this?'

'I'll be all right.'

She looked at him as if he'd lost his mind. 'What if something happened?'

'What?'

'The house could burn down, or someone could come in and do who knows what to you while you're helpless to stop them.'

Julian didn't argue. He just relished the fact that she was willing to stay with him.

By mid-afternoon, Grace could see how much worse the curse had become. Every inch of his body was coated with sweat. The muscles in his arms were taut and he seldom spoke. When he did, it was through clenched teeth.

Still, he would smile at her, his eyes warm and encouraging as she watched his muscles bunch and flex while he suffered through whatever seemed to be gnawing at him.

She kept bathing him, but as soon as she placed the cloth to his skin the cloth would grow so hot she could barely touch it.

By nightfall, he was delirious.

Helpless, she watched as Julian writhed and cursed as if some unseen person were flaying every inch of his body. She'd never seen anything like it. He was struggling so hard, she was afraid he would break the bed.

'I can't stand this,' she whispered. Running downstairs, she called Selena.

An hour later, Grace let Selena and her sister, Tiyana, in. With jet-black hair and blue eyes, Tiyana looked very little like Selena. One of the few white voodoo high priestesses, Tiyana owned a local voodoo shop, and gave cemetery tours on Friday nights.

'I can't thank you enough for coming over,' Grace said as she closed the door behind them.

'No problem,' Selena said.

Tiyana held a drum under one arm, and was dressed in a plain brown dress. 'Where is he?'

Grace led them upstairs.

Tiyana took one step into the room and froze at the sight of Julian writhing on the bed as he cursed the entire Greek pantheon.

Her face paled. 'I can't do anything for him.'

'Tiyana,' Selena chastised. 'You have to try.'

Her eyes wide with fright, Tiyana shook her head. 'You want my advice? Seal up this room and leave him until he goes back where he came from. There's an evil so strong watching over him that I don't dare mess with it.' She looked at Selena. 'Can't you feel the malevolence?'

Grace trembled at the words, her heart pounding. 'Selena?' she asked, desperately needing some way to soothe him. There had to be something they could do.

'You know I can't help,' Selena said. 'My spells never work.'

No! her mind screamed. They couldn't leave it like this.

Grace looked at Julian as he fought against his restraints. 'Is there someone else we can call?'

'No,' Tiyana said. 'In fact, I can't stay here. No offense, this creeps me out.' She gave a flat look to Selena. 'And you know the kind of freaky stuff I deal with on a daily basis.'

'I'm sorry, Gracie,' Selena said, rubbing her hand over Grace's arm. 'I'll do some research and see what I can find out, okay?'

Her throat tight, Grace had no choice but to show them out.

Closing the door, she leaned against it wearily.

What was she going to do?

She couldn't just accept the fact that there was nothing to be done for Julian. There had to be something that could relieve his pain. Something she hadn't thought of.

Heading upstairs, she returned to Julian.

'Grace?' It was an agonized cry that wrenched her heart.

'I'm right here, baby,' she said, touching his brow.

He let out a fierce growl like an animal caught in a trap as he threw his body toward her.

Terrified, she stepped away from the bed.

Her legs shaking, Grace went to her closet and found a copy of *The Odyssey*. She pulled her rocking chair next to the bed and started reading.

It seemed to soothe him. He didn't thrash about quite so severely.

Days went by, and with every one that passed, Grace's hope continued to wilt. Julian had been right. There was no way they could break the curse if he didn't come out of this madness.

Worse, she couldn't stand watching him suffer, hour after hour, without any relief. No wonder he hated his mother. How could Aphrodite allow him to go through this without doing something for him?

And he had suffered like this for centuries.

Grace was at her wits' end. 'How could you!' she shouted angrily at the ceiling.

'Eros!' she called. 'Can you hear me? Athena? Someone? How can you let him go through this and do nothing? If you have any love for him at all, please help me help him.'

As she expected, no one answered.

Grace leaned her head into her hand as she tried to think of something else she could try. Surely, there ...

A light flashed in the room.

Startled, Grace looked up to see Aphrodite materializing next to the bed. She couldn't have been more stunned to find a donkey in her house.

Aphrodite's face was pale and strained as she saw her son convulsing in absolute agony. She reached a hand out to him, then drew it back sharply. Balling her hand into a fist, she dropped it to her side.

It was then she looked at Grace. 'I do love him,' she said quietly.

'I do, too.'

Aphrodite's gaze fell to the floor, but Grace could still see her inner turmoil. 'If I release him you'll take him from me forever. If I don't release him, we'll both lose him.'

Aphrodite locked gazes with her. 'I thought about what you said, and you were right. I made him strong and I should never have punished him for it. All I ever wanted was for him to call me mother.' She looked at her son. 'I just wanted you to love me, Julian. Just a little.'

Grace swallowed when she saw the pain on Aphrodite's face as she touched Julian's hand.

Julian hissed as if her touch burned his skin.

Aphrodite let go. 'Grace, promise me you'll take good care of him.'

'As long as he lets me, I will. I promise.'

Aphrodite nodded, then placed her hand on Julian's brow. He threw his head back as if he'd been struck by lightning. Aphrodite leaned over him and kissed him ever so lightly on the lips.

Instantly, his entire body went limp.

The handcuffs fell open, and still Julian didn't move. Grace's heart stopped as she realized he wasn't breathing. Terrified, she reached a trembling hand out to him.

He took a deep, convulsing breath.

Grace saw the familiar longing in Aphrodite's eyes as she held her hand out to a son who didn't even know she was there. It was the same look of yearning she saw so often in Julian's eyes when he didn't know she was watching him.

How could two people need each other so desperately, and yet not be able to reach out to one another?

Aphrodite vanished the instant Julian opened his eyes.

Grace moved to his side. He was shaking so badly, his teeth chattered. His fever gone, now his skin was as cold as ice.

She pulled the blankets off the floor and covered him up.

'What happened?' he asked, his voice unsteady.

'Your mother freed you.'

Julian stared in amazement of her words. 'My mother? She was here?'

Grace nodded. 'She was worried about you.'

Julian couldn't believe his hearing. Was it possible?

But why would his mother help him now after all the times she'd turned her back on his suffering and left him to it? It didn't make sense.

His frown deepening, Julian started to slide off the bed.

'No you don't,' she said sharply. 'I just got you back, and I–'

'I really have to go to the bathroom,' he said, interrupting her.

'Oh.' Grace helped him from the bed.

His legs were so weak, he needed her support to help him down the hallway. Julian closed his eyes as he inhaled the sweet smell of her. Afraid of hurting her, he tried not to put too much of his weight on her shoulders.

His heart warmed at the way she helped him, at the feel of her arms wrapped around his waist as she walked him down her hallway past the grandfather clock.

His Grace. How would he ever be able to let her go?

After he relieved himself, she ran a hot bath for him and helped him into it.

Julian stared at Grace while she bathed him. He couldn't believe she'd stayed by his side all this time. He didn't remember much about the last few days, but he remembered the sound of her voice soothing him through the darkness.

He'd heard her calling to him. And at times, he was sure he'd felt her hand on his skin, pulling him back from the madness.

Her touch had been his salvation.

Closing his eyes, he enjoyed the sensation of her hands sliding over his body as she bathed him. Down his chest, his arms, his stomach. And when her hand accidentally brushed his erection, he jerked from the force of it.

How he wanted her.

'Kiss me,' he breathed.

'Is it safe?'

He smiled at her. 'If I could move, you'd already be in this tub with me. I assure you, at the moment I'm as helpless as a babe.'

She licked her lips tentatively as she brushed her right hand over his. Her touch was gentle and warm, and she stared at his mouth as if she could devour it. That look went a long way in banishing the chill from him.

She leaned forward and kissed him deeply. Julian moaned at the contact, wanting more. Needing more of her touch.

To his amazement, he got it.

Grace left his lips only long enough to peel her clothes from her body until she stood naked before him. Slowly, seductively, she crawled into the tub with him, straddling his waist.

Julian moaned at the feel of her hairs on his stomach. She returned to his lips with a kiss so hot, it scorched him.

Damn it, he couldn't even hold her! His arms wouldn't budge on their own. And he desperately wanted to hold her tight against him.

She must have felt his frustration, for she pulled back with a smile. 'It's my turn to care for you,' she whispered before burying her lips against his throat.

Julian closed his eyes as she trailed her kisses down his chest. When she reached his nipple, he reeled from the pleasure of her tongue teasing and suckling him. Never had anything touched him more than her actions. He couldn't remember the last time someone had truly made love to *him*.

And no one had ever been so thorough. So giving.

He sucked his breath in sharply as she reached down between their bodies to stroke him. 'I wish I could make love to you,' he whispered.

She lifted her head to meet his gaze. 'You do that every time you touch me.'

Somehow, he found the strength to wrap his shaking arms around her and pull her against his chest. He claimed her lips with his own.

He heard her pull the stopper out with her foot as she deepened her kiss, all the while her hand tormented him with light, gentle strokes against his swollen shaft.

His head reeled from the sensation of her touching him there. He lived for her touch. Craved it in a way that was indefinable.

Once the water had drained from the tub, she left his lips to blaze a scorching trail down his body. Julian let his head fall back against the edge of the tub as she licked his stomach and swirled her tongue over to his hipbone.

Then, to his utter shock, she took him into her mouth.

Julian growled as he cupped her head in his hands and savored the feel of her tongue and mouth swirling around him. No woman had ever done that before. They had only taken from him, none of them had ever given.

Not until Grace.

Her touch shattered the last bit of his will, the last bit of his resistance to her. His entire body shook from the warmth of her actions.

'I'm sorry,' she said, pulling back from him. 'You're so cold, you're shivering again.'

'I'm not shivering from the cold,' he said, his voice hoarse. 'I'm shivering from you.'

Her smile pierced his heart as she dropped her head and returned to her relentless assault on him.

By the time she finished, he felt as if he'd been tortured all over again. He couldn't have been any more satisfied had he actually climaxed.

She helped him out of the tub. Still his limbs shook. And he had to lean on her to get to the bedroom.

She laid him down gently and covered him with all her blankets. She placed a tender kiss on his brow as she tucked the covers around him.

'Are you hungry?'

All he could do was nod.

Grace left him long enough to warm a bowl of soup. But by the time she returned, he was sound asleep.

She set the bowl on the nightstand, then climbed into bed behind him. She curled her body around his and faded off to sleep, too.

It was three days before Julian's strength came back. The entire time, Grace stayed with him. Helping him.

He found it hard to fathom her strength and devotion. All

his life, he'd waited for her. And as every day passed, he realized just how much he loved her. How much he needed her.

'I have to tell her,' he said as he toweled himself dry. He couldn't let another day pass without her knowing just how much she had come to mean to him.

Leaving the bathroom, Julian headed to the bedroom where Grace was on the phone with Selena.

'Of course I didn't tell him what his mother said. Jeez!'

Julian took a step back, and leaned against the wall as Grace continued talking.

'What was I supposed to say? Oh, Julian, by the way, your mother threatened my life?'

He felt as if someone had delivered a staggering blow to his solar plexus. His vision turning dark, he entered the bedroom. 'When did you speak to my mother?' he demanded.

Grace looked up, shocked. 'Uh, Lanie, I need to go. Bye.' She hung up the phone.

'When did you speak to her?' he asked again.

Grace shrugged nonchalantly. 'It was the day you went psycho on me.'

'What did she say?'

She shrugged sheepishly. 'It wasn't really a threat. She just said she wouldn't share you with me.'

Rage coursed through him. How dare she! Who the hell did his mother think she was to make any demand on him or Grace?

What a fool he'd been to ever think his mother had softened her heart where he was concerned.

When would he learn?

'Julian,' Grace said, rising to meet him in front of the bed. 'She changed her mind. When she came here to release you—'

'Don't, Grace,' he said, interrupting her. 'I know her a lot better than you do.'

And he knew what his mother was capable of. Her ruth-lessness made his father's pale in comparison.

His heart heavy, he knew he could never tell Grace what was in his heart.

Worse, he knew he couldn't stay with her. Ever. If he had learned anything it was that the gods would never let him live in peace.

How long before one of them hurt her? How long before Priapus used her to get back at him? Or his mother came to wreak her vengeance on both of them?

Sooner or later, he would pay for his happiness. He had no doubt. And the thought of Grace suffering . . .

No. It was a chance he refused to take.

The days flew by as they spent as much time together as possible.

Julian taught Grace classical Greek culture, and very interesting ways to enjoy Reddi-wip and chocolate sauce, and Grace taught him strip Monopoly, and how to read English.

And after several more driving lessons, and a new clutch, she realized Julian was a hopeless driver.

It seemed to her that only a few days had gone by and yet the last day of the month came so fast that it terrified her.

Even worse, the night before it arrived, she made the most startling discovery of all.

Julian was that one person she couldn't live without.

When she thought of her life returning to what it had been before him, she ached so deeply in her heart that she was sure she would die from it.

But in the end, she knew the choice was his and his alone.

'Please, Julian,' she whispered to him as he slept beside her. 'Don't leave me.'

Chapter Sixteen

Neither one spoke much the entire day. In fact, Julian avoided Grace entirely.

That more than anything told her what decision he'd made.

Her heart was broken. How could he leave her after all they'd been through? After all they'd shared?

She couldn't stand the thought of losing him. Life without him would be unbearable.

At sunset, Grace found him sitting in the rocking chair on her deck, watching the sun as if for the last time. His face was so stern that she barely recognized it as belonging to the playful man she had grown to love so much.

Finally, she couldn't stand the silence any longer. 'I don't want you to leave me. I want you to stay here in my time. I can take care of you, Julian. I make plenty of money, and I can teach you anything you want to know.'

'I can't stay,' he said between clenched teeth. 'Don't you understand? Everyone who has ever been close to me has been punished by the gods. Iason, Penelope, Callista,

Atolycus.' He looked at her as if dazed. 'Dear Zeus, they *crucified* Kyrian.'

'It will be different this time.'

He rose to his feet and gave her a hard stare. 'That's right. It will be different. I'm not going to stay here and watch you die because of me.'

He walked past her, into the house.

Grace clenched her hands into fists, wanting to strangle him. 'You stubborn ... man!'

How could he be so impossible?

It was then she felt the diamond of her mother's wedding ring cutting into her palm. Opening her fist, she took one long look. She was through letting the past haunt her. For the first time in a long time, she had a future to look forward to. One that filled her with happiness.

And she wasn't about to let Julian throw it away.

More determined than ever, she opened the door to the house and smiled evilly. 'You're not going to get away from me, Julian of Macedon. You might have beaten back the Romans, but I assure you, they were wimps in comparison to me.'

Julian sat in the living room with his book in his lap. He ran his hand over the ancient writing, despising it more now than he ever had before.

Closing his eyes, he remembered the night Grace had summoned him. He remembered what it felt like to have no real identity. To just be the anonymous Greek love-slave.

Long ago, he had lost himself in a painful place of dark obscurity, and yet Grace had found him.

Through her strength and kindness, she had braved the worst of him and brought him back to humanity. She, alone, had seen into his heart and found it worthy.

Stay with her.

314

Gods, how easy that sounded. How simple. But he didn't dare. He'd lost his children already. The only part of his heart left alive was Grace, and to lose her because of his brother ...

It would be more pain than he could bear.

Even he had a breaking point. And now he knew the face and name of what could bring him to his knees.

Grace.

For her own sake, he had to let her go.

He felt her enter the room. Opening his eyes, he saw her standing in the doorway, looking straight at him.

'I wish I could destroy this thing,' he snarled, returning it to the coffee table.

'After tonight, you won't have to.'

Her words made him ache. How could she do this for *him*? Her worst fear was to be used, and here he was using her the way he, himself, had been used so many times.

'You're still going to let me take your body just so I can leave you?'

It was the sincerity in her gaze that held him transfixed. 'If it means your freedom, yes.'

The next question stung his throat, but he had to know the answer to it. 'Will you cry when I'm gone?'

She looked away and he saw the truth of it in her eyes. He was no better than Paul had been. He was every bit the selfish abuser.

But then, he was his father's son. Sooner or later, bad blood always showed itself.

Grace turned then and left him alone with his thoughts. Julian let his gaze roam around the room. When it fell to the space in front of the couch, his chest tightened even more.

He would miss those nights of hearing Grace's voice. Her laughter.

Most of all, he would miss her touch.

It was so tempting to stay, but he didn't dare. He hadn't been able to protect his children, how on earth could he protect Grace?

'Julian?'

Julian started at Grace's voice coming from above. 'Yes?'

'It's eleven-thirty. Shouldn't you be up here?'

He glanced down at the swollen lump in his jeans. It was time to finally put it to use.

He should be delighted. It was all he'd wanted since the moment he'd first seen her.

Yet, for some reason it pained him to think of taking her now.

At least you won't hurt her.

Won't I?

Indeed, he doubted if Paul had done half the damage to her heart as he was about to do.

'Julian?'

'I'm coming,' he said, forcing himself to leave the couch.

At the doorway, he took one last look around.

Even now, he could see Grace lying on the couch, her breasts drenched in whipped cream as he slowly, carefully licked them clean. He heard her drifting laughter and saw the light in her eyes as he brought her to climax.

'Don't leave me, Julian.' Her whispered words had scorched him last night when she'd uttered them while she thought he was asleep. Now they lacerated his heart.

'Julian?'

Turning away, he went to the stairs and dragged his hand up the banister. This would be the last time he climbed these stairs. The last time he walked down the hallway to her room.

And this would be the last time he ever saw her in her bed . . .

His chest tightened to the point he couldn't breathe.

Why did it have to be this way?

He gave a bitter laugh. How many times had he asked himself that question?

When he reached her door, he stopped. The room shimmered in candlelight, but what caught his attention most was Grace wearing the red negligee he had picked out.

She was breathtaking.

He suddenly felt the need to pick his tongue up off the floor and roll it back into his mouth.

'You're not going to make this easy on me, are you?' he asked, his voice hoarse.

She smiled mischievously. 'Should I?'

Transfixed by her, he couldn't move as she approached him. 'Aren't you a bit overdressed?'

Before he could respond, she grabbed the bottom of his shirt and pulled it off, over his head. After dropping it to the floor, she reached out and placed her hand on his chest, just above his heart. In that moment, she was the most beautiful woman in the world to him. Not even his mother's beauty could compete with hers.

Julian stood as still as a statue as she ran her hands over his skin, raising chills all the way through him.

No, she wasn't going to make this easy at all.

He felt her fumble with his button and fly. 'Grace,' he said, pulling her hands away.

'Hmm?' she asked, her eyes dark with hunger.

'Never mind.'

She left him and climbed into the bed. Julian sucked his breath in sharply at the sight of her bare bottom through the sheer negligee.

317

She lay down on her side and faced him.

Shedding his pants, he joined her. As he rolled her onto her back, her gown parted, gifting him with her right breast. Julian availed himself of it.

'Oh, Julian,' she moaned.

He felt her quivering under him as he swirled his tongue around the taut peak. His body was liquid fire as it screamed in need for hers. But it wasn't just her body he wanted. He wanted *her*.

And leaving her was going to destroy him.

Julian swallowed as he pulled away. He had waited an eternity for this night. An eternity for this woman.

Tenderly, he brushed his hand over her face, committing every pore and curve of it to memory.

His precious Grace.

He would never forget her.

His soul weeping for what he was about to do to her, he parted her thighs with his knees.

Involuntarily, he shook with the force of how good she felt lying beneath him as their bare skin touched. And then, he made the mistake of looking into her eyes.

The sorrow there took his breath.

'You never had anything in your life you didn't steal from someone else.' Julian tensed at the sound of Iason's voice in his head. The last thing he wanted was to take from the woman who had given him so much.

How can I do this to her?

'What are you waiting for?' she asked.

Julian didn't know. All he knew was that he couldn't tear his gaze away from her sad, gray eyes. Eyes that would cry if he used her and left. Eyes that would cry in happiness if he stayed.

But if he stayed, his family would destroy her.

And in that moment, he knew what he had to do.

Grace wrapped her legs around his waist. 'Julian, hurry. We're running out of time.'

He didn't speak. He couldn't. In truth, he didn't trust himself to speak for fear he would change his mind.

Over the centuries, he had been many things: an orphan, a thief, husband, father, hero, legend, and finally a slave.

Yet, never once had he ever been a coward.

No. Julian of Macedon had never been craven. He was the commander who had stared down an entire legion of Romans, and laughingly dared them to take his head.

It was that man Grace had found, and that man who loved her. It was that man who refused to hurt her.

Grace tried to move her hips to bring his body into hers, but he wouldn't oblige her.

'You know what I'll miss most?' he asked as he reached down between their bodies and gently touched her core.

'No,' she whispered.

'The way your hair smells when I bury my face in it. The way you cling to me and cry out my name when you release. The way you laugh. But most of all, the way you look first thing in the morning with the sunlight on your face. I'll never forget it.'

He moved his hand, then rocked his hips against hers. But instead of sliding into her body, his move ended up as nothing more than a glorious caress that made them both moan.

Julian dipped his head to her ear where he nuzzled her neck. 'I will love you forever,' he whispered.

Grace heard him draw a deep breath in her hair at the same time the clock struck midnight.

In a bright flash of light, he vanished.

For several heartbeats, Grace couldn't move.

Horrified, she kept waiting to wake up, but as the clock continued to chime, she knew it wasn't a dream.

Julian was gone.

He was really and truly gone.

'No!' she screamed, sitting straight up. It couldn't be! 'No!'

Her heart pounding, she ran from the bedroom, downstairs to where the book was still lying on the coffee table. She flipped it open to see Julian standing just as he'd been originally. Only now, there was no devilish smile in place, and his hair was short.

No, no, no! her mind repeated over and over again. Why would he have done such a thing? Why?

'How could you?' she asked, as she cupped the book to her breasts. 'I would have given you your freedom, Julian. I wouldn't have minded. Oh, God, Julian, why would you do this to yourself?' She wept. 'Why?'

But in her heart she knew. The tender look on his face had said it all. He had done this to keep from hurting her like Paul had done.

Julian loved her. And since the moment he'd appeared, he had done nothing but protect her. Guard her.

Even at the end. Even when it meant he'd lose his own freedom from eternal imprisonment and torment, he had placed her first.

Grace ached at the truth and at the sacrifice he had made. Now, all she could think of was him being condemned to the darkness. Alone and in agony.

He had told her of the hunger he felt when he was trapped in the book, the thirst. And in her mind, she saw the way he had been tortured on her bed. But most of all, she remembered what he told her afterward.

'The pain on the bed was nothing compared to what it's like inside the book.'

And now he was in there. Suffering.

'No!' Grace said. 'I won't let you do this to yourself. Do you hear me, Julian?'

Cradling the book to her breasts, she ran to the back of her house. She slung open the sliding glass door and moved to stand in the moonlight.

'Come back to me, Julian of Macedon, Julian of Macedon, Julian of Macedon!' She repeated it over and over again as she begged for his appearance.

Nothing happened. Nothing at all.

'No! Please, no!'

Her heart broken, Grace returned inside her house. 'Why? Why?' she sobbed as she sank to her knees and rocked back and forth.

'Oh, Julian!' she whispered brokenly as memories assailed her. Julian laughing with her, holding her, or just sitting quietly in thought. The feel of his heart as it beat in rapid time to hers.

She wanted him back.

She *needed* him back.

'I don't want to live without you,' she breathed against the book. 'Didn't you understand that, Julian? I can't live without you.'

Suddenly, there was a flash of light in the room.

Gasping, Grace looked up, expecting it to be Julian returned to her.

But it wasn't Julian. It was Aphrodite.

'Give me the book,' Aphrodite said, reaching for it.

Grace pulled it back. 'Why would you do this to him?' she demanded. 'Hasn't he suffered enough for you? I wouldn't have kept him. I would rather he be with you than trapped like this.'

Grace brushed away her tears. 'He's alone in there. Alone

in the darkness,' she whispered. 'Please don't leave him that way. Send me into the book with him, please. Please!'

Aphrodite dropped her hand. 'You would do that for him?'

'I would do anything for him.'

Aphrodite's gaze narrowed. 'Give me the book.'

Blinded by her tears, Grace handed it over, praying Aphrodite would help her join him.

Aphrodite took a deep breath and opened the book. 'I'm going to catch serious hell over this.'

Suddenly, another light flashed, making Grace's eyes sting. Her head spun in a dizzying blur that made her feel sick to her stomach. Everything around her swirled.

Was this what Julian went through every time someone summoned him? She didn't know, but this alone was sheer torture, and terrifying.

Then suddenly, everything went eerily black.

Grace fell into a deep hole where the darkness pressed in on her, stinging her lungs, making her eyes burn like fire.

She reached out to stop herself from falling and felt a peculiar softness beneath her.

The lights came back and she found herself lying on her bed, with Julian on top of her.

He looked around as if dazed. 'How–'

'You two better not screw this one up,' Aphrodite said from the doorway. 'If I try this again, there's no telling what the powers that be might do to me.'

She vanished.

Julian looked from the doorway back to her. 'Grace, I–'

'Shut up, Julian,' she said before he wasted any more time, 'and show me how the gods meant for a woman to know a man.'

Then, she pulled his head down to hers and gave him a hot, penetrating kiss.

He kissed her fiercely, and with one, strong masterful stroke, he drove himself deep inside her.

Julian threw his head back and growled at the warm, sleek heat of her body welcoming his. The feel of it shook him so profoundly that even his bottom lip quivered. Dear gods, she felt even better than he had imagined.

And he remembered what she had said to him.

'I don't want to live without you. Didn't you understand that, Julian? I can't live without you.'

His breathing ragged, he looked down at her face as he felt her body so warm and tight around his shaft. He ran his hand down her arm to capture her hand in his grip and hold it tight. 'Am I hurting you?'

'No,' she said, her eyes warm and sincere as she brought his hand up to her lips and kissed it. 'You could never hurt me by being with me.'

'If I do, tell me and I'll stop.'

She wrapped her arms and legs about him. 'You leave me before dawn and I will hunt you down through eternity and beat you.'

Julian laughed, not doubting it for an instant.

Grace ran her tongue along the column of his throat, delighting in the way he shuddered in her arms.

He pulled his hips back ever so slowly, torturing her with his fullness, and then drove himself so deep into her body she felt the stroke all the way to her toes.

She sucked her breath in at the incredible sensation of him filling her. Of the lithe, agile power of his body thrusting against hers.

Closing her eyes, she savored his muscles flexing against the entire length of her body. She wrapped her legs around his, delighting in the way the hair on his legs tickled hers.

Never had she thought to feel anything like this. She

could only breathe as she felt her love for him flow through her. He was hers. Even if he left her afterward, she would enjoy this one moment of pure bliss with him.

Reveling in the powerful feel of him, she ran her hands over his back, down to his hips where she urged him on.

Julian bit his lip as she dug her nails into his back. How could such tiny hands have the power to break him?

He'd never understand it, any more than he would ever understand why she loved him.

He was only grateful for it.

'Look at me, Grace,' he said, thrusting himself deep inside her again. 'I want to see your eyes.'

Grace stared up at him. His eyes were half shuttered, and she saw how he savored the feel of her in the way he breathed and looked every time he rocked himself against her hips. She felt his stomach muscles contract against hers.

Lifting her hips, she met his frenzied pace stroke for stroke. Never had she imagined anything feeling as good as he felt sliding between her legs as he dipped his head down and kissed her deeply.

Just when she could stand no more, her body burst in a thousand convulsions of pleasure.

'Oh, Julian!' she screamed, arching her body even more against his. 'Oh, yes!'

He drove himself to the hilt and froze as she quivered around him.

When Grace opened her eyes, she met his devilish smile. 'Liked that, did you?' he asked, dimples flashing as he rotated his hips and gave her one luscious caress deep inside her.

It took all her strength not to moan at the sensation. 'It was okay.'

'Okay?' he said with a laugh. 'I guess I'll just have to keep trying.'

He rolled over with her, slowly lest he be forced out of her.

Grace moaned as she found herself on top of him. He reached up and pulled the ribbon in the center of her breasts. The tiny nightie fell open.

The look of pure rapture on his face pleased her even more than the feel of him deep within her. Smiling, she lifted her hips, then impaled herself more deeply upon him.

She felt him quake all around her. 'Like that, do you?'

'It was okay.' But his ragged voice betrayed his nonchalant tone.

She laughed.

Julian lifted his hips then, driving himself even deeper into her.

She hissed in pleasure as he filled her. The sleek power, the hard feel of him. And she wanted more. She wanted to see his face when he climaxed. She wanted to know that she had given him what he hadn't experienced since time immemorial.

'You know, we're going to be exhausted by the time morning arrives if we don't slow down,' he said.

'I don't mind.'

'You'll be sore.'

She stroked him with her body. 'So?'

'In that case ... ' He ran his hand slowly down her body, to her navel, then lower through her moist curls until he found her nub.

Grace bit her lip as his fingers toyed with her in a perfect rhythm to match the thrust of his hips. Faster and faster he went, harder and deeper.

Julian placed his hands against her waist, helping her to maintain their frantic pace. How he wished he could withdraw from her long enough to show her a few more positions. But this was all they were allowed.

For now.

But come morning ...

He smiled at the prospect. Come the morning, he intended to show her a whole new use for the Reddi-wip.

Grace lost track of time as they stroked each other's bodies, and reveled in each other's company. She felt the room spin around her as she surrendered herself to his expert touch. To the wonderful feel of her love for him.

They were both drenched with sweat, but still they savored each other, delighting in the passion they could finally share.

This time when she came, she sprawled on top of him.

His laugh echoed around her as he ran his hands over her back, her hips, then down her legs.

Grace shivered.

Julian delighted in the feel of her naked body lying prone against his. Her breasts were flat against his chest. His love for her welled up inside him.

'I could lie like this forever,' he breathed.

'Me, too.'

He wrapped his arms about her and held her close. He could feel her touches slowing down, her breath becoming smooth and steady.

Within a few minutes, she was sound asleep.

Kissing the top of her head, he smiled as he made sure he kept himself inside her. 'Sleep, precious Grace,' he whispered. 'It's a long time until morning.'

Grace came awake to the feel of something warm and full inside her. As she started to move, she felt arms as strong as steel hold her still.

'Careful,' Julian said. 'Don't force me out of you.'

'I went to sleep?' she gasped, amazed she could have done such a thing.

'It's all right. You didn't miss anything.'

'No?' she asked, wiggling her hips against his to stroke his body with hers.

He laughed. 'Well, okay, you did miss a few things.'

Grace leaned up to look down at him. She dragged her finger along the stubble on his cheek.

As she traced his lips, he nipped her finger with his teeth. Suddenly, he sat up beneath her, holding her in his lap.

'Ooo, nice,' she said as she wrapped her legs about his waist.

'Uh-huh,' he agreed as he rocked his hips against hers.

Lowering his head, he took her breast into his mouth. His tongue toyed with her taut nipple, circling it in a torturous pattern before he blew one long, hot breath across it. She shivered.

He moved to her other breast. Grace cupped his head to her, delighting in his touch. Until she saw that the sky was lightening.

'Julian!' she breathed. 'It's almost dawn.'

'I know,' he said, laying her back on the bed.

She looked up at him as he held himself above her and continued to thrust his hips against hers.

Julian stared at her in wonderment. The feel of her warmth, her love. She had reached him in ways he'd never thought possible. And she had touched him where he had never been touched before.

Deep within his heart.

Suddenly he wanted more. Desperate for her, he rocked his hips against hers.

He had to have more of her.

Grace wrapped her arms around him and buried her face

in his shoulder as he quickened his thrusts. Harder and faster he went until she was breathless from the frantic pace.

Again, sweat covered them both. She ran her tongue over his neck, delighting in the hiss he let out.

Still he filled her, over and over, until she couldn't stand it.

She sank her teeth into his shoulder as her release came fast and furious. He didn't slow down as she lay back.

Reaching up, she cupped his face in her hands and watched his pleasure.

Julian bit his lower lip and moved faster, driving her pleasure on, even deeper than it had been before.

And just as the first rays of sunlight shone through the window she heard Julian growl low in his throat as he closed his eyes.

With one hard, deep thrust, she felt him shudder all around her as he spilled his release within her.

Julian couldn't breathe as his head swam in pure, unadulterated bliss. He shook from the force of his orgasm. His entire body ached, and yet he'd never known such pleasure. He was weak from the night, weak from her touch.

And the curse was over.

He lifted his head to see Grace smiling up at him.

'Is it done?' she asked.

Before he could answer, he felt a tremendous burning on his arm. Hissing, he pulled back from her and covered the burn with his other hand.

'What is it?' Grace asked as he withdrew from her.

She watched, stunned, as an orange glow encompassed his arm. When he let go, the ancient Greek words were gone.

'It's over,' she breathed. 'We did it.'

The smile faded from his face. 'No,' Julian said, trailing

his fingers along her cheek. 'You did it.'

Laughing, she threw herself into his arms. Julian held her tight as they rained kisses on each other.

It was over!

He was free. Finally, after all this time, he was a mortal man again.

And it was Grace who had done it. Her faith and strength had seen him through.

She had saved him.

Grace laughed again as she rolled him over in the bed.

But her relief was short-lived as another, even brighter flash filled the room.

Her laughter dying instantly, Grace felt a malevolent presence even before Julian tensed in her arms.

Sitting up in the bed, Julian forced her back, placing himself between her and the handsome man standing at the foot of the bed.

Grace gulped when she saw the tall, dark-haired man who glared at them as if he could kill them where they lay. 'You bastard upstart!' the man snarled. 'How dare you think to be free.'

In an instant, she knew he must be Priapus.

'Let it go, Priapus,' Julian said with a warning note in his voice. 'It's over and done with.'

Priapus snorted. 'You think to command me? Who do you think you are, mortal?'

Julian smiled evilly. 'I am Julian of Macedon, born of the House of Diokles of Sparta and of the goddess Aphrodite. I am the champion of Greece, Macedonia, Thebes, Punjab, and Conjara. Known as Augustus Julius Punitor to my enemies who quaked in terror at my presence. And you, my brother, are a lesser known god who meant nothing to the Greeks, and only slightly more to the Romans.'

329

Hell's wrath burned across Priapus's face. 'It's time you learned your place, little brother. You took from me the woman who was going to sire my sons to lead my name into memoriam. Now I take yours.'

Julian launched himself at Priapus, but it was too late. He had already vanished with Grace.

Chapter Seventeen

One moment, Grace was naked in her bedroom with Julian, and in the next, she was lying on a round bed in a room that reminded her of a harem tent. Her body was covered in a deep red silk wrap that was so soft and delicate it felt like water sliding over her skin.

She tried to move, but couldn't. Terrified, she opened her mouth to scream.

'Don't bother,' Priapus told her as he approached the bed. He ran a hungry look over her body before he climbed onto the mattress and positioned himself on his knees beside her. 'You can't do anything unless I will it.'

He ran one long, cold finger down her cheek as if testing her skin's texture and temperature. 'I can see why Julian wants you. You have fire in your gaze. Intelligence. Bravery. It's a pity you weren't born during the time of Rome. You could have given me champions to lead my armies.'

He sighed as he ran his hand down the center of her throat. 'But such is life, and the whims of the Fates. I suppose I'll just have to content myself with using you until

I grow tired. If you please me until then, I might let Julian have you back. Provided of course, he still wants you after my children have stretched out your body.'

His eyes burned with hunger. And Grace trembled at his look.

She couldn't believe Priapus's selfishness. His vanity. Terrified, she wanted to speak, but he kept her from it.

Dear heaven, he had complete power over her!

An unseen force pushed her up, setting her back against the pillows as Priapus doffed his robe.

Grace's eyes widened at the sight of his nudity and his erection. Another wave of fear washed over her.

'You may speak, now,' he said as he moved to recline by her side.

'Why do you want to do this to Julian?'

His gaze darkened in anger. 'Why? You heard him. His name was revered by everyone who heard it, while my name was seldom spoken aloud even in my mother's temples. Even now, I am mocked. My name is all but lost to antiquity while his legend is told and retold around the world. Yet I am a god and he is nothing but a bastard seed not even fit to inhabit Olympus.'

'Get your hands off her, you worthless footnote. *You're* not fit to wipe her shoes.'

Grace's heart pounded at the sound of Julian's voice. Raising her head from the pillows, she saw him standing below the dais where they were. He stood in the center of the room wearing nothing but jeans and holding his sword and shield.

'How?' Priapus demanded as he left the bed.

Julian smiled evilly. 'The curse is lifted. My powers are returning. I can now track and summon all of you.'

'No!' Priapus shrieked. Instantly, his body was covered in armor.

Grace fought against the force that held her as Priapus grabbed a sword and shield from the wall above her head and attacked Julian.

Mesmerized by the spectacle, she watched as brother fought brother.

Never had she seen anything like it. Julian whirled gracefully in a macabre dance as he met his brother fierce blow for fierce blow. The floor and bed shook from the intensity of their battle.

No wonder Julian had become a legend.

But after a few minutes, she saw Julian stagger. He lowered his shield.

'What's the matter?' Priapus taunted, using his shield to press Julian back. 'Oh, I forgot. The curse may be gone, but you're still drained from it. It will take days before you reach your full strength again.'

Julian shook his head and raised his shield higher. 'I don't need my full strength to beat you.'

Priapus laughed. 'Brave words, little brother.'

He brought his sword down across Julian's shield.

Grace held her breath as they began hammering blows again.

Then, just as she was sure Julian would win, Priapus tricked him into overextending his reach. As soon as Julian's side was unprotected, Priapus brought his sword up, and sank it into Julian's stomach. Julian dropped his sword.

'No!' Grace screamed in horror.

His face a mask of disbelief, Julian staggered back, but couldn't go far with the sword still in Priapus's hand, and now in his side.

'You're human again,' Priapus sneered as he twisted the sword. He lifted his foot to Julian's hip and kicked him back.

Free of the sword's blade, Julian staggered, then fell to the floor. His shield clattered loudly as it hit the ground next to him.

Priapus was actually smiling as he stood over Julian. 'You may not be able to die by mortal weapons, little brother, but you can die by immortal ones.'

The force holding Grace released her. As fast as she could, she ran across the room to where Julian lay on the floor, covered in blood. His breathing came in short, sharp gasps as his entire body shook.

'No!' Grace sobbed, pulling Julian's head into her lap. Horrified, she stared at the gaping wound in his bare side.

'My precious Grace,' Julian said as he reached one bloodied hand up to touch her cheek.

She wiped the blood from his lips. 'Don't leave me, Julian,' she begged.

He winced in pain. Dropping his hand, he struggled to breathe. 'Don't cry for me, Grace. I'm not worth it.'

'Yes you are!'

He shook his head as he held her hand tightly in his. 'You are my saving Grace. Without you, I would never have known love.' He swallowed and moved her hand to his heart. 'And I would never have known me again.'

She watched as the light faded from his eyes. 'No!' she screamed again, cradling his head to her breast. 'No, no, no! You can't die. Not like this. Do you hear me, Julian! You can't leave me. Please, please don't go. Please!'

Grace held him tight as she wept out the agony in her heart, her soul.

'No!' The fierce scream echoed through the room and shook it.

Grace saw Priapus actually pale at the sound. A clap of thunder sounded and, in a brilliant flash of white light,

Aphrodite appeared in front of her. The agony on the goddess's face was indescribable as she looked down at Julian's cold, pale body.

Her blue eyes filled with disbelief, Aphrodite glared at Priapus.

'What have you done?' she asked him.

'It was a fair fight, Mother. Me or him. I had no choice.'

Aphrodite let out an agonized scream that came straight from her heart. 'I invoked the wrath of Zeus and the Fates to give him his freedom. Who the hell do you think you are to do this?' She looked at Priapus as if he made her ill. 'He was your brother!'

'He was your bastard son, but never my brother.'

Aphrodite shrieked in rage. 'How dare you!'

When the goddess turned her gaze back to Julian, Grace saw the grief on her face.

'My precious Julian,' Aphrodite wept. 'I should never have let them hurt you. Sweet Cyprus, what have I done with my selfishness?' She fell to her knees by his side. 'I left you alone when I should have protected you.'

'Oh, give it a rest, Mother,' Priapus said as if bored by his mother's pain. 'Julian knew what all of us have known since the dawn of time. You think only of yourself, and what we should be doing for *you*. It's who you are. Unlike Julian, the rest of us learned to accept it aeons ago.'

Aphrodite didn't take those words well. In fact, her face turned to granite as she rose to her feet with all the dignity and grace one would expect of a goddess.

She arched a brow at Priapus. 'You said it was a fair fight? Well, let's have one, shall we? Thanatos has yet to claim Julian's soul. It is not yet too late to save him. All I need do is start his heart.'

Grace felt a sudden warmth engulfing Julian's body.

Leaning back, she watched as a golden aura surrounded him, mending the jagged wound in his stomach. His jeans melted away slowly and were replaced by golden greaves and shoes. The golden wave traveled up over his chest, covering it with ancient gold armor and dark red leather and cloth. Dark brown leather bands covered his forearms.

The blue tinge faded from Julian's face.

Suddenly, he took a deep breath that shook his entire body, then opened his eyes. He looked up at Grace and smiled a smile that warmed her all the way to her soul.

Grace bit her lip as happiness swelled inside her. He was alive!

'What the bloody hell?' Priapus roared.

A woman appeared above them, floating serenely. Her black hair shimmered as she glared at Priapus. 'As your mother said, it's time we had our fair fight, Priapus. It's long overdue. And this time, there's no Alexandria to distract Julian from his vengeance.'

'What?' Aphrodite asked. 'Athena, what are you saying?'

'I'm saying Priapus sent her to Julian on purpose to distract him while Priapus fled your temple in fear of Julian's wrath.'

By the look on Priapus's face, Grace could see the truth of it. He curled his lip. 'Athena, you treacherous bitch. You always did coddle him.'

Athena laughed as she appeared next to Aphrodite. 'No one ever coddled him. It's what made him the finest warrior Sparta ever trained. And it's what is going to enable him to kick your ass now.'

Julian rose to his feet. The grim look on his face sent a ripple of chills over Grace.

Aphrodite moved to stand between him and Priapus, and when she looked up at Julian, Grace saw the pride in

Aphrodite's eyes. 'This is the second time I have given you life, Julian. I regret I wasn't the mother you needed the first time. You have no idea how much I wish I could change that. All I can do now is give you my love and blessing.'

Aphrodite looked over to Priapus. 'Now, go kick his spoiled little ass.'

'Mother!' Priapus whined.

Julian turned his gaze to his brother. He twirled his sword around his body as he approached Priapus. 'Ready?'

Priapus attacked without warning. Not that it mattered.

Grace's jaw dropped as she watched them fight. If she had thought Julian skilled before, it was nothing compared to the way he fought now.

He moved with a speed and agility she would never have thought possible.

Athena came to stand by her side. She reached out and ran a light touch over the red wrap. 'Nice dress.'

Grace frowned in disbelief. 'They're fighting to the death and you're admiring my clothes?'

Athena laughed. 'Trust me, I pick my generals well. Priapus doesn't stand a chance.'

Grace turned back to the men at the same time Julian drove his shield sideways into Priapus. The god stumbled back and Julian plunged his sword straight into his side.

'Rot in Tartarus, you bastard,' Julian sneered as Priapus disintegrated into a thousand lights.

Grace ran to him.

Julian tossed his sword and shield aside and grabbed her up in his arms and twirled her around.

'You're alive! Right?' she asked.

'I'm alive.'

Grace surrendered herself to him then. He lowered her down his body, slowly, his armor caressing every inch of her. Until he could claim her lips with his kiss.

Grace heard someone clearing her throat.

'Excuse me, Julian,' Athena said when he didn't release Grace. 'You have a decision that needs to be made. Do you want me to send you home or not?'

Grace trembled.

Julian looked down at her, his gaze searching. He ran his hand gently over her cheek as if savoring the feel of her skin against his. 'In all the centuries I have lived, I've only known one home.'

Grace bit her lip as tears swelled. He was going to leave her now. Dear God, she just hoped she could stand the pain of it.

He leaned down and kissed her forehead. 'And it's with Grace,' he said against her hair. 'If she'll have me.'

Grace rolled her eyes as relief swept through her with such ferocity that she wanted to scream, to laugh, but most of all she wanted to hold on to him forever.

'Gee, Julian,' she said with a nonchalance she didn't feel. 'I don't know. You do take up more than your fair share of the bed. And those noxious boxer shorts you wear ... What is that? If you come back with me, those have got to go. And no more wearing jeans to bed at night, they chafe my legs.'

He laughed at her. 'Don't worry. For what I have in mind, nudity works best.'

She joined his laughter as he cupped her face in his hands.

When he tried to kiss her, she pulled back impishly. 'Oh, by the way, is this your armor?'

He frowned. 'It is, or was.'

'Can we keep it?'

'If you like. Why?'

'Cause, ooo baby,' Grace said, raking a look over his gorgeous body, 'you are one hot tamale in that getup. This outfit alone will get you laid at least four or five times a day.'

Athena and Aphrodite laughed.

In a flash of light, they were back in Grace's bedroom, just the way they'd been before Priapus had shown himself.

'Hey!' Grace said irritably. 'Where's the armor?'

It appeared along with his helm, sword, and shield in the corner.

'Happy now?' Julian asked as he pulled her across his chest.

'Delirious.'

He raised his head and delivered a kiss to her that shook her entire body. Grace moaned at the heat of his mouth on hers. The feel of his body under hers.

She would never again let him go.

'By the way ... '

Julian pulled back from Grace's lips with a groan as he quickly covered the two of them with a sheet.

Grace clutched the sheet to her chin.

'Athena,' he asked testily, 'are you going to keep interrupting us?'

Athena didn't look a bit sheepish as she approached the bed. She held a large gold box in her hands. 'Well, I forgot something.'

'What?' they asked in aggravated unison.

Before Athena could answer, Aphrodite appeared. 'I've got it,' she said to Athena before taking the box out of her hands.

Athena vanished.

Moving to stand by the bed, Aphrodite set the box next to Julian, then opened it. 'If you're going to stay, there are a few things you'll need. A birth certificate, passport, green card ...'

Aphrodite looked at it with a frown. 'No, wait, you won't need that.' She looked to Grace. 'Will he?'

'No, ma'am.'

Aphrodite smiled as it evaporated. 'There's also a driver's license, but if you'll take some motherly advice, I'd let Grace do all the driving. No offense, but you stink at it.' Aphrodite sighed. 'It's a pity we didn't have a god for that, too. But, oh well.' She closed the box and handed it to him. 'Here, you can go through it later.'

As Aphrodite moved away, Julian reached out and took her hand. 'Thank you, Mother, for everything.'

Tears welled in her eyes as she patted her son's hand on her arm. 'I am so sorry I didn't know about your children in time to save them as well. You've no idea how much I regret that I found out only after Thanatos had them.'

Julian squeezed her gently.

'If you need anything at all, you'll call?' she asked.

'I'll call even if I don't.'

Aphrodite lifted his hand to her lips and kissed it. She looked back and forth between them. 'I want six grandchildren. Minimum.'

'Hey,' Grace said as she pulled a college degree out of the box. 'You've given him a Ph.D. in ancient history? From Harvard?'

Aphrodite nodded. 'There's also one in there for languages and classical studies.' She looked at Julian. 'I wasn't sure what you might want to do, so I'll let you pick.'

'Can we really use these?' Grace asked.

'Absolutely. If you dig a little deeper, you'll find his certified transcripts.'

Grace did. Looking them over, she gaped. 'No fair, they're all A's.'

'Of course,' Aphrodite said indignantly. 'My son would never do second-rate work.'

Aphrodite smiled. 'I didn't bother with a marriage certificate. I figured the two of you would want to take care of that one on your own. And as soon as Julian decides on a last name, it'll appear on all the documents inside the box.'

Aphrodite dug to the bottom of the documents and pulled out a small bankbook. 'By the way, I converted the money you had in Macedonia into modern currency.'

Grace opened the book and gasped. 'Holy green guacamole! You're filthy rich!'

He laughed. 'I told you, I conquered well.'

Aphrodite held her hand out. The book that had contained Julian appeared in her arms. 'I also thought you might want to find some safe place to put this.'

Julian gaped as she handed it to him. 'You're giving me custody of Priapus?'

Aphrodite shrugged. 'He killed you. I can't very well let him get away without some form of punishment. He'll get out eventually. *If* he's a good boy.'

Grace almost felt sorry for poor Priapus.

Almost.

Aphrodite leaned forward and kissed Julian on the cheek. 'I always loved you. I just didn't know how to show it.'

Julian nodded. 'I guess it's what happens when your mother is a goddess. You can't very well expect birthday parties and home-cooked meals.'

'True, but I gave you a lot of other gifts that your girlfriend seems to treasure.'

'Speaking of,' Grace said as a thought struck her. 'Can we curb the one that draws other women like a magnet?'

Aphrodite gave her a droll stare. 'Child, look at the man. What woman in her right mind wouldn't want him in her bed? I'd have to blind them all, or make him fat and bald.'

'Never mind. I'll just learn to cope.'

'Thought so.' Aphrodite vanished.

Julian wrapped his arm around Grace's shoulders and pulled her back against him. 'Are you sore?'

'No, why?'

'Because I intend to spend the rest of the day making love to you.'

She nipped his chin with her teeth. 'Ooo, I like the sound of that.'

He kissed her.

'Oh, wait,' he said, pulling back.

Grace frowned as he got out of bed, grabbed the book, then tossed it out into the hallway and shut the door.

'What are you doing?' she asked.

Julian sauntered back to bed with that slow, loose-limbed walk that made her breathless and hot. He crawled up on the bed like a sleek, naked beast and ran a hot, lustful stare all over her body. 'He can hear everything we say. And I personally don't want him in here when I do this.'

She gasped as he flipped her on her side.

'Or this,' he said, sliding his hand between her thighs and teasing her mercilessly with his touch.

He curled himself against her spine.

'And most of all, I don't want him to hear this.'

He buried his lips against her neck as he moved his hand down her inner thigh to spread her legs, then he plunged himself deep inside her.

Grace moaned in pleasure.

'I waited two thousand years for you, Grace Alexander,' he whispered in her ear. 'And you were worth every second of it.'

342

Epilogue

One Year Later

Julian opened the door to the hospital room. With his mother and Selena in tow, he stepped quietly into the room, not wanting to disturb Grace if she was resting.

Fear gripped him as he saw her lying on the bed. She looked so pale and weak that it terrified him. He couldn't stand seeing her like this.

She was his strength. His heart. His soul. Everything in his life that was good.

The thought of losing her was more than he could bear.

Grace opened her eyes and smiled at them. 'Hi,' she whispered.

'Hey, girl!' Selena said. 'How are you feeling?'

'I'm exhausted, but feeling pretty good.'

Julian leaned over and kissed her. 'Do you need anything?'

'I have everything I could ever need,' Grace said, her face glowing.

He smiled.

'So, where are my grandchildren?' his mother demanded.

'They took them to be weighed,' Grace said.

As if on cue, the nurses wheeled the cradles in. They checked Grace's bracelet against the babies', then made a quiet exit.

Julian left Grace's side only long enough to gently pick up his son. Joy spread through him as he cradled the tiny infant in his arms. Grace had given him so much more than he had ever expected to have. And much more than he deserved.

'This is Niklos James Alexander,' he said, handing the baby to his mother. He picked up his daughter next. 'And this is Vanessa Anne Alexander.' He placed her in his mother's other arm.

His mother's lips trembled as she looked at her grand-daughter. 'You named her after me?'

'We both wanted to,' Grace said.

Tears fell down her face as Aphrodite looked back and forth between the children. 'Oh, the gifts I have for you two.'

'Mom!' Julian said sharply, interrupting her. 'Please, no gifts. Just give them your love.'

Aphrodite sniffed back her tears and laughed. 'Very well. But if you change your mind, let me know.'

Grace watched Julian as he brushed his hand over Niklos's bald head. She wouldn't have thought it possible, but at the moment she loved him even more than she had before.

Every day they had been together had been a blessing.

'Oh, hey,' Selena said as she took Vanessa from Aphrodite. 'I went by the bookstore yesterday and Priapus was gone. There was a full moon a few days ago. Anyone want to bet he's making wild monkey love with someone right now?'

They laughed.

344

All except Julian.

'Something wrong?' Grace asked.

'I guess I'm just feeling a little guilty over him.'

'Guilty?' Selena asked in disbelief. 'Over Priapus?'

Julian indicated the children and Grace. 'How can I bear him animosity? Without his curse, I would never have all of you. It was a pain in the ass. But I have to say in the end, it was more than worth it.'

They looked expectantly at Aphrodite. 'What?' she asked innocently. 'Don't tell me you want him free now? I told you, when he learns his lesson ... '

Selena shook her head. 'Poor old Uncle Priapus,' she cooed to Vanessa. 'But he was a bad, bad boy.'

A nurse opened the door and hesitated on the threshold. 'Um, Dr. Alexander,' she said to Julian, 'there's a couple out here who say they're related to you. They ... um ... ' She dropped her voice to a low whisper. 'They're biker people.'

'Hey, Julian,' Eros said from behind the nurse. 'Tell Attila the Hun here that we're okay so we can come and ooh and aah over the babies.'

Julian laughed. 'It's okay, Trish,' he said to the nurse. 'He's my brother.'

Eros made a face at Trish as he and Psyche swept inside. 'Someone remind me to shoot her with a whammy on the way out,' he said as Trish closed the door.

Julian arched a brow at him. 'Do I have to confiscate your bow again?'

Eros blew a raspberry at him as he moved to Selena and took Vanessa out of her hands. 'Ooh, what a little heart-breaker you're going to be. I bet you'll have little boys running after you in droves.'

Julian's face paled. He turned back to his mother. 'Mom, there is one gift I would like.'

345

Aphrodite looked up hopefully.

'Would you speak to Hephaestus about a chastity belt for Vanessa?'

'Julian!' Grace gasped with a laugh.

'She won't have to wear it long. Just thirty or forty years.'

Grace rolled her eyes. 'It's a good thing you have your mommy,' she said to the baby in Eros's arms. ''Cause Daddy is no fun at all.'

Julian cocked an arrogant brow at her. 'No fun at all?' he repeated. 'Funny, that's not what you said the day you conceived these two.'

'Julian!' Grace snapped, her face burning. But then she'd learned a long time ago that he was incorrigible.

And she loved him that way.